THE WITCH OF DAKOTA

C.J. PETIT

Printed in the United States of America

First Printing, 2017

ISBN: 9781983301544

TABLE OF CONTENTS

C.J. PETIT

PROLOGUE

Dakota Territory
October 1876

The Witch huddled under her buffalo robe in the chill at the back of her tipi and knew that they soon would come for her. Before the moon grew full again, they would kill her, and tonight, the man in the moon would be grinning at her as his face was almost complete. Ever since Yellow Sky had been named as the tribe's new shaman in the spring, he had spoken against her because he feared her and worried that her medicine might be stronger than his.

It had taken many bad signs for his words to take root among the tribe. The loss of their antelope herd was the first evil that he had blamed on her. But that had only incited grumbling, but little else. Then this past summer, the crop was dismal, leaving many empty stomachs and the grumbling gave way to open aggression by those who did not fear her medicine, but they had just been threats and words. But last week, with the stillborn birth of White Hawk's much-anticipated first son, Yellow Sky had finally persuaded them to act. She knew they would come to her tipi, take her and burn her in the center of the camp, and she knew that she couldn't speak to them in her defense.

But the Witch was preparing to make a desperate chance at escape. It would be her only small chance to live and it had to be soon. She had been saving some of her food every day,

3

had an extra pair of moccasins, a pack for the food and a wool blanket. She would leave in the night when they were sleeping and go south but had two problems. She didn't know where she was, and she didn't know where she could go. Yet staying was no longer a choice. The Witch wanted to live.

CHAPTER 1

"So, it's true, Lieutenant, you're leaving our merry band?" asked Sgt. Frazier.

"Yup. I think it's time. I don't think they're happy with me anyway."

"Can't say I blame ya. You need anything?"

"I just came down to see if you had any excess weapons that might be useful on my trip."

The supply sergeant smiled and said, "As it so happens, you might be able to do me a favor."

"How's that?" Lieutenant Braxton asked.

"Six months ago, we were supposed to get a shipment of Sharps carbines. We got four cases shipped to our lovely hotel. When we opened 'em, we found that one of the cases had rifles and they weren't even army issue. They were damned buffalo guns, and we don't even have any buffaloes, either. We can't use those damned big guns, and we can't send 'em back because the army insists that they're carbines and the factory only will take 'em back if the army pays to ship 'em. But the army insists they're carbines and we can't ship 'em back. Damned paper pushers! We only got the ammunition that came with 'em, too, and they don't fit in our carbines. We tried to get the quartermaster to take the cartridges back at least, but they said we had to keep 'em. It's another mess that the army seems to be really good at making.

"Anyway, I've been trying to get rid of the damned things ever since. I got rid of all of them except two. Now, if you were a good fella and take both of them off my hands, I'd toss in the last of the ammunition for those cannons. Eight boxes of .45-100 cartridges, and they don't even need percussion caps. You gotta take them both, though. Would you be willing to do that?"

Ross thought about it. They were big guns, and he wouldn't mind one, but they were big and heavy, too. Two would add more weight to his pack horse's load, but the range and the stopping power might be just what he needed on his long journey through hostile territory.

"Throw in a two-man tent and you have a deal," Ross said with a smile.

Sergeant Frazier grinned and said, "Thanks, Lieutenant. How far are you aiming to go, anyway? I heard you were going cross country, but I'm getting all sorts of stories about where you're headed."

"I'm going to my brother's ranch outside of Cheyenne. It'll take me about three weeks, as long as the weather holds, and I get to hang onto my hair."

"You never know out there, do ya? I'll get the guns, the tent and the ammunition. I'll pack them up, too."

First Lieutenant Ross Braxton sat on a packing crate, waiting for Sgt. Frazier to get the weapons. As of tomorrow, he would be Mr. Ross Braxton. He had submitted his resignation from the United States Army after six years of service, and he had finally gotten word of its approval. He had always wanted to be a soldier, and he still liked the army and the men he served with, but the politicians had started sending them to do things that he thought were unacceptable, if not dishonorable.

He didn't have a problem fighting the Sioux. They were worthy opponents, despite having inferior weapons. They usually did have superior numbers, though. What he had a problem with was after the disaster at the Little Big Horn just a few months earlier, the brass sought retaliation. Retaliation in itself was understandable, but retaliation against whole villages when the warriors were out in the field was not. He hadn't gone on one of the raids yet, but as soon as one of his fellow officers had returned from one and told him what had happened, Ross submitted his paperwork. It took a month to get approved, and today was his last day in uniform.

So, tomorrow he would leave for Wyoming Territory. It would mean at least a five-hundred-mile ride across Dakota Territory. A territory filled with hostile Sioux and other tribes that had joined with their traditional enemy to fight the bluecoats.

Sergeant Frazier returned to the big supply counter and laid down his heavy load.

"Here you go, Lieutenant. They still have the original grease from the manufacturer, so you'll need to clean 'em before you pull the trigger in anger. I included the two cleaning kits that came with them, though."

"Thanks, Sergeant Frazier. You take care and keep those officers in line, will you?"

"I'll try. It's been a pleasure serving with ya."

He leaned over and shook Ross's hand.

Ross lugged the tent, heavy guns and ammunition out of the quartermaster's building and returned to his quarters. He shared the bachelor officers' quarters with three others and was the senior man, at least until tomorrow. He laid the heavy guns on the floor near his bed, then sat down in his chair and examined the long rifles. It was two in the afternoon, so he may as well clean the big guns before late chow.

He took the first Sharps, opened the breech to let in some light and looked down the barrel. As promised, the grease was still there, so he began cleaning the weapon to bring it to its deadly utility. It took almost an hour to clean both guns, but he wouldn't be able to test fire the guns until he had left the area, as it might cause a bit of a ruckus. He took out a box of ammunition, removed one of the giant rounds and examined the cartridge. It was a mammoth thing. He pulled a .44 caliber round that he'd use in either of his Colts or the Winchester, and the Sharps round dwarfed the .44. It was only a hundredth of an inch thicker, but the cartridge was about an inch and a half longer, and most of that was gunpowder.

Once he had submitted his resignation, he had started to collect the things he would need for his long journey. The first thing on his list were newer, cartridge-firing weapons. He bought the Model '73 Winchester carbine first, and then he bought two Colt Peacemakers. He bought a two-gun rig and had the left holster reversed so the butt would face forward. He'd cross draw the left gun if he ever needed it. Having twelve rounds in a close in fight is a lot better than six. He also had eight boxes of cartridges that would fit the Colts and the Winchester.

Between the Colts, the Winchesters and the Sharps, he was as heavily armed as any man he knew and hoped he wouldn't need that much firepower, but it was a lot better to have too much than not enough. The Sharps added the long range to the mid-range of the Winchester and the shorter-range of the Colts.

Too bad he couldn't pack a cannon or a Gatling gun, he thought as he smiled to himself, but didn't believe his pack horse would appreciate it anyway.

He had already bought two horses in Britton, and one would serve as a pack horse. The one he would ride was a tall dappled gray gelding but hadn't named it yet and wasn't sure if he would. He used horses and took care of them, but they were still horses. Despite all his fellow cavalrymen's quaint

9

attachment to their mounts, he never reached that level of empathy. Now, dogs were a different story. He loved dogs. Now that he was out, he'd see if he could find one to come on his trip.

He'd still have his uniform, of course, and he'd keep his field glasses, but he'd leave his saber and issued firearms here. He knew he'd never wear the uniform again and that bothered him because retaliatory raids aside, he knew he would miss the army.

Tomorrow would be the start of a new career. What it would be, he wasn't sure. He had his engineering degree from the Military Academy but hadn't really used it since graduating in 1871. He had chosen the cavalry over the engineers, which surprised most of the other cadets. He had taken another step away from the fast track to a stellar army career when he had requested a posting in the Dakotas, which was the only place he believed a soldier could be a soldier.

His new clothes were sitting on the bed, and he idly flipped one of the shirts. He had bought nice neutral colors that would blend in well with background. He never understood the choice of the cavalry uniforms. The dark blue color stood out against most natural backgrounds, and the gold accents made it worse. But it didn't matter any longer, because starting tomorrow morning, he'd choose his own shades.

He began to pack his extra clothes into his saddlebags, leaving room so he could distribute the ammunition equally to balance the weight. Most of the ammo would be on the pack horse, though. He'd have to rig up something for the two Sharps rifles, too.

Ross ran his planned journey to Cheyenne through his mind once more. He'd ride to Britton early in the morning where he'd get breakfast and then buy his supplies for the trip. Then he'd start his journey by turning right around to head past the fort and continue southwest. He planned on making at least forty miles a day, and that would mean about six or seven hours in the saddle for two weeks if nothing intervened to delay him. He knew he'd need to stop every now and then to resupply or take breaks. The only towns on his planned itinerary were Aberdeen, Gettysburg and Pierre. Then it would be a long run of over a hundred and fifty miles without a hint of civilization. Then, he'd drop down to Camp Robinson in Nebraska and onto Scotts Bluff before heading west to Cheyenne.

He pulled out his pocket watch. It was only 4:15, but in another hour, he'd eat his last meal at government expense. From then on, he'd have to pay for his food. He'd saved a good portion of his pay since he had been commissioned and had almost sixteen hundred dollars in his money belt. He wouldn't be eating in a lot of restaurants and cafés on the trip, so he was in good shape.

He had two books, both gifts from his parents when he went to the Military Academy. One was the Bible and the other was Caesar's Commentaries. He still read both often.

After an hour, he went to the officers' mess, and was greeted as the departing comrade that he was. Most of his fellow officers fully understood his reason for resigning and wished they had the sand to do the same. While he shared that last meal with his friends, war stories were told, and memories rehashed. The food was bland and tasteless, but it filled. He'd do better on the trail.

After the handshakes and backslaps, Ross returned to his quarters, cleared his bed and moved everything to the floor, then stretched out on his bunk. Second Lieutenant Oscar Davis arrived and sat on the chair next to his bed and began chatting about things that Ross had no interest in whatsoever. Ross would nod or acknowledge a statement with a 'really' or 'oh' just to appear somewhat interested. Davis was like that. If there was silence, he would fill it. Luckily, Second Lieutenant Eugene Phillips arrived to absorb the conversation. He liked Phillips and knew he would respect his need for private time.

After a while, he pulled off his uniform and set it aside. He had decided to just take the pants and leave the rest. He'd strip off the gold stripe from the side of the pant legs and then be able to wear them at least for their warmth. There were too many shiny objects on the blouse.

At long last, Davis quieted down and recognized that Ross wanted to rest for his long journey.

With silence finally in control of the quarters, Ross was able to close his eyes and just let his mind wander until he drifted off to sleep while his last night as an officer in the United States army faded away.

———

Ross was up early, as he had been doing since he arrived at the Academy and maintained the habit after four years at West Point and then five years on the frontier. He walked to the latrine, relieved himself, washed and shaved, then headed to the barn where he saddled his horse and the pack horse. He led them back to his quarters and began to load the pack horse. The Sharps rifles were a bit of an issue, but he was finally able to tie them at an angle, and knew he'd have to get a couple of extra scabbards when he arrived in Britton. The rest of the packing went quickly, then he mounted his horse, led the pack horse out of the gate of Fort Sisseton waving at the guard, who still saluted even though he wasn't a commissioned officer any longer, and headed toward Britton. He was now officially Mister Ross Braxton.

He arrived in Britton just forty minutes later and stopped at the café where he enjoyed a better breakfast than he had ever had on a post. He ate every bit of his four eggs, six strips of bacon, and two biscuits, and washed it all down with four cups of coffee. After paying for his meal, he went back to his horses and rode them down to the other end of the main street to the general store.

"Good morning, sir. What can I do for you?" the proprietor said cheerfully as Ross entered.

"I've got to pick a lot of supplies for the trail that's going to take me clear down to Cheyenne. If you can think of anything that I might need that I forgot, feel free to let me know."

"Will do," he replied, and Ross was sure that he would.

Ross began piling items on the counter. Two slabs of bacon, ten pounds of coffee, beans, salt, five pounds of jerky, two dozen eggs, some potatoes and some onions. Then he bought a fire grate, a fry pan, a coffee pot, two tin plates, two cups and two spoons and forks, four boxes of matches and a hatchet along with four panniers to carry everything. Then he added a slicker, two blankets, a bed roll, a large spool of heavy cord, and the two scabbards for the Sharps rifles.

When he returned to the counter with the last of his items, he asked the store owner, "Did I miss anything?"

"You might want to add a heavier coat than the one you're wearing. A few pair of those heavy socks would probably be good, too."

"I'll do that."

Ross added the heavy coat, four pair of the socks, two scarves and two heavy union suits. He decided to buy a non-blue hat as well and found two knitted hats that might come in handy.

"So, how much did I damage my wallet?"

"$54.24"

"That's not too bad."

Ross handed him three twenty-dollar notes and accepted his change. He then loaded the items in the panniers, trying to keep them balanced, then when they were finished, lugged them out to the pack horse one at a time and hung them onto the pack saddle, alternating the load until the pack horse was weighed down equally, then used the spooled rope to tie them down. He checked the load balance, then attached the two new scabbards to the pack horse and slipped the long rifles into their new homes, which at least looked less ungainly than having them sticking out at odd angles.

His packing complete, he stepped up into the saddle wearing his new hat, new shirt and his gold-striped cavalry pants inside his army boots, then rode out of town at a slow trot, passing the fort forty-five minutes later and kept going. He didn't look back.

By the time he broke for lunch four hours later, he was already twenty-four miles southwest of the fort and was pleased with his progress. This was even better than he had hoped for, but it was expected at the start of his journey with fresh horses and the featureless terrain of the high plains.

He pulled to a stop, stepped down to rest the horses, letting them crop some grass and drink from a nearby stream. His lunch consisted of two strips of beef jerky and some water. He had three large canteens; two on the pack horse and one on the gray and kept their contents fresh by emptying and refilling them at every stop, not wanting to let the water pick up that delightful metallic taste.

He remounted and continued his southwestern heading. After he was underway, he pulled out his army compass to take a bearing. He supposed he should have turned it in, but the army didn't need it and he did. Without the accuracy of the compass, he could easily add sixty or seventy miles to his trip, and he didn't want to spend an extra two or three days on the prairie if he could avoid it. The one advantage of the prairie is that when he was mounted, he had a wide range of view. If the terrain was level, he could see almost five miles in any direction, but the plains weren't as flat as most people believed. Most of the time, there were a series of undulating rises that would cut down visibility or increase it if you were on the top of a rise. If you were walking, they wouldn't even be noticeable. There were also ridges, gullies, creeks and hills that broke up the landscape.

He hadn't seen anyone else on the prairie so far, and that was a good thing, because the only other humans he would most likely find would try to relieve him of his hair, and he liked his hair. It was just a light brown, but he had grown attached to it and would prefer that it stayed right where it was on the top of his noggin.

He was reasonably tall, an inch or so shy of six feet and well-proportioned. Women liked his handsome face and piercing green eyes, and he was fond of the ladies as well. To be honest, he liked people in general, but he was fonder of the gentle sex. But out here, there were so few unattached white women as to make it irrelevant. And he was travelling west where the numbers didn't increase but dropped even lower.

He kept his pace steady, not trying to wear the horses down. He had passed through Aberdeen two days ago and was close to Gettysburg where he could top off his supplies. He was still making good time and was ahead of schedule, and as long as there weren't any incidents to delay him, he could be there in another ten days.

———

It must be tonight when she made her escape. The Witch had heard the heated arguments and watched as the shaman pointed at her tipi and almost screamed to make his point. She only had a basic knowledge of the Sioux language, but it was enough to understand the gist of what was happening out in by the fire. The shaman was winning the arguments against those few who defended her. What good had the Witch ever brought to them? Her medicine was not as strong as his. He finished his argument by saying that tomorrow night, he would prove that his medicine was more powerful.

To the Witch, that meant that he would show the tribe that he could drag her to the wood pyre they would have to build and burn her alive, which drove her to make her final preparations to leave tonight or she'd never witness another sunset.

The weather was getting colder, and she knew she had enough food for a two-week's journey if she ate little. By then, she must either find somewhere else to live or she would die. She knew they would be able to track her, and her only advantage would be if she had a sufficient head start. But she would be on foot and they would be on their horses, so even if she were to walk twenty miles before they set out after her, they would catch her before noon. It was only a slim possibility that she could escape, but running was her only chance, and it had to be tonight.

The moon hadn't risen yet when the Witch sliced open the back panel of her tipi with a small bone knife that she had kept hidden. They didn't know she had it, and if they had found it on her, she wouldn't have had to worry about what would happen to her on the trail. She silently parted the hide and slipped through, holding her pack in her hand. She would put it on her back when she was far enough away. Now, she just walked as quickly as she dared without making a sound.

She was free, but she knew it probably wouldn't be for long, but death by a bullet or an arrow was preferable to being roasted alive.

———

Ross was shaving in a stream, despite the cold water, but he was used to it. Most men would just grow a beard rather than endure shaving like this, but he never liked facial hair of any form. He had replenished his supplies at Gettysburg, and it was only eight miles further down the trail from Pierre. He'd really stock up there, because after that, it was a long haul to the next place where he could buy supplies. He had measured his consumption rate of food and was pleased that it was lower than he anticipated, but he knew that could change if the snows came early. Out here on the northern plains, he'd seen blizzards show up in mid-October, and it was the seventeenth now. If the weather held and he didn't have any Sioux visitors, he should be able to make it to his brother's ranch by the end of the month.

Ross decided to take a break before packing the horses to try the Sharps rifles. He needed to make sure they both fired accurately and would fire three rounds through each rifle so he could gain confidence with the weapons. He didn't need meat yet, so he'd just pick a target. In some places on his trip, that would be difficult with no trees in sight, but here, next to the big stream, there were a reasonable number of trees, so he just needed to pick one out that wasn't too close.

He found a cottonwood that had been blown over by a strong wind sometime in the recent past, maybe a tornado. It was only about three hundred yards away, though, and he wanted a greater distance to test the length of the long guns. So, he slid six of the long cartridges into his jacket pocket, then picked up both Sharps and walked back another hundred and fifty long strides further away from the tree, which should put the target around four hundred and fifty yards. He then turned and looked at the distant trunk, satisfied that it was far enough away.

He flipped up the rear ladder sight and smiled when he saw the marks go all the way to eight hundred yards and was sure that the rifle could reach that distance. It's what this weapon was built for. He was just amazed that anyone could pick out a target out at a half mile. Maybe he'd get used to it once he started using the rifle.

He set the first rifle down on the ground and loaded a round into the breach of the second, adjusted the ladder sight for four hundred yards and felt the mild wind from the south. He also knew that the four hundred-yard marker on the sight was calibrated for sea level, and estimated his altitude at almost two thousand feet, so he left the range where it was for the four-hundred-and-fifty-yard shot.

He aimed the big gun at the target, held his breath momentarily and squeezed the first trigger, then pulled the second trigger gently. The kick and the rolling thunder of the gun surprised him, as it should, and even though the kick wasn't as bad as he expected, the sound was something else. He had seen the round strike the tree at the point he had chosen, sending splinters flying and was pleased with the shot, so he reloaded and fired his second. When he was finished with the first rifle, he was happy with the accuracy and devastating power of the big gun. *Thank you, Sgt. Frazier!*

The second rifle was just as accurate, so with a new sense of security, he returned to his camp. The horses had been startled with the booms of the large guns but had calmed down after the third shot. He took a few minutes to clean both Sharps before he walked to the targeted cottonwood. When he arrived, he was awed by the amount of destruction that had been done to the tree and was pleased that all six shots were within a one-foot diameter circle. He couldn't imagine what effect it would have on a human target.

He returned to his horses, slid both rifles back into their scabbards and packed up for the day's trip. He expected to be in and out of Pierre before noon.

———

The Witch had made her escape, but knew she was far from being out of danger and estimated she had already walked over twenty miles. She left no tracks that she could see as she walked in her moccasins but didn't think that the warriors that they sent after her would fail to find some sign of her passage. She still didn't hurry, though, nor did she stop to eat. She drank little, so she wouldn't have to make water on the dry prairie but would wait until she found flowing water to relieve herself.

She was tired from the lack of sleep, but her adrenalin kept her going for the first few hours. Once the sun rose, and her excitement of the escape left her, she began to feel the need for sleep creep up on her. Her legs were beginning to tighten from all the walking too, and the two failings combined to lower her expectations of evading her pursuers, but she maintained her resolve, which was the only thing keeping her moving.

———

At the camp, it was Still Water, one of the young warriors who had been assigned to keep the Witch in her tipi that night, who first discovered the slit panel on the back of the dwelling. He carefully opened the cut deerskin and went inside, fearfully at first. He, like many in the tribe, still feared her medicine, but he found that she had gone. He felt a rush of shame in his failure knowing that White Hawk would not be pleased, but he ran to let him know of the Witch's escape.

―――

The Witch crossed the swift stream after taking off her moccasins. She knew that the water would cause them to tighten as they dried and lose some of their strength and all of their suppleness. She finally relieved herself and walked further upstream where she finally found some rocks, stepped out onto them and dried her feet. Then she put her moccasins on and took a few bites of pemmican, drank from the stream, keeping her water supply intact for when there was no water, then continued walking south, constantly checking her backtrail for any signs she might be leaving behind.

―――

White Hawk was not pleased at all and Yellow Sky was furious. He convinced the war chief that having her gone from the village was not enough. They must kill her. White Hawk felt a personal animosity toward the Witch and didn't need the shaman's convincing. She had caused his son to be born without life, so he would go, despite the upcoming campaign against the bluecoats. It wouldn't take long to find her and kill her, and he asked that Yellow Knife accompany him to ward off her evil medicine. He agreed readily, and White Hawk ordered the two guards who had let her escape, Still Water and Running Bear, to join them in the hunting party. It would take them an hour to put together the weapons, food and water for the hunt. Then they would run her down, kill her and expected to be back later that morning, not realizing how early she had gone and how far she had traveled.

———

Ross met his goal and departed Pierre at eleven-thirty. He had really loaded up on supplies, and the pack horse wasn't happy. He continued southwest at a reasonable pace, stopping once for a long break.

He had another hour and a half of daylight, but he wanted to keep the horses healthy and finding a campsite wasn't difficult. There was a decent river south of the town that paralleled his path and its banks were populated with decent growths of trees. He finally settled on a nice spot about twenty miles southwest of Pierre.

He reached his campsite, dismounted and spent thirty minutes stripping the horses and set up for the night. He built a small fire and made himself a reasonably tasty meal of beans, bacon and onions, and coffee. After he finished eating, he cleaned up, then sat back with a cup of coffee and found that he was enjoying the journey. His lack of a garrulous companion, like Lieutenant Davis gave him time to think about what he would do once he settled down. The best option would be to tie on with one of the many railroads looking to expand as they were all hungry for engineers to design bridges and tunnels. Where he went to find the job was another question.

A lot depended on what he found when he got to Cheyenne. Specifically, what would happen when he met his brother and his wife. That would be uncomfortable at least, but he wanted to see how he was doing much more out of curiosity than any filial love. Ross knew that he should have returned to Minnesota to see his parents. It was closer and he was sure that he would receive a warm welcome, but he not only was curious about his brother, he wanted to see that part of the country.

He turned in early, as he expected to get an early start in the morning. From here on, there would be no more towns, and he'd still like to make at least forty miles a day.

––––––––

The Witch was surprised that she had gotten this far, but she was still nervous. She knew that she must have followers, but now it was dark, and she should be sleeping, but she decided to press on for as long as possible. Every mile that she could put between herself and the pursuers was another mile of life. With the full moon overhead that was to be the harbinger of her death but had failed in his duty, she had plenty of light to continue her journey, despite her incredible weariness and her tight legs, but she knew she'd have to rest soon.

––––––

White Hawk was getting frustrated. The Witch had left a poor trail to follow, so it had taken them much longer to track her than they had expected. Despite their advantage of being on horseback, he knew they were not cutting into her lead as much as they had hoped. Now, it was too dark to follow her light trail at all. So, they made a cold camp and waited for the daylight. There was no talk in the camp as each warrior reflected the mood of their leader.

———

The Witch's legs were growing stiffer with each step. She hadn't walked long distances in years. In the past two years, she had barely been allowed to leave her tipi. Finally, she found a good place among some bushes and laid down to get some much-needed sleep. She covered herself as best she could and let sleep take her.

———

After breakfast the next morning, Ross packed up the horses and was loading the Sharps when he decided it might be wiser to take one of the long guns with him, so he moved one of the scabbards to his riding horse's left side and slipped one of the rifles home. He was going into prime Sioux territory ahead and then the Badlands before he reached the Black Hills. Then, there was that long ride south with no settlements at all, but he was enjoying the peace and the solitude and hoped it remained that way.

Once mounted and moving, he was pleased with his decision to move the Sharps because it gave him a boost in firepower that might be necessary sooner or later. The rifle had a cartridge in its chamber, and he had six more of the long cartridges in his pocket. He felt confident he could fight off a band of Indians, as long as there were fewer than ten. He had the Sharps for long range, the Winchester for medium range and rapid fire, and the two Colts for close range. After that, all he had was his knife. If it came to that, he probably wouldn't fare too well.

———

The Witch was up and moving at dawn. She couldn't wait for another stream and had to relieve herself under the bushes and hoped that her followers wouldn't notice. Her legs were already stiff and uncooperative, but she hoped they would loosen as she walked.

Eight miles behind her, White Hawk and his three fellow hunters were on their horses and following at a faster pace than the Witch, but still only riding at a fast walk. Her trail now more visible as her stiff legs made scuffs in the dirt.

The Witch could almost sense their presence. She thought they were closer than they were and increased her pace, leaving a more obvious trail. She knew it was there but didn't think it mattered anymore. She began scanning someplace that she might use to disguise her trail, but knew it was of no use. They would catch her soon, but then, she wouldn't let them take her life easily.

Two hours later, it was Running Bear who found where she had spent the night and whooped to his chief. The other three trotted their horses to where Running Bear stood, pointing.

The Witch heard the whoops from Running Bear in the distance, and knew she was in a bad place as she had nowhere with nothing but grass all around her. The nearest trees were two miles away to the south, and it would be almost impossible for her to reach them before she was run down, but she had to try. She dropped everything she was carrying to help her make this one dash for freedom and started to move as quickly as she could. Her legs were so stiff, it was as if she were running on heavy sticks.

They were only two miles behind her now and gaining rapidly, but she was in the shallow valley between rises and they were on the opposite side and hadn't seen her yet, but she knew it would spot her within ten or fifteen minutes.

She didn't have to even wait that long as she heard them cry out from behind her when they crossed over their rise just a minute later.

———

Ross crossed over the eastern rise to the same shallow valley and saw the open plains below and spotted an Indian running about a mile away. He doubted if he was alone, so he needed to find his companions. He assumed that he was part of a hunting party whose horse had gone lame.

He took out his field glasses, put them to his eyes and was surprised to find that it was a woman, an old woman. She had long gray hair and was moving quite rapidly for an old woman, which impressed him. *But why was she running and what was she doing out here alone?*

He scanned his glasses to the opposite direction of her flight and saw the reason. Four warriors were about a mile and a half behind her and on horses while she was afoot.

Now, he had a decision. She was one of their own, *so why should he get involved at all?* Maybe she did something that deserved retribution, but the thought of some old woman being chased down by four healthy young men bothered him. *Hell, even if she was one of them, this wasn't right.*

He picked up the pace and began closing the gap while pulling his Sharps out of its scabbard knowing he was too far away for the Winchester. The problem was that they were moving across his path, which added to the targeting difficulty. He may have to take out one of their horses to slow them down first.

―――

White Hawk's group didn't pay attention to anything but their quarry. She was only a mile ahead and running for her life, which only proved to him that her medicine wasn't as strong as they had suspected. She could run all she wanted, but they had her now.

The Witch saw them and knew she couldn't make it. She stopped running and turned, the panic she had felt just moments before had evaporated and been replaced by anger. She stood with her arms folded as she defiantly looked back at her pursuers. She would die, but she would let them know she had no fear.

Even without his glasses, Ross saw the old woman turn and face her enemy. It was a display of bravado that reinforced his decision to help her. This old squaw deserved to live. He stopped the horses and stepped down leaving them unhitched and hoping they didn't run when he fired. He trotted a few yards closer with the Sharps and left the ladder sight at four hundred yards. He'd make calculated adjustments off of that.

Ross was confident in the range and knelt on the prairie, cocked the hammer back and watched the drama being played out just three hundred and fifty yards away, surprised that the warriors hadn't spotted him or his horses. They'd know soon enough that he was there.

Even though White Hawk desired retribution for himself, he still harbored a small amount of unacknowledged fear of her medicine, so he sent Still Water to make his attack and kill the Witch. After all, it had been Still Water who had let her escape.

Ross saw the warrior break from the pack, his war tomahawk raised over his head for a killing strike, making him the target for the first .45 caliber round.

He took aim, released the first trigger and led the warrior as he gently squeezed the trigger and the big rifle slapped him in the shoulder as it spat out a heavy slug of lead with a deafening roar that echoed across the open ground.

Still Water never heard the sound. The large bullet smashed into the left side of his chest, crashing ribs before exploding into his heart, the loud report rolling across the plains like lightning-less thunder as he slid off to the side and tumbled to the ground.

Ross was loading another round as the four remaining actors in the unfolding theater below him watched in shock when Still Water met his end.

The Witch was stunned by her sudden reprieve and simply stared at the empty horse and the other three warriors a hundred yards further away.

Ross may have been pleased with his shot, but he wasn't about to stop as he changed his aim, held his breath, released the first trigger and fired at another member of the hunting crowd, sending another large projectile hurtling toward Running Bear who was sitting on his horse just eight feet beside White Hawk.

The three remaining warriors, unlike the Witch, had swung their eyes to find the source of the sudden firing and spotted Ross kneeling on the ground in the distance and were mesmerized as they saw a white cloud bloom from his rifle.

Then, as the boom arrived, Running Bear felt a punch in the upper part of his chest, pulverizing his sternum before the .45 caliber streamlined slug of lead smashed through his aortic arch and lodged in his thoracic spine. The burst aorta dropped his blood pressure to zero instantly and the power from bullet knocked him backward over his horse's rump.

Ross didn't know that he had just taken out the two disposable members of the hunters, but the sudden impact of

Running Bear's sudden death sparked an overwhelming desire in White Hawk and Yellow Sky to vacate the area immediately. They could see the shooter under a cloud of smoke about four hundred yards to the southeast, but to charge at him would be foolish. They would return with a larger party to kill the Witch and if the white man was still near, to finish him as well.

White Hawk challenged Ross with a shake of his rifle, and screamed at him in Sioux, "You will die with the Witch, White Eyes."

Then he and Yellow Sky wheeled their horses and raced north.

The Witch, after hearing the second boom from the Sharps, had spun to the source of the sound and was shocked to see a white man. *What is he doing out here?* There was no settlement for fifty miles. When she quickly turned her eyes back to her pursuers, she saw another warrior fall to the ground, then dropped to her knees. She knew that she wasn't going to die today, and the incredible sense of relief combined with her complete exhaustion overwhelmed her. Her eyes rolled back into her head, and she collapsed face first to the ground.

Ross had watched the defiant war chief and his lone companion wheel their horses and race away, disappearing rapidly into the distance. He slid his Sharps into its scabbard, climbed back into the saddle and started down to see if the old woman was all right. He had seen her collapse and wondered if her heart had failed in the excitement. He was already wondering if he was going to take the time to bury her as those Sioux would probably be back and they'd be angry.

He took a roundabout track to see if he could gather one of the two Indian horses that were wandering loose and was able to snare the pinto that the attacking warrior had ridden. It seemed almost docile, as he tied the pinto to the pack horse and walked the horses the three hundred yards to where the old woman had fallen, her face hidden under her long gray hair. He still hadn't decided on what to do if she was dead but put it off until he checked her condition.

He stopped about fifty feet from the woman, dismounted, and ground hitched the gelding, took a canteen and approached the old woman warily. As far as she knew, he was just another evil white man, and if she was alive, she might pull a knife on him and end his good Samaritan ways.

The Witch had awakened and had heard his horses as they approached and wasn't sure if she was in a much better situation. The only white men who would dare travel alone out in these parts were little better than savages, so she stayed put.

Ross could see her hands extended to her sides, and he stared, noticing that they weren't wrinkled at all and there was no mottling that he had expected to find on the old woman. He crouched down next to her and touched her shoulder.

"Ma'am, are you all right? Would you like some water?" he asked.

She stirred and then came the most stunning word he would ever hear.

"Yes."

It was such a shock that he almost fell back on his haunches.

"Ma'am, you can speak English?" he asked.

Her hand pushed up from the ground and then pulled back her hair as she tried to sit.

"Of course, I can speak English," she snapped, with more anger than he expected considering she would be dead by now if he hadn't arrived when he did.

She slowly sat up and glared at him. If the discovery that she spoke English wasn't enough, when he saw her face, he found himself looking into the bright green eyes of a young white woman. A pretty, young white woman who happened to have gray hair, which he had never seen before on anyone under sixty.

He regained enough of his senses to hand her the canteen.

She pulled the cork and took several deep swallows letting the cooling liquid quench her thirst.

As she drank, she looked at her rescuer, and Ross was surprised to see anger rather than gratitude in her eyes, a confirmation that her earlier response wasn't a fluke.

"Ma'am, if you don't mind. I'll be moving on, but I don't believe those Sioux will take this defeat easily."

"So, you're just going to leave me here, then?" she asked angrily, again confusing Ross.

"I was going to leave you this horse and give you some food. Pierre is only about forty miles northeast."

"Listen, mister," she snarled, "I was caught by those bastards three years ago and they finally had a bellyful of me and were going to kill me. So, you think a horse and some food is going to let me live longer than a few more hours?"

Ross had no idea what to say next but gave it a try.

"Well, what do you want from me, ma'am? If you want to tag along, you're welcome, but, either way, I don't think it'll be wise to stick around here for very long. How far is it to their village?"

"I'd guess about twenty-five miles or so."

"Then, if they need more warriors, I'm guessing it'll be at least twelve hours before they'll be back because more than a simple hunting party like he had would require approval of their council and chief, then they'll have to wait for daylight to be able to track."

"What are you? What are you doing out here?"

"I just got out of the army and I'm heading to Cheyenne."

She glared at him, but with less anger as she asked, "Did you desert?"

Ross sighed. *Why would she accuse him of being a deserter?*

He replied, "No, ma'am. I resigned my commission, but I'd rather not stay here and discuss my military career. Are you coming along, or did you want to go your separate way? I can give you some food and a pistol with some ammunition."

The Witch thought about it. She had trust in no one but had no options.

"Alright. I'll follow you, but don't get any ideas. I'm a married woman," she replied as she continued to glare at him with her piercing, bright green eyes.

Ross stood and said, "Trust me, ma'am. That was the farthest thing from my mind,"

"My hair scares you too, does it?" she asked vehemently,

"No, not at all, but your attitude sure sets me off. Now, do you think you can ride the horse, or do you need a saddle?"

"I'll ride the horse."

He untied the horse and brought it to her as she struggled to her feet.

He hated to do it, but asked, "Do you need help, ma'am?"

"No, I can do it myself and don't watch when I climb onto its back, either," she said as she took the pinto's reins.

Ross didn't bother replying as he turned away, walked to his horse and stepped up into the saddle, not looking her way at all as he nudged the gelding to the southwest at a walk to allow her to catch up.

The Witch had some difficulty getting mounted with her legs in such poor condition, but she kept her eyes focused on the disappearing rider to make sure he didn't watch her as she managed to get climb on the horse's back, exposing her legs. Once she was on the horse, she tugged her buckskin skirt as far as it would reach and started after the ex-soldier.

They rode southwest, and he listened to hear the softer approach of the unshod Indian horse. Ross knew he was leaving an easily tracked trail behind him, but it really didn't matter now. He had no doubt that he'd soon have to deal with a large band of angry Sioux warriors.

She finally trotted the horse next to him and said loudly, "You know you're leaving a trail that a blind Irishman could see, don't you?"

He kept his eyes focused ahead as he replied, "Yes, ma'am, I'm aware of that. The Sioux that tried to kill you will backtrack to our starting position quickly, and I would rather put as much distance between us and them as possible. If I spent a few hours trying to hide the trail of three horses, it would buy us maybe a half an hour if that. Oh, and you're welcome, by the way. I must have missed your expression of appreciation for saving your life at the risk of my own."

As harsh as she appeared to be, his comment still hurt. She knew that she hadn't thanked him, and that if he had done nothing, she would be dead, and he could ride on in safety. Now, he would have hostile members of the tribe chasing him because of her. But the feeling of guilt wasn't enough to get her to say anything.

He finally turned to the gray-haired young woman and said, "My name is Ross Braxton, by the way."

She thought about it for a solid minute, then judged it not to matter and finally said, "Amy Childs."

"Well, Mrs. Childs. I hope your demeanor improves somewhat because it's going to be a long trail to go where I'm headed or even until we reach the next settlement. Now, I don't mind riding in silence, but I don't want to ride along thinking I'm going to get waylaid by a knife in the back."

"I won't kill you," she replied.

"Well, thank you for that positive comment."

Amy wanted to reply but kept silent.

They rode on for three more hours before Ross found a spot near a horseshoe lake that he could use to water the horses and let them rest.

Without turning, he said loudly, "We're going to stop here to let the horses rest."

She said nothing as he pulled over to the small lake, its shape a remnant left over when the river changed channels.

After he stepped down and led the two animals to water, Ross looked over at the woman, still sitting astride her horse.

"Are you going to let the horse drink?

"I would if it could get down."

Ross wasn't sure if he could trust her promise not to kill him but walked over to her horse and put his hands around her waist and lifted her to the ground, keeping his eyes diverted, knowing she would let him know if she thought he might take a glance. He could tell that her legs were almost useless, when after he had put her onto the ground, she wobbled and leaned on the horse trying to stand. She didn't complain, but she didn't take a step, either.

"Stay there for a second," Ross said.

Ross jogged over to his horse and pulled off his bedroll, returned and stretched it out in front of her feet and picked her up again. He put her feet down on one end of the bedroll and keeping his hand on her shoulder as a brace, he walked around to her back.

"Now, just lean back slowly."

He didn't expect her to comply, but she did, and Ross lowered her slowly to the bedroll.

Once she was on the bedroll, he said, "Now, try to stretch out your legs."

He watched her face grimace as she tried to straighten them.

"Okay. Now, I know you don't like me and probably think I'm Satan incarnate, but we need to get some blood flowing in your legs, or they'll stiffen more. This will take me five minutes, and you'll have to trust me when I tell you I'd prefer not to do this. I'm going to have to rub your legs to get the circulation restored. If you'd rather that I don't do it, just tell me."

Amy thought about it. Her legs hurt badly, and she knew that more time riding would make them even worse, so she said, "Can you give me a gun to stop you if I think you're going too far?"

Now, it was Ross's turn to think about the consequences of agreeing with her request, so he said, "I'll give it to you, but first you need to promise me that you'll just tell me to stop and give me a chance to back off. It wouldn't be fair for you to just shoot me and not let me know that you thought I had overdone it."

"Alright. But if I tell you to stop, you'd better stop quickly."

Ross let out a sharp breath, rolled his eyes, and handed her his left-hand Colt.

She laid back on the bedroll with the Colt in her left hand. She had no idea how to shoot it, but he didn't know that and was surprised he had agreed to give it to her in the first place.

Ross pulled back her deerskin skirt and noticed how bunched up the muscles were. It was like they were permanently cramped and must be extraordinarily painful.

"I know this is going to hurt. Your muscles are all knotted up worse than I thought possible."

She didn't reply as he began with the right calf. He worked his fingers slowly into the muscles, rolling them gently at first, and could feel them spasm.

Amy felt the pain, but she also felt her muscles begin to relax. It was an unusual sensation with both pain and relief at the same time. The more he worked on the right calf the better it felt. Then he began on the left side. Again, the pain, and again, the relief. It took more than five minutes for each calf.

"Ma'am, I'm going to have to do your thighs now. I won't look. You can watch me to make sure."

She did just that, keeping her eyes focused on him, but the soothing relief from his magic hands would be worth it even if he had gone too far. She watched him anyway, and he kept his word as his head turned away and never even tried to peek.

Ross noticed that her thighs weren't as bunched up as the calves, but because they were bigger muscles, they took just as long. When he finally finished, his arms felt like they were going to fall off.

"Okay, I'm done. Is that better?"

"Yes," she answered, then after a pause, said, "Thank you."

"You're welcome. Now stay there for a few minutes. Try and stretch your legs. I wouldn't bend them yet. They may cramp up again. Would you like something to eat?"

"Yes."

"I normally have a cold lunch, but you look like you could eat, so I'll cook something. The Sioux would already know where we are anyway, so the smoke doesn't matter."

Ross dug a small fire pit, filled it with kindling and set it ablaze. He took out his grid, placed it over the fire then went down to the lake and filled the coffee pot with water. When he returned, he threw a can of beef into the frypan and added a can of beans, let them get warm until the mix began to simmer, then added some salt, removed it from the fire, added some coffee to the boiling water and removed the coffeepot as well. He filled a plate with the beef and bean mix, put a spoon onto the plate, filled a cup with coffee and brought them to her. He set them down next to her then walked to the pack horse, pulled a pannier free, returned and placed it behind Amy.

"Alright, sit up and I'll slide this pannier behind you for support."

She slowly sat up, and Ross slid the pannier against her back. She leaned back as he put the plate on her lap, left the coffee next to her and without a word, went back to the fire where he filled his own plate and cup, and silently had his own dinner.

When they had finished, he tossed the remaining coffee on the fire and began putting things away. He went back to the woman, who simply handed him the plate and cup without a word.

He shrugged and took them down to the lake to clean them before putting them away. Then he went back to her and asked, "May I have my Colt back now, please?"

She gave him the gun, and he slid it back into its holster and pulled the hammer loop in place.

"Can you stand up, or do you need help?" he asked.

She tried to stand, but her legs were still stiff, despite the pain being gone.

Ross sighed and picked her up and sat her on the horse, again keeping his head averted while she adjusted her skirt, and without a word, she turned the horse southwest and began riding away as Ross stood there in surprise watching her leave.

Ross shook his head, then walked back to the camp, picked up the pannier, lugged it back to the pack horse, hung it in place and tied it down before returning, rolling up his bedroll and securing it to the back of his horse, then finally mounting and starting out southwest. She was already two hundred yards ahead, and Ross let her go. At least he wouldn't have to worry about having her drygulch him if he kept her in view.

———

White Hawk and Yellow Sky trotted their horses back to the camp, taking four hours of time they didn't want to waste. When they arrived, White Hawk called for a council meeting to seek the approval of the chief, Walking Buffalo, to mount a larger expedition to hunt down the Witch and her white-eyed protector.

————

It was getting dark, and Ross had to find someplace to camp for the night; someplace he could build a fire without having it seen for three miles, but the small river he'd been following was long gone and the White River was still about twenty miles away and there were no trees here at all.

He had cut into her lead, so he could at least get her attention. It had been a peaceful afternoon ride, but he knew that was about to change.

Finally, he said loudly, "Ma'am, there's no place near where we could set up a proper camp, so we'll set one up here. I'll dig a decent hole for a fire and that should hide it well enough. I don't think they'll be back for a while anyway."

Ross stopped the horses and stepped down, glanced her way and saw that she had turned and was riding back to the new campsite.

When she was close, Ross looked at her and asked again, "Can you get down or do you need help?"

She didn't answer, but she didn't dismount either. Ross shook his head and walked to the horse and lifted her down.

At least she didn't wobble this time when he set her on the ground.

After she was standing, she tried some small steps.

Ross noticed and said, "Well, you seem to be doing better. I'll get the bedroll and you can lie down and try to stretch your legs."

He didn't get a response and frankly he was puzzled. She had said thank you once and he thought she was going to begin to behave more sociably, but apparently not.

Ross untied his bedroll and stretched it out on the ground near her feet.

"Did you want to try to sit down, or do you need some assistance?"

She slowly bent her knees, waiting for the cramping in her legs to start, but it didn't, so she knelt, then put her hands on the bedroll and turned, sitting down on the soft sleeping bag and took in a deep breath.

"Good. Go ahead and relax. I've got to take care of the horses and unpacking. I'll make something to eat later."

Amy felt useless. She felt as useless as she had in the past three years at the Sioux village. She didn't want to be so obnoxious, but it had been her salvation for so long that she found it to be the best defense. She didn't understand why she continued her behavior after being treated with so much consideration, but didn't change it either.

Ross unsaddled the horses and removed the loads from the pack horse. He led all three horses to a small wallow that had some muddy water, let them drink and then crop grass.

He took some of the wood he had gathered on his journey because he knew there wouldn't be any for long stretches along the way, started the fire and set the cooking grate on top, poured a half canteen of water into the coffeepot and put it on the grid. For dinner, he cut up a potato into small cubes, opened a tin of beef and dumped it into the frypan then dropped the small cubes of potatoes in the frypan and added some onions and salt. Then he let it simmer for a while to let the potatoes soften. The coffee was ready, so he pulled it from the cooking grate and set on the edge to keep it warm. After ten minutes, he pulled the stew from the fire and spooned more than half onto a plate. He poured a cup full of coffee and brought both to a sitting Amy, handing her the plate with a spoon and left the coffee on the ground beside her.

He returned to the fire for his own dinner, keeping his back to her so she wasn't offended by seeing his face as she ate.

She tasted the stew. She hadn't said anything earlier, but the lunch he had given her was the tastiest thing she had eaten in years. She knew it was canned beef, but still, it was so good, and the stew was even better with their long-missed potatoes and onions. She savored every bite. And then there was the coffee. She had forgotten how much she had missed it.

Ross finished his dinner, then walked over to Amy to take her empty plate and asked, "Would you like some more coffee?"

It almost hurt her to say the words, but she replied, "Yes, please."

Ross was mildly surprised but didn't say anything. He just took the pot over to her and refilled her tin cup, brought it back and handed it to her.

She held it tightly in her hands and began to sip.

Ross returned and used some of the coffee to clean the plates and frypan and left the cookware out for breakfast.

The coffee made Amy realize she needed to empty her bladder, so she rolled over and pushed herself into a standing position and began to take some wobbly steps. Ross watched her from the other side of the camp to make sure she didn't fall but remained sitting.

She waddled over to an area far enough away in the dark, managed to relieve herself without any problems, and felt better, so she tried to walk around for a few minutes and with each step, she felt a little better than the last.

After she returned, she arched her back, put her hand on her lower spine and then walked back to her bedroll. Things were working better now, and she felt almost human again.

Ross was relieved when she returned but turned his eyes away to avoid conflict.

When she returned to the bedroll, she managed to sit down and then stretch and bend her knees without too much discomfort.

Ross noticed that she was doing better, so he walked over and said, "Ma'am, I think we need to turn in early, so we can get an early start in the morning. Do you think you can get into the bedroll all right?"

She nodded and slid her feet into the opening and wiggled inside, feeling warmer already as the bedroll kept the cool breeze off her bare legs.

Once she was inside, Ross said, "Good night, ma'am," then turned away.

Ross walked to the other side of the camp, impressed that she hadn't threatened to do him bodily damage if he came within twenty feet, then pulled off his boots and slid under the blanket. He had placed his slicker on the ground to keep out the dampness, but it would still be cold on his back. It was going to be a cold night in the front side too.

———

White Hawk had been given permission to chase down the Witch and the white-eyes and would be allowed to take Yellow Sky and six other warriors. He was pleased, although he had silently wished for ten warriors. He had witnessed the devastating effect of the white man's loud rifle and already knew that he would lose some warriors in the attempt. They had never even seen him before he fired and then when they did, he was far beyond the range of any of the rifles they had. But six was the best he was going to get, and he still believed it would be more than enough. He planned to depart in the morning and begin hunting his prey.

CHAPTER 2

Ross was up early, the predawn sky just beginning to lighten, and it was cold, which was no surprise at this time of the year in the Dakota Territory. He wondered just how cold the woman was with her bare legs as he looked over and saw Amy snuggled in the bed roll. Maybe she'd be in a better mood after a good night's sleep. *Who knew?* Maybe it would be worse, although he didn't see how that was possible unless she sprouted horns. He had been calculating how many days to reach Cheyenne before, but now his goal was Fort Robinson in Nebraska where he could drop her off and proceed on the rest of his journey in peace.

He went to his pack and took out a half slab of bacon and six of his eggs, restarted the fire and poured water in the coffeepot and laid some strips of bacon into the frypan, hovering over the fire for the heat.

As the bacon began to sizzle, the aroma floated across the camp. Amy's eyes popped open and couldn't believe the smell. *Bacon!* She hadn't had any for years, but she closed her eyes again and just inhaled the intoxicating scent. It would be too much to expect bacon and eggs, not out here.

She opened her eyes and slid out of the bedroll, feeling the full effect of the cold air as she did, so she left her legs in the bedroll when she sat up. She was still stiff, but not nearly as bad as yesterday.

Ross saw her sit up and said, "Good morning, ma'am. I'll have breakfast ready shortly. If you want some privacy you can go over on the other side of the horses. I won't look."

Amy definitely needed the privacy, so she pulled her legs out of the bedroll and stood, her legs feeling almost normal. She walked easily toward the opposite side of the camp on the other side of the horses to use them as an obscuring wall.

After she finished, she walked back to the campfire, and as she approached, Ross took a piece of cooked bacon and held it out to her. She accepted the piece of savory meat, closed her eyes and took a bite, letting the long-missed flavor fill her mouth.

Ross watched her almost serene face as she chewed. Maybe he should just keep giving her bacon the rest of the day.

He returned to the fire and added some more bacon to the frypan. Normally, he'd cook two slices, but this morning, he cooked six. He was still only planning on having two for himself, though. When the last of the bacon was fried, he cracked open the eggs into the popping bacon grease, then after they were cooked, he lifted out each one on a fork and laid them on the plates, putting four strips of bacon and three of the eggs on her plate.

Amy had heard him cooking, finally finished her one strip of bacon, and had then watched the east for followers as the first hints of dawn brightened the horizon.

Then she heard Ross say, "Here you go, ma'am," and she turned to face him.

Her eyes must have been deceiving her when she saw a miracle. There were bacon and eggs on the plate he was holding out for her.

She said nothing as she took the plate. She should be bouncing around for joy at the sight, or at least saying 'thank you', but she didn't.

Ross ate his breakfast quickly and began cleaning up while Amy took a little longer to savor her larger helpings, but soon finished her bacon and eggs and sipped her coffee. She returned her plate, cup and fork to Ross and was going to say something but stopped herself.

Ross saddled his horse and loaded the pack horse in record time and just kicked the dirt back into the fire pit. The Sioux could easily find the tracks anyway.

Ross stepped up into the saddle and waited until he heard the woman's horse moving, not wanting to offend her this early in the day by looking at her. Once he saw her pass in his peripheral vision, he started southwest at a fast walk.

Amy took her accustomed position fifty yards ahead, which he found odd. He would think she's stay close for protection, but if she was afraid of him, which she obviously was, then why wasn't she behind him? He shrugged off the question, and Ross thought how odd this whole trip was becoming. He just hoped it didn't include a confrontation with any pursuing Sioux, although after recalling the rage on the face of their leader, he was sure they were back there. The questions were: how far back they were, and how many were in their party?

––––––––

The answer to Ross's questions were twenty-three miles back and eight pursuers, including Yellow Sky. They were moving at a good pace, about half again that of Ross and Amy. They had ridden quickly to the spot where Ross had picked off two of their warriors, but they stopped to bury both men and that slowed them down. Then they easily picked up their trail from there. They could tell by the prints and the condition of their horses' droppings that they were less than a day behind. White Hawk was further incensed that the Witch was riding Running Bear's horse.

––––––––

Ross thought again about trying something to throw them off the trail, but realized it was a waste of time. Even the unshod horse left deep imprints, and there aren't any streams to try to go up or down, either, but that wouldn't slow them down much anyway. Maybe they'd get tired of the chase after a day or two, but he didn't think so. Their leader had called her the witch when he'd shouted. At least he understood the reason for that, but the anger behind the threat wasn't directed at him so much as it was at her. It had all the earmarks of a blood feud and he wondered what she had done to anger them. She said she had been kept there for three years, and suspected it had something to do with the gray hair and those remarkable green eyes. He'd never seen anyone with either feature before, despite his own lighter, less noticeably green eyes, and imagined that the Sioux had put great store in her appearance and kept her alive because of it, but she sure did get them angry over something. Maybe the one who was so mad tried to make her his wife and she turned him away. He had to admit, aside from her witch-like behavior, she was a very attractive young woman. He wondered if he'd get the full story of why she was running for her life before those Sioux attacked.

An hour later, he saw something on the horizon ahead, so he halted the horses, pulled his field glasses, looked ahead and smiled. It was a line of trees which heralded the arrival of the White River. They'd be able to find a good place to camp with water nearby and plenty of wood for a fire for the next few days.

Momentarily forgotten were the eight hostiles now less than twenty miles behind.

He returned his field glasses to his saddlebags and started forward again. The woman had continued riding away when he stopped to look and was more than a hundred yards ahead now. Ross was going to yell at her to turn southwest toward the trees but decided to just let her go. He was tired of having to worry about where she was going, and if she didn't want to stay close, or even bothering to check behind her, then he'd just let her go wherever she wanted. He angled his horses to his left and set them to a medium trot.

After ten minutes, the distance between Amy and Ross was more than a half a mile as she kept going without once turning to see where he was.

Ross could see the White River beyond the trees, and despite himself, did keep an eye on the woman in the distance to make sure she wasn't surprised by any other Sioux.

It was Amy's stomach that finally caused her to realize that she was riding alone. She knew it was almost time for the noon break and turned slightly to see if he had closed her gap. She was suddenly terrified to see no one there. *She was alone again! He had deserted her!* She quickly turned to her left and with relief and anger, saw him and the pack horse angling away from her and were about eight hundred yards away. She turned the horse and put him into a fast trot toward Ross, seething at his thoughtlessness. *He was trying to get rid of her after all!*

Ross saw her coming and quickly read the fury on her face. Well, that was just too damned bad. He wasn't going to put up with it any longer. Either she would be civil, or she could go back to the Sioux.

She finally pulled up next to him and let him have it with both barrels.

She shouted, bordering on a scream, *"What the hell was that all about? Were you trying to get rid of me?* That was a nasty trick to pull! *How far were you going to let me go, all the way to Wyoming?* I can't tell you how angry I am! If I had a gun, I'd shoot you through the heart, assuming you had one!"

Ross kept riding, looking straight ahead as he loosed the left Colt's hammer loop, pulled the pistol and handed it to her, never saying a word.

Amy was taken aback by his response. He didn't yell back at her or threaten her, but when she said she was going to shoot him, he just gave her his gun.

She took felt the heavy weapon in her hand and shouted, "Maybe you didn't understand me. I said I was going to shoot you, and I meant it!"

Ross halted the horses, turned to her and said loudly, "Go ahead. I gave you a pistol, and frankly, I don't care if you shoot me in the heart or in the head. At least I won't have to put up with your lousy attitude anymore. I've tried to be considerate because you're a woman. If a man had treated me as badly as you had, he'd be either dead or waiting for those Sioux before now. You've been rude, heartless and unforgiving. Now, I can deal with the silence. That's fine. But when you do things like ride off, so you don't have to see my sorry ass and expect me to come trailing after you, begging for you to return, that's a bit too much. Now, I spotted the White River to the south a few minutes ago and I wanted to change direction to get there quicker so the horses could get water and there would be firewood. If you had been where you should have been, I could have just told you without having to ride fast just to catch up with you and tell you what I was going to do. If you think that I was asking too much, then go ahead and put me out of my misery, because, Mrs. Amy Childs, riding with you has been nothing but annoying agony."

Amy was speechless. She wanted to be offended and scream at him, but she knew he was right. She had been all those things and more.

She took a deep breath, and said, "I'm sorry. I'll try to be more civil."

"Good. That's all I'm asking. You don't have to be friendly. I'll be more than happy with just civility."

"Okay," she replied quietly as she handed him back his Colt.

Ross accepted the pistol, slipped it into his holster and lashed it down.

A short time later, they reached the White River. Ross stepped down and Amy slid down from her horse, then he led them to the bank and let them drink, before leading them to a large grassy area to let them have their fill.

With the horses peacefully grazing, he built a small fire and set up the cooking grate, then chopped up some bacon into the frypan and when they were cooked, he dumped in a can of beans. He estimated that at their current rate of consumption, now that he had to cook for two, they had maybe a week of food left, which should be enough to get them to Fort Robinson. He added some onion and let it simmer while he took the coffeepot from the grate and then the frypan. He filled Amy's plate and brought it to her as she sat on a fallen tree trunk.

Amy accepted the food, but said nothing, as she was deeply miserable for her hostility and despicable behavior. He had treated her as if she were a good person, feeding her and even curing her of her aching muscles. He had given her the bed roll while he slept on the hard ground under a blanket, not to mention that minor detail of saving her life when he didn't have to, and she had been nothing less than a complete bitch.

She knew she wasn't that way at all, but after three years of not trusting anyone and having to maintain the fearsome demeanor to enhance her position as the Witch, it had become second nature. She sighed and decided that she had to try and return from being the Witch to being Amy again.

Ross sat near the fire eating, wondering how far away the Sioux were. If they were within fifteen miles, they could cover that in one night and be on them in the wee hours of the morning, but they'd have to guess where they were. He shook his head and figured that they'd attack in the day unless they became desperate. Still, he'd better keep checking their backtrail.

He then changed his view, looked to the west and saw the line of clouds crossing the horizon. It looked like snow or freezing rain in their future.

He put down his plate and walked over to Amy.

"Ma'am, if you'll notice to the west, there's a line of clouds heading this way. Now, it's pretty early for snow, but it's not out of the realm of possibility. But it surely will be getting colder. You aren't exactly dressed for the cold. To be honest, you're not even dressed warmly enough for the mild weather we've been having, and your deerskin dress isn't very good for riding, either. If I could offer a suggestion, I'd recommend that you change into something a lot warmer. Now I have some spare britches and a shirt you can have. I also have some new heavy socks and a spare pair of boots. I'd really recommend is a heavy union suit underneath it all, too. I have two new ones in the packs as well and other cold weather gear you could wear. I have a scarf, a knit hat, some gloves and a heavy jacket."

She looked at him and answered, "A union suit wouldn't be very practical for me, would it? I'm a woman, remember?"

"So much for civil," Ross thought.

"Yes, ma'am. I'm aware of that. Understand that they're not very convenient for men, either. So, what I do is cut them in half at the waist. The top half becomes a nice warm inner shirt, and the bottom becomes a pair of inside pants. I cut small holes along the waist of the bottom half and tie them to the belt loops of the britches. Then, when you take off one, the other comes off."

"Very innovative," she replied in an obviously sarcastic tone.

"Never mind, ma'am. I just thought I'd offer. If you start getting too cold, let me know," he said before quickly turning, then walking back to the fire and his lunch.

Amy watched him leave and wondered why she had answered as she had. She was just chastising herself for being a witch and she did it again. She already was cold and if those clouds held snow, and they probably did, she'd get even colder. *What was wrong with her?*

Ross was through trying to be nice. He tried. He had really tried. From now on, he'd let her stew in her own meanness. He'd talk as little as possible and just let her tag along, or he'd tag along if she insisted on riding ahead again.

When he finished his food, he glanced over, noticed she was done eating, so he walked over, took her plate and cup and returned to the fire, dumped the coffee onto the embers, then washed everything and put them away. He walked to the horses, mounted the gelding and began riding, acting as if the woman didn't exist. If she wanted to come along, she could.

Amy had been deep in thought and didn't even notice what Ross was doing until she heard the horses' hoofbeats, looked around and saw him riding away. She quickly then popped to her feet, hurried over and mounted her pinto then trotted to catch up. She decided to ride behind him so she could keep him in sight, and stayed closer too, riding only twenty yards back.

———

Sixteen miles south, the eight Sioux also noticed the increasing clouds, and kicked their horses into a fast trot to close the gap and ate as they rode rather than stopping.

The clouds now covered the sky, and the temperature had dropped a few more degrees as they rapidly closed the distance between them and their prey.

———

Amy was decidedly cold, and her open skirt was letting the wind blow right between her legs. Her only heat was from the pinto and it only warmed her butt and inner thighs. She wanted so badly to ask for his help, but she couldn't do it. She just couldn't and didn't understand why.

Even though Ross promised himself that he wouldn't do anything for her anymore, when he glanced behind him to see if she was there, he saw her chattering teeth and her loose arm wrapped around her and changed his mind. This was just getting silly.

He stopped riding, stepped down and walked to the pack horse as Amy pulled up alongside wondering what he was doing.

Ross untied one pannier, lifted it free, lowered it to the ground, then rummaged around and pulled out a scarf, one of the knitted hats and his spare pair of gloves, then stepped over to Amy and handed them to her.

"Now, you put these on. I don't care if you hate me till doomsday, I am not going to let you freeze to death."

She said nothing but put on the hat, wrapped the scarf around her neck and pulled on the gloves.

While she was doing that, Ross went to a different pannier and pulled out the heavy coat. He brought it to her and handed it to her.

"Now, put this on," he said almost daring her to argue.

She took it, then pulled it on and immediately felt the warmth take over, or at least the lack of cold until her body heat made it warm inside.

Finally, Ross took two blankets from a pack and walked to her horse. He tossed one across her lap and then wrapped it around her left leg. Then he walked to the other side of the horse and tossed the second blanket across her lap again and wrapped that around her right leg.

He didn't wait for the curses to start for getting so close to her, so he just walked back to the gelding, mounted and started him walking again.

Amy followed on the pinto, feeling much better physically, but even worse inside than she had before. She wondered if he just enjoyed being treated so poorly. It was a stupid idea, but what else could explain how he treated her, despite how she treated him. But he sure didn't seem happy with her when he asked her to be civil, yet she had to admit that she hadn't even managed that.

It was difficult to see which came first, the snow or the dusk as both started at the same time. It wasn't a driving snow, but a gentle drifting snow with large flakes that initially melted when they hit the slightly warmer earth.

They pressed on for two more hours, still riding into the growing darkness. That gave them five more miles over their followers, who had to stop after nightfall or risk losing the trail. They were back to a twenty-mile gap, and by then the snow had accumulated to over two inches, hiding the trail that had been so easily followed earlier.

Finally, Ross pulled them toward the river and the trees, where he found a spot hidden among the trees with easy access to the river and where the trees kept the snow from accumulating.

Ross didn't say a word as he began unloading the horses. Amy rode close and took off the blankets, so she could slide from the horse and was instantly appalled how cold it was when she did. When she did get on the ground, she wrapped one of the blankets around her waist and draped the second across her shoulders.

Ross led the horses to the river and let them have some water, and after they were satisfied, he led them back to a grassy area where they could eat.

Ross went back down to the shelf on the riverbank to build a fire pit and knew that between the snow and the bank, no one could see a fire unless they were fifty feet away, and if they were that close, he'd be dead anyway. So, he dug a hole and built a good-sized fire, put on the cooking grate on top, filled the coffeepot with water and set it on the grate before digging out the frypan and dumped in a can of beef before adding a can of beans and a can of tomatoes and some onions.

While that was simmering, he went back to the packs and took out the tent. He laid it down and spent five minutes to set up. Setting up a two-man army tent was something he could do blindfolded, and once the tent was finished, he returned to the fire, took the coffee and the frypan from the grate and poured a cup for Amy and filled her plate with food. He brought them to her and set the coffee next to her and gave her the plate, not waiting for a thank you. There was no point anyway.

He returned to the fire and ate his own meal and drank his coffee, then, after he was finished, he cleaned up his plate, walked over to Amy and took her empty plate and returned to wash hers, leaving her the cup so he could give her a refill, knowing he would want one as well.

He went to the horse and took out the bed roll, carried it to the tent and rolled it inside, then returned to the packs and found a spare pair of pants, and one of the extra heavy union suits which he promptly cut in half with his knife. He also took one of his spare shirts, a pair of heavy socks and his spare pair of boots, returned to the tent and tossed them all inside before returning to where Amy was sitting.

"Ma'am, now I know you don't want me talking to you, but I need to tell you this, so I apologize in advance. Your bedroll is in the tent. I've also put a pair of pants and that cut union suit I mentioned earlier. There's also a shirt and a pair of socks and boots. Now, the boots may not fit well, and if you don't want to wear them, just leave them in there, and I'll pack them back up in the morning. You may as well get some sleep."

Ross turned and went down to the fire, madder than he had been in years, but held it inside. If she had been a man, he would have beaten her until next Sunday, instead, he sipped at his coffee as he sat on the log stewing in his frustration.

As he sat staring at the flowing river with snowflakes still drifting past his eyes, he heard a noise behind him, knew it had to be her and was expecting another tirade, so he steeled himself.

Any brushed off some snow from the log and sat down next to him.

She lowered her head and began to speak in a normal, conversational voice.

"Three years ago, I was in a wagon train with a married couple named Everson. We were going to Oregon. They were acting as escorts to take me to my husband. We were attacked by the Sioux, and they killed everyone there but me. The warriors saw my gray hair and green eyes and it scared them. They were going to leave me and then decided to take me into their village because they thought I had great medicine. I was terrified. Once I arrived at their village, no one would go near me because they were afraid of me. Nothing bad had happened so they didn't know if I was good medicine or bad, but they thought I was powerful, so I became what they expected me to be. I was mean and vicious and had to keep them worried enough to leave me alone.

"The following year, things were good. An antelope herd arrived, and they ate well and had plentiful crops. So, they thought I was good medicine, and I grew meaner and more distant. I would go into trances and not say anything for days, and it terrified them. It was that way the next year as well. There were no disasters at all, not even big blizzards.

"Then, last summer, things changed. Their old shaman died, and his replacement, Yellow Sky, had hated me from the start because I took away some of his power. Anything bad that happened was blamed on me, no matter how trivial. The antelopes continued their migration leaving the tribe low on meat, then there was a long drought and their crops of corn shriveled away. And then, a few weeks ago, their war chief, White Hawk, lost his son when he was stillborn, and Yellow Sky blamed me for his death.

"I heard them talking and knew they were going to kill me, so I ran. It was White Hawk and Yellow Sky along with two others that trailed me and were about to kill me when I heard the thunder of your rifle and watched the warrior fall from his horse. In just seconds, everything changed. That second loud boom was as if God had spoken to me, but it was your rifle that had done the talking.

"But after having spent three years being angry and mean to survive, and not trusting anyone, it was just so hard for me to get over that. It was difficult to believe that there was someone who didn't want to kill me or take advantage of me. I kept trying to convince myself to stop behaving that way and I wouldn't even listen. I don't know why I kept doing it. You've been nothing but generous and considerate to me and I've treated you horribly and behaved stupidly. I am so sorry for how I've acted, and I'll try not to do it anymore."

Ross was stunned but her story explained everything, and he went from hating the sight of her to feeling enormous compassion for what she had undergone for three long years.

He turned to look at her sorrowful green eyes and said, "Amy, I'm sorry I acted the way I did. Forgive me, I just didn't know."

"You didn't know because I didn't tell you. I don't have to forgive you for anything. May I call you Ross?"

"That's my name, so of course, you can. Now, if you'd asked me if you could call me Clarence, I'd have to think about it."

Amy laughed.

Ross smiled as he watched her. Now there was a sound he hadn't ever expected to hear from her, then saw her wipe a tear away from the edge of her eye.

"I haven't laughed in three years," she said quietly.

"Well, Amy, if we carry on normal conversations, I'll make sure it won't be another three years, okay?"

"Thank you for everything, Ross. I'll try not to be a bitch anymore."

"Amy, it's all water under the bridge. Now, you should go to sleep. We need to get under way early, so we can take advantage of the snow."

"Where are you sleeping?"

"I'll stay out here. I have my slicker. I'll be fine."

"Okay."

Amy had thought about sharing the tent, but she was a married woman and that just wouldn't do. But she knew he'd be cold while she was warm, and that wasn't right, either.

"Ross, if you understand that I'm married, you can share the tent. I know you'd be cold and wet outside. That's not right."

"Amy, I really don't mind sleeping outside. I've done it before. I'm from Minnesota, you know."

"No, I didn't know that. We weren't talking very much. But I'd prefer that you sleep in the tent. I'd feel better knowing you were warm."

"Alright. I'll give you about twenty minutes to put on your new clothes except for the boots, of course. Keep the flap down and I'll let you know before I come in. How's that?"

"That'll be fine. Thank you for the clothes, too. I really was freezing."

"I know. You go ahead."

She smiled at him and returned to the tent.

Ross was still uncomfortable with sleeping in the tent with her. *What if she had a nightmare and saw him less than a foot away?* A lot of bad things could happen. The only good thing was that she was right. He would be warmer and drier and having Amy being a normal human being was much better than what she had been before.

Twenty minutes later he walked over to the tent and noticed that her deerskin dress had been unceremoniously tossed outside and smiled at the sight.

"May I enter, Mrs. Childs?"

"Yes, you may, Ross," she replied from inside the tent.

He pulled back the tent flap and ducked inside. He had his spare blanket under his arm, and she was already scrunched up inside the bedroll.

Ross duck-walked to the back of the tent and then stretched out, pulled off his boots, then noticed that she had already spread out the two blankets that he had covered her legs with earlier.

"That was very thoughtful to put out the blankets, Amy. So, I think I'll turn this one into a long pillow."

He unrolled the blanket and folded it twice until it was almost four inches thick.

"Lift up your head, Amy."

She did, and he slid the blanket under her head.

"Thank you, Ross. That's very comfortable."

"Good. Now you get some sleep."

He slid under the blankets and found himself a foot away looking into her green eyes.

Amy asked, "I'm not that tired, Ross. Now that we're talking, could we talk for a while?"

"Sure. What do you want to talk about?"

"Why are you here? I mean, where you found me, there aren't any white settlements for more than fifty miles."

"I was on my way to visit my brother. He has a ranch near Cheyenne. I had just resigned my commission in the army and had no particular place to go, so I figured I'd head that way."

"Why did you resign? Didn't you like the army?"

"No, it's just the opposite. I loved the army and I still do. It's all I've known, really. I left the family dairy farm in Minnesota ten years ago to go to West Point, then, after I was commissioned, I spent six years at Fort Wadsworth, which was changed to Fort Sisseton just a little while ago. I enjoyed the camaraderie and even the discipline, but after Custer's fiasco, the army brass decided to initiate reprisal raids against the Sioux. Now, I had no problem whatsoever fighting against their warriors, but I objected to orders that were sending us to ride through villages with only a few warriors and lots of women and children. I was told either go on the raids or resign my commission. So, I got out."

"Oh. Did you do well at West Point?"

"Yes. But the class sizes were a lot smaller after the Civil War ended."

She smiled again and asked, "So, you finished pretty high, then, didn't you?"

"If you must know, I finished at the top of my class. That's probably why I was given the option of resigning my commission rather than face a court martial. If I was just a run-of-the-mill lieutenant, they probably would have hanged me."

That startled her and she asked, "They would have hanged you for not killing women and children?"

"Yes, ma'am. They saw it as a lawful order, but I disagreed. They didn't want it to get out that one of the Academy's best and brightest wouldn't follow the order, so they let me go."

"That's terrible."

"I thought so, but I got out and here I am on my way to Cheyenne."

"What's your brother like?"

"Now, that, Amy, is an interesting question. He's five years older than I am. It was ironic, really. He had a chance to fight in the war, but said he was needed on the farm. I wanted to go but was too young. Anyway, when I was very young, my big brother was like a hero to me. He was much bigger and stronger than I was, and all the other boys seemed afraid of him. It wasn't as if he was my pal or anything, it's just that he didn't pay attention to me.

"Then as I grew older, he did begin to notice me. He was big, and I was small. Suddenly, he went from hero to bully in just a month or so one summer when I was eight. What really bothered him was that I liked to read. He hated it and thought I was a sissy. So, he'd do what he called the 'girlie dance' on me two or three times a week and kept it up until I was ten."

"Then what happened? Did you beat him up?"

Ross laughed and replied, "Hardly, he was still a lot bigger than I was. But I discovered I was a lot faster than he was, maybe because I was so skinny, and he was a lot bulkier. So, from then on, when he tried to catch me for one of his 'girlie dances', I would run like crazy. He couldn't say anything about it, either.

"He dropped out of school in the sixth grade and got a job at the local lumber mill, and never gave a dime to my parents. He said it was his money, and my parents were well off anyway, so they didn't object. Well, I continued reading and enjoyed my time in school now that he was gone, and when I finished high school, I applied for West Point. I took their entrance examination, did well and left home."

"Did you have any girlfriends?"

"A few. But that's another interesting story. My first girlfriend was Bessie Petersen. She was a typical Minnesota schoolgirl with blonde hair and blue eyes. Anyway, she was my girlfriend and she thought it would be exciting to be an officer's wife, until I explained to her that I wouldn't be an officer for four years and that ended the relationship. Then in my sophomore year at West Point, I found out she had married."

"Did that bother you?"

"Not in the least. By then, I had seen her as just a girl with blonde hair, blue eyes and cute dimples but no force of personality. There was nothing there. Ask her about the weather and that was about the depth of conversation you could have with her. The funny thing was who she married."

"Who?"

"My older brother. Our great uncle Joe out in Cheyenne had died and left him a ranch, and Bessie thought it would be exciting to be the wife of a rancher, so she batted her eyes at him and off they went. The last time I knew they had two children, too."

"So, why are you going? Do you want to see her again?"

"Heavens, no. I really don't want to see him either. But for some reason, deep down, I'm insanely curious about how that worked out. I mean, I could have gone back to Minnesota much more quickly. It's only a two-day ride from where I was, but it just tickled my fancy to go and see what they're like. You never get to see that in letters. Not that I have ever gotten one from him in six years. I've written him a number of times, but never got a reply. Besides, I really wanted to see the country more before I decided what to do with the rest of my life."

Then he said, "So, Amy, as long as we're talking childhood memories here, tell me about yours."

She sighed and said, "I grew up in eastern Dakota Territory. We lived on a small farm south of Jamesville. My parents had me and my two younger brothers. It was hard, because we didn't have much money. Like you, I loved to read and would walk three miles to the town library. It wasn't big, but it had enough to keep me happy. I had to drop out of school in the third grade when the school closed, and they closed the library a few years later when I was thirteen, but I was able to get a lot of books when they closed it.

"My husband was raised on the next farm and I was the only girl within five miles, so we were married four years ago. His older brother had gone to Oregon three years earlier and had built a lumber mill and asked his brother to join him. Aaron, that's my husband, left four months after we were married and said he'd send for me as soon as he found someplace to live. His brother only had a small place, so he had to find another one for us. He wrote to me six months later to join him and so I was able to join up with Mr. & Mrs. Everson. We just never made it. I watched them die in front of me."

"Amy, tell me, what was your favorite book," Ross asked wanting to change the subject.

"I loved Ivanhoe and I always pictured myself as Lady Rowena, but I felt closer to Rebecca. How about you?"

"I enjoyed Caesar's Commentaries more than most. Julius Caesar was an amazing man. When I was at West Point, we'd get into arguments about who was the greatest general all the time. Most of my classmates would choose an American general: Washington, Jackson, Sherman, Grant, or even Robert E. Lee or Stonewall Jackson. I chose Julius Caesar.

"He fought and won so many battles against superior forces. My favorite was the battle of Alesia. He had trapped a Gallic army in their mountain fortress city, and they outnumbered him, but he laid siege. His legions build this enormous breastwork complete with towers and trenches on both sides of their encampment. It was seventeen miles long and surrounded the entire mountain. Can you imagine that? Building an entire defensive work around a mountain!

"Then Caesar was attacked by another army with more than double his numbers from the outside of his encampment, and as his legions were engaged with the new forces, the besieged army charged out of the fortress and attacked from the other side. His army was now outnumbered four to one and being squeezed from both sides. When it looked like the Romans might lose, Caesar rode to the front of the army in his bright red battle cloak, so all his men could see him. It turned the tide and the Gauls were defeated and never challenged Rome again."

Amy had listened, mesmerized by the story and watched his excited eyes dance as he spoke, even in the dim light of the tent.

"Ross, that's one of the best stories I've ever heard. It surpasses many of the tales I've read about and what makes it fascinating is that it's true."

He smiled at her. "History is often that way, with extraordinary stories that are more amazing because they really happened."

"I wish I wasn't so stupid, though. I only went through the third grade."

"Amy, you're selling yourself way too short. You are far from stupid. In fact, you sound very intelligent. Education is a funny thing. You only went to the third grade and my brother went to the sixth grade. Now, who is better educated? Technically, it's my brother because he was in school three years longer than you were. Now, I'm telling you this in all honesty, because in reality, it's not even close.

"You are much better educated than he is, because you read. I've met officers who had college degrees that were quite ignorant. Daddy paid their way through college and they got their piece of paper at the end. I'm surprised that some of them could read it. You are not only not stupid; you are very well educated. So, enough of that."

"I never looked at it that way."

"You should. Never equate lack of intelligence with ignorance. We are as smart as we will ever be the day we are born. You were born very smart, and I'll admit that I was as well. After that, it's just a question of replacing ignorance with knowledge. We can go to school, we can read, learn from other people or learn from our mistakes. We all have a lot to learn, Amy, including college professors and generals...especially generals. I've had privates that were smarter than me, but just needed to learn. Now, before we get to sleep, is there anything else you want to know?"

"Just one. What happens to me after we get to Cheyenne?"

"When we get there, I'll buy you some clothes, give you some money, and buy you a train ticket to Oregon."

"The train goes all the way to Oregon now?"

"Yes, ma'am. I hear that the Northern Pacific is going to build another route right across the Dakotas soon, too. Too late to be any use to us, though.

"Unfortunately."

"Okay, let's get some sleep. And Amy? One more thing."

"What's that?"

"I'm really happy we're not enemies anymore."

"Me, too. Goodnight, Ross."

"Goodnight, Amy."

Amy rolled onto her back, closed her eyes and felt immensely better for being Amy again and talking to Ross. She also was pleased that he thought she was smart.

———

White Hawk was explaining to his warriors how he planned to make up the distance, despite the snow. He said that the two whites were following the river and they could do the same and not even bother tracking. When the snow melted, they'd pick up the trail, then move at a fast pace and not even worry about losing them. His men agreed, not that it mattered as their war chief had told them of his plan.

CHAPTER 3

The next morning, Ross woke up before dawn and wondered if he would ever be able to sleep past six o'clock. He lifted the flap to check on the depth of the snow and found that it must have stopped shortly after they had gone into the tent, as its depth hadn't increased over the two inches that had already fallen. He reached down, picked up his boots, pulled back the blankets and put them on, then donned his coat and slipped outside, trying not to wake Amy.

He walked through the snow and found a private spot, made some yellow snow, then he returned to the location of his previous campfire. He noted that it wasn't as cold as it had been yesterday and guessed that the snow was going to melt soon which would make the ground tougher going for the horses.

He started the fire and put the grate over it, and soon he had coffee water heating and bacon frying.

Amy smelled the bacon and knew Ross was anxious to get moving, so she slid out of the bedroll and pulled on her boots. She had been so warm last night and had a peaceful, contented sleep for the first time that she could recall. She was glad that she and Ross had talked for so long and was happier they were friends and not silent enemies. She knew that she was the reason they had been at each other's throats, but that was over now. She was Amy again and would be as pleasant as she'd been when she'd been just a girl before she was married.

She quickly put on her coat and her hat, then put her gloves into her pocket with the scarf. She walked around behind the trees and tried out Ross' union suit modification. She was pleasantly surprised that it worked exactly as he said it would, and her bottom didn't have to stay exposed that long at all.

By the time she hustled down to the fire, Ross had two bacon strips for her and more bacon and eggs.

"Good morning, Amy. Are you ready for breakfast?"

"I'm starved," she replied with a smile.

"Good. We're going to make this quick,"

He spooned out the food and poured some coffee, and they ate quickly.

The plates were cleaned, and they carried the camp necessities back to the panniers, before Ross removed the bedroll and blankets from the tent and put them where they belonged, then he collapsed the tent and quickly rolled it into its stored condition, loaded the pack horse and they were ready to leave after thirty minutes. Having Amy helping made it quicker, not to mention much more pleasant.

―――――

White Hawk and his warriors had started thirty minutes earlier, just following the river and not bothering looking for signs as their horses' hooves left their prints in the already melting snow.

———

Ross had them moving at a good clip, almost as fast as the Indians despite the mud. White Hawk had gained distance by getting started earlier but were no longer gaining substantially. Ross's plan for continuing for a couple of extra hours the evening before had added to the separation, and they were still eighteen miles behind when Ross and Amy began moving.

As they kept the horses moving at a steady trot, Ross said loudly, "Amy, sometime today, I'm going to start looking at our back trail using the field glasses. I don't know how far behind they are, but if I get a good vantage point, I'll stop for a few minutes and look back with my field glasses. If I see them, I know they're within ten miles. If I don't, we know we have at least that much of a gap."

"Okay."

Ross kept the pace as fast as possible and kept looking for a high spot that would allow him to check their backtrail. He would have climbed a tree, but the leaves would be obstructions. Then they began a gradual climb up a gentle rise. It wasn't much, but when they reached the top of the incline, he'd stop and stay on his horse to look behind them.

"Amy, when we reach the crest of this incline, I'm going to take a quick look. You can too, if you'd like."

"Oh, I'll be looking. Trust me," she replied.

He kept the horses moving at a good clip and soon reached the almost undetectable summit, stopped the horses, then twisted in the saddle and using his field glasses, scanned the backtrail, not seeing any sign of the Sioux.

But as he scanned to his left and then back to the front, he stopped. He looked more closely in the direction they were headed, and saw four Indians, most likely Sioux, coming in their direction. He couldn't see if they were a war party or a hunting party, but with only four, it was almost assuredly a hunting party.

"Amy, we have visitors, and not the ones we expected. There are four Indians directly in front of us. It looks like they're following the river as well. It's probably a hunting party, but we can't avoid them."

"Are we going to have to fight them, too?"

"Let me think for a minute."

Ross thought of possible ways to get past them without slowing down too much. After a minute, he turned to Amy.

"Amy, can you mess up your hair to make it look crazy?"

"Of course, I can," she said.

She began rustling her hair with her fingers and pulling it up and out. After a few seconds, it was flying everywhere.

She asked, "How's that?"

"Perfect. Now here's what I plan to do. We are going to ride straight at them like we don't have a care in the world. That is because you are controlling me like a puppet. I'll speak to them, but I want you to just glare at them. Don't say a word. I'm going to tell them how I ran into you out on the prairie and you had just killed some warrior by chanting and then took his horse. Then, I'm going to point to the direction we want to go.

"When I do that, I want you to say my name, loudly. Screech it if you can. Then after I react, I want you to say something in gibberish, or at least in English that even if they understand English, they won't recognize. I'll take it from there. Now, I'll have my Colt's hammer loop off as a precaution, but I'd rather not use it if I don't have to. I'd rather we just take a minute to talk our way past them than get into a fight. Are you ready?"

"Yes."

"Let's go, crazy woman. Stay to my left. If I need to use my Colt, I want you out of the way."

She moved over to his left side and they began their descent. Ross could see them pointing at him and Amy and he thought, "Let the drama begin."

As the two groups of actors closed the distance between them, Ross could see that three were armed with single shot carbines and one had a bow. None of the hammers were back on the guns, so that was a positive. He never even glanced at Amy as they came with a hundred feet and Ross stopped.

In an almost catatonic voice, he said in Sioux, "My name is Ross Braxton. I was traveling and found this woman. I thought she needed help, but then she cursed me and now I need to be free. She has too much magic. I watched her curse a warrior and take his horse. She wants me to go there,"

Then, he pointed to the southwest signaling Amy's entrance onto the stage.

"Rossssssss!" Amy screeched.

Even he felt a chill down his neck, as he saw the four Sioux shrink back.

Ross grabbed the left side of his head like he had been struck with a tomahawk and screamed.

Then she pointed southwest and blurted, "Ivanhoe Rowena Robin Hood Julius Caesar!"

Ross began nodding his head violently and then at last said to them, "The woman demands to go forward. Please kill her for me. She will kill me soon in much pain. I cannot fight her medicine alone. Kill her, please!"

Finally, one spoke, "It is your fate, white eyes. We will not help you. We go."

With that the four turned to the north and quickly rode off, throwing wary glances backward as they rode. Amy kept staring at them as they trotted away.

Not a minute later, they were moving southwest again. After five minutes, Ross took out his glasses to make sure the Sioux were still moving north and was relieved to see that they were still moving away at a rapid pace.

"Amy, you were spectacular. I was scared to death myself."

"I've had experience acting the crazy woman," she said as she began smoothing her hair back down.

"I've got to wash this mess sometime. You don't have a comb, by any chance, do you?" she asked.

"No. Never use one. Sorry."

"That's all right."

"Would a hairbrush be alright, though?" he asked innocently.

"*You have a hairbrush*?" she exclaimed.

"I figured it would come up sooner or later."

"Can I use it now?"

"Sure. I have it right here in this saddlebag, where I keep the soap."

He handed her the brush and she began stroking it through her long gray hair as they rode.

"Amy, I don't want to cost me our new friendship, but could I ask why your hair is gray?"

"To tell the truth, I'm wondering why it never came up before. Usually that's the first thing that anybody asks. The simple truth is that I was born with it for no reason that we know of. It was a lot of trouble for me growing up, if you can imagine. When I was small, I was considered a freak. Maybe that's why I read so much, so I could escape."

"Amy, I hate to tell you this. But I actually like your hair."

That startled her, so she turned in mid-stroke and said, "You have to be joking. Nobody, including me, likes my hair."

"I may not have liked it when you had it all over the place when you were the crazy lady, but when you brush it, it glows. It's like the final stage of blonde hair. I've seen some women up in Minnesota that have blonde hair so light, it's almost white. All those Scandinavians, you know. Maybe that's why I like it. I was used to lighter shades. But looking at you now, I think if you had brown or even blonde hair, it wouldn't suit you as well, but your gray hair really makes your green eyes stand out. Again, it's just my opinion."

"Ross, I still don't know what to make of that. Are you just trying to be nice?"

"Not at all. I don't lie or exaggerate, Mrs. Childs. If I thought you were homely or your hair was hideous, I wouldn't comment at all. I'm just telling you what I see."

"Well, then, thank you."

"You're welcome."

They continued riding as Amy continued brushing her hair with a smile on her face. No one had ever told her that her hair looked nice before, and she knew that Ross meant it, too.

———

The interlude with the Sioux hunting party had allowed White Hawk and his band to close the gap. They were within fifteen miles now and soon would reach the spot where Ross and Amy had camped. The temperature was rising close to forty degrees and the snow was melting faster.

The trail would still be there, with or without snow. The only thing that would make a difference would be if the two white eyes had changed direction in the snow and they hadn't noticed. If the snow continued to melt, they would know soon.

Ten minutes later they spotted the new, even easier to follow trail in the melting snow and White Hawk felt vindicated when the hoofprints appeared, so they picked up the pace.

———

"We should see the Badlands coming up on the right in another five or six miles. There are two spots near the river where we'll have to cross strips of the Badlands, but not very far."

"Are you sure we should stay by the river?"

"It's a good idea. Besides, it'll cut down the distance to Cheyenne. I'd guess we're about two hundred and fifty miles away now."

"Do we have enough food for that?"

"We're okay. I can always shoot some game if we need meat. But we're only about seventy miles from Camp

Robinson and another hundred from Scotts Bluff. So, food shouldn't be a problem."

"Speaking of food, do we stop for lunch?"

"We can. It'll have to be quick, though. The horses need the break and some water themselves anyway."

"That sounds good."

The day was warming, and the sun felt good. The snow was gone, and the ground was muddy as Ross turned them to a small lake where grass grew right up to the shoreline.

"Let's stop here, Amy. This is as good as it gets."

They pulled up and after dismounting, Ross let the horses drink and feed while he took off one of the panniers and built a quick fire, popped on the grate and frypan and dumped in some beans and some cut up jerky. He made some coffee and let the beans and jerky simmer. Soon he was spooning the quick mix onto their plates and pouring coffee. They ate quickly, and Ross had everything repacked in just ten minutes. The entire stop took forty-five minutes.

But those minutes brought White Hawk's band three miles closer, and they were now within fourteen miles. Since they had found the trail after the snow melted and picked up the pace, they had been gaining, but their horses were tired. They hadn't been fed as much, nor as well-rested as Ross and Amy's mounts, and they had been pushed harder. The six warriors assigned to the hunt weren't pleased with the treatment their horses were undergoing, nor were they happy with their own lack of food. They hadn't brought enough for an extended hunt because they had expected to return after two days.

White Hawk had undergone a transformation that was noticeable to all of his men. He had ceased being a practical, thinking war chief, and developed an almost maniacal sense of revenge against the Witch. This change was fueled by Yellow Sky who constantly reminded White Hawk of the Witch's part in the stillborn death of his son.

———

Ross took a long look at their backtrail, then said, "Amy, I have a feeling that our friends are closing the gap."

"Why? Did you see something?"

"No. I think they're running out of time. They probably didn't pack much food because they probably figured they'd run us down a lot faster. If they're still behind us, their horses must be more tired than ours because it's always harder to chase. It's possible they turned around, but I have feeling that they might make a run at us while we're sleeping if they are still back there. Say they're fifteen miles behind us. If they give up tracking and are willing to push their horses to the limit, they wait for us to stop and they keep going. If we stop at seven o'clock or so, and they keep going, they'd catch us by ten o'clock. Then, it's just a matter of finding us."

"I can see that. What do you think we should do?"

"I know that I said we were going to stick to the river, but I think for tonight, we swing into the badlands a mile or two. Nothing more than that. We don't make the turn until it's dusk. That way, if they plan on a late-night attack, we won't be where they think we are. If they aren't going to attack and wait to start tracking in the morning, we may lose a mile or two, but they'll still be behind us. I'm even thinking of setting up an ambush if we spot them, but right now, with the badlands just a few miles ahead, that's where we should go. We should see the badlands in another hour or so and we can scan them for a good place to go and when sunset starts, we can make our turn."

"That's a good plan, Ross. I'm glad you're on our side. When we turn, do we do anything different?"

"No. But I think I'm missing something. Can you think of anything?"

She thought about it for a minute, then replied, "Not a thing. We're buying some security and sacrificing some time. Besides, if they ride all night, their horses won't be able to follow us anyway."

"That's true. If you think of what I may have missed, let me know."

"Yes, sir."

"You know, that's funny."

"What is?"

"For almost six years, I have heard 'yes, sir' probably thousands of times. That's the first time I've heard it since I left, and I don't miss it one bit."

She laughed, and they pressed on.

———

Eleven miles back, White Hawk was telling them of his plan to attack them while they were sleeping. The only one who expressed doubt in the plan was Yellow Sky. The others wanted to get this chase over with and get back as their horses were close to exhaustion. If they had to ride five more hours to finish the job, so be it. Yellow Sky said something about the Witch's medicine being too strong to allow for them to sneak up on them at night, but White Hawk's position as war chief allowed for no more discussion. The Witch and her companion had not deviated from their path along the river for three days. Why should they change in five hours?

———

The sun was going down, and they were getting ready to make their change in direction. Ross and Amy were scanning the badlands to their right. It was rough terrain with high walls of rock.

"Amy, let's turn right here," he said loudly.

"Alright."

"When we get far enough away from the river, about two miles, we'll turn back to the southwest. It'll take us out of the badlands, so even if they catch our turn somehow, turning again may really throw them off."

Amy nodded before she turned her pinto to stay on Ross' right side. She glanced into the dusk to the east expecting to see White Hawk and his men but couldn't see anything.

———

It was getting darker and White Hawk was getting tense. He knew they were close, but how would he know that he had found them? Their horses would smell his and could give them away, but if they were that close, it wouldn't matter, so they pressed on.

He could have had a warrior walk and follow their trail on foot, but that would add hours to their hunt, and he wanted to get them as soon as possible. He wanted to end this hunt tonight.

———

Ross and Amy had gone two miles, turned southwest again and exited the badlands and after another two miles, Ross thought they were safe enough. There were no trees, but there was a remnant of the badlands that offered a small box canyon that would be ideal. They walked the horses into the canyon to the very end and stepped down. Ross hitched the three horses and they unloaded the pack horse and unsaddled the gelding. Ross estimated the distance to the small canyon's opening was around only about sixty yards across and four hundred and fifty yards from where they'd set up camp. As a precaution, he loaded both Sharps and laid them across the packs.

"I apologize for the cold camp tonight, Amy. I just think we're hitting the danger time. They're close enough now that they could mount an attack at any time."

"Is there a chance that they've given up and returned?"

"Maybe. I just don't feel it. When you were on the ground and I had just killed two of his warriors, the chief made a few gestures and threats in my direction. He sounded like he really wanted to get you. It sounded like a blood feud and he's never going to let this go."

"I can live with not having hot food," she said.

"We'll be all right, Amy."

―――――

The danger was very real. In that twist of fate that changes lives, the moon appeared and the angle was perfect as the moonlight outlined the tracks of their first change in direction toward the badlands.

White Hawk whooped and pointed out the change, and they began following north. He tried to speed up his horse, knowing they were close, but the mare could give him no more. All eight horses were spent, but they continued to ride them into the badlands. Then, thirty minutes later, they made a mistake when they kept going after Ross had made the second turn, missing the change in the trail, even in the moonlight. It could have been a disastrous mistake if they had fresh horses and kept going deep into the Badlands, but they stopped when their horses simply gave up less than a mile from the second turnoff.

———

"Did you hear that, Ross?" Amy asked when she heard the loud whoops issued by White Hawk as he discovered their first direction change.

"Yes. I think they found our new trail, Amy."

"What do we do now?"

"You will get some sleep. I'm going to stay up for a while. That old myth about Indians not attacking at night is just that. The good news is that our little canyon is a very good defensive location. They can't climb behind us or on top. With their rifles, they can't hit us from the end of the canyon either, but I can hit them. If they're stupid enough to try a bull rush, I'll pick them off with my Winchester. So, you go and try to get some sleep. Okay?"

"Okay. I am tired."

She smiled, slipped into the bedroll, and closed her eyes as Ross sat and watched the end of the canyon.

———

In the badlands two miles east, White Hawk was trying to convince his warriors to tie down their horses and make their attack on foot. None of them were enthusiastic about the idea.

It was night, and although they would attack at night, it was only when they knew where the enemy was and what his disposition was, and this was neither. They weren't even sure which direction to go.

It was Yellow Sky who finally squashed the idea by telling White Hawk that at night, the Witch's medicine was stronger than his because she received her powers from the moon while his strength was from the sun. White Hawk thought about it and gave in but told them that they would make their attack with the sunrise.

————

After an hour or so of waiting, Ross judged that it was unlikely they would be coming tonight. He set his pocket watch's alarm for five o'clock just in case his mind's normal wake up alarm failed him for once, then pulled a blanket over himself, falling asleep around two o'clock.

The next thing he knew the light dinging from his pocket watch announced the arrival of five o'clock, and he pressed the button to silence the chiming.

He shook off the blanket, finding it not as cold as he would have expected. He stepped behind the only sizeable rock on the floor of the small canyon and relieved himself, then he stepped back around and began making a fire. He knew the only ones who could see the flames had to be at the mouth of the canyon, and he could already see the opening in the pre-dawn light, so he felt having a fire was no disadvantage. The tracks led directly into the canyon anyway, so the fire wouldn't make any difference.

By now, he wanted them to come so this could be over. He was confident in their position and the amount of firepower he had. They knew about the Sharps, but they'd be shocked when he began using his Winchester, if they were stupid or angry enough to try a frontal assault. More than likely, they'd lay in wait for him and Amy to leave the canyon, assuming that they hadn't heard the whoop announcing that they were still following.

If that were the case, then he'd give Amy a pistol and a quick lesson on how to fire it and then walk out to the mouth of the canyon with his Winchester, one of the Sharps and spare cartridges in his coat pockets and face them there. He still didn't know how many were there and if it was a large group he'd take out as many as he could and hope that no more than one or two survived and Amy could surprise them with the Colt.

He really hoped that they were so angry they'd make a bull rush, but wishes and hopes didn't usually come true, especially not in the Badlands of Dakota Territory.

He put the grate on and put a half canteen of water into the coffeepot, sliced some bacon and put the frypan on the fire.

Amy smelled the cooking bacon, knew she should get out of the bedroll, but decided to spend an extra few minutes luxuriating in the warmth of her cloth cocoon and her newfound friendship with Ross.

Finally, she opened her eyes, saw Ross pouring beans on the second chunks of bacon he had put into the frypan after removing four strips of cooked bacon. She smiled and slid from the bedroll.

"Good morning, Amy. If you're looking for privacy, the only place is behind that rock over there."

"Good morning, Ross. I'll be right back," she said as she scurried behind the rock.

Ross smiled at the sight of the baggy-dressed Amy trying to move quickly.

She returned shortly, and as she sat, she asked, "I appreciate the hot breakfast, but why did you build a fire?"

"They know we're in here anyway, so I thought that we'd have ourselves a nice breakfast to start our day. The other small advantage is that by building the fire it's almost like sending them a signal that we don't know they're there and that will build their confidence."

She nodded, then waited and watched Ross cook, and a few minutes later, he presented her with her large breakfast.

The sun was breaking over the horizon when they began to eat.

———

White Hawk's hunting party had been up when Ross first began cooking. They were annoyed when they discovered that the trail they had been following was no longer there and had to backtrack. The warriors all knew it was at White Hawk's insistence that they continue on after the initial sighting of the trail that had added to their delay. They walked their horses as they continued backtracking their own trail, then found the turn to the southwest made by their soon-to-be victims. Dawn was breaking as they began to follow the trail.

Ross packed all their things into their respective panniers, assisted by Amy.

"When do we get going?" she asked, noticing he was making no move to pack the items onto the pack horse.

"We're not. We'll stay right here and wait. I'll give them three hours to find us. I want them to rush at us through that canyon mouth. If they do, I'll wait until they've committed themselves to the attack and then I'll shoot every last one of them. But it's much more likely that they won't do that. They'll probably just wait for us to leave and then I'll have to go get them, and if I have to do that, I'll tell you how that's going to work later if it's necessary. Right now, we prepare for them to come into the canyon."

"So, what do we do?"

"Here's what I'm planning on doing. The Sharps rifles are both loaded and ready to fire. The Winchester has a full tube of fifteen cartridges. I'm going to put a box of ammunition by the Sharps and another by the Winchester. Both Colts will have all six chambers filled. Then we wait and watch the canyon mouth. If they're stupid enough to come in, we let them. There is only one way in or out. We both stay low, and I want you flat on your back and I'll be sitting between the two Sharps. If they come, I'll let them get as close as they dare so they can't run back and escape."

"Okay," Amy replied, looking grim but determined.

Then he pulled his left-hand Colt and said, "Amy, I know you don't know how to fire a pistol. I could tell by the way you held it a couple of days ago, so I'm going to give you this for personal protection if any of them make it past me. I don't know how many there are. To fire it, just pull the hammer all the way back, point it at your target and pull the trigger. You'll want to use both hands, so the kick doesn't knock it free from your grip. This is only as a last resort, okay?"

She accepted the pistol, looked at it through different eyes than she had before, and said, "Okay."

He gave her a warm smile to alleviate her fears that he was sure were there, and said, "Alright, Amy, let's kill those bastards."

Amy looked at Ross, felt a flush of confidence and smiled back before lying on the ground, but she pulled a blanket over, folded it into a pillow and slid it under her head, so she could watch what was happening.

Ross was calm, as he always was just before a fight, and if they came into that canyon, it wouldn't even really be a fight, it would be a massacre, but a massacre of their own making. It would turn the canyon into a shooting gallery.

———

White Hawk was getting excited. He knew they were nearby. He could feel it. Then he saw the trail turn into the small canyon, and he stopped his warriors before he slid from the horse. He pointed out the change and told them to move forward on foot.

After they were all dismounted, White Hawk said, "This white man has a big rifle that can shoot at great distance, but it takes him time to ready the rifle for a second shot, and he may be still sleeping, or perhaps he is enjoying the Witch as a woman even as we stand here."

He waited for the expected laugh, and when it finished, he continued.

"He will not expect us to attack so soon, if he even suspects we are here, but it does not matter. One or two of us may die, but no more. We will be welcomed into the great gathering as warriors and will have ended the evil that this Witch has brought to our tribe. I will go and see where they are. Load your guns and prepare to make our attack."

He looked at each of his warriors, and except for Yellow Sky, saw anticipation in their eyes for the upcoming fight. Yellow Sky didn't matter to him anymore.

He left the group, and walked quickly to the edge of the canyon, slowed down at the end canyon wall and peered into its length. *He saw them!* They were at the far end of the canyon, and there was smoke from a small fire, but he spotted no movement, so he waited, still staring trying to pick up the white man and the Witch, but in the shadows of the canyon wall, all he could pick out was the fire, and he didn't like the idea of a fire.

If they were sleeping, the fire shouldn't be there, unless they had built it during the night for heat and kept it going. It would be so like the white man to do something so stupid. White Hawk had seen their campfires all along the trail and they were much too large. He began to believe that they didn't even expect his warriors to still be behind them.

He was so anxious to kill them both that he threw aside even the smallest amount of all of the tactical training he had received that allowed him to become a war chief. He began fitting the evidence he was seeing into what he wanted to see. He convinced himself that the fire was from last night and that they were asleep.

He knew that the best way to kill them was to set up outside the canyon and wait for them to run out of water, but his obsession prevented him from making the correct decision. He wanted them dead and he didn't want to wait, and then rationalized his decision by their lack of food and the tired state of their horses.

He returned to his war party and told them there was no movement and it was a good time to make their attack. They would move swiftly and scatter across the sixty-yard-wide opening. They could reach the end of the canyon in less than a minute.

As they prepared their weapons, and began to move toward the canyon's mouth, Yellow Sky held back expecting disaster but not saying anything. White Hawk was mired in a deep blood lust of Yellow Sky's making, but the shaman only blamed the war chief for his poor decision to attack.

———

Ross had his eyes trained on the canyon mouth and said, "Our friends are here, Amy. I just saw movement on my left at the far end. It was probably just a quick look to see where we were. I'm picking up one of the Sharps and just leaning back on the pannier. You just stay there and get ready."

"I'm ready."

"Alright. Let's see how long they take to start the show."

He knew better than to stare. He kept scanning back and forth across the canyon's mouth looking for any sign of motion and didn't have long to wait.

———

White Hawk took the lead. He had his rifle in one hand and his war tomahawk in the other. His other warriors followed and immediately began spreading out as much as possible in the narrow opening, moving quietly in a trotting crouch.

Ross watched them come, was surprised that there were only seven and wondered if some were holding off in case these seven failed. But that was for later concerns, so for now, he just let them come closer until they couldn't turn back. He wanted them to enter further into his shooting gallery, still appalled that they made the decision to attack, but wasn't about to give up his advantage.

The Sharps was cocked now, and he began to measure distance. He knew that he was within range of their rifles now, but they'd have to stop to fire, and he'd shoot anyone who stopped. They were well into the canyon now, but he wanted them closer still. They were less than three hundred yards away and still coming.

White Hawk was exhilarated. They were almost halfway there and still no fire from the white man. Maybe he really was in bed with the Witch after all, he thought with a smile as he moved forward.

Then the world exploded.

Ross took his first shot at the lead attacker, guessing he was their war chief.

White Hawk felt the .45 caliber bullet smash into the upper left side of his chest, destroying two ribs and making mincemeat of his left lung and then crashing through two more ribs in the back before leaving his body. The war chief lived long enough to know he was dying as he spun counterclockwise and rolled onto the ground.

Before White Hawk had stopped rolling, Ross exchanged one Sharps for the second and aimed at the man on the far left then fired. At a range of a little over a hundred and fifty yards, the power of the big gun was devastating.

The second warrior to discover the power of the Sharps took the hit dead center, only high in his gut, blowing apart his abdominal aorta before mangling his spine. It would have caused him an immense amount of pain if he'd live long enough to feel it, but he simply collapsed onto his face.

Hearing the second shot so quickly after the first unnerved the remaining attackers who had been expecting a delay after the first shot. White Hawk had been wrong, but he was dead, and their rage exploded.

Three of them stopped almost in unison and raised their rifles to fire where they had seen the muzzle flash as the back of the canyon was now enshrouded in a fog of gunsmoke.

But all of his training in the army had conditioned Ross to move after he fired if visibility was poor, so after his second shot, he'd dropped the second Sharps, grabbed his Winchester and moved ten feet to the right.

The three warriors fired, and after getting no return fire began to run at their adversary, thinking he was dead.

Ross opened fire with the Winchester as they drew within eighty yards. His first shot was wide, but they were more accurate with each following shot, so none of the next three were off target.

Each warrior was met with a .44 round, two in the chest and one in the neck, and all were fatal hits.

The three went down, and the remaining two warriors refused to give up the attack because to turn and run was a sign of cowardice. They were close now, and one stopped to aim his rifle and was immediately cut down by a round from Ross's Winchester.

The remaining Sioux screamed, raised his war tomahawk high over his head and raced the last fifty feet to kill the deadly white man.

Ross knew he couldn't bring the Winchester to bear, so he quickly dropped the repeater, and yanked out his Colt, cocked it and fired twice rapidly.

The warrior felt the two .44 caliber rounds ram into his chest and as his eyes rolled back into his head, he fell and tumbled to the ground at Ross' feet.

Ross stood, then stared down at the warrior wondering why they had chosen to attack.

From the time they had made their first incursion into the canyon until the last warrior hit the dirt was less than three minutes, and the smoke and smell from the powder hung over the end of the canyon in the early morning.

After a minute of silence, Amy stood, looked at Ross, who was still looking down at the Sioux warrior at his feet, then turned to the horses who had been spooked by all the gunfire, went to them and began to calm them down and make sure none had been hit by stray rounds.

Ross picked up the Winchester and walked over to his gelding and unleashed it as Amy had her hand on the pinto.

"Amy, stay here. I'm going to ride out of the canyon to make sure there aren't any more out there. Seven is an odd number to send. If I ride out fast and low, I can surprise any that are waiting outside of the canyon. I'll be right back."

Amy was going to protest but understood that Ross knew what he was doing, as evidenced by the seven dead warriors scattered across the canyon floor.

"I'll be here," she said and then felt foolish for saying it. *Where else would she be?*

Ross slid onto the gelding's bare back and took the reins. He walked the horse past each of his victims to ensure they were all dead, even though he was reasonably sure he had hit each one with a fatal shot. With a Winchester at that range, it wasn't difficult to do. After he had given each one a quick look over, he started the gelding at a fast trot until he reached the canyon mouth, then slowed him down to a walk and hunkered down on the horse's neck. Once outside the canyon, he quickly sat up and scanned the area quickly finding no one there, but he saw movement to his left about a half a mile away and soon identified a Sioux trotting away toward some waiting horses.

He shifted the gelding to that direction and set him to a canter.

Yellow Sky knew they were all dead, and now he needed to get back and tell his people what had happened. He would tell them that he had killed the Witch, despite White Hawk's failure.

Then he heard hoofbeats, turned and saw the white man approaching rapidly, cursed and ran to get to the horses. He only carried his war tomahawk, believing that firearms were cursed because of their source.

Ross saw him and knew that any shot from the back of a fast-moving horse would be futile but risked one anyway, knowing he had plenty left in the Winchester's magazine, so he took the shot.

Yellow Sky had almost reached the horses when he felt a hammer blow to his right shoulder, spinning him around. The rifle report arrived a fraction of a second later.

Ross couldn't believe the shot found its target and kept going. He knew he didn't kill this one, not with a snapped shot like that. He slowed the gelding to a trot, then a walk, before he halted the horse, slid to the ground and walked to the man, identifying him as Yellow Sky by the symbols of his position. He saw that this right shoulder had been shattered and blood was pouring from his armpit. He may not be dead yet, but he didn't have long.

He looked down at Yellow Sky, and said in Sioux, "You are Yellow Sky, the one who caused all this death. I will let the carrion come and eat your face and eyes. You were a coward and shamed yourself and your people. You are not worthy of a proper burial."

Yellow Sky was fading but heard the words of the white man. He had spoken of Yellow Sky's two greatest fears, being known as a coward and being eaten by the creatures of the night. He tried to say something, but just wheezed away his last breaths.

Ross reached down and picked up Yellow Sky's knife and war tomahawk, sliding them under his belt. Then he returned to the gelding and climbed aboard. He'd come back for the horses and maybe release them to the wild later. He headed back to the canyon, then turned into the mouth and saw Amy's gray hair reflecting the early sunlight. He waved his arm high above his head with the Winchester and was rewarded when she did the same.

It was over. There would be no more pursuit. Now, all they had to do was ride another two hundred and fifty miles of travel over hostile Indian territory. It would be a walk in the park.

He trotted the gelding to the end of the canyon, passing the dead Sioux. He would bury them all, even their bastard chief. At least they all died as warriors, unlike that coward outside the canyon.

He slipped from the gelding and approached Amy.

"It's all done, Amy. They're all gone. Yellow Sky was out there and was probably going to run back home and say how great he was. I shot him and left him bleeding to death. Before he died, though, I told him in Sioux that he died a coward, and then I told him I wasn't going to bury him, but let the carrion eat his face and eyes. He didn't live long enough for the terror to last long, though."

"So, are we going to bury the others?" she asked.

"Yes, I'll take care of that shortly. I don't want to waste much time, though. They'll be shallow graves, but it's the best I can do."

"Did you want me to help?" she asked, hoping that he would say no.

"No, Amy. I'll take care of it. This is my job. I made the mess and I'll clean it up. You go ahead and start packing," he answered, knowing she really had wanted no part of it.

He walked over to the closest warrior, the one he had taken down with the Colt and removed his knife. Then he simply snapped off the hammer of the rifle and tossed it away. He dragged the body over to the canyon wall, placed him as close as possible, then took the warrior's tomahawk and began hitting the almost white dirt of the canyon wall and it crumbled on top of the body. It took only a couple of minutes to finish the job. He then proceeded down the canyon, repeating what he had done for each warrior. He kept their knives and tomahawks, and also added Yellow Sky's knife and tomahawk to the stack. In less than an hour, all seven warriors were under dirt. He had done the best that could be done, all things considered, and he knew it was more than they would have done for him or Amy.

He carried the weapons back to their camp, set them on the ground and then took off one of the panniers.

Amy noticed the stack of knives and tomahawks and asked, "What are those for?"

"Exchange. You'd be surprised how much those go for back East. I'll bet I can get fifty dollars for them in Scotts Bluff. They'd sell them for three times that in the cities in the East."

"Really?"

"Yup. Let's get going. First, we'll head back to the river and take a short break. We owe it to ourselves."

They mounted their horses and headed out of the canyon just two hours after the last shot had been fired.

As they exited the canyon, Ross asked, "What do we do with the eight horses from our Sioux friends? I don't know if I want to just let them loose or bring them along. I'm leaning toward just letting them loose."

"Are any of them nicer than this one?"

"I'll tell you what, you stay here, and I'll whip over there and take a look. If I see one that looks better, I'll bring it along."

"Okay."

Ross and the pack horse started toward the horses who were all chewing on prairie grass as he approached. He passed the corpse of Yellow Sky, paying it no mind, and examined the horses. One stuck out from the others. It was tall for a Sioux horse, so he stepped down, and out of curiosity, picked up its front hoof and found it was shod, and they were fairly new shoes, too. He wondered where they had gotten the animal. It was a gelding, about six years old, then he checked its rump and found no brand. He began taking off the bridles of the other seven but kept the gelding. He hooked a rope around the gelding's neck and tied it to the pack horse. As he began riding back, he noticed the other horses beginning to drift off.

He picked up his pace, caught up to Amy before they turned and headed for the river.

"What do you have there?" she asked, pointing at the gelding.

"That could be your new ride, if you'd like. He's shod and about six years old. He seems like a gentle sort."

"If it's all right with you, he's too tall for me to ride bareback. I'll stick with the pinto."

"That's fine, but I'll keep him with us. He's too nice to let go. Plus, I don't know how he'd do out there by himself. He was owned by a white man until very recently. I just don't know where they could have gotten him from this far from any settlements."

After reaching the river, they turned southwest again, keeping the waterway on their left.

"How bad was it, Ross? The shooting?" Amy asked.

"The shooting itself wasn't bad. In fact, it was too easy. If anything, I feel a bit guilty for that. I've been fighting the Sioux for six years, and I've never seen any of them make as many mistakes as this group did. They made a frontal attack against a heavily armed enemy. They knew I had the Sharps at least, yet they still came on. I don't know if it was fatigue or an obsession. It was almost shameful it was so easy."

"The first one you shot was White Hawk. I could tell by the single white feather he wore."

"That makes me lean toward thinking he was obsessed with killing you. If he blamed you for the death of his son, then that might have pushed him into making the bad decision."

"I'm just glad they won't be chasing us anymore. It does kind of wear you down to be always on your toes like that."

Ross smiled and said, "It's always like that when you're out in the field engaging hostiles. You spend a few days or a couple of weeks out there always nervous about surprises, then you get back to the fort and collapse for a day. Pretty soon, you get bored and want to go back out again."

Amy shook her head and said, "Not me. I'd rather not have any more excitement, thank you."

Ross laughed, then replied, "I'll grant you that, Amy."

They continued for another hour and then pulled over for lunch. It had warmed up nicely and was already over sixty degrees. Ross had heard that the southwest corner of Dakota was a lot warmer than the surrounding area for some reason and today was shaping up that way.

After Ross had cooked and served lunch, he looked over at the river and felt the temptation that if offered. He knew the water would be frigid, but he had grown used to it. Even as a boy he would run out and dive naked into a pond with snow on the ground.

"Amy, I feel the need to do something that may embarrass you, so I'll ask you to do something to keep yourself busy for about fifteen minutes. Just so your curiosity doesn't cause you to look, I'll be taking a bath in the river."

"That water must be freezing!" she exclaimed.

"It will be, but I'm used to it. Once I'm used to the water's temperature, it'll be a lot more pleasant. I just need fifteen minutes of privacy. Okay?"

"Fair enough."

"I'll be back shortly."

Ross reached into his saddlebags and pulled out his bar of white soap and a towel. He trotted down to the water and sat on a log at the water's edge. He never looked back to make sure Amy wasn't watching, as he didn't mind one way or the other. He wasn't that shy after four years at West Point and six years in an army fort.

He pulled off his boots and then his socks, took off his shirt and union suit's upper half. Finally, he peeled off his pants, the lower half of the union suit and walked into the icy water. It wasn't too bad, although the mud was pretty deep. He lathered himself and dropped under the water, rose and repeated the process, this time adding a good lathering to his hair. His ablutions completed, Ross walked out of the water and stood for a moment in the warm sun and ran his fingers through his hair, feeling a lot better. He stepped over to the log and began drying himself with the towel, then, after wiggling his muddy feet in the water to rinse them free, he pulled on his socks and then his boots.

Amy had tried to resist the temptation. *She was a married woman, for God's sake!* But she couldn't resist and managed to hold back almost a full minute before she watched the show. When he stood facing her with his eyes closed and ran his fingers through his hair, she felt a warm rush run though her and her knees weaken. She'd never seen a man naked before and she wasn't sure she'd ever see one as masculine as Ross was.

As he began to get dressed, she turned away again. She was flustered more than she had ever experienced before. She knew it was a warm day, but she felt tropical and was ashamed of herself. *What would Aaron say?* But, all that aside, she was very happy she had done it.

When he returned to the campsite, he smiled at Amy and wrapped the towel around the soap before putting them away in the saddlebag.

"That felt good. I needed that. So, are you ready to mount up?"

Amy was distracted as she let the images dance in her mind and didn't hear him.

"Amy? Are you ready to go?" he asked again.

"Oh. What? Yes, of course."

Ross could guess the cause for her disorientation, but let it go. He was actually flattered that she had not only looked but was flustered so much as well.

They rode heading southwest for a few more hours in relative silence as Amy wrestled with herself about the excitement that she had felt at seeing Ross without clothes and the shame that she wasn't nearly enough as it should be.

Ross finally broke the silence when he said, "In a couple of more hours, we'll lose the river. Then we turn south and head to Camp Robinson. We can get some more supplies there, and you can buy some clothes if you'd like and anything else you think you need. Then after leaving Camp Robinson, we hit Scotts Bluff, then turn due west for three more days, and then we'll be in Cheyenne."

"So, how many more days do we have on the trail?"

"Nine or ten, I'd guess."

"Oh," was her only response.

Ross wondered why she seemed saddened by the answer. He would have thought she would be excited about going on to Oregon to see her husband that she hadn't seen in almost four years.

"Amy, let's have a nice long stop tonight. We don't have anyone chasing us and it's a beautiful day."

Amy turned and smiled as she replied, "That would be marvelous."

"Good. As soon as we see the river begin to leave us, we'll pull over and set up our camp, and now that we don't have to worry about those Sioux followers, I'll go find us a nice rabbit or something for dinner."

"Now, that does sound good," she said with a smile.

"Great. Now we'll just hunt for a nice camping spot."

It was less than an hour later that Ross found an ideal spot near the river. There was a grove of cottonwoods nearby and good grass for their four horses.

They stopped and began to set up camp, and after the animals were all stripped and taken care of, Ross set up the tent, just in case the temperature dropped suddenly, as it was wont to do on the Great Plains at this time of year.

Ross pulled the Winchester out of its scabbard and said, "I'll go and get our dinner, Amy. I should be back soon. If you want to pass the time, my copy of Caesar's Commentaries is in my right saddlebag."

"Maybe I'll do that," she said as she smiled again.

Ross smiled back, then waved and trotted north. He had seen rabbits running through the grass about a quarter mile off, so he walked up to the crest a small hill to get a better view, but didn't see any rabbits, so he slowly walked down the far slope.

He knew he had seen them, so he shifted to the west slightly, began walking more slowly and after a few more minutes saw two large jackrabbits chasing one another. He raised his Winchester and led them, hoping they didn't make one of their sudden turns, squeezed the trigger and watched the lead rabbit's head vaporize. The second one veered off, and he let it go. He walked to the dead rabbit and picked it up by its hind legs.

Ross smiled and turned back. The small hill was to his left now, so he walked straight and as he cleared the hill, he saw something that he didn't want to see, and was worried that he had. There were two tall black horses with saddles hitched a couple of hundred yards in front of him and recognized them immediately as army mounts. This wasn't good. They must be deserters, and they had to be in his and Amy's camp.

His problem was how could he get into the camp close enough to take them down. He couldn't go in with firing his Winchester, not with Amy there. He needed to get close and surprise them somehow, which would be difficult as they must have heard him shoot the rabbit and knew he was there.

So, he walked back to the other side of the hill, took off his gun belt and removed his right-side Colt. He tucked the pistol in his waist at the small of his back, then he took the Winchester in his right hand and the rabbit in his left. He took a deep breath, then started whistling as he topped the hill and started back to the camp acting oblivious to the two deserters who must be there. He glanced ahead and could make out three people. Amy was easy to spot, and the other two were wearing faded, dirty blue uniforms. He kept walking toward them acting as if he was ignorant of their presence.

When he got within fifty yards of the camp, he heard one of the deserters shout, "Hey, you! You'd better drop that Winchester right now or we'll fill your woman full of lead. Then you walk slow-like this way."

Ross looked up with a surprised look on his face and shouted back, "Don't hurt my wife. I'll do as you say."

He bent at the knees and slowly lowered the rifle to the ground then stood straight again and began walking toward them with his hands up.

One had his Spencer carbine pointed at Amy. The other's Spencer was pointed at Ross.

Amy was shocked at his meek obedience. She had expected Ross to drop and fill them both full of holes. *How could a man who had just killed eight Sioux warriors a few hours ago give up so easily? And did he just call her his wife?*

Ross continued to walk slowly toward them. When he got within twenty yards, he saw that the two deserters hadn't even cocked the hammers of their Spencers, and he saw his advantage.

"What do you want?" Ross asked, his voice shaking as he closed the gap to be even closer, "We can give you some food. Just take some food and leave us alone. Please? There's no need for violence. My wife is pregnant, and I want us to live and have our baby."

Amy was appalled. *Where was the brave man who had taken on eight Sioux warriors?* Then she noticed that he didn't have his gun belt on. Maybe that was why. *And she was pregnant? Why would he say that, which was even more strange than saying he was his wife?*

"Oh, we're gonna take some food and a whole lot more. Maybe we'll even dally with your woman 'cause we don't care if she's gonna have a baby or not. But first, mister, you're gonna tell us where them Black Hills are."

Now there was a surprise. The surprise wasn't that they had deserted to go hunt for gold in the Black Hills. That had been an issue at many posts in the region. The surprise was that they missed it and missed it by plenty.

"You men are off course, you already passed it. It's about eighty miles northwest of here. Now, boys, I really don't want to hurt you. So, I'd rather you just leave."

His change in tone surprised the two deserters.

"What are you talking about, mister. We're gonna kill you and then take your woman with us while we go hunt us some gold and get rich."

Ross stared at them both and said clearly, "One more warning, boys. That's all you get. If you don't get on those stolen army horses and ride away, then you'll both die where you stand."

Ross's eyes and steady, threatening voice should have warned them, but they had the guns and he didn't, so they were unfazed. Amy, however, was thrilled to hear the power and authority of his voice. This was the Ross she expected to hear.

The taller of the two, shouted, "To hell with you, mister," and began to aim his rifle.

Then, in his most commanding voice, Ross shouted, "Ten-hut!"

Both men, with years of military discipline and repetition, began dropping the butts of their rifles to the ground and bringing their heels together. It was only a fraction of a second, but it gave Ross the edge. He whipped the Colt from behind his back, cocked the hammer before it was even halfway, then quickly pointed it at the one on the left, who had pointed his rifle at Amy and squeezed the trigger from less than twenty feet, cocked the hammer again, moved the front sight five degrees to the right and fired again at the second deserter. Both shots were almost dead center in their chests as they fell over backwards, a look of absolute shock on both of their faces. One squirmed for a few seconds, while the only motion from the second was when his left boot twitched once.

Ross ran up to them to make sure they were dead, which didn't take long and then trotted over to Amy who was still stunned by the sudden, unexpected shooting.

"Amy, are you all right?" he asked as he took her by the shoulders and looked into her unfocused green eyes.

Then she blinked, focused on Ross and said, "I'm fine, Ross. I was just surprised. I thought you were giving up."

Ross removed his hands from her shoulders and said, "Amy, giving up is not in my nature. I wasn't sure how big of a threat they were. I needed to get close, and I couldn't do that if I arrived wearing my pistols. I was worried that they may have a gun pointed at you, so I couldn't risk a long shot with the Winchester. So, I took off my gun belt behind that hill and put one pistol behind my back. Then, when I was close enough, I saw that they weren't as big a threat as I had thought, so I gave them a chance to leave."

"But they had their rifles pointed at both of us!"

"They didn't even have them cocked. I doubt if they even had a round in the chamber. It would take them a half of a second to cycle the lever, or at the very least to cock the hammer and fire. I needed a little more of an edge, so when the tall guy sounded like he was going to shoot me, I counted on their ingrained training to throw them off. When I called them to attention, did you see them automatically start shifting their rifles to the ground? I was counting on it."

"I was wondering why you did that. So, who are they?"

"Deserters. The army's been having a big problem with desertion since they discovered of gold in the Black Hills. We had it at Fort Sisseton. Most likely, these jaspers came up from Camp Robinson in Nebraska. There is some good news, though."

"What's that?"

"They were riding army mounts. They hitched them about a quarter mile west of here. They have saddles, so we can switch a saddle to the gelding, and you can ride normally. But first, I'm going to see who they were, and where they stole the horses."

Before he left, Amy smiled, tilted her head and asked, "My wife is pregnant?"

Ross grinned, then looked at her and said, "I thought I'd see if I could play on their sympathies by telling them you were going to have a baby. Even deserters might have a soft spot for soon-to-be mothers, but apparently, these two were beyond even that. I apologize for saying it if it embarrassed you."

"No need to apologize, Ross, I was just curious."

"Then, with your permission, ma'am, I'll go and find out about those two."

He walked over to the tall man and immediately noticed his foul odor that had nothing to do with being shot, so, with his eyes watering, he held his breath and quickly began searching his pockets. He found $2.65, and a letter he had received six months earlier, glanced at the address on the letter, then pocketed it and the money. Now he knew they had deserted from Fort Fetterman in Wyoming. That explained why they were so destitute and so far off target. It's a lot farther to Fetterman than Camp Robinson. Ross then removed his belt.

Then he walked away to breathe some fresh air before he stepped over to the other dead trooper, who may have smelled even worse, and found the he had all of $3.10 in money, but no letters. He checked the inside of his shirt and found his name on the inside. John Humboldt. Willie Ellison was the name of his fellow deserter.

Ross returned to Amy, wiping his eyes and gulping clean air.

"It looks like they deserted from Fort Fetterman about two months ago. That one over there was Willie Ellison. This one was John Humboldt. They had all of $5.75 between them. Now, I'm going to go and bring their horses into our camp. I'll be back in a few minutes and I'll bury them both. Can you clean the rabbit?"

"I'll do that down near the river," she said.

Ross pulled out his pocketknife and handed it to her before saying, "I'll be right back."

Ross walked the four hundred yards to the two horses, and checked their haunches to be sure, and found the USA brands on them both.

He checked the first horse's saddlebags and found two cans of beans, some dirty clothes and some cooking utensils, including another coffeepot, and a box of ammunition for the Spencer. These guys had a poor future, even without getting killed. The second set of saddlebags had a half box of matches, some old uniforms, two more cans of beans and another box of cartridges.

Both had bed rolls, but they smelled so badly, Ross just tossed them aside. It was the same for their blankets. He added their old uniforms to the pile, too, but he kept the two canteens. He checked the saddlebags to make sure they didn't smell as bad as the bedrolls or blankets. They weren't bad, but they needed cleaning.

He led them back to the camp, swinging around the hill to pick up his gun belt. He put it back on, feeling not so naked and took a minute to reload the two chambers, telling himself to clean the gun and the Winchester when he had a chance.

After reaching their campsite, he took the saddles off both mounts and led the horses down to the river, and after they were finished, he walked them back to their four horses and let them graze with the others before he approached Amy who was skinning the rabbit.

"These two should never have joined the army in the first place. They didn't plan anything. They had almost no money left, and they would have been starving in a week. They got lost and what even if they made it to the Black Hills, what were they going to use to dig for gold? But we did get some useful things from them. They had four more cans of beans and some ammunition for the Spencers. Have you ever shot a gun before?"

"I shot my father's rifle once, but that was a long time ago."

"We'll have the two Spencers with us until we get to Camp Robinson, then I'll turn in the horses and their rifles and ammo. I'll try to beg the saddle from them, but they shouldn't care. When I was at Fort Sisseton, we always had a surplus of saddles. Horses were hard to come by."

"The rabbit's ready. Where do you want me to put him?"

"Follow me and I'll take out the frypan and we'll put him on that until we cook him in a little bit."

He went to the pannier with the cooking utensils and gave the frypan to Amy.

After she laid the rabbit in the pan, he said, "I'm going to go and dig those graves."

"Ross," she said, "Did you notice something else about those two?"

"You mean the smell. I'd imagine that they haven't washed since they deserted, and maybe before that. I didn't want to say anything, but that's one of the reasons I wanted to get them under the ground."

"Thank you. I'm going to head over toward the river where it's not so bad."

"That, ma'am, is a very wise decision. Here I go," he said as he walked toward the bodies.

He looked around for a place to dig that was far enough from the trees, so he didn't run into roots. He walked back the way they had come and noticed that one of the big cottonwoods was ready to fall into the river and had created a ready-made hole where its roots had pulled back the earth. He'd still have to cover them up, but it would be a lot easier than having to dig the hole by himself.

Now came the hard part. He'd have to get close to those two stinking corpses, so he walked back to the first body, and as he drew stood close, his stomach revolted at the vile odor, and he wondered if they ever bathed at all in the past year.

He grimaced, held his breath, then grabbed the shoulders of the first man and began dragging him the two hundred yards to the hole and was gasping for breath by the time he reached it, but then had to get close so he could roll it into the hole. He crouched down, put both hands under the bloody body and rolled him it unceremoniously into the wet soil. He returned to the second ex-soldier and his eyes watered when he got close.

He had to stop several times to walk away and breathe as he dragged it to the natural gravesite. Finally, he gratefully dropped the second body into the hole, before spending a couple of minutes twenty yards away to get his breath.

They were so malodorous that all Ross did was kick some surrounding piles of earth onto the bodies until there was two or three inches of dirt covering them before he turned and left the area. If any critters could stand to get close enough to eat them, more power to them.

He returned, pulled the soap out of his saddlebag and walked down to the river. He took off his shirt lathered himself

125

everywhere to get rid of any remnants of the two, then quickly washed the shirt, wrung it out and walked back to the camp. Once he returned, he shook out his shirt and spread it over a bush to dry.

Then he noticed Amy watching him and walked close to her.

"Amy, if I had been their commanding officer, I would have had some of the other men throw them into any nearby water. They were the raunchiest smelling human beings I have ever encountered, especially the small one."

"I know. I was upwind and still could smell them. I'm surprised you could stand being that close."

"I was really close to losing control of my stomach when I was dragging them away for burial."

"How did you get them buried so fast, anyway?"

"There was a big cottonwood over there that had tipped over and had ripped its roots out of the ground. All I did was kick some dirt on top of them. They didn't deserve anything more."

"That's true. It makes me want to have a bath myself, but I'm not like you. I'm not fond of icy water."

"I'll see what I can do before dinner. It's the least I can do after your performance with those four Sioux hunters. I was thoroughly impressed."

Amy smiled and said, "It was a natural act."

Ross laughed, then stepped over to the two sets of army saddlebags. He knew that they were almost waterproof because he had used a pair as miniature watering troughs for his horse on one expedition. So, he took the two sets of saddlebags, emptied the contents and set them aside. Then he started a fire, filled the two coffeepots with water and then half-filled the saddlebags and hung them from a low tree limb.

Amy watched him and wondered what he was building and wondered why he was still shirtless, not that she minded at all.

Once that was done, he went to his saddlebags and pulled out two towels and a shirt, then headed back to where Amy was sitting.

"Amy, this is the best I can do. It's not a real bath, but when I finish, you will have four saddlebags of nice, warm water that you can use to bathe. Here are two towels and my bar of soap. If you'd rather not, then I'll find another use for the setup."

Amy smiled broadly and said, "No, this is great. I'll be very grateful to use it. Now, where will you be?"

"I'll stay on the other side of the trees. I'll give you about twenty minutes. Will that be enough?"

"That'll be fine. I can't wait."

Ross pulled on his new shirt, before he checked the coffeepots and found the water boiling. The boiling water and the cold water should make a good warm bathwater temperature. Amy had left the campground to undress in the trees to prepare for her impromptu bath.

"Okay, Amy, I'm going to add the hot water in a few seconds, then I'll get out of your way."

"Alright" she shouted from behind the trees.

He poured a half pot of boiling water into each saddlebag and then put the coffeepots down and walked quickly to the other side of the trees.

"I'm out of the way. Enjoy your bath," Ross shouted as he continued to walk away.

"Thank you," she yelled back as she sprinted toward the suspended saddlebags.

She had already removed all of her clothes and had them in her arms as she ran as she didn't want to waste any of the precious warm water while she undressed.

Ross thought it best if he just took a walk. That way, she'd feel more comfortable knowing he was further away.

Amy used one towel to dip into the water and moisten herself, then plunged the soap into the water and worked up a good lather and started to work it over her dirty skin, then she tipped one of the saddlebags over her and let the warm water flow across her. What she really wanted more than anything was to clean her hair, but she still spent two more minutes scrubbing and rinsed herself once, the second time pouring the water onto her head. Using the bar of soap, she began lathering her hair and when she was done, she squatted under a saddlebag and dumped the contents onto her head. The water flowed over her and took most of the soap away, then she repeated it using the last water-filled saddlebag. It was still warm and made her feel amazingly clean.

She turned and faced the trees, expecting to see Ross spying on her, but he wasn't there. She took the dry towel and began drying off, feeling so good that she wanted to start singing. She used to sing a lot when she was young because it made her feel better. Now, she felt better and wanted to sing again.

Finally, she felt sufficiently dry and began to dress. She was impressed that Ross hadn't tried to peek and guessed that even though he was no longer an officer, he was still a gentleman.

Finally, completely dressed again, she hung both towels from the limb with the saddlebags to dry and walked to where Ross should be, but he wasn't there. She looked around and finally spotted him about a half a mile west and still walking away. *What was going on?* Then she saw him look at his watch and turn around. He saw her and waved. She waved back, still wondering why he was so far away.

She went back to the camp and found Ross's hairbrush and began to work out the kinks she knew would be there. And they were definitely there…in spades.

She was still untangling when Ross entered the camp. He smiled at her, so at least he wasn't mad.

"How did it work out, Amy?" he asked.

"It was different, but it was marvelous. I feel really clean for the first time in years."

"Good. I'm glad it worked out. Now, I'm going to start setting up a spit to roast our rabbit, then I'll cook our dinner. Okay?"

"You're spoiling me, Mr. Braxton. A bath and now a rabbit dinner."

"Just trying to keep you happy, Mrs. Childs," he said as he grinned at her.

Ross made the spit easily and soon had the rabbit roasting on the fire as the coffeepot and frypan with beans and onions sat underneath to the left of the rabbit. The way he had it set up, some of the grease from the cooking rabbit would drip into the bean and onion mix for added flavor, and he would periodically sprinkle salt on the rabbit, being careful not to use too much.

After he pulled the rabbit from the skewer and onto one of their spare tin plates, he carved chunks of meat off the side and cut the legs off separately. He put the two hind legs and a piece of meat on a plate, added scoops of beans and handed it to Amy along with a cup of coffee.

Amy heard her stomach rumble as she accepted the plate, then used the fork on the meat and savored every bite before eating some beans. Then, after the meat had cooled, she took the legs in her fingers and ate every bit of meat from the bones and finished before Ross did.

"That was exquisite, Ross."

"Thank you, Amy. Maybe we'll do it again sometime on the trip."

"I'd like that. Ross, could I ask you something?"

"Sure."

"Why were you so far away from camp a little while ago? You must have been a half mile away when I saw you."

Ross answered, "It was a way of making you sure that I hadn't been spying on you. You haven't known me long enough to believe that I never lie, or break promises. This way, you could be sure that I hadn't broken my promise to give you your privacy."

"Oh. I was wondering."

"Well, it's time to set up for the night."

Ross set up the tent, bedroll, blanket and pillow combination. He let Amy slide into her bedroll first before joining her when she said she was ready.

Once they were settled in and were just inches away and looking at each other, she asked, "Ross, what will you do after we get to Cheyenne? You know, with your life?"

"That's a good question. I thought I'd see if the Union Pacific could use another engineer. It's what I was taught to do. Usually, West Point trained engineers are highly sought, I'm just not sure I'd be happy sitting behind a desk."

"For a second there, I thought you were talking about a train driver, which I thought was odd, but that sounds like it could be a challenge if you wanted to do it."

"How about you, Amy? What would you like to do with your life when you get to Oregon?"

The question immediately reminded Amy of what awaited her in Oregon, and it slammed into her like a sledgehammer. This was becoming a thrilling adventure and she would soon be returning to a much harder and less satisfying life.

"Well, I'd like to have some children. And then, sometime, maybe when I'm older, I'd like to do something that is a bit of a fantasy, really."

"And what is that?"

"No, it's just a silly dream."

"No dreams are silly, Amy. What is yours?"

"I want to write books. Now you see what I mean. That's an impossible dream."

"Why do you think that's impossible? I think you'd be more than capable of becoming an author."

"Ross, I didn't get beyond the third grade, remember?"

"Do you know some others that didn't make it out of elementary school? Try Mark Twain, or one of the greatest authors of our time, Charles Dickens."

"Really? They didn't go to college?"

"No, they didn't even go to high school, but they both had what you have, Amy, a gift with the language. You speak very well, and I'm sure you'll write just as well. All you need is a vivid imagination and a story. What do you want to write about?"

"I wanted to write a story set in medieval England, like Ivanhoe, but I think that's been overdone. I've been searching for a different time frame and location, but I'd like it to have a powerful, evil force being thwarted by a heroic champion who leads his people to defend their land. Probably with some romance as a part of the story, too. I just don't know where to go."

"How about a warrior queen who raises up her people against a great army and does something that no other monarch had ever done when she defeats them."

"That's not very realistic, Ross. Readers have to believe that it is at least possible."

"It happened, Amy. Have you ever heard of Queen Boudica?"

"No. Who was she?"

"Boudica was made queen of the Iceni tribe in Britain when her father died in 60 A.D., during the reign of Emperor Nero. The Romans had occupied Britain, and her kingdom was supposed to be independent, but Rome ignored her father's will and her kingdom was annexed. Boudica was flogged and her daughters raped. Boudica led her people and others in revolt. They destroyed several Roman cities, including London. She led an army of over a hundred thousand.

"But the Romans had a great general named Suetonius, and like Caesar, despite being heavily outnumbered, defeated Boudica's forces in the Battle of Watling. She counted on her superior numbers, but Suetonius had positioned his men well, leaving Boudica no other choice but to mount a frontal attack, like the Sioux warriors did, with the same results.

"Her army wasn't disciplined like the Romans, and they fell apart. Boudica then either killed herself to avoid capture or died of illness, depending on which ancient historian you read. It's an amazing story, Amy. I'm sure you could find a lot there to write an exciting book."

Amy was mesmerized by the tale, then said, "That's an astonishing story, Ross. Like you said before, history has stories that sound more like fairy tales than fact. You're right, too. It would make a great basis for a novel. I'm already getting excited."

"See? You can do it, too, Amy. You just need confidence in yourself. You're smart, too, so don't worry about your lack of formal education, and I think you can make something out of your life."

"Thank you so much, Ross. This has turned out to be the best day of my life."

"I'm happy for you, Amy. Now, let's get some sleep and tomorrow may be even better."

"I don't see how. Good night, Ross. And thank you again."

"You're welcome, Amy. Good night to you, too."

Amy closed her eyes and dreamt of ancient queens, and despite her own prohibitions, she fantasized about the man just inches away from her.

CHAPTER 4

When she opened her eyes again, the sun was streaming through the tent flap opening and Ross was gone.

She stretched and found herself happy and content. Two words she couldn't have ever believed that she could apply to herself three weeks ago. She didn't want this trip to end, because she knew what was waiting for when she arrived in Oregon, and it wasn't going to be encouragement to do what she wanted desperately to make of her life. There would be no more interesting, lively talk, no more laughter or being able to exercise her own wit. She'd be a housewife and no more.

But today would be another good day, whether it brought Sioux or deserters or maybe even a grizzly bear. She didn't care about the dangers anymore. Ross was here.

She slid out of the bedroll and put on her boots. When she exited the tent, she was greeted by a smiling Ross and the smell of bacon.

"Good morning, Amy. Glad to see you had a good night's sleep. I'll have breakfast ready in a few minutes. It looks like another warm day, so enjoy them while you can."

"Good morning, Ross. I'll be right back," she said as she hustled around to the back of the trees.

He was finishing their breakfast preparation when she returned, so he handed her a plate with some beans and two strips of bacon. Then he handed her a cup of coffee before she took a seat next to him as they ate.

"So, what is the plan for today?" she asked before putting a spoonful of beans into her mouth.

"We head southwest for a while and then south toward Camp Robinson. It's not that far. We should get there tomorrow sometime. We'll drop off the horses and get something to eat and pick up some more supplies. Then, we hit the road for Scotts Bluff. That'll take us three or four days. Then we can spend a day there to relax, and then it's on to Cheyenne, which is another three or four days west."

"Okay."

After breakfast and cleanup, they started packing for the ride. Amy noticed that the saddlebags were gone from the branch, but the towels were still there. Ross must have forgotten them, so she went to take them down and found them to be still damp. They should be dry by now. Unless…

"Ross, the towels are still wet. What happened?"

"I took advantage of the nice weather and took another bath."

"Oh," was all Amy said, but she almost blurted out, 'and I missed it!'. Luckily, she caught herself in time.

Ross brought the gelding sporting an army saddle over to her.

"Well, Amy. Did you want to try your new horse? I've adjusted the stirrups to your height, so that will make it a lot more comfortable than riding bareback on the pinto," he said as he smiled at her.

She grinned and stepped into the stirrup and swung her leg around the gelding's rump.

Once high up on the saddled gelding, she said, "This is quite an improvement. I feel like I can see another mile."

"Let's see how this works out."

He climbed aboard his horse and they started southwest again. He let the pinto loose, but it followed on its own accord.

Amy noticed and said, "I guess the pinto doesn't want to leave."

"He must like you," he replied.

She laughed as they left the White River behind after filling up all six canteens and turned toward Camp Robinson about fifty miles south.

It was different having Amy almost at his height, but it was a good different.

"So, tell me about Aaron, Amy." Ross said, asking what he thought was a perfectly innocent question.

Amy sighed and replied, "Aaron, as I mentioned before, he lived on a neighboring farm. He was two years older than I was. He was close and didn't seem to mind my gray hair. So, we got married."

Ross raised his eyebrows and said, "That doesn't tell me much. Is he tall or short? Is he some big, strong farm boy that swept you off your feet? Is he eloquent? Just saying he was near isn't much of a selling point."

"Honestly? That was the only selling point. That, and he didn't seem to care about my hair. He was average height and build. He never went to school at all. He could write his name but that was about all. He was pleasant enough, and he didn't beat me or anything. He was just there. My parents wanted me out of the house, so they didn't have to feed me. I was taller than he was, and I think that bothered him more than my gray hair."

"Sorry. I thought a pretty lady like you would have had the pick of the boys in the area."

She laughed and said, "Now, Ross. Quit being nice. I thought you said you never lied?"

Ross was taken aback and replied, "I don't. Why do you think I lied?"

"Ross, we're being honest here, aren't we?"

"Always."

"Then why did you say I was pretty? We both know that's not true."

"I have no idea why you would think that. You are a very pretty woman, maybe the prettiest woman I've ever met. I thought you knew that. How could you not know?"

"When I was thirteen, I saw myself in a glass window in town. I was anything but pretty. I could never look at that face again. I figured between that, my gray hair, and my green eyes, I looked every part of the witch that the Sioux thought I was."

"People change over the years, Amy. I don't know what you looked like when you were thirteen, but I do know what you look like now, and I'm telling you that you are a very handsome woman."

"Sorry, Ross. I'm not buying it."

"Just a minute."

Ross turned as the horse plodded along and he reached into his left saddlebag. He pulled out a small, thin pouch, opened it and slid out his signaling mirror and handed it to Amy.

"You keep a mirror with you?"

"We all did. It's for signaling other officers. It's why we all know Morse code. Now, look at your face."

Amy really didn't want to. She knew Ross was exaggerating, but she looked anyway. As she rode, it was difficult, so she stopped the horse and took a closer look without the bouncing horse. Gone were the buck teeth, the freckles, and the fat cheeks. *She wasn't homely at all!*

Ross watched her finally acknowledge her fine features and smiled. Imagine going through years of your life thinking that you're both stupid and ugly and not knowing you were smart and beautiful. It was like a fairy tale, but much better than *The Ugly Duckling.* Swans were mean and Amy wasn't anymore.

Amy was looking at herself and saw a reflected tear appear in her left eye before she felt it. She didn't know what to say. She was pretty, but it didn't make any difference in her life. She would be going to Oregon and assume her duties as the wife of an ordinary man and would grow old. She was a mixed bag of emotions, feeling happy and sad at the same time.

She wiped the tears from her face and handed the mirror back to Ross.

"Thank you, Ross. It was a revelation. You really never lie, do you?"

"I simply can't. For one thing, I'd feel so guilty about it I'd be easily caught. Second, it's always easier to tell the truth."

"I'll remember that the next time I want to ask you a difficult question."

"Fair enough."

They stopped for lunch and found a suitable location near the base of a small hill, so, after they stopped, Ross climbed to the top of a hill and scanned the area in all directions to see if anyone was within sight, but not a thing moved.

He trotted back down the hill, and led the horses to a small pond, really nothing more than a large puddle made from melting snow from a storm that must have missed them. They let the horses all drink at the pool, just about draining it while they had a cold lunch and rode on.

All afternoon they discussed everything from politics to family. She told him of her family, and how her parents and two brothers had worked the farm and never had much money. He told her of his parents, still working the family farm in Minnesota. It was a very successful dairy farm that also produced garden vegetables.

As the sun was setting, they had to settle for a spot that offered some water, but nothing else in the way of protection. Nonetheless, Ross built a fire in a hole to minimize the visibility. The weather was growing colder again after the brief respite with temperatures in the fifties. It was early November, after all.

After dinner cleanup was done, he set up the tent, unsure of the weather.

Amy crawled into the tent and took off her boots, then Ross ducked inside when she was tucked into the bed roll.

"Have you ever been to Camp Robinson?" she asked when they assumed their now customary face-to-face positions.

"No, but it's probably set up like most of the others. We'll go to the commanding officer to report the deaths of the two deserters and the recovery of the two horses. Then we can go and get something to eat at the sutler's. We'll stock up on supplies and then we can leave for Scotts Bluff. It may be a little late when we depart, but I'd rather be away from the fort."

"Why? I thought you liked the army?"

"I did and still do. But I have you with me now. And now that you're aware of your good looks, it might cause some trouble. Remember there aren't many white women around, and none with your looks and your, um, femininity."

Amy laughed and said, "So, now you're trying to say that under all these baggy clothes, you know that I'm well formed?"

Ross was decidedly uncomfortable but replied, "Well, um, I'm just saying that, well, that, you know, well, everything is where it should be and in the proper proportions."

She laughed harder and said, "Well, Mr. Braxton, I'm not going to punish you any further. I won't argue that point. I know that I do have the proper proportions. So, if it will make you feel better, we can leave the camp as soon as we're restocked."

"Good. Let's change the subject. When we get to Cheyenne, did you want to meet my brother and sister-in-law? It should be enlightening. I have no idea what to expect. They could be very happily married with two perfect children. The ranch could be prosperous, and they could be living the lives of well-to-do ranchers."

"But you don't think so."

"No, I'd expect just the opposite. Henry was bigger than me, but he was tending toward fat when I left. He didn't like to work, either. So, it's possible he sold off the ranch and spent the money. He may not even be there. Now, Bessie will be harder to predict. When I knew her, she was just a teenager, and now, she'd be twenty-six. Maybe she's more mature and not so frivolous. She was smarter than Henry, and that would be a problem for him later.

"He'd had been infatuated with Bessie's blonde hair, blue eyes and rather noticeable bosom, but when he got past that and realized that she was smarter than he was, it would bother him. He hated people who were smarter than him. Unfortunately, that was most people. So, how she is now would be a mystery. She could go one of several ways."

"What if she changed? What if you get there and she's become a very thoughtful, mature woman? Would you regret your decision?"

"Maybe, but I doubt if she has. Besides, she'd be married with children. She probably forgot all about me, anyway."

"I doubt that, Ross."

"Well, it doesn't matter what she is or isn't. My job now is to get you to Cheyenne safely and get you on your train."

"I suppose."

"Maybe I'll come and visit you sometime."

Amy was suddenly horrified with the thought of Ross seeing her in some old dress with a baby on her hip as she swept the floor of their one-room cabin.

"I don't think that would be a good idea."

"Why not? I thought we were friends now, Amy."

"We are. That's why I thought it would be a bad idea. Aaron might get jealous."

"You're probably right. Can I write to you, at least?"

Knowing that Aaron couldn't read helped, so she replied, "Yes, you can write to me."

"Good. I don't want to lose touch with you after our little adventure together."

"You won't."

"Well, I suppose we should get some sleep now. Tomorrow should be interesting."

"They always have been since we've been together."

"That's the truth. Goodnight, Amy."

"Goodnight, Ross."

Amy rolled over. She closed her eyes and felt drawn into the vortex of emotions swirling through her. Here she was in the middle of the prairie with danger all around, yet she felt alive and content. She was a married woman sleeping in a tent with a handsome, virile young man next to her, yet felt no shame. Yet the thought of what awaited her in less than two short weeks depressed her. No more fairy tales. No more dreams about writing books. And worst of all, no more Ross. But she was a married woman and must return to her husband.

Ross wasn't quite as torn as Amy. He was getting very fond of her, and to be completely honest with himself, it was well past simple fondness. But she was a married woman and would be leaving him in another ten days or so, and there was nothing he could do about that. He would just have to try to forget her and move on with his life, but he knew better. He could never forget Amy, but he would have to watch her ride away on that train.

They both eventually slept, but neither rested very well.

———

Ross, as usual, was the first up. He slid his boots on and slipped outside. It was another sunny, not-so-cold day, making him wonder how much longer their luck would hold.

After taking care of his morning hygiene, he started the fire and was soon cooking breakfast. As he knew they would be stopping at Camp Robinson in a little while, he made a nice breakfast of bacon and beans with onions and tomatoes.

Amy awakened to the smell of frying bacon, now accustomed to the wonderful wakeup. She stayed in her bedroll a little while longer. Not because she wanted to stay warm, she just wanted to think. She knew that there was nothing to think about, but it was a mental exercise. *What would she do when she got to Cheyenne?* She'd wire ahead to let Aaron know she was coming and wondered how he might have changed. Finally, she slid out of her bedroll still without an idea of what to expect.

They had breakfast saying little beyond normal conversations about the weather and the camp, as an unexpected tension now existed that had nothing to do with witches or foul tempers or even pending danger.

After breakfast, they mounted and headed south to Camp Robinson.

Once on the road, they did start talking again, avoiding topics like marriage, children, or anything that might lead to any feelings of affection.

They talked about growing up in the north country, and how they would combat the cold. Ross knew he had it infinitely better than Amy because his family was prosperous, and he always had plenty to eat. He enjoyed the outdoors as most boys did and didn't hide in the house during those frigid Minnesota winters either. He'd be out in the snow and ice doing boy things.

Amy told him how they had to cope with a drafty house, and how those winds would come howling down from Canada shaking the poorly constructed farmhouse. She and her brothers would huddle near the fireplace for heat, and yet, in the summer, there would be that oppressive heat. People from the East could never understand that. *How could someplace that far in the north be so hot?* It just was. But it made the wheat and corn grow fast and tall. Theirs was such a small farm, though, even in good years they had little money.

Ross knew they were close to their destination, so he told Amy they'd keep riding past noon.

––––––

The first buildings of Camp Robinson came into view around two o'clock. It was an active post, and even from two miles out, soldiers could be seen moving about the camp.

Amy hadn't seen a group of white people in three years, so it was a different experience for her.

To Ross, it was just another army post.

"Stay close, Amy," he said as he turned to her.

"Always, Ross," she replied as she smiled back at him.

They wound their way through the buildings, Amy drawing more than her share of stares, and Ross doubted if it was because of her gray hair. Ross soon found the headquarters building and they stepped down, then tied the horses to the rail. The pinto was still there, standing behind the others, but they didn't bother doing anything with him.

Ross and Amy walked into the office and found a middle-aged corporal behind the desk.

"Good afternoon, Corporal. Is the commander available?" Ross asked.

The corporal was looking at Amy and missed the question.

After ten seconds of silence, Ross asked in an officer's voice, "Corporal, could I see your commanding officer, please?"

Ross's command voice shook him out of his trance, and he said, "Just a moment, sir. What would you like to speak to him about?"

"Deserters."

"Very well, sir."

He walked to the next office and knocked before entering. Ross could hear the standard military jargon before the corporal returned.

"The colonel will see you now."

"Thank you, Corporal."

He led Amy to the commander's office, and as he entered, he read the nameplate at the desk: Lieutenant Colonel Richard L. Mason.

Ross suppressed a desire to salute.

"Good morning, Colonel. I'm Ross Braxton and this is Mrs. Amy Childs. We've just come down from Dakota Territory and ran across a couple of deserters."

The officer shook his hand and told them to have a seat, which they did.

"You say you ran across two deserters?"

"Yes, sir. Both privates. One was named Willie Ellison and the other was John Humboldt."

"I got a wire about those two a few weeks back. Where were they headed?"

"Well, they were headed to the Black Hills to seek their fortune, but they actually missed them by eighty miles. They invaded our camp and threatened harm to Mrs. Childs and myself, so I had to shoot them both."

"They're dead? Well, that saves the army some time hunting for them. Did you recover any of the army's property?"

"We have their mounts out front as well as their Spencer carbines and some ammunition. I do have one request, though. If possible, I'd like to purchase one of the saddles. Amy was riding bareback when we came across the two men and was happy to be able to ride using a saddle again."

"You can keep the saddle. The army owes you that much at least. If you want a receipt, see the quartermaster. Is there anything else?"

"No, sir. We're going to get some lunch and then resupply before heading down to Scotts Bluff."

The colonel smiled and said, "I won't hold you up any. I'll have the corporal send someone to take care of the horses. Thank you for what you did."

They shook hands, then Amy and Ross stepped out of the office and past the corporal who was being summoned by his commanding officer.

They returned to their three horses and the pinto, mounted the saddled animals and turned them to where Ross had seen the sutler's store earlier. The pinto followed.

When they arrived, it was almost three in the afternoon. Because they had skipped lunch in order to reach Camp Robinson earlier, they were hungry, so they took a seat at a table and ordered chicken dinners with mashed potatoes and gravy and biscuits. Amy thought she would die when the food was set before them.

Ross enjoyed the food as well, but not as much as someone who had been deprived of good food for at least three years. Being a witch doesn't entitle one to the same food as valuable members of the tribe.

After they had finished their meal, Ross began piling items up for the last ten days of travel. He bought cans of beans, beef, onions, and potatoes. Then he added two slabs of bacon, ten more pounds of coffee, three dozen eggs and a small pepper grinder and a can of pepper corns. He even snuck in two cans of peaches. He also bought two large pads of writing paper and six pencils. All except the paper and pencils was placed in large cloth sacks, but he had the paper and pencils put into a paper sack.

They returned to the horses and hung the new sacks on the pack horse for now and then rode out of Camp Robinson. The pinto still trailing behind.

Ross turned and watched the camp receding into the distance and noticed the pinto still trailing quietly behind them.

"You know, that pinto's still back there. I thought maybe he'd stay at the post. I guess he just likes being part of our herd."

"How much further to Scotts Bluff?" she asked.

"About eighty miles or so. We'll get there in three days. When we arrive, I'll wire my parents and tell them what's going on. They knew I was going to visit Henry, but they were worried about the ride. Oh, and did you notice what I bought at the sutler's store?"

"I saw you bought two cans of peaches."

"I also bought two big pads of paper and six pencils, so you could start writing your novel."

There was a reason that Amy hadn't noticed. She had been keeping an eye on a man who was leering at her. She didn't mention it to Ross because she didn't think it mattered, besides he was a civilian.

"Really, Ross? You did that for me?"

"Amy, never keep putting off a dream if you don't have to. You have the internal tools in your mind, so I thought if I bought you the external tools to put your ideas down on paper, you could begin to realize your dream."

Amy was excited and grateful. She had always put her hopes into the pipe dream category, but Ross believed in her and was giving her the impetus that she needed to begin to take that dream from being a pipe dream to being reality.

"Thank you so much for that, Ross. I've been running through different scenes in my head and I'm getting closer. Thank you for being so thoughtful, Ross."

"You're welcome. You can thank me by writing that book. How did you miss it when I was buying the paper and pencils?"

"I didn't want to say anything at the time, but there was a man who was looking at me that made me feel uncomfortable. I finally walked close to you, so he could see that I was protected."

"Was he army?"

"No. He was wearing regular clothes."

"Well, I'll keep an eye on our backtrail."

They continued talking for another ninety minutes. The sun was getting low on the horizon, so Ross stopped and turned his horse around and pulled out his field glasses and quickly noticed that there was a lone rider about four miles behind them.

"It looks like we may have a visitor, Amy."

"Not again, Ross. When will we be able to just ride along peacefully?"

"Soon, but maybe not tonight. He's about thirty minutes behind us and we can't do a lot of hiding, but neither can he. It's possible that he's just heading down to Scotts Bluff himself, though. We'll pull over in a few minutes and start setting up camp. I'll keep my Colts ready and the Winchester nearby. If he stops by, and I think he will, be ready for anything."

"Alright," she replied, already feeling nervous.

Ross found a decent campsite with small stream but no cover. They pulled over and began unsaddling the horses as the pinto wandered into the camp and over to the stream when Ross let them all drink. He'd been monitoring the approaching visitor for ten minutes now but acting as if he didn't see him. As he drew nearer to the camp, Ross turned, took a good look, so the stranger knew he had been seen, then turned back to the horse and finished unloading him.

The stranger was fifty feet away when Ross walked toward him.

"Hello, the camp!" the stranger shouted from horseback.

"C'mon in," Ross yelled in reply as his hand stayed next to his untethered Colt.

They hadn't built a fire yet, but there was enough light for Amy to recognize the man who had stared at her in the store. She wished she had a pistol and knew how to use it.

"Name's Louis Campbell," he said from his horse.

"I'm Ross Braxton and that's my wife Amy."

Amy knew he was just saying that to justify being alone together, but still it gave her a thrill that made her feel disloyal to Aaron, making her ashamed of herself yet again.

Mister Campbell smiled at Amy, tipped his hat and said, "Pleased to meet you, ma'am. I'm on my way to Scotts Bluff and wanted to share your fire and maybe some friendly conversation."

Ross replied, "Louis, if it was just me, that would be fine, but my wife and I need our privacy, so I'd appreciate it if you just kept riding for a bit. No bad feelings or anything, we just need to be alone."

"Well, just trying to be neighborly," Louis said, before he wheeled his horse and kept heading south.

Ross watched him disappear into the darkening evening.

Amy approached Ross and stood next to him as they both watched where he had gone, then said, "That's the man who was staring at me in the store."

"I figured that. When I introduced you, he had a funny look in his eyes. Like the one you see on a kid's face when he's standing in front of the penny candy display."

"It was much worse in the store. It was like he was undressing me."

"I think tonight we need to be ready for his return."

"You think he's coming back?"

"He has to. He was lying about going to Scott's Bluff. Even traveling alone, he'd have to stop at least once, and he wasn't packing any supplies at all. He knew we'd probably be setting up camp close, so he thought he could just stop in, take me out when my back was turned and do what he wanted with you. He'll be back. Probably within a couple of hours.

"Now, we ate late, so we can skip a meal, but we can share a can of peaches in a little while, and there's something else we can do. We'll set up the tent, then when he comes back, he'll expect us to be there, you know, doing husband and wife things. We'll build a fire and let it burn down, so he has enough light to see it and we can see him. Then, I'll take it from there."

"Where will I be?"

"You will be in the bedroll right behind me. I'll be sitting in the dark with my Winchester cocked and ready. We'll be about fifty yards from the tent and the horses. He'll be on foot, so our horses don't smell his horse. I'm going to give you my second

Colt. Remember what I told you before; just pull back the hammer, point it and squeeze the trigger."

"Okay."

First, Ross set up the tent. Then, he built a small fire about thirty feet off to the side, so he could still see clearly, but would still be a beacon for the stranger.

After they had picked out a spot about fifty yards away from the fire, Ross stretched out the bedroll and had Amy lie down to present as low a silhouette as possible. Ross would just sit with his Winchester cocked and had already given Amy his second Colt.

Then they waited. An hour and a half passed before Ross heard something, and it came from his one o'clock position. He kept his eyes away from the dying fire and watched as the man slowly crept out of the shadows. His pistol was drawn, so Ross raised his cocked Winchester.

The stranger stood in front of the tent, with his legs spread as he pointed his revolver at the tent.

Then he shouted, "C'mon outta there, mister, before I start filling that tent full of lead. I might kill that woman of yours first, so you'd better come out now. I ain't waitin' very long."

Ross waited as the man thought about which direction to shoot, left or right. He was preparing to gamble shooting Amy in the hope he'd kill Ross and then have Amy alive.

"This is your last warning," he yelled.

Finally, Ross shouted, "Drop it, you bastard! I've got you covered."

Ross never found out if the man thought Ross was bluffing or just had a pistol and might miss. It didn't matter as he turned and opened fire. Ross already had him in his sights and didn't care where the stranger's shot went as he squeezed the trigger.

After traveling one hundred and forty-four feet, the .44 punched into the stranger's chest, shattering his breastbone and amazingly, missed his heart, but did massive damage before shattering his seventh and eighth thoracic vertebrae and then cutting his spinal cord.

The man's Colt dropped from his fingers, he took two awkward steps, tripped over the tent stake and fell face first into the ground. His right hand shook for five seconds and then stopped.

"Amy, you stay here. I'll go make sure he's dead," Ross said as he stood quickly.

"I know."

"I'm sorry this keeps happening, Amy."

"So, am I."

He walked over to the corpse lowering his Winchester when he was within ten yards. Men don't fall on their faces when they're trying to pretend that they were hit. He dragged him over to the almost dead fire before Ross added some more kindling and it crawled back to life. After he had tossed on some larger wood, it became a full-sized fire again.

Ross knelt next to the body. Surprisingly, the man had a money belt with over three hundred dollars inside. Ross tossed it aside and kept searching for something to identify the man. Finally, when he took off his hat, he could see some writing inside. He couldn't make it out in the dark, so he put it with the money belt. The other $11.45 cents he had on him he put in his own pocket. The man's empty gunbelt was added to the stack near his dropped Smith & Wesson Model 3.

Then he had to figure out where to bury him. He slid him over a small sand dune to the other side, then began digging a shallow hole like a dog would using his hands. It was only a foot or so deep when he finished. Then he rolled him into it and began paddling the sand back on top.

He then stood, brushed his hands on his britches and walked back to where Amy was sitting on the bedroll.

"So, what's this one's story?" she asked almost mechanically.

"I have no idea. The odd thing was that he was pretty well off. Usually, these types are so down in their luck, they get desperate. This guy had over three hundred dollars on him. He had a good revolver, too. I can't identify him yet, but I have his hat that has some writing inside. Did you want to go to the tent while I get his horse? That might help, too."

Amy thought she might prefer staying where she was but decided she'd be safer with Ross.

"If it's alright, I'll just walk with you."

"That's fine."

Ross offered her a hand and helped her to her feet, then took the bedroll and tossed it over his shoulder, and when they passed the tent, he put it inside. Then they went looking for his horse, and it wasn't hard to find. Two hundred yard away, the horse stood looking at them, his reins tied to a small bush. Ross hadn't closely examined the horse before when the man had arrived as he had spent most of his time watching the man's eyes and looking for indications of his true intentions. They led the horse back to the camp, and over to the fire. The first thing he noticed was the nice Winchester in the scabbard.

Ross hitched him to a tent stake, pulled the surprisingly heavy saddlebags free and set them on the ground and flipped open the flap. Inside were four boxes of .44 caliber ammunition. There was also a bag with First National Bank of Scotts Bluff on the outside.

He pulled the bag out and looked over at Amy with raised eyebrows.

"Now this is a surprise. Do you want to count it, or do you want me to do it?"

Amy replied, "You do it. I'd probably drop money all over the place."

Ross reached inside the bag and pulled out the large wad of cash and began counting, quickly arriving at a total of $1245. He put the money back into the bag and put the bag in the saddlebags.

He looked back at Amy and said, "I'm almost afraid to see what's in the other side," but still opened it.

The other contained a second pair of pants and a shirt. There was a second gunbelt with another Smith & Wesson Model 3, and two more boxes of ammunition. Then, he found a folded wanted poster.

Ross unfolded it and found a remarkable likeness of the man he had just buried. Under the picture, it said:

WANTED
DEAD OR ALIVE
ALBERT TALBOT
$1000
WANTED FOR MURDER, RAPE,
ROBBERY AND ASSAULT

Amy walked up next to him, looked at the poster and exclaimed, "That's him!"

Ross noticed something else on the sheet and said, "Look at what he wrote across the wanted poster. He scrawled, *its Alfred not Albert, you morons*. I guess he wanted the fame and notoriety that goes with being a bad man assigned properly. I think we'll get a warm welcome in Scotts Bluff, and I think we have a large reward coming our way."

"We get that money?"

"The thousand dollars? Yup. I'm not sure about the loose money he had in the money belt, though. We'll find out when we get to Scotts Bluff. Now the horse is outstanding. Outlaws always seem to have good horses. We also picked up two nice pistols. I'll want to train you on how to use it when we get the chance. From now on, you'll wear one. I want you to be the most dangerous woman in the West."

"I definitely want to wear one. I'm tired of feeling helpless."

"I doubt if you were ever helpless, Amy, and now, you'll be downright dangerous. So, after all this, did you want to eat?"

"For some reason, I'm starved."

"Alright, then. Let's eat."

Ross put the cooking grate over the fire and added a few more pieces of wood. He made coffee and a beef, potato and onion mix. They both ate well and then Amy cleaned the plates as Ross unsaddled their latest addition to their growing herd.

"You know, Amy. At this rate, by the time we get to Cheyenne, we'll have a regular herd of horses."

"Please, no more. I'd rather collect something else, maybe rocks."

"I can understand that," he said as he smiled at her.

They finally put out the fire and after Ross collected the rest of the outlaws things from the pile and put them with the panniers, they crawled into the tent. Their nightly conversation was short this time as Amy was emotionally drained and quickly fell asleep.

Ross stayed awake just looking at her peaceful face and wishing that she didn't have to go to Oregon before he finally slipped into dreamland twenty minutes later.

————

Early the next morning, Ross fixed a breakfast of bacon and eggs, with salt and now, pepper.

"One of these days, one of us is going to have to figure out how to make biscuits," Ross said as he handed the plate to Amy.

"I make very tasty biscuits. I'm actually quite a good cook," she replied.

"Then why are you putting up with my cooking?"

"I just thought you wanted to, and you never asked."

Ross stood, bowed at the waist, and asked, "Pardon me, ma'am. Could you please cook us a tastier dinner tonight than I've been making?"

"I'd be honored, sir," Amy replied with a smile.

"Good. Now, before we hit the road, there's something I need to do."

Ross walked over to where he had buried the outlaw and looked around. He found three branches, made a tripod, tied them together at the top and then returned.

"That's in case the authorities want to come and dig him up," he said as he saw her curious eyes.

"Oh."

Ross saddled all the horses except for the friendly small pinto and loaded the pack horse. Then he took money belt and put it in the same saddlebag with the bank bag. He looked in the hat and saw the same scrawl that he had seen on the wanted poster...Alfred Talbot.

He tucked the hat under one of the ropes on the pack horse and then he called Amy over to the horses.

"Are we ready to go?" she asked.

"First I need you to stand in front of me. Now, I'm not trying to be familiar, so don't take offense."

She didn't take offense, and wanted him to be familiar, but knew he wouldn't and was even ashamed for hoping he would.

Ross picked up the gun belt, sans pistol, and wrapped it around her waist. Then, he adjusted the belt until it was comfortable on her hips. He reached down and picked up the

Smith & Wesson and dropped it into the holster, then he locked the hammer in place with the leather loop.

"There. Now you're packing iron. This gun shoots like my Colt, so if you need to use it, just unhook the hammer loop, draw the pistol, use your left hand to pull the hammer all the way back, then slide your left hand under your right hand for support and pull the trigger. I'll be more specific later."

Amy tugged the belt a little firmer onto her hips.

"Now that you've armed me, are we leaving?"

"It's off to Scotts Bluff, milady. Let's get mounted."

They mounted their horses, and soon the parade was riding south.

They set a good pace, hoping to cut down most of the distance to Scotts Bluff today. By the time they stopped for a short lunch break to take care of the four horses and the trailing pinto, they had already covered twenty miles. The humans satisfied themselves with some jerky followed by a can of peaches that they shared. When they finally called it a day, they had covered just over fifty miles. Fifty miles that were filled with pleasant conversation and more than a few laughs. Amy was having Ross tell her more stories from history and he never seemed to run out of them.

They found a nice camp site at sunset and set it up quickly as they've begun to work more as a team. Ross pitched the tent and put the blankets and bedroll inside, then he took care of the animals while Amy began to cook dinner. She had the added benefit of pepper to add to whatever she made, but still, it did taste much better.

The weather had turned back to typical November weather earlier in the day when the wind had picked up and clouds had covered the sky. They scurried into the tent as snow began to fall. They were small pellets rather than the large, soft snowflakes they had seen when they were being chased by the Sioux.

With the lowered temperatures, Amy was pleased to have the bed roll and felt a little guilty that Ross only had the blankets, but she knew he'd never accept a different situation and eventually fell asleep.

What she didn't know is that after her eyes closed, Ross repeated last night's fantasy to look at her serene face for quite some time, and again wished she didn't have to get on that train when they arrived in Cheyenne, but there was nothing he could do to prevent it.

———

When they awakened, the wind had died down to a barely detectable breeze and the snow had long since stopped, but the temperature had plummeted. It was well below freezing when they dressed under the blankets and finally emerged into the Nebraska freezer.

Ross quickly got a big fire going and started breakfast while Amy took care of personal business. Ross found her heavy jacket and gave it to her, then she put on her knit cap and the scarf, and Ross could barely see her pink cheeks under the wrapping.

They ate breakfast quickly and Ross loaded the pack horse and saddled the horses. He decided to put a loop around the pinto, just to protect him from becoming 'lost' when they arrived in Scotts Bluff.

They were on the road by seven o'clock, and when the sun finally broke through by mid-morning, Ross guessed that they were within five miles of Scotts Bluff. Their conversation was limited because of the cold, but they knew they'd be warmer soon after they reached the town.

Just under an hour later, when they arrived in Scotts Bluff, Ross told Amy that their first stop needed to be at the sheriff's office, so they pulled up in front of the jail where they both stepped down and tied their horses to the hitchrail. They hurriedly entered and closed the door quickly, deeply appreciating the warmth from the heat stove.

They were greeted by a middle-aged man with a receding hairline in his light brown hair.

He seemed pleasant enough and said, "What can I do for you, folks?"

"Are you the sheriff?" Ross asked.

"Sheriff Amos Hanratty, at your service."

"Sheriff, my name is Ross Braxton. We were on the trail down from Camp Robinson and we ran afoul of a man who seemed intent on assaulting Amy. He drew a pistol on our tent and was threatening to fire unless we came out. I was behind him at the time, having guessed his intent when he stopped by our camp earlier. I shouted for him to drop his weapon and he chose to fire. I put one Winchester .44 cartridge into his chest from about fifty yards. I buried him out on the trail, but I marked where I had buried him about sixty miles north of here."

"Glad you got the bastard, but that's out of my jurisdiction."

"I understand that. But when I was going through his belongings, I found something that you might be interested in. Was the First National Bank held up recently?"

That spiked the sheriff's interest, as he replied, "Yes, just about a week and a half ago. Why?"

"How much did they get?"

"He got about twelve hundred dollars. It was a lone robber. We believe it was Albert Talbot."

"Well, you're mostly right. His name is actually Alfred Talbot. He seemed to be annoyed that the wanted posters had it wrong. That was the man I shot. I have your bank's money in his saddlebag outside. I'll be right back. You stay in here and stay warm, Amy."

"Thank you, Ross," she replied.

"So, ma'am, how did you find yourself on the trail?" the sheriff asked after Ross had gone outside.

"I had been held captive by the Sioux for three years up in Dakota Territory. I escaped and was about to be killed when Ross shot the Indian who was about to kill me. Then he shot another from about four hundred yards. We began heading southwest and were pursued by eight more Sioux warriors. Ross killed all of them. Then, two days later, we ran afoul of two army deserters. Ross had to trick them to shoot them before they shot me, then we ran into Mister Talbot. Now, we're here."

The sheriff sat there with his mouth open having heard the most remarkable fifteen second speech he had ever heard before and most likely would ever hear its equal.

The door opened and closed again rapidly, and Ross noticed the blank look on the sheriff's face.

He turned to Amy and gave her a quizzical look.

"He asked how come we were on the trail. So, I gave him the quick version."

"Oh."

The sheriff refocused on Ross as Ross laid the bank bag on his desk.

"I counted it, sheriff. There's $1240 dollars in there."

"All of it? You got all of the bank's money back?" he asked in astonishment.

"He must not have had time to spend any of it yet. He saw us at Camp Robinson, and he watched Amy for a few minutes. I guess he decided he would like to have her, so he followed."

"How do you know it was Talbot?"

"Quite a few things, really. The man I buried looked like the man in the wanted poster I have in my pocket. His hat has his name on the inside label, he had the bank's money, and he wrote this on the wanted poster."

Ross took out the wanted poster handed it to the sheriff, who saw where the outlaw had written his protest of the incorrect use of his name.

"Well, I'll be damned. Looks like you have a hefty reward coming, Mr. Braxton. It'll take me a couple of days to get authorization to release the money. Is that okay?"

"Sure. We need a break anyway. We'll be heading over to Cheyenne when we're done here. What about his horse and other stuff?"

"You keep 'em. You sure earned them."

"Thank you, Sheriff. I'm going to go and drop off our horses at the livery and we'll head over to the hotel."

"Sounds good. I can't wait till I tell the bank president. He's been giving me grief for letting that bastard give me the slip for ten days."

"Well, enjoy your vindication, Sheriff," Ross said.

The sheriff was grinning as he shook Ross's hand, and then they made a hasty exit to keep the cold out of the office.

Once outside, the sheriff trotted away to the bank, so Ross turned and said, "Amy, why don't you go and wait for me in the hotel? I'll be down shortly. Okay?"

"Considerate as always. Thank you, Ross. I'll meet you there."

She hustled across the street to the hotel and Ross watched with a smile on his face.

He led his four horses down the street to the livery. Once he arrived, he told the liveryman that he'd be in town for a few days, and he needed him to shoe the pinto and check the shoes on the others. He also asked that they be given extra oats. The liveryman said it would be two dollars per day for stabling the horses plus the cost of the shoes. Ross gave him twenty dollars.

"Do you need help in getting them free of their gear?" Ross asked.

"No, I'll take care of that. Your stuff is safe here as well."

"That's good to know."

Ross pulled off three of the saddlebags and walked back down the street to the hotel.

Amy was inside staying warm and had taken off her hat and scarf, but still had pink cheeks. She smiled when Ross walked inside, and he smiled back.

Ross and Amy then walked to the reception desk and Ross asked if all the rooms were the same, and the clerk told him they had two larger suites at the end of the bottom floor, so Ross told him they'd take one of those and the adjoining room then paid for three days.

He was given two keys and Ross led Amy down the hallway and opened the door. It was a nice room with a sink. The bathroom was right next door at the end of the hallway. It even boasted a water closet and a bathtub with hot and cold spigots.

"This will be your room. I'll be next door if you need anything. But before you go running off to the bath, why don't we go across the street and you can buy some new clothes and anything else you need."

"Even though I'll freeze on the way over there, the thought of getting new clothes will keep me warm," she said.

He smiled at her grinning face but avoided any show of being a couple as he turned then escorted her out of the hotel and quickly walked across the street.

When they got inside, Amy gave a big smile to Ross and trotted down to the women's clothing section. Ross walked to a different section and bought two toothbrushes, two cans of tooth powder, some more white soap and some scented soap for Amy along with some peach scented shampoo for her as well. Then he bought her a hairbrush and mirror set, bought himself a new razor and shaving mug, brush and soap kit. He added two good-sized travel bags for the clothes she would be buying. Ross smiled at the proprietor and told him that Amy would be buying quite a few clothes unless he missed his guess.

He paid for his purchases while they waited, and the proprietor put them into a cloth bag. It took a while, but finally Amy waddled up the aisle with an armload of clothes. Ross ran over to her and relieved her of the tonnage.

"Amy, you could have brought some over to the counter and gone back."

"I'm sorry, I couldn't stop," she said just short of giggling.

Ross laughed and dropped the load onto the counter next to a beaming store owner. He began going through Amy's purchases. Ross looked over at her and she seemed to feel buyer's remorse.

"That will be $42.15."

Amy looked shocked.

"That's fine."

Ross counted out two twenties and a ten dollar note, handed them to the proprietor, then accepted his change and waited while all of Amy's items were packed.

There were two large bags in addition to the middle-sized bag that Ross had bought which contained the collapsed travel bags.

"Amy, if you'll get the smaller bag, I'll take these two. Go ahead and bundle up."

She did and then she lifted the smaller bag and Ross hefted her two larger ones as the proprietor held the door for them, and they walked across the quiet street to the hotel. Amy opened the door, let Ross in, and after closing the door, walked beside him as they passed by the desk, then walked down to Amy's room where Ross unlocked the door and handed her the key.

Ross left the door open after they entered, and Amy began taking off her cold weather gear. Ross set down the two big bags and hunted for his shaving gear and one toothbrush and can of powder in the small bag and set them aside on the dresser.

"Ross, I'm so sorry. I never meant to spend that much."

"Amy, don't worry a thing about it. We're in fine shape for money."

"I know, but still."

"Now, why don't you find what you want to wear to dinner and then you can go take a real bath. When you're ready to eat, come by my room and knock on the door."

Amy wondered what was in the smaller bag.

"What did you buy, anyway? We don't need any more bullets."

"Come here, and I'll show you."

She sat on the bed as he began pulling items out of the bag.

He handed her a bar of scented soap, then the bottle of peach shampoo, a toothbrush and the can of tooth powder. Then he gave her the brush and mirror set.

When she had them all in her lap, he smiled at her and said, "No, Amy, I didn't buy any more bullets."

She was starting to tear up at the sight of all these things to make her transformation complete.

"Thank you so much, Ross. Here I am worried about spending so much money on myself, and you go and buy more things for me."

"I did buy some new shaving gear for myself, so don't feel too bad. Now, go and take a nice bath. I'll be in my room shaving. Let me know when you're ready."

He smiled and gave her a short wave before leaving the room with his shaving gear, toothbrush and powder. He closed the door behind him, walked next door, opened his room, and stepped inside, closing the door behind him. It wasn't as nice as Amy's room, but there was a sink.

He took off his jacket, hat and scarf and hung them on the hooks near the door, poured some cold water from the pitcher into the sink, and whipped up some lather in his new shaving cup, brushed it on his face and scraped off his whiskers, before he stretched out on his bed and waited for Amy.

Amy selected one of her new dresses and the female underpinnings she needed and laid them on the bed. She almost floated into the bathroom and closed the door. The young woman who emerged forty minutes later was almost unrecognizable compared to the woman who had entered. She carried Ross's clothes with her when she returned to the main part of the room.

She spent ten minutes brushing her hair with the new hairbrush. Even though there was a mirror in the room, Amy felt obligated to use her new mirror, but she still used the larger room mirror to inspect herself and was astounded by the change. Just a few days ago, she thought she was an unattractive woman and now, with her hair brushed and wearing a new dress, she felt so very feminine.

Now, she wanted to impress the man who made this all possible, even though she knew he could never be hers.

She opened the door and walked down to Ross' room and knocked. She waited anxiously for the door to open to see the expression on his face, still feeling guilty for the pleasure she was already feeling. This behavior had to stop. She was almost ready to return to her room and put on a less attractive dress when his door opened, and Amy had her wish as Ross stood there looking at her with wide eyes.

Ross was stunned. Amy was pretty, he'd already told her that. But she looked well beyond just pretty as she stood before him now. Amy was spectacular, but he couldn't go overboard. He must refrain from appearing to be wooing her. He kept reminding himself that she was a married woman.

Amy noticed the pause and finally asked, "Well, how do I look?"

"Amy, I have to admit, you look very nice, indeed," he replied.

Amy knew it was an improvement, but she was disappointed. She had hoped to impress him, but perhaps it was just as well. Now she didn't have to feel guilty about it.

"Did you want to go and get some lunch?"

"I really don't want to go out in the cold so soon."

"We don't have to. We'll be eating our meals in the restaurant just off the lobby."

"I didn't even notice it."

"Well, it'll be a nice change. We don't have to do anything but enjoy our food. We won't have to get cold or do any cleanup."

Despite his earlier commitment not to appear as a couple, Ross offered her his arm, which she accepted, then smiled as they walked down the hallway to the restaurant. As they walked, the gentle, flowery scents he picked up from Amy were having further impacts on Ross and he was having problems thinking straight.

They walked all of one hundred feet to the restaurant and were shown to a table. The waitress was a young lady about Amy's age. She was pretty and seemed nice, but, Ross thought, she couldn't hold a candle to Amy, and he couldn't imagine that any other woman ever would.

They ordered some chicken for lunch, and it came with all the sides. It was so pleasant to be able to just eat and talk normally without having to worry about someone trying to kill them. They enjoyed their coffee and stretched out the meal for almost an hour. The waitress didn't mind as they only had one other customer, and she really didn't mind when Ross left a fifty-cent tip.

They returned to the rooms and Amy began to put away her clothes, while Ross availed himself of a hot bath down the hallway and enjoyed it a bit more than the icy baths he had been taking recently.

When he returned to his room twenty minutes later, he thought he'd consolidate his money and get a total on how much he had to finish the journey.

Ross dumped out both money belts on the bed. He followed that with all the currency he had in his pockets.

He began to count it out and came up with $1692.55.

He decided to put fifteen hundred dollars into the money belt and carry the rest. That should get them into Cheyenne with over a hundred dollars in his pockets plus the reward money that would be added to his money belt

Ross decided to send that telegram to his parents while he remembered, so he put on his hat and jacket and left the room.

He walked out to the hotel lobby where he was met by the sheriff and another gentleman.

The sheriff grinned at him and said, "We were just coming to look for you, Ross. This is Andy Hostetler, our bank president. He wanted to thank you personally for returning the bank's money. Not too many folks would do that."

"Really? That's kind of sad because it isn't even the bank's money. It belongs to the folks."

As he shook Ross's hand, the banker said, "I wish more people had that attitude. Yes, sir. I do sincerely appreciate the return of the bank's funds. Of course, you're correct in that it is really our depositor's money, so they'll all be relieved."

"I'm glad to be of some help."

"Well, thank you again, Mr. Braxton."

The banker waved as he left the hotel.

Ross turned to the sheriff and said, "So, you seem to be on good terms with the banker again."

"That's an understatement. When I walked into the bank with that bag of money, he almost peed his pants. He counted every dime like he might be cheated. I sent off the information to the folks that put up the reward, so I should hear back by tomorrow authorizing payment. Is a bank draft okay?"

"Absolutely. I'd prefer a draft."

"Good. Are you heading outside?"

"Yup. I need to send a wire to my folks to let them know that I'm here and will be in Cheyenne in a few days."

The sheriff thanked him again and shook his hand before they both left the hotel. Ross turned left toward the Western Union office.

He entered the office and took out a sheet. He wrote:

WALTER AND EMILY BRAXTON SEXTON MINN

REACHED SCOTTS BLUFF
WILL BE HEADED TO CHEYENNE TO SEE HENRY
WILL WRITE SOON

ROSS BRAXTON SCOTTS BLUFF HOTEL NEB

He handed it to the clerk and paid fifty cents, then returned to the hotel.

He walked back to his room and quietly opened the door. He was going to go inside when he decided he really just wanted to talk to Amy, which he thought was silly as he'd just had lunch with her. But rational reasoning was pushed aside as he turned back down the hallway and knocked on her door.

Amy was lying on her comfortable bed. She knew she was only a few days from Cheyenne, and she was getting to hate that name. It meant the end of the trail…literally. She would board the train and go to Oregon and never see Ross again. He'd probably get married and forget all about her, as he should. She was a married woman.

Then there was a knock on the door, and she jumped from the bed, knowing who had probably just arrived.

She almost yanked the door off its hinges and smiled as she saw Ross standing before her wearing his own broad smile.

"I just got back from sending that wire to my parents letting them know that I had arrived in Scotts Bluff safely and would be heading to Cheyenne. I thought you might want to go and have some coffee, so we could just talk."

"I'd like that, Ross."

He smiled at her and offered her his arm again. She closed the door, then they returned to the almost empty restaurant where they soon were sitting at the same table with cups of coffee. He told her about his meeting with the sheriff and the bank president and the sheriff's comments about the banker's reaction to getting his money back.

She laughed at the story, which made Ross laugh in return. He told her that the bank draft for the reward would probably be issued tomorrow and they'd leave the following day.

She nodded but quickly slid into a mild depression with the reminder of their short hiatus.

But that disappeared when he changed the subject to one that surprised her…dogs.

"Have you ever had a dog, Amy?" he asked.

Amy was a bit taken aback by the shift, but replied, "No, have you?"

"Not personally. But the boy in the next farm did. The boy's name was Bobby Fulton and he had this large dog with golden fur. It was really friendly, and I'd go over there just to play with him. I couldn't stand Bobby, but the dog was a real friend. Bobby didn't even like the dog and didn't play with him or treat him right, either.

"Once, I saw him kick the dog, so, naturally I punched him in the nose and yelled 'How do you like it?'. He went running into the house and I was banned from visiting. I missed that dog. I felt like sneaking over there and bringing him to my house, but he wasn't my dog. I still miss him. So, when I settle down. I know I'll have to have a dog."

Amy wondered if he was just telling her a story or sending her a message, but either way, Amy understood what the story meant to her. To Ross, maybe it was just a story of something that had happened when he was a boy, but to Amy, it was the story of their relationship. She belonged to another and even if he wanted to take her home, he couldn't. She wasn't his.

He had asked her a question, but she had missed it.

"Excuse me, Ross. I missed that one."

"I was asking if you ever had any pets at all when you were young."

"Oh. No, not unless you count a few scrawny chickens. I don't think that qualifies, because we ate all of them."

Ross laughed, and said, "No, I guess not. After the dog incident, I figured I'd wait until I was grown up and find one that I could take care of. We never had any chickens, but we had plenty of cows. Have you ever milked a cow?"

"No. I imagine you've done that a few times."

"Every day. It's what made my hands so strong. They were really soft, too. Until I went to the Academy, it was almost embarrassing."

"Are they still soft?"

"I don't think so."

"Let me feel your hand."

Ross put out his hand and Amy put it between her two hands and began gently sliding her fingers across his palm and fingers, unsettling Ross in grand fashion.

"It doesn't feel soft at all, Ross. It feels like a man's hand."

Ross answered quietly "That's because it is. It's been a long time since I milked cows."

Ross became conscious of Amy still holding his hand after her brief inspection.

Amy had asked to feel his hands just to feel them, whether they were soft or not didn't matter. Cheyenne was just a few days away, and she felt as if she was acting like a shameless hussy but didn't care anymore.

Finally, she released his hand and asked, "So, what else did you do besides milk the cows?"

"We moved them from place to place. Helped them have their calves. Milk cows have to give birth once a year to produce milk, so we always had a lot of calves and heifers around. The young boys were sold off to cattle ranches, but most of the girls we kept for more milk cows."

"Did you brother help with that?"

"Not much. He always had one excuse or another until he went off to work in the lumber mill. We had hired hands to do a lot of the work. I helped because I was grateful to my parents for providing for me. Plus, I liked to work."

"How many cows did you have on the farm?"

"The last time I knew it was close to eighty, but that was some time ago. I'm sure that there are many more by now. We sold milk, cream, butter, and cheese. My father said he was going to really expand the cheese operation when I saw him last, and he'll do it, too."

"Sounds like you had a nice childhood."

"Except when Henry was beating me up," he said with a smile.

"Then, you ran."

"I ran," he said, then he looked at her bright green eyes, then continued, saying, "Until I was sixteen. Then, I stopped running. He expected me to keep running. But I made a decision that day. He was bigger than I was, but it didn't matter. I would no longer run...ever.

"At first, he laughed and tried his usual tactics. As soon as he took his first swing, I hit him in the stomach...hard. He was soft and hadn't expected it, so he went down and started crying. I was tempted to stand over him and say something, but instead I offered him my hand to help him up. That was a big mistake. He took my hand and pulled me to the ground then started kicking me. So much for being compassionate with Henry.

"I rolled over, taking the kicks until I could get some leverage. I finally grabbed his foot and yanked him onto his back. He fell as I scrambled to my feet and then when he stood, I started hitting him. I was so angry. I've never been that angry again.

"Finally, I stopped. Henry was a bloody mess, and I just looked at him and said, 'Never again, Henry. Just leave me alone.' And he did. He hated me even more after that. I think that added to the reason for wanting to marry Bessie. So, now I'll be seeing him again in a few days. I'm not worried, just curious. Maybe he's changed, but I doubt it. But since that day, I have never backed down, not to him or anyone else."

Amy had watched his eyes as he told the story. She wondered why he hadn't told her that when he had first told her of the 'girlie dances' that Henry had inflicted on him.

"Ross, why didn't you tell me that story the first time you told me about your brother?"

"I'm not too sure. Maybe I didn't want you to be afraid of me. I just don't know."

"I could never be afraid of you, Ross."

"Not now, maybe, but back then, I wasn't so sure."

"So, you'll be seeing him when we get to Cheyenne, him and Bessie together."

"Yes, ma'am, and I expect it to be very interesting."

"Where is their ranch?"

"It's the Box B and it's on the northeast approach to the city. We should pass it on the way in."

"Do we stop then, or do you want to go into Cheyenne?"

"It depends on the time of day and the day of the week. A lot of things will determine whether or not we'll stop to visit."

"Now you've got my curiosity aroused, so I'll have to see them, too."

"It might be scarier than any other part of our trip," he said.

Amy smiled and realized that he was serious.

They finished their coffee and Ross escorted Amy back to her room.

"I'll knock on your door when it's time for dinner."

"Thank you, Ross," she said as she smiled at him.

"You're welcome, Amy," he replied as she closed the door.

He let out a long breath, then walked back into his room, put on his hat and coat, then left the hotel and walked outside. He had seen a small shop when he had gone to the livery, and he wanted to go explore.

Five minutes later, he stepped inside the small bookstore, and smiled at the proprietor when he entered.

"Good afternoon, sir. Looking for anything in particular?"

"Do you have any Dickens?"

"Of course, sir. No bookstore should be without copies of his works. Any one in particular?

"Do you have *Nicholas Nickleby?*"

"Of course, sir. Anything else?"

"Yes, I'd like a copy of *Jane Eyre* as well."

"Very good choices, sir."

He placed both books in a heavy bag. Ross paid the bill and left the store in a good mood. Amy would appreciate them both.

Amy was in her room, sitting in the comfortable chair near the window. She was looking outside, almost not paying attention and then saw Ross walking back toward the hotel and had a bag with him and wondered what he had bought. He didn't need any more weaponry, and the dry goods store was the other direction. But she had a feeling that whatever it was, he'd be bringing it to her shortly. She stood, smoothed out her dress, and couldn't hold back the smile as her heart picked up its pace in anticipation of his pending arrival.

Two minutes later, there was a tapping on her door, and she quickly stepped to the door and opened it more carefully this time.

He stood before her grinning, which seemed to be all either of them did when in each other's company now.

"Come in, Ross. Is it time for dinner already?"

"No, Amy. Not for another hour or two. I just thought you'd be bored, so I thought I'd drop these off."

He handed her the bag, and as soon as she felt the weight and the shape, she knew what was inside.

"You bought me books?" she asked.

"I thought you might find *Caesar's Commentaries* a bit dry, so I picked these up at the bookstore near the livery. I saw it earlier when I dropped the horses off."

She pulled out the two books and smiled as she hadn't read either.

"Ross, I can never keep thanking you enough."

"One is by Dickens, our undereducated great author. The second is by Charlotte Bronte, whose sisters were also writers. So, Amy, here are two great novels by people just like you. There is one giant difference, though."

"And what's that?"

"They are both English. I think it's time for a great American woman author to emerge."

"Now you're getting carried away, Ross."

"Just go ahead and read these. Maybe you'll find more inspirations. I'll be back when it's dinner time."

He turned and closed the door behind him, and not because he wanted to leave, but because he felt he had to.

Amy knew it was proper and he couldn't come into her room, yet that didn't mean she hadn't wanted him to enter and close the door behind him, propriety be damned. But what she wanted didn't matter, as she looked down at the books and read the bindings. Two precious books and they were hers. She set Dickens aside and decided to begin reading *Jane Eyre*.

Ross returned to his room, satisfied that he had chosen correctly. He removed his jacket and hat and sat down on the bed then realized that he should have picked up something for himself, so he figured that tomorrow he'd be able to buy something to read.

Then the day after tomorrow, it would be onto Cheyenne. It would take three days if the weather held and they kept the pace slow. Maybe he could stretch it to four. After all, there was no need to rush. He knew that whenever they arrived, he'd be saying good-bye to Amy, probably for the rest of his life. At least she'd always have the books to remember him by. That led to all sorts of scenarios of what her life would be like in Oregon and none of them involved him.

After brooding for close to an hour, he decided that it was time for dinner, or close enough, so Ross left his room, stopped in front of Amy's room and rapped on her door. Fifteen seconds later the door was opened, and he was greeted with those smiling green eyes.

"Ready for dinner, ma'am?" he asked.

"Thank you, kind sir," she replied as she took his offered arm.

They walked across the lobby to a well populated restaurant, and after entering, the waitress arrived and showed them to their table.

After they had been seated, they ordered two steak dinners with baked potatoes and they had coffee while they waited for their food.

Amy had noticed that as they walked through the restaurant, heads were turned in their direction.

"Ross, why did everyone keep looking at us?"

"Don't you know?"

"No."

"I'll bet every one of those husbands who looked at you is getting a swift kick under the table from his wife. The women are just plain jealous."

"You think so, do you?" she asked as she beamed at the compliment.

"Absolutely."

Their dinners arrived a few minutes later, and Amy enjoyed her first steak dinner in a long time.

They were on their way to their room when the clerk called Ross over and said he had a telegram for him. He quickly read it and handed it to Amy.

She read:

ROSS BRAXTON SCOTTS BLUFF HOTEL NEB

SAY HELLO TO HENRY AND FAMILY FOR US
WRITE WHEN YOU CAN
LOVE ALWAYS

WALTER AND EMILY BRAXTON SEXTON MINN

She returned the telegram and asked, "Ross, if you find bad things when we go to the ranch, will you tell your parents?"

"Yes. I've never kept secrets from them, and I'm not about to start now, but I hope it's not as bad as I suspect."

"Do you really think it'll be that bad?"

"I don't know, Amy. I hope that it's not, but I really don't know."

"I guess we'll find out soon."

Ross nodded, then escorted her to her room and she smiled a goodnight to him as he smiled back and then returned to his room asking him the same question that Amy had asked him. *Will it be as bad as he expected?*

————

The next day, the ferocious cold left again, having just provided an early taste of what was to come and not leave for a few months once it took up residence.

After a nice breakfast, Amy returned to her room to read, and Ross left the hotel and went back to the book shop.

"Back again, sir?"

"I just needed something for myself. The other two were gifts. Do you mind if I browse?"

"Not at all. Most customers do."

Ross picked two books for himself. One was a quick read, *Twenty Thousand Leagues Under the Sea* and the second a longer one, *Les Miserables*.

He handed them to the proprietor who said, "Quite a variety in just two books."

"I know. One I needed for a quick read, the second for more in-depth reading."

"Exactly."

Ross paid a dollar and sixty cents for the two books and returned to the hotel.

Again, Amy saw Ross through the window. She had been reading and had paused and looked up just as he crossed her line of vision. She smiled as she watched him pass, knowing that he'd probably gone back to buy something for himself to read. She was suddenly aware of how well she knew Ross yet knew almost nothing of her husband. She barely even remembered what he looked like, but she must return to him. She was his wife, after all.

Ross had no sooner settled down and begun reading Verne when there was a polite knock on the door.

Ross got up and opened the door to find the sheriff standing before him holding out a small folded sheet of paper.

"I received authorization for payment, so the bank issued you the draft," he said as he handed it to Ross.

Ross accepted the draft and said, "Thank you for all your help, Sheriff. We'll be heading out for Cheyenne in the morning."

"Well, good luck to you. Hope everything goes smoothly."

"Me, too. I've had a lifetime of trouble on this trip."

"Sounds like it."

He shook the sheriff's hand and then closed the door behind him, then walked next door and knocked gently

Amy opened the door a few seconds later and smiled.

"Looks like we'll be leaving his lap of luxury tomorrow, Amy."

Even though she knew it was likely, she still felt her heart skip a beat before asking, "What time will we be leaving?"

"I'll knock on your door at seven-thirty, we'll go have a nice breakfast, and then I'll check out. I'm going to go down now and tell the liveryman that I'll be down at eight to pick up the horses. You just relax, and I'll take you to lunch when I return."

"Okay. I'll be waiting," she said and smiled a smile that she didn't feel as Ross turned to leave.

She closed the door and returned to reading, but as she pulled out her book, she just sat looking at the words, but not understanding them. So, she closed the book again, closed her eyes and took in a long, slow breath, then let it out just as gradually.

Tomorrow, they'd be leaving for Cheyenne. In less than a hundred miles this magic journey of terror, discovery and then she finally used the word that she feared to admit to herself, love, would end. She was close to asking Ross to not send her back and to keep her with him, but she knew he wouldn't let her. Not because he didn't want her, because she was sure now that he did, but because he wouldn't want her to feel guilty for the rest of her life for breaking those vows, and he would be right.

For three long years, she had been kept in a tipi prison and now that she was free, she'd be returning to another prison for the rest of her life knowing what she was losing.

She hugged her copy of *Jane Eyre* to her chest, closed her eyes and let the tears she had been holding back flow freely.

———

Ross left the hotel and glad he wasn't freezing when he walked down the street. He entered the livery and saw his four horses, and all of his gear, including the two Winchesters and Sharps that were stacked neatly in the corner.

The liveryman saw him enter and stepped out of a stall.

Ross said, "I just wanted to let you know that we'll be leaving around eight o'clock tomorrow. How much is the bill?"

"At the risk of sounding like a swindler, all four horses needed to be reshod, so minus the twenty you gave me, it'll be another two dollars."

"I don't think you're a swindler at all. Those poor animals have gone a long way."

"Did you want another pack saddle for the pinto? I have one I can let you have for ten dollars."

"That's not a bad idea. I'll take it. I'll have to redistribute the weight, but that shouldn't take me long."

"Don't worry about it. I'll have them all saddled and packed by the time you get here."

"Well, I appreciate it. Here's fifteen dollars. Keep the change."

"It's been a pleasure doing business with you, sir."

"Same here. I'll see you in the morning. Let's hope the weather holds."

"It should. My bones will tell me when it's gonna change three days ahead of time."

"I'll bet on your bones, then. See you in the morning."

Ross waved as he stepped back out into the street. The sun was out, and it was already over forty degrees, which wasn't bad for the Great Plains at this time of year.

He walked into the hotel and told the clerk that they'd be checking out in the morning after breakfast. He had already paid up, so he was told to just leave the key at the desk if no one was there.

He returned to his room and read Verne for a while and was pleased with his choice. A little past noon, he stood and left the room, walked down the hallway and tapped on Amy's door.

She opened the door and was still holding her book that she had finally been able to begin reading again. Her red eyes told him that she had been crying, and he assumed that she had read a particularly emotional section.

"Are you enjoying *Jane Eyre*?" he asked.

She smiled and replied, "It's wonderfully written. She is a great author."

"They'll be saying the same thing about you some day, Amy."

She closed the book and smiled at him again, then said, "Maybe."

"Let's go get something to eat."

He escorted Amy to the restaurant where they were seated, and after placing their orders, he looked at Amy.

197

"We're all set with the liveryman. I told him I'd be back after eight o'clock to pick things up. The horses have all been shod, and I bought another pack saddle for the pinto. As long as he's coming along, he may as well do something. I figured it would be handy for all your clothes."

"My clothes! I just realized I have nothing to pack them in."

"You didn't notice the two good-sized travel bags I bought? They're for your clothes. We can just hook the handles over the hooks on the pack saddle on the pinto. I'll lash them down, so they don't get bounced off."

"Thank you again, Ross. It seems like I'm always having to thank you."

"It's okay. I'm enjoying myself. I like making you smile, Amy."

Now, every time Ross said something like that it made everything worse. She had a firestorm mix of feelings between guilt, shame, happiness and dread. Suddenly, she thought of an issue that could create a real mess later. *How could she explain to Aaron about having all these nice clothes?* The impact of the thought made her shudder.

"Amy? Are you okay? You just turned as white as a sheet."

"No, I'm all right. I just thought of something. It's okay now."

"Is it something I can help you with?"

"No. It's fine. Really."

Their order came, and they ate in silence. Ross wondered if he had overstepped those delicate rules of society by telling a married woman that he liked making her smile. Maybe that was it. He had gone too far, so he'd have to watch it from now on. In a few short days, she'd be on the train returning to her husband, so he'd have to behave himself a little longer, but it was so hard to do. He wanted to tell her so much more that he made her smile.

They finished their lunch then returned to their rooms and read for a while, although neither of them absorbed the prose nearly as much as they thought about the quickly approaching end of their journey and their relationship.

Ross knocked on her door at five o'clock, a bit early, but he had spent the last half hour pacing in his room waiting to go next door.

Amy opened the door, took his offered arm, and they strolled slowly down the hallway, across the lobby and into the restaurant. Amy still turned heads, but she didn't notice anymore.

After they were seated and placed their orders, Ross asked, "Do you have any ideas for your book yet?"

"No, not yet. I'm still trying to get my thoughts together."

Then he looked at her and said, "No matter what happens, Amy, never give up on your dream. Will you promise me that?"

Amy was fighting back those damned tears again as she nodded and then said, "I promise."

Ross quickly lightened things by asking, "Did you want some tea instead of coffee this time?"

Amy smiled and replied, "Tea sounds wonderful."

When their order arrived, Ross asked for the tea and Amy was able to enjoy it with her meal.

But now it seemed as if every time either of them spoke, it just reinforced the knowledge of their imminent separation, so it was a relatively quiet dinner.

―――

Ross said goodnight to Amy and returned to his room an hour later, lit the kerosene lamp and took out Verne.

Amy couldn't concentrate at all. She packed her clothes after selecting tomorrow's riding wardrobe, and even packed one book in each of the new travel bags. It was a tight fit, but she managed, and the bags were bulging when she finished. While she was packing, she tried to come up with excuses to her husband for having so much clothing. Maybe if they weren't so new, she could pass them off as hand-me-downs from some charity. But they not only looked new, they were very nice. Maybe she should just leave them with Ross in Cheyenne, and he could give them to his new wife. When that thought crossed her mind, she sat down on the bed, put her face into her hands and simply sobbed as she shook.

――

The next morning, Ross tapped on her door at seven-thirty, and Amy opened it almost immediately as she had been anticipating his arrival. She was wearing her women's riding pants and a nice blouse, which affected Ross nearly as much as the nice dresses. They'd have breakfast and then return for their winter clothing for the ride.

Ross noticed how much different her pants were as opposed to the men's pants that she had been wearing. In keeping with his promise to himself, he just said good morning and escorted her to breakfast avoiding the compliments that were bouncing around in his head and threatening to pop out of his mouth at any moment.

They made small talk during breakfast to avoid the difficult separation issue, and as they left the restaurant, Ross said after he retrieved his saddlebags, he'd walk to the livery to get the horses and Amy could stay in the lobby with her travel bags.

So, Amy returned to her room to get the bags while Ross walked to the livery with his saddlebags over his shoulders.

Ten minutes after he left, Ross walked the four well-rested horses to the front of the hotel, walked inside, and picked up the two bags while Amy carried the lone remaining bag that carried all her toiletry items. He hooked the two large bags onto the pinto, then he added the smaller bag and tied them all down.

They mounted their horses and set out for Cheyenne, the last leg of their long ride across the Great Plains, and the most painful.

CHAPTER 5

It was chilly when they left, but after a couple of hours, the sun warmed them to a comfortable level.

Once outside the town, Ross reached into his saddlebag, pulled out the gunbelt with the Smith & Wesson, handed it to Amy, and she strapped it around her waist under the heavy coat.

"Amy, once we get out of the area, I want you to start to practice with the pistol you're wearing. When it's unloaded, you'll be able to dry fire for a while until you get the feel of the gun. Then, after you're comfortable, you can start shooting live rounds. I have a cleaning kit for the gun, so I'll be able to keep it in good working order."

"Alright. Is it loaded now?"

"Yes, it is. Give it to me butt first."

She pulled the gun from the holster and handed it to Ross.

"The interesting thing about the Smith & Wesson is how it loads and unloads. It's totally different than the Colt. Watch," he said as he snapped the gun open and the four full cartridges and one spent cartridge popped out. He closed the pistol and handed it back to Amy.

"Now, you'll be able to practice dry firing. Get used to unlooping the hammer loop, sliding the pistol out smoothly, and then cocking the hammer with your left hand and then sliding the left hand down to the bottom of your right hand to provide support. Don't worry about using the sights. Just point it at the target and squeeze the trigger gently. When the hammer snaps back, it should be a surprise. Another thing that you need to know about guns. Even though we both know that the pistol is empty, never under any circumstances, point that gun at anyone you aren't planning on killing."

"I understand."

Amy began to practice. She was very awkward at first, but by the early afternoon, she was much smoother. When they stopped for their break, she practiced even more, and Ross was pleased with the way she handled the pistol.

The rest of the afternoon, as they rode due west, was spent alternating practice and talking, both designed to keep their minds off the looming arrival at Cheyenne.

They stopped for the night, and Ross unloaded the two pack horses and removed all the saddles. He let the horses drink and graze as he set up the tent while Amy made dinner. After they ate, Ross set up a target for Amy to try shooting with a live weapon. Initially, she was surprised by the kick, but she adjusted to it and soon was able to hit the target regularly.

"Amy, you're doing really well. How do you feel?"

"I'm more at ease with the gun than I thought I'd be. And I hate to admit it, but I enjoy shooting."

"You shouldn't be embarrassed to admit that you like shooting a gun, Besides, I'll feel a lot better knowing you can protect yourself if I'm not around. Now, today we did about twenty-five miles. I plan on doing another twenty-five tomorrow. We'll make two more stops and get into Cheyenne before noon on the third day."

"Ross, why are we going so slowly? We were doing at least forty miles a day before?"

Ross couldn't tell her the real reason; that he didn't want to see her get on that train, but he knew the best he could do was to advance a secondary reason. It was as close to a lie as he ever told, but he knew he couldn't tell her the real reason because she was a married woman.

"The horses have those new shoes and I didn't want to risk one of them, especially the pinto, throwing one."

"Oh," Amy replied.

She was glad for the added time but wished he had told her it was because he didn't want her to leave, but that wouldn't be right either. It would make everything worse, because if he had told her that, she would stay, and that just couldn't happen.

"Where is your brother's ranch exactly?" she asked.

"It's about six miles northeast of the city, so we should see it on the way in."

"Are you nervous?"

"Not nervous. Just curious."

"Me, too. But I'm a bit nervous, too."

―――――

The next morning, they were on the move by seven-thirty. Ross had them moving at a steady, but slow speed, and the horses appreciated it, although none of them commented.

Amy continued to dry practice with her revolver. Her speed and smoothness were both increasing with the added practice. She may never be as good as Ross, but she was more than satisfactory.

They found a nice spot to stop for lunch. It was in the lee of a small hill that kept the northeasterly wind away. It wasn't a strong wind, but it was annoying.

Ross built a fire and Amy made a fast lunch as the horses grazed, but they only stayed in the noon camp for forty minutes before leaving and continued to Cheyenne. They were just short of thirty miles at the end of that day, despite their best efforts to waste time.

Ross set up camp and started the fire that evening, and because they only needed supplies for one more day, Amy prepared a bigger dinner than usual. Ross set up the tent and rolled out Amy's sleeping bag. Each simple task reinforced in his mind that they were that much closer to separation. He didn't think it was going to be this difficult, but it was getting worse by the hour.

Amy had been aware of how hard it was going to be for some time now because she already knew her fate and hated the thought of it, which made her guilt even greater. She swore she could see Cheyenne rising above the high plains already with each passing yard and felt caught in a cave with only one way out, a way she didn't want to go. She felt trapped, but she had no options.

As they ate, Amy asked, "So, what books did you buy for yourself?"

"I bought something light and fast, so I picked up Jules Verne's *Twenty Thousand Leagues Under the Sea*."

"So, is it?"

"Light and fast? Yes. I've already finished it, in fact. You should take it with you. It's an interesting story."

"What was the second?"

"Victor Hugo's *Les Miserables*."

She asked him about the plot to the second book and then they discussed *Jane Eyre,* which Amy had almost finished.

It passed the time, which was what they both wanted and didn't want. It was the most unusual of situations. Each held back so much and wanted the time to go quickly before they said something that they knew they shouldn't, yet even that danger didn't stop them from slowing the pace even more just to extend the time they could spend together.

Finally, they turned in, and even that last night in the tent together, looking at each other, they only made conversation in a narrow band of topics that didn't include anything in the future or their past.

―――――

They woke early, and despite themselves were on the road by seven o'clock. They were so used to doing everything quickly, it was difficult to slow down.

They picked up a road to Cheyenne by mid-morning, and for the first time since Ross left the fort, he was traveling on an honest-to-goodness roadway.

Once on the road, Amy continued her dry firing. She was getting so it was second nature. It also kept her mind occupied, so she couldn't spend any time thinking that this was the last day. She wouldn't be spending the night with Ross and may even be on the train to Oregon later if it was late enough.

Ross was aware of it as well. He was almost hoping for something momentous to happen, like another Indian attack. Now that was stupid, he thought. Hoping to be set upon by some vicious, angry red men just so they didn't reach Cheyenne, but anything seemed preferable to putting Amy on that train. They'd seen the black smoke from passing trains further south, which didn't help as it reinforced their proximity to Cheyenne.

When they stopped for lunch, Ross led the beasts to a rushing stream. While he was standing there, he saw a large trout fighting to get out of a small pool. Bad luck for him, Ross thought as he reached into the cold water, grabbed the large fish and tossed him onto the bank where he continued to flap vigorously.

"Amy, do you fancy some nice, fresh trout for lunch?" he asked loudly.

"You caught a trout?"

"Yes, ma'am. I'll clean him if you want to set up the side dishes, then we'll fry him up with a little salt and pepper."

The seasoned trout cheered them both somewhat. It was a wonderful last lunch together on the trail.

They wound up spending a little longer for lunch than usual because of the fish, but it was well spent.

They returned to the road and kept moving. A little after three o'clock, they saw a road sign that read: CHEYENNE 25 MI.

They both looked at each other but said nothing.

Two hours later, Ross directed them off the road to a pleasant field with the same stream that had produced the trout, although it was much wider now.

They set up camp and Ross built the fire. They had a mundane dinner of beans and canned beef.

After cleanup, they sat facing each other across the fire.

"Well, Amy, it looks like we're going to make it. No more Sioux, deserters or murderers. I think we only have another ten miles or so to the ranch. How do you want to handle this? I can take you to the Railway Hotel and get you a room, then I'll buy your ticket. Speaking of the ticket, where will you be going, exactly?"

Amy dropped her eyes to the fire before she quietly replied, "Estherville, Oregon."

"So, after I buy your ticket, you should be all set."

"I suppose so."

"Amy, I want you to have another hundred dollars when you leave. This won't be for your husband, although you're free to give it to him if you want. It's for you to keep with you for emergencies. I don't want you to get on that train and have nothing."

Amy exploded when she shouted, "I won't have nothing, Ross! I'll have clothes and books and most of all, I'll have my memories!"

Ross was taken aback by the violence of her response.

"I didn't mean it that way, Amy. I meant I wanted you to be able to take care of yourself. It's still a long train ride. I'd like you to keep that revolver with you, too. Keep it under your coat so you won't look so conspicuous. Okay?"

"Fine," she replied, her eyes still glued to the flames.

Ross knew she was really upset. It was as if she thought he was abandoning her again or trying to buy her.

"Amy, I really don't know what I said that hurt your feelings. I'm sorry. I really am. I was hoping that our last night together would be more special. We've become very close these past few weeks and I don't want to ruin that."

"I'm sorry, Ross. I'm just an emotional female who can't control herself. I'll be all right."

Ross knew that neither of those statements were true but wasn't about to correct her.

"So, tomorrow we get to meet my brother and sister-in-law. The last time I knew, there were over seven hundred head of cattle on the spread, according to what my parents told me when he left. There should be over a thousand by now. Of course, with Henry running the place, I won't be surprised if there are a thousand grasshoppers and not much else."

Amy laughed. It was a weak laugh, but it was something.

"Well, I suppose we should turn in, Amy."

"Okay. I'm sorry I'm not very nice tonight, Ross."

"I understand, Amy. Trust me, I really do."

After they settled into their respective sleeping slots, they wanted to say so much more but knew they couldn't, so they didn't.

———

The last morning was the warmest of the trip. Temperatures were already above fifty degrees when they left camp.

An hour later, Ross figured they were close to the ranch and said, "Let's start keeping our eye out for the Box B."

Twenty minutes later, they found the ranch and pulled to a stop. They sat on their horses and stared at the ranch house four hundred yards back from the road.

"Well, Amy. Here we go. Lord only knows what we'll find."

Ross turned their convoy down the access road with Amy riding alongside.

The ranch was quiet. Ross didn't know what it normally looked like, so he wasn't sure. He realized that there weren't as many cattle as there should be, and there were no signs of ranch hands either. A working ranch with a thousand head of cattle should always have noise somewhere.

"Amy, does this look right to you?"

"No. It seems dead," she replied.

"That's what I thought, too. It looks like there's only about three hundred cattle, and no ranch hands. I don't see any movement at all, but there is smoke coming out of the cooking chimney and the fireplace chimney, so someone must be in the house."

"That's something, I suppose."

They trotted down the access road and pulled up in front of the house and dismounted. Ross waited for Amy to reach his side.

After tying off their horses, they stepped up the stairs and onto the porch and even Ross felt some butterflies as they reached the door.

Ross knocked loudly on the door, and they waited. Finally, after almost a minute, the door opened.

Standing behind the half open door was a six-foot tall, two-hundred-and-forty-pound man with a week's growth of beard.

"Yeah, what do you want?" he snarled.

"Is that any way to greet your brother, Henry?"

Henry squinted his eyes and stared at him for a second, then he leaned back and grinned.

"Well, well. If it ain't my sissy little brother. What are you doing here, Ross?"

"I've just come to visit my older brother and his family. Is Bessie in? Could I come in and say hello to her and my niece and nephew?"

Henry acted as if he hadn't asked.

"I thought you was in the army?"

"I was. I got out six weeks ago."

"Why do wanna see Bessie and the kids?"

"Because our parents asked me to stop by and let them know how everyone is."

"They did, huh?"

"Yes, they did. So, are they in?"

"Yeah. Who's that with you?"

"This is Mrs. Amy Childs."

"You married?" he asked Ross.

"No. I rescued her in Dakota on the way here. She had been captured by the Sioux and escaped. I had to kill a few to get her out of there, and she'll be leaving tomorrow to go to Oregon and join her husband."

"And I suppose you ain't been diddlin' her all the way here, have you? That would account for the gray hair, 'cause seein' you naked would scare any woman," he said then started to laugh at his own joke.

Before Ross could respond, Amy spoke.

"No, Mr. Braxton, your brother was a complete gentleman the entire trip."

"I'll bet. I suppose you can come in."

"Thank you, Henry," Ross replied as he glanced at Amy to see how she had reacted to his brother's insult.

Ross and Amy entered the main room and waited while Henry closed the door. Amy was now just curious, but Ross felt surprisingly nervous about seeing Bessie again after all these years.

"Bessie! Bring the kids out here. We got a visitor," Henry bellowed.

When they emerged from the hallway thirty seconds later, Ross was stunned. *This was Bessie?* Aside from the blonde hair and now tired, but still blue eyes, the only other attribute that marked her as the Bessie he had known was her height.

He kept his eyes on her as she and the children almost timidly entered the room, and he noticed Bessie taking quick glances at Henry as she looked at him and Amy.

Ross finally passed his initial shock, smiled and asked, "Hello, Bessie. How are you?"

She stared at Ross for a few seconds, before her face transformed into a closer resemblance to the old Bessie as his voice finally let her make the connection.

"Ross? Is that you?" she asked.

"Yes, Bessie. How are you?"

She took several steps toward Ross, and the closer she drew, the thinner she looked.

"Hello, Ross. I almost didn't recognize you. You've filled out and you're not in uniform. I thought you'd be an officer by now."

"I was, but I got out of the army about six weeks ago. I just came here to see Henry, you and your children. How are they, Bessie?"

She turned to the children and said, "Alice and David, come and meet your uncle Ross."

The two children slowly walked forward, their eyes almost fearful as they shifted them between their uncle and the gray-haired lady. They were thin as well, and Ross was already feeling his anger bubbling inside him.

Ross sat on his heels to reach their eye level, smiled and said, "Hello, Alice. Hello, David."

Alice said, "Papa said you died."

"Well, nobody told me. The last time I knew I was still okay. Do I look okay to you?" he asked as he scrunched up his face.

Alice giggled and replied, "No. You look funny."

Ross poked her in the tummy and said, "That's because I am funny."

She giggled again and David smiled, probably hoping for a tickle of his own.

He stood, turned to Bessie and said, "Say, Bessie. Maybe you can help us out. We just rode in from Scotts Bluff, and I have a lot of food that I need to get rid of. Can we leave it with you? We sure don't need it anymore."

She glanced at Henry who was glaring at Ross, before turning her eyes back to Ross and said, "If you don't need it, I guess that would be okay."

"I appreciate it. We'll go out front and move them around the back, so you can put it right in the kitchen. Alright?"

"Sure. I'll go to the kitchen and open the back door," she said, then quickly turned and trotted down the hall with Alice and David behind.

Henry was fuming over Ross's surprising arrival, and now his brother was sticking his in nose where it didn't belong. He wasn't even asked, not that he cared that much. If she wanted some food for those brats, he didn't care, as long as he didn't have to pay for it.

Amy and Ross then turned and left the front room, closing the door behind them, crossed the porch and approached the horses. After unhitching the pack horses, they led them to the back of the house.

As they slowly walked along, Ross asked, "Amy, what do you think?"

"It looks like the only one getting fed is your brother."

"I know. I wonder what he's doing with all the money from selling the cattle."

"He sure isn't spending it on the house, either."

Ross blew out his breath and said, "I know."

They arrived at the open back door and Ross and Amy began unloading the food panniers onto the porch. Knowing his brother as he did, he hadn't expected a happy household, but finding Bessie and their children in this state was horrible, yet also very frustrating. As the man of the house, Henry legally could do damned near anything to impose his version of discipline. Ross knew he had no right to do much more than what he was doing now, but he was already convinced that he couldn't let this continue. He had to at least try if he ever wanted to live with himself.

He carried the first two panniers into the kitchen and set them on the floor as Bessie and Amy began unloading the food. Amy could see Bessie almost crying as she unloaded bacon, beans, beef, tomatoes, onions, potatoes, sugar and coffee as Henry stood with arms folded near the hallway entrance.

Ross brought in the last food pannier and after lowering it to the floor, glanced over at Bessie and could see relief written over her face.

He walked over close to her and asked softly, "Is there anything else that you need, Bessie?"

She looked quickly at a scowling Henry and said, "No, thank you, Ross."

"Okay. If there's anything you need, I'll be back periodically to see how you're doing. Okay?"

"No, we're fine. Really."

Ross nodded, then turned to Henry and asked, "Henry, could I talk to you in the main room a minute, please?"

Henry had a good idea what Ross wanted, but asked, "What about?"

"Nothing for women or children to hear."

"That leaves you out then, doesn't it?" he said as he laughed.

Ross exhaled sharply and replied, "Just come into the main room. It's not going to kill you."

"It if means gettin' rid of you faster, I'll do that."

Ross glanced quickly at Amy, whose eyes were on him, before he turned and walked into the main room to wait for Henry.

After reaching the main room, he turned and faced his older brother, who had a combative, threatening demeanor as he stopped four feet away.

"Henry, there is no excuse for Bessie or the children to look like that. They're hungry and they need new clothes. What have you been spending your money on? You seem to be well fed."

Henry growled, "That ain't your business, little brother. What I do with my money is up to me."

Ross's eyes narrowed as he stared into Henry's and said in a cold, controlled voice, "Maybe. But if I come back and see Bessie and your children being treated this badly again, I'll make you wish you were never born. Don't doubt it for a second."

Henry grinned, then snickered before saying, "Oh, suddenly you're mister tough guy?"

"No, Henry. But you know how violent I get when I get mad, or have you forgotten? I'm bordering on being that mad right now. Now in the past month, I've killed thirteen men. Ten Sioux warriors, two army deserters, and a murderer named Alfred Talbot, and I won't hesitate to add a wife beater to the list, even if he is my brother."

"I'm sure you did all those things…in your dreams. I ain't afraid of you, Rossie."

"If you had a half a brain, you would be. I'm just warning you this one time. You had better take care of your family."

While Ross was laying it on the line for Henry in the main room, Amy was trying to pry more information from Bessie. She was sure that was what Ross had expected of her after he'd caught her eyes before leaving with that bastard of an older brother of his.

"Bessie, Ross can help you and your children if you'll let him. He's an amazing man."

"I know. I should have married him instead of Henry, but I was stupid. Are you his wife?"

"No. I was captured by the Sioux three years ago and escaped. They were getting ready to kill me when Ross showed up and shot two of them from long range. Then eight of them chased us for four days, but Ross killed all of them. He escorted me all the way here, so I could catch a train to Oregon where my husband is. He had to kill two deserters who were going to kill me and a murderer to tried to kill him and do other things to me. He's so brave and smart, and I know he'd handle your husband without a problem if you'd just ask."

Bessie looked at Amy, smiled and said, "So, you're in love with him, too."

Amy blushed, and hurriedly replied, "No. No. Not at all. I'm very grateful for all he's done, but I'm a married woman. I can't be unfaithful. It's not right."

"I'm a married woman, too, Amy, and I'm not ashamed to admit that I'm still in love with him, and always have been. It started out so superficially because I wanted him so badly. That's what drove him away, I think. I was just too possessive. Then he left, and I realized what I had lost. I married his brother thinking he might be like Ross, but he was at the opposite end of the rope."

Amy needed to change the subject and asked quietly, "Does he beat you or the children?"

"Not too badly. I get on his nerves a lot, though. Lately, I've just tried to keep him calm, especially after he returns from town."

Amy knew the private time with Bessie was growing short, so she asked, "What happened to all of the cattle?"

"He's been selling them to the Rocking M over the years. I don't know what he's doing with the money. There were over eight hundred when we got here."

Amy was about to ask if she wanted a pistol when they heard footsteps coming down the hallway, and Bessie said softly but almost in a panic, "He's coming back. Don't tell him I said anything. Please."

Amy quickly launched into a cooking lesson, saying, "The best way is to use the onions first. Fry them a bit and then add the beef."

Henry and Ross entered the room and Henry was still angry about what Ross had said. He wasn't worried about him, despite his claims, but he never knew what his sissy brother would do. But he was the husband and father and Ross couldn't go to the sheriff or anything, so he finally just pushed Ross's warning aside.

"That's enough girl talk. I think Ross wants to get going to Cheyenne. Ain't that right, baby brother?"

"We'll be heading out shortly. I need to get Mrs. Childs ready for her train trip. Just remember what I told you, Henry," he said before looking into Bessie's blue eyes and saying, "You take care, Bessie, and if you need anything, I'll be at the Railway Hotel."

Then he surprised everyone in the room when he took two long strides, then leaned over, wrapped Bessie in his arms, then kissed her on the cheek.

While he was close, she whispered in his ear, "I've always loved you, Ross."

Ross held her for another two seconds, then released Bessie and looked down at the two children.

"Alice and David, you listen to your mama. She's a good lady."

Both children nodded before he turned to Amy and said, "Amy, let's get going to Cheyenne."

Amy nodded, then turned and said, "Goodbye, Bessie. Be good, Alice and David."

Ross and Amy then gave them short waves, picked up the empty panniers, stepped through the back door onto the porch, and after closing the door, stepped down to the horses and hooked the panniers over the pack horses.

They silently led the horses to the front and after Ross tied them to the trail rope, they mounted and started walking their horses toward the access road.

Once they were fifty feet away, Ross turned to Amy and asked, "What did you find out?"

Amy was almost in tears when she replied, "It was what you might have expected by looking at them, but it still hurt to hear it. She said that he didn't beat her too badly, but I could see the bruises. I asked her where all the cattle had gone, and she said he sold them off over the years to the Rocking M but doesn't know where the money went."

Amy didn't tell Ross of Bessie's confession of continued love for him as she thought it might inspire him to act rashly.

"Do you know why I hugged Bessie?" he asked.

"I assumed it was because you missed her."

"No. I did feel badly for the way she's being treated, but I wanted to see how thin she really was under that baggy dress. Remember I told you before how Bessie was well endowed?"

"Yes."

"Did you see any evidence of that?"

Amy realized that she hadn't, and replied, "No. Now that you mention it."

"Amy, I felt ribs. Bessie probably doesn't even weigh ninety pounds, and I saw the bruising as well."

"What did you talk to Henry about?"

"I told him that I'd come back periodically to check on Bessie and the kids and that he'd better start taking better care of them or I'd make him wish he never lived. Amy, you know I never make a promise that I don't keep, and he knows it, too. I don't know if it'll do any good, though. I can only hope that I haven't pushed him to do something worse. He's a sorry excuse for a man."

"That is an understatement."

"Well, I think I'll be paying a visit to the land office first and then go and talk to the Rocking M. If they're a normal operation, they should be able to tell me a lot about what is going on, but they still won't know what Henry is doing with the money. I may have to trail him a few times."

"I wish I could help, Ross."

"I know. You've already done a lot by talking to Bessie. At least she and the children will get something to eat for a while. I'll check on them and bring more food from time to time until I get to the bottom of this whole sorry affair. But enough of that problem, I'm sure you're anxious to get going. I wish this hadn't been such a depressing situation."

"Me, too," she replied, but didn't comment about the 'anxious to get going' part of his statement.

They rode at a decent pace and arrived in Cheyenne an hour later. It was just after ten o'clock when they arrived.

"Let's hunt down the railroad station and the Railway Hotel first."

"Okay," Amy replied as she started slipping into depression again.

She had been hoping that the seriousness of Bessie's situation would make him ask her to stay to help, but that wasn't going to happen. She was going to Oregon.

The station was easy to find, as was the Railway Hotel, once you find railroad tracks. They stopped at the station first, and after dismounting, Ross and Amy walked side by side to the ticket agent.

They reached the window and Ross said, "I'll need a first-class ticket to Estherville, Oregon."

"One way, or round trip?" asked the agent.

When Ross said, "One way," Amy felt her knees weaken but managed to stay upright.

'That'll be $47.50. The train departs at 9:35 in the morning."

"Fine," Ross said as he paid for the ticket and gave it to Amy.

Then he said, "Let's get you checked into the hotel. Then I can buy you lunch."

Amy just nodded. It was finally happening. She had her ticket in her hand and now she was going to the hotel. Tomorrow morning at 9:35, she'd be on board a train waving goodbye to Ross forever, and the finality struck her hard.

Ross led the four horses to the hotel-assigned livery with Amy walking almost in a trance beside him, then after dropping them off, he removed Amy's two clothing bags as she stood waiting.

They left the livery, stepped onto the boardwalk and headed for the nearby hotel, and Amy felt as if she wasn't even herself any longer. Someone else must be walking in her body.

Ross was pretending that he wasn't in the least upset, despite his own churning emptions. He had to be almost remote now, so Amy didn't get upset. *What else could he do?* He knew he'd most likely never see Amy again once she stepped on that train.

They crossed the hotel lobby, and Ross took a deep breath and approached the desk clerk.

"Mrs. Amy Childs needs a room for the night. She'll be leaving on the 9:35 train tomorrow morning."

"Very good, sir. Does Mrs. Childs have any special needs?"

"She needs the best room you have."

"Yes, sir. We have a full suite available. It'll cost four dollars for the night."

"That's fine," he said as he paid the clerk.

"That'll be room 112. Just down the hallway on the left," the clerk said as he handed her the key.

Amy accepted the key and said, "Thank you."

Ross picked up Amy's two bags and carried them down the hallway as Amy followed almost in a daze. He opened the room and carried the bags inside, and as he set them on the floor, Amy sat on the bed, putting her toiletry bag beside her.

"Are you all right, Amy?" he asked.

"I'm okay," she lied.

"I know you probably want to relax or take a bath, but would it be okay if I spent some time with you?"

Amy had expected him to just leave, so she quickly replied, "Of course, it's okay. I wouldn't want it any other way."

"Now that you're all checked in, why don't you go ahead and change, and I'll wait for you in the lobby. I'll take you to lunch and then we can go look around and talk."

She smiled at him weakly and said, "That sounds nice."

"Okay, I'll be in the lobby."

He smiled down at her and closed the door behind him as he left.

Amy wanted to break down in tears, but she had to be strong. It was going to be worse tomorrow. She knew she'd be getting on the train and wave goodbye to Ross forever but tried not to dwell on it as she rose to get changed. She decided to wear her nicest dress. The one that had stunned Ross when he first saw her wearing it but hadn't said anything about it. Tomorrow, she would be wearing her plainest dress, the one that Aaron would see her in. She had thought of wiring him to let him know she was coming but decided she didn't want to do it until she had to. Maybe she'd get lucky and the train would derail over a tall bridge.

She dressed quickly and put her key into the small purse she had bought in Scotts Bluff and smiled at the memory of walking down the aisle with her arms full, and how Ross had still bought her more things.

She left the room and walked down the hallway to the lobby.

Ross had been sitting in the lobby in a bit of a mood himself. All he kept thinking was that there was nothing he could do about tomorrow morning. Then he looked to his right and saw Amy coming out wearing the same dress that she had worn when he first saw her wearing a real dress. She looked just as spectacular this time as she had then. All he could do was to admire her but couldn't say anything.

She smiled at him as he stood, smiling back.

"Shall we dine, Mrs. Childs?"

"Let's, Mr. Braxton."

She took his arm and they entered the hotel restaurant, were quickly seated and placed their orders. There were only six other diners.

"Amy, while we have this private time. I'd like to say that even considering all the near-death experiences we've encountered these past six weeks; I've never had a happier experience. You have been a wonderful traveling companion, well, except for the first few days, but we won't talk about that."

Amy smiled and replied, "No, we definitely won't talk about that."

"So, what will we do after lunch? It's not too chilly, so I could rent a buggy and we could tour the city."

"That sounds like a wonderful idea."

Ross smiled at the thought of having Amy close for a couple of more hours.

The waitress brought them their lunch, and they talked about everything but the nearing apocalyptic departure.

"What will you do about Henry?" she asked before taking a bite of the roast pork.

"A little investigating. Find out where he's going and hopefully finding out how he's spent so much money. You can run a household on five hundred dollars a year. He's sold upwards of eight hundred cattle over the eight years. That's a hundred a year. That's over two thousand dollars. I need to figure out where the money's going. I'll also be keeping an eye on Bessie and the kids to make sure he doesn't hurt them anymore."

"You have a lot of work in front of you."

"I know. But I'll get it done."

"I know you will."

They spent the rest of the meal talking about the horrible situation that Bessie and the children were in before finishing the last of their coffee.

Ross set down his empty coffee cup and asked, "So, Amy, are we ready to go touring?"

"I can't wait."

Ross paid the bill, then led Amy back to her room, so she could bundle herself in some warm clothes.

They left the hotel and walked to the hotel livery, rented a buggy and once seated on the red leather seat, Ross laid the included blanket across their laps and rolled onto the cobbled streets. It was a cold day, but not as bad as it would be in another month.

————

Back at the Box B, Henry had grilled Bessie about what she and Amy had talked about and ended his interrogation by teasing her about his little sissy brother hugging her and giving her a kiss. Finally, he told her that he was going into town and would be back late.

Bessie had been grateful for the non-violent inquisition and even more thankful when he said he was leaving for the night. She wondered if his lack of punishment was because of whatever Ross had told him, but right now his pending departure was the best news she could have hoped for.

After he left the house and she'd heard his horse ride away, Bessie called the children into the kitchen and began to cook. As the aroma of frying bacon filled the air, they were as excited as if it were Christmas.

————

Even with the heavy blanket, Amy still slid over next to Ross, ostensibly for the heat, and he wasn't about to object.

Cheyenne was the largest city Amy had ever seen, and she was like an excited schoolgirl pointing at all the large buildings as the buggy rolled across the cobblestones. One of the buildings was a large clothing store, and when Ross saw it, he quietly asked Amy if she'd like to go in and look around. Amy said she wouldn't buy anything but would really like to look inside.

They pulled over and Amy was grinning as she took Ross's offered arm and clutched it tightly. Ross was enormously pleased that he had come up with the idea.

Amy walked through the aisles admiring the many clothes, and Ross couldn't let her go without buying anything. So, he found a beautiful pair of kid gloves that would keep her hands warm and still be stylish. He picked up a pair and walked to where she was admiring a green silk dress.

"Amy, these won't take much room and they'll keep your hands warm."

He handed her the gloves and she gushed, "Oh, Ross. They're beautiful."

"Good. Now, I've got to run outside for a minute. Here's ten dollars to cover the cost of the gloves. I'll be right back."

"I think I'll manage to keep myself busy."

Ross smiled, then said, "I'll be back in ten minutes," before waving then trotting out of the store.

He turned left and went two doors down and entered D. Miller's Jewelry. He couldn't let her leave Cheyenne without something to remind her of the journey they shared.

For five minutes, he looked through the display cases looking for something as unique as she was, but just couldn't find what he wanted. There were many fine pieces, but nothing that was exactly right. He was about to give up when he saw a necklace with a large stone that was green but had dancing veins of orange and black. It was fascinating.

"Excuse me, what is that necklace?" he asked the clerk who had been standing silently nearby watching as Ross examined the merchandise.

"That is an opal, sir. It's the only one we have at the moment. Would you like to see it?"

"Yes, please."

The jeweler took it out of its display case and held it before him, letting it catch the beams of sunlight. As the light reflected off its surface, it seemed to be alive. The green was always there, but the veins danced and changed hue.

"That's perfect. I'll take it."

"It's rather expensive, sir. $105.00"

"That's fine. I'm sure it's worth it."

"As is the recipient, I'm sure."

"Yes. Yes, she is."

Ross paid for the necklace and the jeweler placed it in its presentation case. He shook the man's hand and slid it into his pocket, then almost danced out of the store and headed back to the clothing store where he found Amy still wandering the aisles.

She saw Ross and waved happily, melting his heart as he smiled at her, then waved back and stepped quickly to her.

As he came near, he asked, "Find anything else you can squeeze into your bags?"

"No. It's just staggering how many wonderful things they have here. I paid for the gloves already, so we can leave when you're ready. Did you find what you wanted?"

"It wasn't what I needed," he replied honestly.

"Well, let's go back out to the buggy and see if my new gloves keep my hands warm. I know they certainly feel nice."

"Good."

With her new gloves on her hands, she clutched Ross's arm as he escorted her out of the clothing store, then once outside, helped her into the carriage, where she sat holding the blanket up for him to slide under and join her, as closely as he dared.

Once he was beside her, she held out her covered hands and said, "These are beautiful gloves, Ross. Thank you so much."

"I knew you'd need something to keep your hands warm. Sometimes those trains can get chilly."

At the mention of the train, Amy's joy deflated faster than a pricked balloon.

Ross was concentrating on the traffic and missed the change in Amy, but suddenly he was very interested in the crossing traffic.

He turned to look at her and said quickly, "Amy, look who's riding past right now."

She suddenly looked up and saw Henry trotting his horse along the intersection street, not thirty feet away.

"Let's see where he's going. He won't look for us in a buggy," Ross said as he snapped the reins and the buggy rolled into the roadway.

The excitement of the chase made Amy forget her depression momentarily as she watched Henry ride before them before he turned left down a side street. Ross followed at a discreet distance. After two blocks, Henry made another turn, but to the right this time. Ross wasn't familiar with the town, so he didn't know where he was headed.

When Ross turned right down the street that Henry had taken, he suddenly knew where his brother was going even if he didn't know Cheyenne. At the end of the street he noticed the change in signs from English to Chinese. Henry was headed for Chinatown.

Ross, turned at the next turn, allowing Henry to go to wherever he was headed, and Amy wondered why Ross had ended the chase.

Ross said, "Well, I think I have an idea what Henry's dabbling in."

"What is it?"

"Opium."

Amy was surprised and asked, "How is he involved in opium?"

"I have no idea. They need to get it into the country, but Henry hasn't got the brains to handle that. He's not using it, either because he's too fat. Opium users tend to be thin because they prefer opium to eating. If I'd have to guess, he's just an investor. He supplies money for the buy and then makes a profit."

"But what does he do with the money he would make?"

"Another good question, and now that you mention it, I might have this wrong. I can't think of anything else in Chinatown that he could get involved in that would require money, unless he's gambling it away. I'll have to keep checking out what he's doing later. At least I have a clue now. Let's head back to the hotel. It's almost dinner time."

As he turned the buggy toward the hotel, Amy felt as if a doomsday clock was ticking loudly in her head marking down the last hours, minutes and seconds before she stepped onto that train.

He drove the buggy back to the hotel's livery, helped Amy down from the buggy and they returned to the hotel.

Once inside, Ross grinned and said, "I forgot that I'll need a room myself, unless I camp on the lobby floor, and I don't think they'd appreciate that."

Amy laughed and said, "They would probably be annoyed when you started pounding tent stakes into the wood."

Ross laughed as well, then smiled at her before he said, "Let's go to the reception desk."

After he paid for a room on the third floor so there would be no question of impropriety, he escorted Amy to her room.

"Amy, I'm going to go out back to the liver to get my saddlebags and put my things in my room. I'll be back down in about ten minutes, so we can go to dinner."

"That's fine. I'll see you then."

Amy closed the door, then leaned back against it and immediately started crying, then she walked slowly to her bed and sat down. She took off her new gloves and just stared at them as the tears kept flowing. They would be the last thing she ever received from Ross, and she knew she would treasure them always, even if she could never wear them again. When she got to Oregon, she would first place her bags in storage somewhere, maybe at the depot storage. She'd only take the toiletry bag and add one more plain dress. All her nice dresses and the wonderful gloves would be stored away. She would think what to do with them sometime in the future.

She dried her eyes as she knew Ross would be back soon, and he must never know how badly she wanted to stay or how willing she would be to throw away her marriage to be with him.

Ross had gone out to the livery again and pulled two saddlebags, returned to the hotel and climbed the stairs to his room, entered and put his things away, thinking he could be here for a week or two. He'd probably have to expand his wardrobe as well, but at least his cooking days were behind him for a while.

He took out the small box from his jacket pocket and opened it, then took a sheet of paper from the room's desk and wrote a short note, folded it, placed it inside, then slowly closed it and took a deep breath.

Ross left the room, went down the two flights of stairs and knocked on Amy's door. When she opened the door and smiled at him, he could see the red in her bright green eyes but didn't acknowledge it because he understood what had caused the color and knew that talking about it would only make it worse.

"Ready for dinner, milady?" he asked as he smiled at her, offering his arm.

"Thank you, kind sir," she replied, taking his arm.

They walked to the restaurant, finding it almost full. Again, Amy attracted attention, and knew it was because of her hair, despite what Ross said, but she knew he believed it was because she was beautiful, and she didn't care what anyone else thought, only what he thought.

They were seated, and a waitress came and took their orders.

After the waitress left, Ross asked, "Amy, what would you like to do after dinner?"

"I hadn't really thought about it."

"We have time. If it's alright with you, I'd rather spend the time talking with you more than anything else."

"I'd really like that."

Harry nodded, then said, "Amy, I've been thinking about Henry's time in Chinatown. If he's going there to gamble, it would take a lot of money. If he was losing, and they always lose, he could go through twenty dollars a night easily. That would account for the losses. There is an advantage to gambling in Chinatown. The local law enforcement really doesn't care about what happens there, whether its gambling, prostitution, or opium dens. They can all be found easily, and there's no concern of being arrested. The law only cares if it spreads out of Chinatown."

"It sounds like you're going to have your hands full."

"It'll keep me busy until I find a job. I'm still thinking about the railroad. They have an office in Cheyenne, so I could apply here. I'm going to hold off until this is taken care of, though."

"Don't let it ruin your life, Ross."

"It won't. It should be done in two weeks."

"I hope so."

The waitress brought them their dinner, a perfect prime rib. There were baked potatoes with butter and sour cream on the side, too. Amy had never tasted sour cream before, and as Ross explained how it was made, she found that she loved the tangy, rich taste.

The prime rib was so delicate that it didn't require a knife, and Ross was glad that their last dinner together was turning out so well. But when he thought of the significance of that description, it tempered his good mood. Tomorrow he'd lose Amy.

They were reaching the end of the prime rib when Ross said, "Amy, let's try some dessert. Does that sound good?"

"What do they have?"

"They have apple pie a' la mode. That sounds good."

"What's the a' la mode part."

"You'll see."

Ross ordered two and more coffee as he waited in smiling anticipation of Amy's reaction to their after dinner treat.

When the dessert arrived, Amy's eyes opened wide.

"Ross, I've never had ice cream before. This looks amazing."

Ross smiled at the waitress before she left, then Amy took her spoon and cut through the ice cream and the apple crust into the apples inside, put it into her mouth and closed her eyes as Ross just watched with a grin on his face. There was so much that Amy had been deprived from enjoying, and he wished he could give them all to her.

When she opened her eyes again, he began eating his own serving, and they finished about the same time, then just sipped their coffee to end the supper.

"Ross, that was a perfect ending to a perfect meal. Sour cream and ice cream in one meal."

"Now you know what my life was like for my youth. If you could make it from milk, we had it."

"I'm amazed you aren't all fat little round men," Amy said with a smile.

"Some of us are. I just never overindulged."

"Where do we go now?"

"They have a nice sitting room just off the lobby."

"That sounds perfect."

Ross paid the bill and left a large, well-deserved tip.

He escorted Amy to the sitting room, and they sat in opposing easy chairs rather than the couch or the setee as it would be inappropriate.

Amy said, "Ross, you never did sell those Sioux knives and tomahawks."

"No. I don't think I will, either."

"I agree with you. They are worth more to us than anyone else."

"Exactly."

"So, where will you go after you're finished with Henry's problem?"

"I don't know. If I get the job, I'll go where they send me."

"Can I write to you?"

"I'd really like that, Amy. I'll give you my parents' address. That way, they can forward it to me no matter where I am. But I don't think it would be a good idea for me to write to you. It might make Aaron angry."

Just hearing Ross say her husband's name reminded her of her marital vows, so all she could say was a weak, "That's true."

"I know I told you this before, but it's so important to me. Whatever you do, Amy, don't forget your dream. You can do it. You have the ability and a lot more."

Amy knew she would never forget her biggest dream, and it wasn't writing a book. Her dream was sitting across from her.

"I won't, Ross. I'll always keep my dream alive."

"Good."

They spent another two hours talking about things that had no connection to tomorrow's departure, what awaited Amy in Oregon, or even about Bessie and Henry. It was just an opportunity to hear each other's voice.

Finally, around ten o'clock, Ross escorted Amy back to her room and told her he'd knock on her door at seven o'clock to take her to breakfast. The hotel would send her luggage to the train, and he told her to make sure she wore her warm coat.

Ross returned to his room, undressed and washed, then stretched out on his bed and just looked at the ceiling. He couldn't sleep, and really didn't want to. He wanted to live in those incredible green eyes of the woman sleeping two floors below him.

That green-eyed woman was having the same problem. She was in her nightdress and looking at the ceiling as well, knowing that Ross was thirty feet away, but was resigned to her fate. It was just the way it had to be.

Eventually, they both fell asleep anyway, finally ending their long journey together.

CHAPTER 6

Ross woke at five-thirty, went down the hallway and took a bath and shaved. He returned to his room and dressed, putting on his heavy jacket with the flat box still in its pocket, before putting on his hat and walking out of the room five minutes before seven o'clock.

He walked down two flights to Amy's room, tapped on her door, and it opened almost instantaneously.

"Good morning, Ross," she said smiling while wearing her plain dress.

Ross thought she was just as beautiful in the plain dress as she was in the nice dress, because it wasn't the dress that made the woman, it was the woman that made the dress, but what he thought and what he said had to be different.

"Hello, Amy. Let me get your bags and drop them off at the front desk."

He went inside and picked up the two heavy bags. Amy had the toiletry bag that now contained her other plain dress. Ross hadn't commented on her choice of wardrobe for the trip because he knew what kind of problems it would cause in her home life if she walked in wearing nice clothes. He was sure that Aaron would think that she'd been unfaithful and after seeing how Henry treated Bessie, he didn't want Amy to fall into a similar situation.

Ross carried out the two bags, left them at the desk and told the clerk they needed to be on the 9:35 train westbound train. The clerk asked to see her ticket, and Amy presented it to him. He filled out two tags and attached them to the bags, then he returned her ticket with the other half of the tags.

Amy took Ross's arm and they went to the restaurant for breakfast. Even though it was a very good breakfast, neither could even tell what they were eating.

They stayed at the table and talked as long as they could. The waitress refilled their coffee three times without comment, accustomed to lengthy departures.

Near the end of their extended breakfast, Ross took Amy's small purse, opened it, reached into his pocket, took out some bills, then put them inside and closed the purse.

"That will be enough money to take care of any needs you may have. Like I said before, it's yours to do with as you wish. I also wrote out my parents' address on a sheet of paper."

Amy nodded, unable to speak and trying desperately not to cry.

Finally, just before nine o'clock, they stood, Ross offered her his arm and they went outside. It was a cold morning, but not nearly as bad as normal for this time of year.

They walked slowly to the platform, Ross holding the toiletry bag. The train whistle sounded in the distance, and they both turned to watch its approach. Neither could talk, as Amy clutched his arm, her doomsday clock ticking ever louder as the train grew larger from the east.

The locomotive reached the far end of the platform, the large bell clanging loudly as if anyone couldn't hear the squealing metal wheels or hear the loud hissing as steam was being vented. There would be twenty more minutes before the train left the depot after filling its coal bunkers and its water tanks, but those minutes were passing so very quickly.

The train was taking on water as the passengers disembarked, and soon the departing passengers would begin to climb aboard.

Ross noticed one gentleman in particular who was scanning the passengers and called him over.

"Sir, you are a Union Pacific railroad special agent, are you not?"

"Yes, sir."

"This is Mrs. Amy Childs. She will be traveling unaccompanied to Oregon and I'd appreciate any efforts that could be made to ensure she arrives safely. She is very dear to me."

"We'll make sure of that, sir."

"Thank you," Ross said as he shook his hand and then turned to Amy.

For the first time since that day in Dakota Territory, he wrapped his arms around her. Amy hugged him closely and didn't want to let go as her emotional reservoir was close to bursting through the rational dam holding it back.

She was so overwhelmed that she didn't feel the small box that Ross slipped into her heavy coat pocket.

Finally, the blast of the locomotive's steam whistle followed by the conductor's loud cries of, "All aboard!", shattered the moment.

The passengers were climbing the passenger car's steps, so it was finally time for them to part, and they both knew it would be their last parting and they would never see each other again.

Ross stepped back just a bit and looked into those amazing green eyes for the last time and simply said, "Good-bye, Amy."

Knowing that anything more would be improper, Amy replied, "Good-bye, Ross."

Amy then quickly turned, rapidly walked to the end of the wooden platform and stepped onto the first-class car's steel platform. She waved once and disappeared inside the passenger coach as the train's whistle blew again and it began slowly moving forward.

Amy sat in the last row and looked out the window for Ross as the train gained speed. She begged herself to maintain composure for just a little longer as she turned her head and found Ross looking at her. For those brief, horribly memorable seconds, their green eyes locked and shared their unspoken love, before the Amy found herself looking at the back of the depot building, and he was gone. She turned to face the front of the seat in front of her, bowed her head and let the tears flow freely now that it didn't matter. She was alone.

Ross managed better, but still had to turn and quickly walk to his room managing to keep himself under control until he passed the desk, and barely made it to his room before he succumbed to his own incredible sense of loss. Amy was gone.

———

The train was accelerating, and soon Amy could only see prairie. She had finally stopped crying when she realized that it didn't make any difference. She was going back to her husband in Estherville, Oregon, a place she had never seen or wanted to see. Tomorrow evening, she would arrive in Oregon and meet her husband and become a dutiful, boring wife with no dreams and no future.

———

Once he'd recovered, Ross went back downstairs, left the hotel and walked to the livery and saddled the gelding. He had things to do.

Ross's first stop was at the bank. He created an account and deposited most of his remaining money, including the voucher and making a balance. His next stop would be the land office.

He walked into the land office and was greeted by an amiable clerk when he approached the counter.

"Good morning, sir. How may I help you?"

"Good morning, I was wondering if you could point me to the Rocking M ranch?"

"Quite easily, sir. Just take the eastbound road out of town and it'll be about four miles on the left. It's owned by Arthur and Mildred Mandrake. Both are very nice people."

"Thank you. I also need to check on my brother's ranch, the Box B. Is he the only one on the deed or is my sister-in-law, Bessie, on there as well?"

"Let me pull that record. I'm familiar with that property. Joe Braxton was a good friend. I just want to make sure nothing has changed."

He walked to a large file cabinet, opened one drawer, then after thumbing through some folders, pulled the record, then returned to the counter, reading the sheet of paper.

"It's unchanged, and I assume you are Ross Braxton?"

Ross was wondering how he knew his name, but replied, "Yes, I am."

"There are two names on the deed, but they are your brother Henry's and yours, not his wife's. When Joe passed away, I know he willed the ranch to you both and I always wondered why you never came to claim your share."

Ross was taken aback, but replied simply, "I was in the army."

"Oh. That explains it. Well, I'm glad you've returned, so maybe you can reverse the trend for the ranch."

"I hope so. Could I get an official copy of the deed, please?"

"You don't need one. This is actually your copy that I have right here, but if you could, I'll need your signature on both copies. Do you have any proof of who you are?"

Ross replied, "I just opened a bank account and I have all of my army paperwork, like my commissioning certificate, my discharge papers and my West Point degree."

The clerk smiled and said, "Excellent. Any of them would be sufficient"

The handiest was the bank book, so he showed that to the clerk, then after he handed it back to Ross, he walked to his files and pulled out the second copy of the deed and Ross signed both. They waited for the ink to dry, then Ross slipped the deed into his pocket.

He shook the clerk's hand and said, "Thank you very much. This will help immensely."

"I was hoping it would," he replied.

"I'll be heading out there now. I have things that I need to do."

As he left, the clerk smiled and under his breath, said, "I'll bet you do."

Ross pulled out his watch and found it wasn't even eleven o'clock yet. Now that he had some real power over Henry, he knew that he could help Bessie legally. The only question was how to go about it.

After leaving the land office, he rode back to the livery and saddled both pack horses and trailed them back onto the cobbled streets.

———

Seventy miles away, Amy was sitting in her reasonably comfortable seat as the train continued to take her away. She had taken along *Nicholas Nickleby* to read on her journey but hadn't opened the book yet. She hadn't cried as long as she thought she would, but was just numb now, and decided to do some reading. As she took it out and put it on her lap to read, there was a noticeable thump when it struck her jacket pocket. She reached into the pocket and pulled out a small, flat blue box. Having never seen a jewelry box before, she had no idea what it was or how it got there, although just by the fancy velour cover, she strongly suspected that it was something nice and Ross had slipped it into her pocket on the train platform.

The sun was pouring in through the windows as she opened it, saw the note and when she removed the covering scrap of paper, the sun struck the opal, and was hypnotized when the sun's light bounced off the stone. She turned it different directions and watched the colors dazzle her eyes.

Then she looked at the paper in her hand, and her hand began to shake as she opened it, knowing who had written it and hoping against hope of what feeling is might express.

She read:

My Dearest Amy,

I couldn't let you go without giving you something to remember me by. I know you can't wear it, but please keep it with you always. Like you, the opal is rare. Like you, it has incredible beauty. But it can't compare to you on either count. I will treasure the time we were together as I will always treasure my memories of you.

Forever yours,

Ross

She didn't break down into a sobbing mess, as just a single tear left her right eye and meandered across her cheek, but she didn't brush it away. She felt it wind its way to her chin and fall away, then folded the note gently and placed it in the box, laid the box inside her toiletry bag and began to read.

———

Ross led his pack horses and his folded panniers to the clothing store, then after tying them off, went inside to the children's department and sought out a salesclerk and told her what he wanted. While she was assembling that part of the order, he found a second clerk in the woman's department and asked her to pick up the second part.

When both orders were completed, he asked that they not be boxed, just placed in heavy bags, and wrote a draft for the order. He took the three heavy bags and went out to the horses, packed the bags into the panniers and tied them down.

Next, he led them to the grocery store he had seen when he and Amy had toured the city. All they sold was food and Ross had never seen one before.

He bought tins of beans, beef and peaches, fifty pounds of flour, twenty pounds of sugar, ten pounds of oatmeal, a smoked ham, two slabs of bacon, three dozen eggs, ten pounds of coffee, two pounds of tea, some baking powder, five pounds of salt, some ground pepper, five pounds of brown sugar, some cinnamon, and molasses. Then he added a large bag of potatoes, some onions, and peppers. Finally, he added two large containers of milk, one of cream, and three pounds of butter. He also bought six bars of lye soap and four scented ones for Bessie. As he was paying for his order, he added a large bag of penny candy.

They had a young man help him load the large order onto his pack horses, which took a while.

253

When the horses were loaded, Ross walked over to a café and had lunch and checked his watch. It was after one o'clock. He paid for his lunch and went back to his horses, turned them east, and an hour later, he saw the sign for the Rocking M, and turned down the access road.

It was a large and prosperous ranch, and he could hear cattle in the distance. Ranch hands were moving about doing all sorts of work. This is how the Box B should have looked.

He rode up to the hitch rail, pulled up and shouted, "Hello, the house!", then waited for someone to invite him to step down.

A middle-aged woman with brown hair opened the door. She had an open, kind face and was quite handsome.

"Can I help you?" she asked.

"Yes, ma'am. My name is Ross Braxton and I was wondering if I could speak to Mr. Mandrake."

"Are you related to Henry Braxton?" she asked, as her friendly face lost its mild expression.

"Yes, ma'am. He's my brother."

Ross noted an even more serious cooling effect after his reply.

"And what would you be wanting, Mr. Braxton?" she asked sharply.

"Ma'am, I just left the army a few weeks ago. I left Dakota Territory and rode to Cheyenne just out of curiosity about my brother. I didn't particularly care about him, but after six years, I began to wonder what was going on. I arrived at the ranch yesterday and wasn't happy with the state of the ranch. I know your husband could help me clear some of my questions."

"Well, as you don't seem to like him either, go ahead and set and come in."

"Thank you, ma'am."

Ross stepped down and followed Mrs. Mandrake into the nicely furnished house.

"You have a marvelous home, Mrs. Mandrake," he said as he removed his hat.

"Thank you. Obviously, at least one of the Braxtons has manners."

"Henry was the exception, ma'am, not the rule."

"Glad to hear it. Would you like some coffee?"

"That would be welcome, ma'am."

As she walked into the kitchen, she shouted, "Arthur, you have a visitor!"

She returned with the cup of coffee and set it down on a flat stone square on the table.

"He'll be out in a minute. I'll let you two discuss business."

"Mrs. Mandrake, I'd like you to stay and hear what I have to say. I've found that women understand these kinds of things better than men do."

"Well, that's a refreshing viewpoint. So, it doesn't involve cattle, then?"

"It does, but only as a marginal topic."

"You certainly are better educated than your brother as well."

"West Point, ma'am," Ross replied with no small amount of pride.

Arthur Mandrake strode into the room, and Ross rose and offered his hand. Arthur was the image of a successful rancher and Ross was sure that he'd be a success at whatever endeavor he chose.

"Good morning, Mr. Mandrake, I'm Ross Braxton," Ross said and watched Mr. Mandrake's expected sour reaction to the name.

His wife intervened, saying, "He's the opposite of his brother, Arthur, so please be polite."

"Alright, Mildred. Did you want to have a seat, Mr. Braxton?"

"Thank you."

Arthur noticed that Mildred had taken a seat as well and pretended that this was an everyday occurrence.

"So, what can I do for you?"

"Yesterday morning, I arrived at the Box B. I had ridden from Dakota Territory after leaving the army and had been asked by my parents to see how things were with my brother and his family."

Mildred interrupted, asking, "You rode across the Dakota Territory?"

"Yes, ma'am. When I arrived, we found the place in disarray, to be kind. My brother initially refused to allow me entry. When I finally convinced him to allow us inside, I found that his wife and children were emaciated and in a sad state of dress. I was appalled. I had noticed on entering the ranch that the herd was a lot smaller than it should have been.

"I estimated that there should have been over a thousand head by now. Instead it looks like there are fewer than four hundred. When I was finally able to talk to his wife, Bessie, whom I have known since childhood, she told me he had been selling the cattle to you during the past few years. She had no idea what he was doing with the money, but I assure you that he surely wasn't spending any of it on the care of his wife and children. She said that he had beaten her, and I wouldn't be surprised if he was also beating the children."

"That's reprehensible!" growled Arthur as Mildred's face pursed in anger.

"I aim to start correcting that now. I have my two pack horses outside loaded with food and new clothing for each of them. I think his wife weighed about ninety pounds. I don't know if you've ever met Bessie, but when I knew her, she probably weighed around a hundred and twenty."

"So, what can I do to help?" asked Arthur.

"Mr. Mandrake, I need to know about the cattle sales. Now, my brother, among his other bad traits, was notoriously lazy. I can't imagine him doing all the work to run the ranch, nor can I see him parting with any money to hire hands. I'm guessing that he had an arrangement with you to sell you a hundred head each year and as part of the deal, your hands would do the castrations, branding, and countless other chores."

"You hit it right on the head. He'd give me a bargain basement price on the cattle, fifteen dollars a head, and I'd let my hands work over there. What was odd was that just a week ago, he stopped by and asked me to buy the entire remainder of the herd at fourteen dollars a head. It was a bargain, and I agreed. He'll be getting payment for the last lot when we move our next shipment to market in a couple of weeks. My hands already counted the animals and there were four hundred and fourteen. The total was $5796."

"There's another twist to this story. This morning, I went to the land office to find out where your ranch was located, and then I asked the clerk if my brother still owned the ranch outright or had put Bessie on the deed. He checked the deed and told me that the ranch had been left to my brother and me and my name is on the deed, not Bessie's."

Arthur looked horrified when he realized the legal jeopardy he might be in and said, "I didn't know. I hope you don't try to sue me."

"No, sir, not at all. You didn't do anything wrong. Besides, it's not about the money, it's about justice, justice for my sister-in-law and her children. What I would like you to do is hold onto the draft. If he shows up, tell him that I claimed the money as my inheritance. Tell him I showed you a copy of the deed. He'll believe you because he hates me so much."

"I can do that. What will you do if he comes to the ranch looking for you?"

"We'll talk, and I'll essentially blackmail him. If he puts Bessie's name on the ranch and puts three thousand dollars into an account that only she and I can access, I'll let him have the money and sign over my half. I'm not sure if he'll agree to it, but he might. If not, he'll probably try to kill me. Then we'll see how that works out."

"Honestly, I wished you had taken that ranch. We would have enjoyed having you for a neighbor."

"Neighbor?" Ross asked.

"Sure. The back end of our northern border is the southern border of the Box B. You can ride straight north and be on Box B land in twenty minutes."

"That'll save me some time. Is it all fenced?"

"We put in a gate when he began moving cattle on a regular basis."

"Well, that will make it easy. I'll be heading over there now. I appreciate the hospitality, Mr. and Mrs. Mandrake, and I'll let you know how things go."

"We'd like that. And call me Arthur and my wife's name is Mildred."

"Call me Ross. If you hear anything, just pop over and let me know."

"We will, Ross."

"Thanks again, Arthur and Mildred. It has been a real pleasure meeting you both."

He shook their hands, left the house and returned to his gelding. They waved goodbye as he headed north to the Box B.

The size of the ranch meant it took him ten minutes before he found the gate, crossed over to the Box B property and passed the remaining cattle. It was getting onto winter and the cattle were beginning to run out of grass. The Rocking M already had hay out for their cattle and Ross wondered why Henry was so anxious to get rid of all the cattle and had a strong suspicion that he was going to run. He could only hope that his surprise arrival didn't spur Henry into moving more quickly.

Once that thought entered his mind, his brain automatically began to imagine all manners of terrible things that Henry might do, and his level of concern skyrocketed.

When he got within a mile of the house, he saw smoke from both chimneys, so he calmed down thinking that everything was normal on the Box B.

But when he was less than a half a mile out, he saw Henry riding down the access road away from the house leading a full pack horse. *Was he abandoning his family?* He gave Henry enough time to get down the road to avoid any conflict that might endanger Bessie or the children, although he did seriously think of chasing after Henry.

After Henry was gone from sight, Ross rode the rest of the way to the house, stopped at the kitchen door, tied off the gelding and the pack horses outside, leapt onto the back porch and opened the door without knocking. It was his house as well, after all.

He walked into the kitchen and startled a half-naked and bloody Bessie who was sitting hunched over at the kitchen table with Alice and David standing next to her crying. Ross was furious as he stepped up to the table and put his hand on Bessie's shoulder who either hadn't noticed him enter or thought he was Henry returning to finish what he had started.

"Bessie, what happened?" he asked.

Bessie was startled when she heard Ross's voice, and hurriedly tried to pull what was left of her clothes around her.

Ross took off his coat and draped it over her shoulders before asking a second time, "What happened, Bessie?"

She finally sobbed, "Henry…Henry left. I told him not to leave us with nothing and he told me that everything here belonged to him and he'd take what he wanted. I had just told him I was pregnant, and he was furious and said he was going to kill me. I was terrified, but didn't think he'd really do it, but he knocked me down, then kicked me a few times and stomped on my stomach so hard that I passed out for a little while.

"When I came to, he ripped my dress and pulled the wedding ring from my finger almost taking my finger off, then he kicked me one more time. He said he'd leave me with nothing, Ross, and he did! Ross, I don't know what to do. I hurt so bad."

He wrapped her in his arms and said softly, "Don't worry, Bessie. I'm here now. No one will hurt you again. If he comes back, I'll beat him so badly he'll beg for a bullet, but I don't think he's coming back. Now, you stay right there, okay. Try to calm down. I have some things I need to bring in. Okay?"

She nodded, still sniffling, but Alice and David had both stopped crying as they looked at their uncle.

Ross smiled at both of the children before walking to the back door and going outside to get the pack horses unloaded.

Even without his coat, Ross was steaming as he reached the pack horses, feeling angrier than he had ever been in his life. If Henry had been there, he probably would have killed him. He took the clothing panniers down first and began leaving them on the back porch. When all of them were on the porch, he moved the clothing panniers through the open door, setting them down before his wide-eyed niece and nephew. When they had all been brought inside, he closed the door, walked to the sink and pumped some water over a towel.

He sat down next to Bessie who had barely glanced at the mass of panniers on the floor and began wiping the blood from her face.

He said softly, "Let's get you cleaned up. How are you otherwise? Tell me where it hurts."

She pointed to her left side of her chest and her stomach.

Ross then asked, "Does it hurt to breathe?"

"A little."

"Take in a deep breath and tell me how that feels."

She did and grimaced before saying, "It hurts a lot more when I do that."

"It sounds like you might have some broken or cracked ribs. The good news is that all we can do is just let them heal. Don't exert yourself. Do you think you can go back to your room and get changed?"

"I don't have anything else to wear."

"Sure, you do. Let's see what we can find."

He found the pannier with all the women's clothing and dragged it closer to the table, then opened the cover.

"I didn't know about a lot of these things. I just told the clerk your size and that I needed three dresses, something to keep you warm, and all those other things ladies wear. So, let's take this back to your room, and you can pick what you need."

Bessie's eyes widened as she asked, "You bought me clothes? Why?"

"Bessie, it was obvious that you and the children needed food and clothing. I have two more panniers full of clothing for the children as well. Let's get you taken care of first. Besides, I need my coat back."

He smiled at her and she weakly smiled back before she slowly rose then with his free arm around her slumped shoulders, he guided her slowly back to her bedroom. He set the pannier on the floor, then sat her down on the bed and said, "Go ahead and take your time, Bessie. I have a lot of food out there, so it'll take me a while to unload it all."

"You brought more food?"

"What we gave you yesterday was just what we had left from our trip. This is to fully stock your pantry and cold room."

"Okay," Bessie said.

She must not have cared what Ross saw, because she took off his coat and handed it to him, grimacing as she did. Ross was angered when he saw her naked body. She had so many more bruises all over her body and she was so thin! He took the coat and closed the door behind him.

He walked out to the kitchen still shaken by what Henry had done to Bessie. Her two children watched him as he entered.

He crouched down and looked into their faces, saying, "Alice, I'm going to start bringing in a lot of food now. I don't want you or David to get cold, so I have new jackets for both of you to keep you warm."

He reached in one of the panniers and pulled out a pink coat for Alice and a black one for David. He slipped them on each child, who seemed too numbed by what had happened to their mother to react.

He began transferring the massive quantity of food to the kitchen. Some, like the milk, cream and butter, went straight into the cold storage room. The rest he began piling up and tossed more wood into the cook stove in between trips. The children sat in chairs and just watched as the food began to accumulate.

He had almost all of it moved when Bessie reappeared. She looked a lot better in the new dress but failed to fill it out and Ross knew that would have to change if she were to get better and return to the Bessie he knew.

"Ross! That's so much food!" she exclaimed weakly.

"You and the children have been deprived long enough, Bessie. Now, I have one more trip to make and then I'll cook you all something good and filling."

He went out and got the last pannier of smaller items and brought them inside.

"Now, Bessie. I don't want you to worry about anything anymore. Alright?"

"If you say so, Ross. I won't."

"Good, because I am not leaving this house until I'm sure you're safe."

Bessie managed a genuine smile and asked, "You're going to stay now?"

"I'm not leaving until I see the same round-faced, well-endowed girl that I remember sitting in front of me at the kitchen table laughing at one of my bad jokes."

Bessie actually laughed lightly and asked, "I was well-endowed, wasn't I?"

Ross grinned at her and replied, "Very, and I want you to eat until you are again, and you can dazzle my eyes."

Bessie then sighed and said, "I love you, Ross."

Ross just smiled at Bessie, took one step over to her and gently touched the side of her face that wasn't bruised, before returning to the panniers.

He went to one knee, reached into the pannier and pulled out the bag of penny candy.

"Alice and David, would you like to have something to keep you busy while I make you some oatmeal?" he asked as he opened the bag and showed the contents to the children.

Alice let David take one first. He put it into his mouth slowly and turned to Bessie and smiled. She smiled back as Alice took a piece and grinned as well.

"Would you like one, Bessie? I seem to recall you had a bit of a sweet tooth."

Bessie smiled, and asked, "I still do. Is there a cherry one in there?"

"Of course, I made sure of it."

Bessie found a cherry candy and placed it softly on her tongue, then closed her eyes and began to cry.

Ross gently patted her on her shoulder. *How bad does it have to be when a piece of penny candy can make a grown woman cry?*

Ross emptied the pannier and took a pot and half filled it with water, set it on the stove and began to put away the food. He knew he'd have to do some serious cleaning in the house, and Bessie was in no shape to do much more than eat and sleep.

He wished Amy was here to help, and then quickly modified the thought to just wish that Amy was here.

———

Amy was reading as the train pulled into Boise, Idaho for passengers, coal, water and some routine maintenance. It was going to be an hour and a half stop and all of the passengers got off the train to get something to eat. Amy thought she may as well do what she had to do and walked off the train to the Western Union office.

After she reached the nearby building, she quickly wrote out a message and handed it to the operator.

He read the message and his eyebrows went up, but didn't say anything beyond, "That'll be forty cents, ma'am."

She handed him the money but didn't wait for him to tap out the message. She left as he began sending:

AARON CHILDS ESTHERVILLE OR

CAPTURED BY SIOUX THREE YEARS
ESCAPED TWO MONTHS AGO
WILL ARRIVE ON AFTERNOON TRAIN TOMORROW

AMY CHILDS BOISE IDAHO

She decided to have something to eat after all, so she stepped into the diner and had a nice lunch before returning to the train.

————

Ross had the oatmeal bubbling and added some brown sugar and cinnamon. He spooned it into three bowls and then added a pat of butter to each stirring it just enough to mix it before added some cream to finish the oatmeal. Then he poured two glasses of milk for the children and a mug of coffee with cream and sugar for Bessie, then set the food on the table in front of each of them with a spoon.

"I know it's late for breakfast, but this is all I'm really good at making, so eat up. There's more if you want some."

"Thank you, Ross, this smells delicious," Bessie said as she picked up her spoon.

Alice added, "Thank you, Uncle Ross."

Even David murmured a thank you.

They each dove into the oatmeal like it was their last meal, and Ross knew that they needed more. There was enough food here to last them for a while, and maybe finally begin putting on some much-needed weight. He was concerned about Bessie's injuries though. He really did want to see her back to her well-rounded figure, but not for the reason that she may have thought. But then again, without Amy, maybe he should think about it, but for now, his only concern was to get Bessie and her children healthy again.

Bessie finished her oatmeal first and asked Ross for more. He smiled at her and brought the pot over, added more 'fixings' to the oatmeal and spooned it out to her bowl and the now empty bowls of the children until the pot was empty. When they had finished their second bowls and the children had emptied their glasses of milk, Bessie led them into their bedroom and let them lay down for a nap. She was tired herself but didn't let Ross know, but he knew just by looking at her.

She re-entered the kitchen and sat down, wincing in pain.

"Why are you doing all this, Ross?"

"Bessie, this is all wrong. When Henry married you and fathered those two small human beings, he had an obligation to care for you, and he failed miserably. I'll deal with him later. Right now, I'm trying to rectify his failings. You all need food and clothing. I'll do some cleaning because you're in no shape to handle it."

"What about Amy?" she asked.

That question shot into Ross like a shotgun blast, but he calmly answered, "She's gone. I put her on the train to return to her husband in Oregon this morning."

"Oh."

"Right now, Bessie, we need to get you into bed. You're exhausted. You need to go and sleep peacefully for a while. No one will ever hurt you again."

"But if Henry comes back, he can throw you out!"

"No, he can't. This is my ranch, too, Bessie. Uncle Joe left it to both of us. I don't know why my parents never told me, but I have my suspicions that it was to try to save Henry from himself. But now he has no legal authority to have me tossed out of here. I'll stay as long as I like, and it will be as long as it takes to get you and Alice and David healthy and happy again."

"I didn't know."

"I know you didn't, Bessie. Now, you go and lie down."

He walked over to Bessie, put his arm over her shoulder, then led her down the hallway. As they walked, she was half bent over from pain and she was breathing rapidly. When they reached the bedroom, he sat her on the edge of the bed, then leaned her back softly onto the mattress and swung her legs over the bed before covering her in blankets.

She looked at him with her moistened blue eyes and whispered, "Thank you, Ross."

She paused, then asked softly, "Ross, promise me that you will take care of my babies."

Ross was shocked by the question and wondered if she was hurt more than she let on.

"Of course, I will, Bessie, but I'll take care of you, too."

She closed her eyes, and whispered, "I'm happy now. You always keep your promises."

Ross leaned over and kissed her gently on her forehead as a small smile crossed her lips.

He left quietly, closing the door gently behind him, knowing that she'd sleep for a long while. He thought about going to get a doctor but was concerned that Henry may return, so he walked out to the kitchen and began cleaning.

———

A few miles to the west, Arthur and Mildred Mandrake were talking about Ross's visit.

"Arthur, how can anyone treat children like that?"

"There's no excuse, Millie, none whatsoever. Henry was always a boorish, crude man, but even at that, I didn't believe he was capable of such things."

Arthur and Mildred had never had any children, and now with Mildred approaching forty, it was unlikely they ever would. It was an ache in Mildred that she knew she never would have the joy of young children running through the house hugging her and calling her mama, and now she was hearing that at the neighboring ranch, someone had two precious gifts and treated them terribly.

"You know, Arthur, Ross did say we could pop over anytime. Did you want to pay them a visit?"

Arthur was inclined to say no because it was so soon, but he could never deny his Mildred anything and knew she wanted to go and see the children.

"Alright, Millie. We can do that."

She grinned and stood quickly, saying "I have some cookies I just baked this morning, too. I'll put them in a bag and take some with us."

She turned and trotted into the kitchen as Arthur watched her and smiled as he put on his heavy coat then left the house to go and saddle their horses.

Mildred had packed the cookies, then returned to their bedroom and changed into her riding clothes, almost as giddy as a schoolgirl about seeing the children.

A short while later they were riding north, crossing their pastures which were filled with healthy, well-fed cattle. They arrived at the gate a few minutes later and passed onto Box B land.

———

Ross had to take out a bar of soap that he had bought to start cleaning as he hadn't found any in the house. He filled a bucket with hot water and started with the dishes and the pots and pans. That took an hour, then he began cleaning the shelving and everything else he could.

Alice came out of her room and padded into the kitchen.

Ross saw her enter and said, "Hello, Alice. Are you wide awake now?"

"Yes, Uncle Ross. It looks nice and clean in here. It smells nice, too."

"I'll have it all done soon. Can I do anything for you?"

She plopped down on a chair, and asked, "Is my papa coming back?"

Ross put down the cloth he was using and sat next to her.

"I don't know, sweetheart. I don't think so."

"That's good. He was mean to mama."

"I know. He was mean to me when I was a little boy, too."

"He was?"

"Yes, ma'am. I was a lot smaller than he was, so he used to beat me with his fists and kick me a lot."

"Did it hurt?"

"Yes, it hurt. But then, when I was ten, I found that I could run fast, and he couldn't hit me anymore."

"That's good."

"But when I was sixteen, I didn't run anymore. I stood up to him when he tried to beat me."

"Did he beat you up again?"

"No, never again. I beat him very badly. I made him all bloody and left him crying."

"Good."

"What did he do to your mama today?"

Alice dropped her eyes and said, "He slapped her very hard and then she fell down. He kicked her a lot and stepped on her tummy till she fell asleep. Then she woke up and he pulled off her dress and kicked her again. Then he left with all of our things."

David had wandered into the kitchen, and Ross looked at him and said, "David, I'll tell you what. Why don't you have a seat and we'll decide what we'll do next, okay?"

He nodded, then Ross heard a rap on the kitchen door, so he hopped up, crossed the floor and opened it to see a smiling Matilda Mandrake and Arthur standing behind her.

"Come in, Mildred and Arthur. It's cold out there."

"We saw your horses in back and thought you were dropping off all that food and I couldn't resist bringing something over for the children," Mildred said as she and her husband entered.

Ross closed the door behind them and said, "Let me introduce you to Alice and David."

Then he turned to the children and said, "Alice, bring David over and I'd like to have you meet our neighbors, Mr. and Mrs. Mandrake."

Alice took David's hand and they stepped shyly over to the Mandrakes.

Millie was all smiles as she bent over and said, "Hello, Alice. Hello, David. I'm Millie. This is my husband Arthur."

"Hello, ma'am," replied Alice.

"Hello," said David.

Millie could see how thin they were, and their clothes were in a terrible state. She wanted to either cry or shoot Henry Braxton, maybe both.

"Would you each like a cookie?" she asked.

Their eyes lit up and they both nodded vigorously.

Mildred reached into the bag and gave them each a big oatmeal raisin cookie.

"Thank you, ma'am," said Alice.

David had the cookie in his mouth and mumbled, "Tank ooh."

Ross could see Millie's heart melting, and so could her husband.

Millie noticed the cleaning and all the new food Ross had brought and said, "Ross, you're a good man."

'Probably no different than your husband, Mildred."

"That's very observant of you. Did you say you brought some clothes for the children?"

"Yes, right over there in the corner. I didn't get them dressed yet because I thought they needed a bath first."

"That's a very un-manlike decision, and a very correct one. Is Bessie around?"

"She's sleeping. I noticed that she had been severely beaten when I came in and she was half-naked from Henry ripping her dress just to humble her. He said everything belonged to him, and even took her wedding ring. He took whatever he wanted and left. I saw him leaving when I came down the rise from your place. Both children have seen it all, and I didn't know how bad it was until she told me. He really beat her badly. I was going to go and get the doctor, but I was afraid he might return and harm the children, and did you know why he beat her and left? Because she had just told him that she was pregnant."

"That bastard beat her because she was going to have another baby?" Mildred asked, aghast at the thought.

Ross nodded.

"We'll stay if you want to go and get the doctor. Did you want to see how she is?"

"I think that's a good idea. I gave her one of her new dresses and two bowls of oatmeal to build up some strength, but she was really hurting. I'll go see if she's awake."

Ross walked to her bedroom and gently tapped on the door. There was no response, but Ross knew how tired she was and wasn't surprised by the lack of response.

He knocked louder and called, "Bessie?"

There was still no response, and he was suddenly very worried.

He slowly opened the door finding Bessie still asleep under the blankets. Mildred had walked behind Ross as he stepped slowly to the bed and reached over.

He said softly, "Bessie? It's Ross, we have visitors."

He touched her cheek. It was cold, and the sudden realization of her death slammed into him. *No! It couldn't be!*

He quickly sat on the edge of the bed and felt her neck, then leaned over and put his ear to her thin chest and heard nothing.

He sat up and tears rolled down his face as he tried to control himself. That bastard brother of his had murdered Bessie.

Mildred walked close to Ross, knowing what he had found. She put her hand on his shoulder and didn't say anything as he just sat and sobbed.

Finally, he spat out two words.

"That bastard!" he growled and then stood.

"Ross, we need to worry about the children now," said Mildred softly.

Ross cleared his eyes and nodded.

He turned to Bessie and looked at her and pulled the blanket over her small, thin face. He remembered the smiling round-faced blonde girl from his youth and had a hard time connecting it to the Bessie lying dead under the blanket.

He and Mildred left the room, and he closed the door behind him.

When they returned to the kitchen, Alice looked up at Ross and wondered why he was so upset as Mildred looked at Arthur and just shook her head.

Ross sat down opposite Alice and took a deep breath. Now was not the time to start lying.

"Alice, I just went to see your mama. Your bad father hurt her too much when he hit her today. She just died and is now with God and the angels in heaven. Do you understand?"

"Yes. When papa was kicking her, he said he would kill her, but then she woke up and was better. Why did she die?"

"Because when he stepped on her tummy or kicked her too hard, he broke something inside her. Sometimes it takes a little while for that to make you die. Now, I'm going to have to go and talk to the sheriff, so he can arrest your papa for killing your mama."

"Are we going to be alone? What if papa comes back?"

Mildred stepped in and said, "No, sweetheart, I'll be here. Arthur will go back to our house and tell them to watch to make sure your father doesn't come back and then my husband will come back. We'll watch over you until your Uncle Ross returns. You'll be safe, okay?"

"Can I have more cookies?"

"Of course, you can."

Arthur said, "I'll be back as soon as I can. I'll have Rich watch the house and keep the fires burning while we're here."

"Thank you, Arthur."

Arthur nodded then turned and quickly left the house.

"Mildred, can you handle a pistol?" Ross asked.

"Better than most men."

"Good. I'm going to leave you one of my Colts. If my brother comes back, don't hesitate. Blow a hole through him."

"Trust me, I wouldn't hesitate."

He handed her the Colt, checking that there were five rounds before he did so.

"I should be back in a few hours with the sheriff."

"Go ahead, we'll be fine."

Ross stepped out of the house, disconnected the trail horses, then mounted the gelding and was on his way in less than a minute. He set the horse at a fast trot and made it to the sheriff's office in twenty minutes.

He stepped down and entered the door and was greeted by an affable deputy.

"Good afternoon, sir. What can I do for you?"

"I need to report a murder," Ross replied as he managed to restrain his deep anguish and anger.

The deputy's genial smile quickly changed to a business-like firmness.

"Follow me. The sheriff is in his office."

They walked into the sheriff's office after the deputy had rapped quickly on the door jamb to let the sheriff know they were coming.

"Sheriff, this gentleman would like to report a murder."

The sheriff looked up. He was a middle-aged man with graying temples on an otherwise thick head of black hair.

"Have a seat and tell me what happened. Deputy Brewster, take a seat as well and take notes."

Ross waited until the deputy had pulled a pad off the sheriff's desk and a pencil from a cup.

"Yesterday, I arrived from Dakota territory to visit my brother and his family at the Box B. Now, it's important that you know right from the start that my brother and I never got along. My parents had asked me to check up on him when I got here."

Ross then told the lawmen everything that had happened since he arrived in Cheyenne, including Amy's departure which hadn't helped his melancholy mood.

He was shaking when he finally drew to the conclusion, and the reason for his visit.

"I started cleaning the kitchen when the Mandrakes arrived. They came in and Mildred gave the children cookies. I suggested that the children have baths, so Mildred and I went to wake Bessie up, and we found her dead."

Ross started to tear up again, so he wiped his eyes and blew out a breath.

"Mildred stayed with the children. Arthur went home to arrange for his foreman to mind the house and then he would return. I left my Colt with Mildred and told her that if Henry returned to shoot him."

The sheriff sat back and took almost a minute to digest the story.

Then he said, "John, notify the doctor that we're going to need his work as a coroner," before looking at Ross and adding, "Mr. Braxton, I'm sorry you had to see that."

"You know, Sheriff, on the trail back with Mrs. Childs, I killed ten Sioux warriors, two deserters and one murderer. None of those deaths bothered me at all. But this, seeing Bessie lying there, her short life ended because she dared to be carrying a child just made me sick. When I knew her, she was a lively, pretty, young girl, but had all that life taken from her long before Henry murdered her."

"Don't worry. We'll find the bastard. Let's go back to the ranch, and we'll swing by the undertaker to arrange transport for her body back to the city. The doc will perform an autopsy to determine the cause of death. Stay here until I get my horse."

Ross nodded as the deputy and the sheriff both rose and left the office.

Ten minutes later the sheriff and Ross started back, and after a brief stop while the sheriff talked to the undertaker, they set off at a trot to the Box B.

It was getting dark when they arrived and walked in the front door.

"I see what you mean about the house's condition," the sheriff remarked as he looked around.

Mildred and Arthur stepped out from the kitchen.

"Ross, I'm making dinner if you and the sheriff want to join us in a few minutes."

"Thank you, Mildred."

They walked into Bessie's bedroom and closed the door behind them. The sheriff removed the blanket and Bessie looked at peace, but the bruises on her face were still evident, if not more pronounced.

The sheriff sighed and covered her again.

"Sights like this make me want to retire. Let's go out to the kitchen. I'd like to talk to the little girl."

"Her name is Alice. The little boy is David."

"Thanks."

They arrived into the warm and clean kitchen.

"I see you've been busy, Mildred," said the sheriff.

"Ross cleaned most of it before I got here."

The sheriff sat on a chair next to Alice, as Mildred handed Ross his Colt.

"Alice, I'm the sheriff. Do you know what I do?"

"You arrest bad men like my papa."

"Yes, I do. Can you tell me what happened to your mama?"

"Papa wanted to leave, and mama said he couldn't take all those things. He slapped her and pushed her down, then he kicked her two times. She was crying, and it made me sad, but I was afraid. Then he yelled at her and said he was going to kill her. He ripped her dress and pulled her finger to take her ring. He got madder and kicked her two more times and stomped on her tummy. She went to sleep for a while, but papa kept yelling at her, and she woke up. He kicked her one more time and left. I thought my mama was all right, but she went to bed and died, so she went to heaven to live with God and the angels."

"Thank you, Alice. You're a brave little girl."

The sheriff wrote his notes down and put them in his pocket.

Mildred served a complete dinner that helped calm the mood but did little to quell the anger that still raged inside of Ross.

They had barely finished when the undertaker with an assistant arrived, and the sheriff and Ross directed them to Bessie's room. They wrapped her body in their own cloths, placed her in a temporary coffin, then carried it outside to their hearse. They told the sheriff that the doctor would perform the autopsy in the morning, then boarded their hearse, drove down the access road and turned back toward Cheyenne.

The sheriff made his farewells and soon followed the hearse back to Cheyenne.

Mildred gave the children a hot bath and dressed in the new pajamas that their Uncle Ross had bought for them. Alice was pleased, but David was unsure about the pajamas.

After they were put to bed, Ross walked out to the kitchen with Mildred and Arthur.

"What will happen to the children now, Ross?" Mildred asked hopefully.

"That's a good question. They only have one set of grandparents, my father and mother. Bessie was an only child, so that leaves me as the only other relative. Their father will be hung for murder unless I get to him first."

"Ross, I know this is asking a lot, especially as it's so recent, but do you think that, you know, after everything is settled, um, I don't know how to put this," she stammered.

285

"Mildred, from what I've seen of you and Arthur, I think that after we track down Henry, I should recommend that you be allowed to adopt Alice and David, if that is okay with you both."

Mildred began to cry as she looked at Arthur, who was smiling broadly at his beloved wife.

"Thank you, Ross. That would make me so happy," she said with a smile as if Ross didn't know.

"Mildred, this world needs every bit of happiness to outweigh all of the ugliness."

"So, are you going to stay here?"

"Tonight. Tomorrow, I don't know where I'll be staying. I have a room at the Railway Hotel."

"Can we move the children to our house tomorrow? We'd be able to keep them safe and give you the freedom to do what you need to do."

"That's an excellent idea. I think they'd follow you anywhere. You gave them cookies, after all. By the way, did they leave any for me?"

———

Halfway across the continent, in Estherville, Oregon, a messenger boy was standing on the porch of a small house in town and knocked on the door. When it opened, a young woman holding a baby on her hip looked at him with curious eyes.

"What do you want?"

"I got a telegram for Aaron Childs. Is this his place?"

"Yeah. Give it to me. I'll hand it to him."

The messenger stood there, waiting for his tip, and got a door slammed in his face instead. He sighed, then turned around and left. It had happened before.

As the woman turned into the front room of the two-room house, a toddler stepped in front of her almost, tripping her.

"Aaron! You got a telegram!" she shouted as if Aaron were on the other side of town.

"I got a what?" he asked as he walked out from the small kitchen.

"A telegram."

"I got a telegram?"

"That's what I keep trying to tell ya. Come and get it and you can tell me what it says."

"Aww, Gladys, you can read it."

"Not if it's writ fancy."

"Give it here."

She handed him the telegram. He opened it and froze.

Gladys saw the shock on his face and said, "Did somebody die or something?"

"No. Somebody didn't die. I thought she did three years ago."

"What are you talking about?"

Aaron hesitated, knowing what would happen, but still explained the meaning of the short telegram. Gladys hadn't heard the story before and started slapping him.

CHAPTER 7

The next morning, Ross was up early and made some oatmeal for everyone, including himself. It was quick, nutritious, and with the add-ins, mighty tasty. He even had a glass of milk.

He told the children that they would be moving in with the Mandrakes, so they could be protected while Uncle Ross took care of some things.

As expected, the first thing that came from David was when he asked, "Can she make more cookies?"

After being assured that it was highly possible, they readily agreed.

Arthur and Mildred showed up with a carriage on the regular access road an hour later. They packed all the children's new clothes into a bag, and everyone walked to the carriage. Mildred was still grinning as she got into the carriage and both children sat close beside her. They waved at Ross and drove down the road.

With the departure of the children, that gave Ross free reign to do what needed to be done.

He saddled his gelding, leaving the pack horses in the barn. He would bring Amy's horse back with him from the hotel livery when he returned. Amy's horse. He figured Amy was just a few hundred miles from meeting her husband, but he smiled at the thought of her finding the opal necklace.

He started toward Cheyenne at a fast trot, and it was after ten o'clock when he arrived. First, he went to the hotel and told them he was checking out and to let them know that he'd be at the Box B if the sheriff or anyone else needed to find him, then went next door to the livery and saddled Amy's horse and added the remaining saddlebags and other packs, including the Sioux weapons.

Just before noon, he stopped in front of the sheriff's office, dismounted and stepped through the door.

"Good morning, Deputy Brewster. Is the sheriff in?"

"Yup. Go ahead. The doc just left."

Ross walked to the sheriff's office. The name on the door read Elias Winston. He knocked, and the sheriff waved him in.

"Mr. Braxton, the doc just gave me his preliminary report."

"Call me Ross, sheriff."

"Fine, call me Elias," he replied as Ross took a seat.

"Anyway, it was pretty much as you said it was. The young woman was suffering from severe malnutrition. She had multiple fractures in her hands and feet and one in each forearm. Those were all old injuries. The new ones were three broken ribs and a ruptured spleen. He said that she was so small, he was surprised she didn't die right away. For her to do as much as she did afterwards was remarkable."

Ross nodded and said softly, "She stayed alive for her children."

There was a brief pause as both men took a few breaths.

"Anyway, the prosecutor has issued a warrant for the arrest of your brother for murder. Do you have any idea where he might be?"

"When I first got here, I found him heading into Chinatown. I have no idea what he was doing there, but it was costing him a lot of money."

"There are a lot of things that could cost him money in Chinatown. Do you think he was a user of opium?"

"No, he was too fat. I think it might be gambling."

"That sounds about right. There are some fancy gambling houses over there. We don't raid them because they keep to themselves. Some white folk know that and visit the places. Regular customers like your brother would get special treatment. You know, food and women. So, you're probably right about that."

"There's something else. He's getting low on money by now. I think he took everything he could lay his hands on in the house to get him through a few days in the gambling house. He's waiting on Arthur Mandrake to sell his herd and expects Arthur to give him over five thousand dollars."

"That'll be a tough legal situation. They're still his cattle. He has a right to sell them until he's convicted."

"That's where I can stop him. I found out yesterday that the ranch had been willed to both of us by my Uncle Joe. So, he's been selling our joint property over the years without my permission to the tune of almost fifteen thousand dollars. Now, I really don't care about the money, but if it can keep him from doing anything like skipping town then that's one more weapon.

"I told Arthur to tell him that I forced him to give me the bank draft, and that will force Henry to confront me. I'll try to talk him into giving himself up. If not, so be it. One other thing. As a safety precaution, the children will be staying with Arthur and Mildred Mandrake. I could see when Mildred first saw the children that she was in love with them, and I can't provide the kind of home that they need, so after this is all over, I'm going to allow them to adopt Alice and David."

"That would make Millie very happy. She always wanted to have children but never did. You're a hell of a man, Ross."

"We need to make as much right as we can out of this mess that my brother has created."

"So, what are you going to do now?"

"I'll send a telegram to my parents advising them of the situation. Then, I'll head back to the ranch and start cleaning the house. I'll just wait for Arthur's crew to come and move the cattle and then see if Henry makes his appearance. Arthur told me he'll move them next week because he doesn't want to feed that many cows over the winter."

"Arthur always ran a good operation."

"It's what the Box B should have been and probably was before Henry got his hands on it."

Ross stood and shook the sheriff's hand, then left the sheriff's office and stopped by a mercantile on the way back. He bought four new sheets, two new pillows, four new pillowcases, two new blankets and a quilt. It was bulky, but it didn't add any weight to the load already on Amy's horse. The two Sharps and their bullets were heavier.

He stopped at the Western Union and sent the following message to his parents:

WALTER AND EMILY BRAXTON SEXTON MINN

ARRIVED IN CHEYENNE
FOUND HOUSE IN SHAMBLES
BESSIE MURDERED BY HENRY
STILL AT LARGE
CHILDREN THIN BUT BEING TAKEN CARE OF
SORRY FOR BAD NEWS
WILL KEEP YOU UPDATED

ROSS BRAXTON BOX B RANCH CHEYENNE WYOMING

It was harsh, but there was no other way to do it. All the time he had been growing up, he had kept Henry's abuse from his parents. He knew that they probably suspected it, but as long as Ross could deal with it, they didn't interfere. When he did finally whip Henry, he complained to them, but they never mentioned it to Ross. Even with all those years of bullying, he couldn't imagine that his parents would believe Henry to be capable of such horror.

He returned to the ranch and took his Sharps and other weapons into the kitchen and stood the two big guns in the pantry. It was already two o'clock, so he decided to skip lunch, but did grab a couple of cookies and a glass of milk, and thought it was a better lunch than many of the others that he'd had to eat over his years in uniform. He went into the bedroom and replaced all the old bedding with the new. He didn't throw the used linen out, though. He'd wash them later and then store them.

Then he returned to the kitchen and began cleaning his guns.

————

Over at the Rocking M, Arthur had told his foreman to move the cattle starting in the morning. He wanted this whole Henry thing over and done. Mildred was partly to blame. She loved having the children there and wanted the issue resolved, so they could adopted Alice and David. So, the next morning, the crew would move the cattle to the holding pens in Cheyenne. It was only a nine-hour drive.

———

Amy was getting despondent again. She had almost finished the book and had enjoyed it immensely. The fact that it was a gift from Ross made it even better.

But the train was slowing as it was pulling into Estherville. In a few minutes, she would meet her husband and he would take her to his home. He'd be kissing her and then wanting to take her to bed, and the thought nauseated her, but there was nothing she could do.

On the platform, Aaron Childs waited nervously. *How could he tell his Amy what had happened?* He had to be blunt. He had to tell her right off. It would break her heart, but he had to. He would tell her that she would find someone new in time. Where she would stay was the problem. Gladys had already laid down the law on that front. That woman wasn't going to set one toe in her house. His brother's house was a bit bigger, but he already had three children. Amy would be bringing so many problems with her on that train, and he watched as the locomotive slowed as it approached the small depot, dreading the moment he met her again.

Amy was dreading it for an entirely different reason. The train had finally stopped moving and she knew she had to leave. A few other passengers were already walking down the aisle, so she let out her breath, straightened and tried to smile, but she just couldn't. So, she just put on her grim Witch face and walked down the aisle to her fate. Maybe she would scare him away.

Aaron watched the passengers exiting, knowing that he would recognize her easily with her gray hair. Suddenly, there she was, and he began to walk toward her as he still ran through different explanations in his mind.

Amy, on the other hand, had a hard time picking out Aaron. He was never much of an impressive figure before and she doubted if he was now. She scanned the platform and saw him. *My lord!* How could she go back to *him*? She took a deep breath and stepped toward Aaron.

Aaron took his deep breath and shuffled four more feet toward Amy. He had forgotten just how pretty she was and regretted having married Gladys, but it didn't matter.

When they were close, neither was ready to embrace for essentially the same reason, so it stayed that way.

"Hello, Amy," he said as he looked past her to the train beyond.

"Hello...Aaron," she stammered.

"Um, Amy, before we go much further, um, there's something you have to know."

Amy could see the stress on his face and wondered what was causing it. Maybe he had forgotten her gray hair, although she thought that highly unlikely.

"What's that Aaron?" she asked.

"Um, well, see I, well, um, when I got the news about your wagon train being attacked by them Indians. Well, see, the army said that everyone died."

"Yes, they all did except me. I was captured."

"Yes, yes, I can see that. But when the army said that, I thought, well, you know, I needed to move on. So, I well I, um, had our marriage annulled and I got married. I have two kids now, too. So, um, Amy, I know that you're disappointed and all, but…"

Aaron never got another word out. Amy heard the word 'annulled' and every worry she had in the world evaporated like the steam venting from that big locomotive sitting fifty feet away.

Amy dropped her travel bag and grabbed Aaron by the shoulders.

"*Annulled? Annulled?* That means I'm not married to you anymore!" she shouted with a wild look of complete exultation.

"I know. I'm sorry, Amy, but Gladys said…"

Amy didn't let him finish. She didn't care who Gladys was or what she else he had to say.

She leaned across, kissed Aaron on the lips and practically shouted, "Goodbye, Aaron! Congratulations on your marriage, by the way. You go home to Gladys now. Goodbye!"

Amy released a confused Aaron, grabbed her travel bag, turned and ran, not delicately either, to the ticket window.

Aaron stood there dumbfounded not knowing what had just happened. Finally, he shrugged his shoulders, turned and walked back to his mule. Gladys was waiting.

Amy scampered to the ticket window and asked breathlessly, "When is the next train going to Cheyenne?"

The ticket agent said, "The next eastbound train will be coming by at 7:20, just under four hours from now."

Amy's mind was racing. This will work.

"I'd like a one-way first-class ticket to Cheyenne please."

"That'll be $41.10, ma'am."

Amy wondered briefly about the disparity in costs when there was only a change in direction but didn't dwell on it.

She reached into her purse and handed the agent fifty dollars. He gave her the change and her ticket as she silently blessed Ross for giving her the money. Maybe he was hoping she'd come back.

"Could I have someone take my bags to the hotel, please?" she asked as she handed him her luggage tags.

"Yes, ma'am."

She scurried across to the hotel and rented a room, even though it was only going to be a couple of hours. Her bags arrived ten minutes later, and she tipped the young man.

She told the clerk she'd be down in about two hours and asked if he could keep an eye on her one bag.

298

He nodded, before she snatched her room key and carried the heavy bag and toiletry bag to her room, pulled out what she thought of as the 'Ross dress', and laid it on the bed. She walked down the hallway to the bathroom and locked the door. Thirty minutes later, she came out with her hair still wet and was almost bouncing as she walked back to her room. She took ten minutes brushing her hair with the brush Ross had given to her, and began to think she was acting way too silly for an adult woman and then said out loud, "Who cares?"

She put the dress on and finally, for the first time, she put on her opal necklace. She carried her two bags back to the lobby and asked that both heavy bags be sent to the station then went into the restaurant and had a very happy dinner.

It was six when she returned to the train station. The Western Union office was right there, as they usually were, and she stepped inside.

Unlike the last message that she had sent, this one was filled with hope. She wrote:

ROSS BRAXTON RAILWAY HOTEL CHEYENNE WY

MARRIAGE WAS ANNULLED AARON REMARRIED RETURNING TO CHEYENNE
WILL ARRIVE ON SATURDAY MORNING TRAIN
LOVE THE NECKLACE AND I LOVE YOU
MAIDEN NAME BELOW

AMY SORENSEN ESTHERVILLE OREGON

She handed it to the operator who said nonchalantly, "That will be fifty cents, ma'am."

She paid the fee and left the office smiling.

She checked with the station manager who assured her bags were correctly tagged before taking a seat on the platform to wait for a train that wasn't due to arrive for another hour.

———

In a small backroom in Cheyenne's Chinatown, Henry Braxton was lying stretched out on his bed thinking. He was annoyed that the miserable Chink bartender was charging him five dollars a day to stay in this small room. He brought him some lousy Chink food every once and a while, but Henry still had to pay for his drinks. *Bastard!* But in three days, he'd go and collect that big draft from Mandrake, then he could go anywhere he wanted to go and live the way that he wanted to live.

He had been in Chinatown for more than a day when the word filtered down that he was being sought for the murder of his wife. *That stupid bitch! What did she go and get pregnant for?* They already had two brats. He should have stuck with those Chink whores. They were free, too, until he ran out of money again. He figured those tables might be rigged a long time ago, but he'd get so close to a big killing every so often, that he knew his luck had to change. But then that bitch had to go and die. Now he was really screwed, and he only had enough money for another week. But by then, he should be loaded and out of the territory. He'd go to California or maybe even Mexico. A man could live pretty good in Mexico with that kind of money.

But now those cheap-ass Chinks acted like he was an outcast. He hadn't been out of the room for two days, and hadn't taken a bath in a few weeks, so he knew he was smelling bad, but he didn't care. In a few days, he'd be a bad-smelling rich man, and they could all kiss his ass.

———

The next morning found another change in the weather. The winds had picked up as the temperature dropped, and Ross thought this time it wouldn't be going back up. There had been some snow overnight, but the wind had swept most of it clear off the flat spaces, making it accumulate in drifts around buildings or trees. It was still cold. Not the bone-chilling cold of mid-winter, but cold enough to make travel undesirable.

But the Rocking M had cattle to move. Arthur had added three hundred of his own to the Box B cattle. It was a short drive to the Cheyenne holding pens, so it wouldn't be too much of a problem, he just wanted them out of his pastures. He had already negotiated a price of $21.75 a head for the cattle, and Mildred had convinced him to pay twenty-one dollars a head for the Box B cattle rather than the fourteen that he had promised, as long as the money was going to Ross and not Henry. If Henry got the money, he'd get the fourteen dollars a head. Arthur didn't need that much convincing, as the seventy-five cents would cover any added costs for moving the cattle. He just hoped he never saw Henry's face again.

———

Ross spent most of the morning cleaning the house. Four years at West Point do not allow for messy quarters. Around ten o'clock, there was a knock at the door, so he walked across the room and opened the door, finding a very chilly messenger there with a telegram.

"Come on in and get warm. It's cold out there."

He scampered inside as Ross closed the door.

"Thank you, Mr. Braxton. You are Ross Braxton?"

"Yes, that's right."

"I have two telegrams for you, sir."

"Two? Let me guess. One is from Minnesota. Where is the second one from?"

"Oregon."

Ross figured Amy must be wiring him to let him know she had arrived and to thank him for the necklace. He got part of it right, anyway.

"Give me the one from Minnesota first."

He handed him the telegram. It read:

ROSS BRAXTON BOX B RANCH CHEYENNE WY

WILL BE ARRIVING FRIDAY NIGHT AT SEVEN THIRTY

WALTER AND EMILY BRAXTON SEXTON MINN

"Well this ought to be interesting," he mumbled, then said, "Okay, give me the one from Oregon."

He took the proffered sheet of folded paper. He unfolded it and read:

ROSS BRAXTON RAILWAY HOTEL CHEYENNE WY

MARRIAGE WAS ANNULLED AARON REMARRIED
RETURNING TO CHEYENNE
WILL ARRIVE ON SATURDAY MORNING TRAIN
LOVE THE NECKLACE AND I LOVE YOU
MAIDEN NAME BELOW

AMY SORENSEN ESTHERVILLE OREGON

He stared at the message, looked up at the messenger and then dropped his eyes down again and reread it.

Finally, he turned to the messenger and said, "Son, what is the largest tip you have ever earned?"

"I got a silver dollar once."

Ross reached into his pocket and tossed him a ten-dollar gold piece.

"You've earned every penny of that," he said with a giant grin.

The young man was beyond words, but eventually spit out, "Thank you, SIR!"

He managed a horrible imitation of a salute and then he stumbled out of the house and climbed onto his horse.

Ross closed the door, sat down and reread the telegram. *Amy was coming home!* He had almost forgotten the other telegram sitting on the floor as he wondered what he could do to make her arrival special. He knew one thing. He'd need to have a long, hot bath before she arrived.

Then he picked up his parents' telegram and realized that they were arriving in just nine hours.

He picked up his cleaning pace and finally stopped to have lunch. He continued his tidying after lunch until three o'clock. The house was in as good as condition that it been in years, and he needed to do some outside work, but not in this weather.

Rather than make himself dinner, he figured as he was going to go into Cheyenne later, he'd share dinner with his parents. It'd be later than he was used to, so he filled the gap with the last of Mildred's cookies and a cup of coffee.

———

At the Bar M., Arthur was back from the cattle pens. He had his bank draft from the buyer for $15,529.50 and wrote out a draft payable to Ross Braxton for $8694.00 and put both drafts in his wall safe. He heard giggling in the other room followed by Mildred's laugh, and couldn't recall her ever being this happy. He went into the kitchen and found Alice with a dollop of sugar frosting on her nose and David chasing her trying to lick it off.

He watched, but he knew that now that the children were in the house and constantly near Mildred, he'd have to set up some sort of system to notify her if Henry did show up. He knew he'd have to pretend not to know that Henry was wanted, too. It would be hard because he despised the man.

––––––

By five o'clock, Ross washed and shaved, put on a new shirt and then donned his heavy clothing. It wasn't too bad outside right now and guessed the temperature was around twenty degrees when he mounted his gelding and rode into Cheyenne. As he did, he passed the full holding pens, and took a short detour, riding close enough to the pens and saw some Box B cattle inside which meant that Arthur had moved up the transfer. If Henry got wind of that now, he'd be visiting soon. He had to tell his parents of his plans, and still didn't know what their views would be would be about Bessie's murder, and then, to counter all of that worry, was his overwhelming excitement of Amy's imminent return.

After leaving the cattle pens, he trotted alongside the tracks and crossed them near the railroad station, then pulled out his watch. It was 7:10, so he decided to stay on the horse until the train was almost in the station as he appreciated the heat from the animal.

Ten minutes later he heard the whistle and could see the lights from the approaching train in the distance. He stepped down and tied the horse to the hitchrail in front of the Railway Hotel, then walked over to the platform.

Three minutes later the engine passed him, releasing clouds of steam as it slowed its drive wheels. When the last car had stopped in front of the platform and passengers began disembarking, he began scanning the platform and spotted his mother first and waved. She smiled widely and waved back as his father stepped beside her then smiled and waved too. Ross guessed he wasn't in trouble after all.

He walked up to them and scooped up his small mother and hugged her.

"Hello, Mama. I've missed you."

"And I've missed you, Rossie."

His father came up to him and enveloped him in a bear hug, asking, "How are you, Ross?"

"Fine, Papa. How was the trip?"

"Boring. But it's the plains, so it can't be anything else."

"Did you want to have dinner in the hotel restaurant?"

"That would be fine. The food on the train is not good."

"I try not to eat it, myself," Ross replied.

Ross put his arm around his mother's waist and his father's shoulder as they walked into the hotel.

First, his father walked up to the desk and arranged for a room and to have their luggage brought up. He was given a key, then he joined Ross and his wife.

They entered the restaurant, which was only about a third full, and after they were seated, the waitress brought coffee for the men and tea for his mother, and they placed their orders.

"So, Ross, tell me about Henry," said his father.

Ross told them what he had found when he had first arrived at the Box B.

He was just finishing and had reached the part when he had followed Henry to Chinatown when their food arrived, and he continued as they ate.

It was still hard to describe what he found when he walked into Bessie's bedroom.

After he finished, he continued eating, waiting for their questions.

"Where are the children now, Rossie?" asked his mother.

"They're staying with the Mandrakes at the Rocking M. They've already asked if they could adopt the children, and I told them they could. I don't know where my life will take me, and you couldn't ask for two nicer people, Mama. Mildred never had any children of her own, and she felt so deprived. You had to see her face when she helped them. I think that's the best solution for both the children and the Mandrakes."

"I understand, son. You've handled this all as we've grown to expect. I think the children will be happy there," his father said.

"So, about your long journey across Indian lands. Tell us about the young lady you traveled with," said his mother.

"Mama, you are going to love her. She was born with gray hair that made people think there was something wrong with her. But it wasn't her that was at fault, it was those who saw her hair and didn't look beyond it. She is the most remarkable woman I have ever met. She's smart, enjoyable to be with, witty, well-read and just an absolute joy. It broke my heart to put her on the train to Oregon two days ago."

"You love her, don't you, Rossie," she asked softly.

"Like I've never loved anyone before, Mama."

"And now, you've lost her forever."

"That's what I thought until a few hours ago. The messenger that brought me your telegram also brought me one from Amy. It seems that when she got off the train, her husband told her that because she had been reported killed in the Sioux attack, he had the marriage annulled and married again and has two children. Amy is on her way back here and will be arriving on the morning train. When she arrives, I'm going to take her down to the courthouse and I'm going to marry her before she gets away. You know, I've never even kissed the woman, but it doesn't matter. By tomorrow at noon, she'll be my wife."

Both parents went into a state of shock again, only this time from hearing wonderful news.

"Does she know this yet?" asked his mother.

"No. I haven't asked. I've never told her that I love her, either, but she knows. Those long weeks on the trail were so hard on us both. We both knew she was married, so all we ever did was talk. Maybe that's the best way. The last few days were like a death sentence for both of us, but now, my Amy is coming back to me and I can't be any happier."

She smiled as she said, "Then I'm happy for you both. We will be at the wedding, won't we?"

"You'd better be," he replied, then said, "Early tomorrow, I'm going to run over to the jewelry store and get our wedding bands. Then I'll come back here and meet you in the hotel lobby. Her train gets in at nine o'clock."

"Sounds like a good plan," his father agreed.

"I'll rent two buggies and we can ride to the ranch. I've spent some time cleaning it up."

"So, we'll see you in the lobby tomorrow morning," his father said as Ross paid for their meal and they rose.

Ross smiled, then replied, "I'm very happy that you came, and you'll get to meet Amy."

His mother smiled at him and said, "So, are we."

He kissed his mother on the forehead, shook his father's hand, then escorted them back out to the lobby. His father hadn't objected when Ross paid for their dinner and left a generous tip.

After leaving his parents, so they could have some time to recover from the long train ride, Ross left the hotel to make the ride back to the ranch.

————

In Chinatown, Henry continued to seethe. It was only two more days, but he was tired of the lousy food and the lack of mobility. He had heard talk from one of white customers that there had been a bunch of local cattle moved into the holding pens, and he wondered if they were the Box B cattle. If he had heard more, he might have gone to see Arthur Mandrake today, but he decided he'd go a day earlier anyway. He'd go and see Mandrake tomorrow, get his money and get out of Cheyenne for good.

CHAPTER 8

The next morning broke bright and considerably warmer. Ross had barely slept the night before for reasons that were no mystery and took a long bath around six o'clock before he made himself a quick breakfast.

He left the house a little before seven o'clock, saddled the gelding and set him on a fast trot, arriving in Cheyenne at a quarter of eight. He was waiting for the jewelry store to open and when the jeweler saw him waiting, he opened his door early. Ross chose their rings quickly, made sure that his fit properly but he had to guess Amy's size. The jeweler assured him they could resize it easily, and Ross paid for the rings, left the jewelers with a bounce in his step, mounted his horse, and trotted to the Railway Hotel to meet his parents. He was giddy and enjoyed every second of the euphoric feeling. His Amy was coming back to him.

———

Amy was staring out the window, hoping to catch a glimpse of Cheyenne in the distance. She remembered how the very name 'Cheyenne' would cause her unending distress. Now, it was the hope at the end of a dream. The train was on time and it was only twenty minutes before she would see Ross again. She wondered how he would react. He had never said that he loved her, but the necklace did. She knew that he

311

couldn't say it because he believed she was a married woman, and she couldn't say it until she knew she wasn't. Now there were no more restrictions.

———

Ross walked into the hotel, saw his parents waiting in the lobby and both rose when they saw him enter.

"Were you able to find the rings, son?" his father asked.

"Yes, Papa. Now, in fifteen minutes, you'll meet your future daughter-in-law. Forgive me if I take my time with introductions. There may be some delay."

"I would hope so!" exclaimed his smiling mother.

When they heard the whistle in the distance, Ross broke into a smile, took his mother's arm and led her out onto the platform.

Amy heard the whistle and could see the first few buildings of Cheyenne pass by her window as her heart pounded against her ribs almost demanding to escape. For a fleeting moment, she thought that Ross might not be there, but it was only that and nothing more. If he had received the telegram, he would be there.

The train began slowing as Ross moved close to the edge of the platform and began scanning the cars, his smile frozen in place.

Amy was watching the platform slowly appear into view, then she saw Ross looking hopefully at the cars. He was looking for her and he was smiling as much as she was. She wanted to get up and run off the train but had to wait.

When Ross saw her smiling at him through the window, he waved frantically. She waved more sedately but reached down and pulled her opal necklace toward her face to show him that she was wearing it. He stopped waving and just continued to smile at her.

The train stopped, Amy scooped up her small bag and walked quickly to the back of the car as Ross walked on a parallel path along the platform.

At long last, even though it had only been two and a half days ago, Amy and Ross found each other. She leapt down from the last step, tossing her bag aside, and Ross clutched her so tightly he thought he might hurt her. He relaxed a little and kissed her for the first time. Amy was crying so much she could feel the tears building up pools under her eyes.

As soon as their lips parted, Ross said, "You're home, Amy. I loved you for so long and could never tell you. Now, I'll never stop."

"Ross, I love you so much it almost hurts. I've never been so happy."

He kissed her again and picked her off her feet. People were staring with smiles on their faces and Ross and Amy didn't care. For weeks, they had refrained from the display of affection, now they were going to display that affection for all to see.

At last, the initial welcome was over, and Ross lowered her to the platform, reached over and picked up her small bag, then he offered her his other arm.

He stopped and turned to face her and said "Amy, an awful lot has happened since you've been gone."

Amy saw the sadness appear in his eyes and wondered what could have hurt him so much that he had to tell her now.

Ross said softly, "The day after you left, Henry murdered Bessie. They have posters and a warrant out for him. The children are safe and staying with Arthur and Mildred Mandrake at the Rocking M."

"Ross, that's horrible! What happened?"

"He beat her to death in front of the children because he found out she was pregnant."

That stunned Amy more than all of the horrors she had witnessed, and she quietly asked, "What kind of monster is he?"

"The worst kind, Amy. I telegrammed my parents with the news, and they arrived last night."

"Your parents are here? Where are they now?" she asked as she looked behind him.

"About six feet to your right."

Amy spun and faced Ross's parents, who were both smiling broadly.

"Hello, Amy. I'm Walter Braxton, Ross's father, and this cute little lady is his mother, Emily."

Emily approached the much taller Amy and gave her a hug before Amy bent down and kissed her on the cheek.

Emily smiled at her future daughter-in-law and said, "Ross understated your appearance, Amy. You're much more than simply beautiful. You are radiant. That is a beautiful necklace as well."

"Ross gave this to me when I left, but just slipped it into my coat pocket. It was his way of telling me that he loved me because he couldn't say it."

Walter stepped forward and hugged Amy as softly as he could, and Amy kissed him on the cheek as well.

Walter turned to Ross and said, "So, where do we go now, Son?"

Ross took Amy's hand and led her a few feet away, then turned to gaze into those bright green eyes.

"Amy," he said quietly, "I know that we just kissed for the first time ever, and I've only told you I loved you once, but more than anything else I'd like to take you to the courthouse and marry you, so you can never leave me again."

The tears started falling again as she hugged Ross.

All she could say was, "Please."

So, with two kisses behind them, Ross and Amy walked to the livery leading his gelding and rented two buggies. Ross had picked up one of her large travel bags and his father had collected the second, so Ross put her two large bags on the shelf in the back of their buggy and tied them down, then tied the gelding to the back. She put the small bag on the floor and the two buggies rolled to the courthouse.

They parked them in the assigned area and tied them off, then everyone entered the building and Ross asked the clerk how they could arrange a marriage. He pulled out a form that they filled out, then directed them to the office of the justice of the peace. He said to simply give the license to the gentleman in the outer office.

They did just that and the outer office clerk knocked on a door and went inside for a minute before returning. He left the door open and led them all inside. The justice of the peace was a very short man, but it didn't matter. He said the right words and he had the legal authority to perform marriages, which is all that did matter.

Amy was surprised that Ross had the rings when the time came. He put the ring on Amy's finger, and she placed it on his. The justice of the peace pronounced them man and wife, and Ross needed no cue to kiss Amy.

His parents signed the witness form and the justice of the peace signed it. They stopped in the outer office and signed some more forms. The man in the outer office, whose name they never learned, signed the marriage certificate and they became Mr. and Mrs. Ross Braxton just forty minutes after entering the courthouse.

As they walked out of the courthouse, his father asked, "What now, Ross?"

"Now we can all go to the Box B and talk about everything we need to talk about. I think Amy probably has an interesting story about her brief stay in Estherville, Oregon."

"I do," said a laughing Amy.

"We're not spending the night," said Emily.

"Absolutely, not," replied Ross, "but we have plenty of time. It's only about ten-thirty. We can make a nice leisurely drive to the ranch house. It's clean and there is more food there than most restaurants."

They untied the reins of the two buggies, and with the weather about forty degrees warmer than the day before, it was a pleasant ride, especially in Ross and Amy's buggy. Two people couldn't sit any closer as they drove to the Box B.

An hour later the two buggies arrived at the ranch house and were parked in front of the house. Everything was so quiet when they entered, it was almost eerie.

Stomachs had to be satisfied, so Amy and Emily went into the kitchen to fix lunch. Amy was impressed with the amount of food that Ross had brought into the house. There would be plenty for them to have a long honeymoon in their private home, and the thought of what would soon await her made her almost weak-kneed to the point of losing her balance.

"Amy, tell me, Ross just glossed over everything concerning the trip. Was it that bad? He made it out to be so easy," Emily asked.

"I'll let him tell the story, Mrs. Braxton, but I'll tell you this. Every time there was a life or death situation, Ross was nothing less than spectacular. I'd be worried but when I looked into his eyes, I would calm down and knew he'd prevail."

"When did you two fall in love?"

"For me it was the third day, after I dropped my Witch act. The Sioux thought I was a witch because of my gray hair and green eyes. That's why they didn't kill me at first. I became a nasty, vicious person to scare them and keep them away from me. It worked for three years, but when they decided to kill me, I escaped. When Ross saved me, I couldn't go back to the way I was before I had been captured. I was so mean to him. All he did was save my life, then he fed me, eased my pain, gave me clothes to keep me warm, and treated me with respect that I didn't deserve.

"Then, because I was so obstinate, I wound up riding so far away, I thought he had left me. I actually got mad at him, even though it was my fault and not his. So, I trotted back and started yelling at him. I told him if I had a gun, I'd shoot him, and what did he do? He handed me his revolver. He said that if I didn't start treating him civilly, I may as well shoot him. I gave him back his gun and I realized he was right. All the reasons for our falling out belonged to me. The next day, I told him what happened and then I knew how special he was. The longer we traveled the more I fell in love with him. I think he felt the same way too, but we knew all we could do was enjoy being with each other.

"The closer we got to Cheyenne, the more I dreaded it. I couldn't stand being away from him and was sure he felt the same way. It was torture for us both, but he was always the gentleman. I know that if he had kissed me or even asked me to stay with him, I would never have gone back, but he didn't do that. He knew that if I gave in, I'd never outrun my guilt and shame. You have an incredible son, Mrs. Braxton."

"Please call me Emily or Mama. You are Mrs. Braxton now."

"Thank you, Mama," she said as she kissed her new mother-in-law.

Out in the living room, Walter and Ross were discussing radically different topics.

"So, Ross, you actually made that shot at five hundred yards? What kind of gun were you using?"

"It was a Sharps rifle, Papa. They're in the kitchen now. I can show you one later. Would you like to shoot one tomorrow?"

"You bet! I haven't fired a real gun in ages. How are you with those Colts?"

"Better than most. I taught Amy how to shoot a pistol, too. She has her own Smith & Wesson Model 3. She's really good, especially for a woman."

"I don't even own a pistol anymore. The last I had was an old Colt Dragoon."

"If you'd like, I can give you a Smith & Wesson Model 3 like Amy's."

"You'd do that for your old father?" he asked with a smile on his face and a gleam in his eye.

"Of course, the story behind the gun is pretty good, too. It belonged to an outlaw named Alfred Talbot. He had a thousand-dollar reward on him for murder, assault, rape and bank robbery. He tried to sneak up on our camp to kill me and assault Amy. But we tricked him.

"I thought he might sneak back, so we left the tent empty and we stayed fifty yards away while he snuck into camp. He drew the Smith & Wesson and pointed it at the left side of the tent and threatened to kill me if we didn't come out. I had my Winchester already on him and told him to drop his pistol. He turned and fired, so I shot him. He's buried in the sand about sixty miles north of Scotts Bluff."

"Wow! That is some story."

"So, Papa, I'll make you a package deal. You can have a Sharps and a box of ammunition, Talbot's Winchester and his Smith & Wesson."

His father's eyes sparkled as he replied, "You're joking, son. You'd give me those guns?"

"Absolutely. I have no need for the extra firepower. I'd still have my two Colts, Amy's Smith & Wesson, a Winchester and a Sharps."

"Now, that would make my day," he said as he slapped his son's back.

The ladies told them that lunch was ready and to come and get it.

It was an outstanding lunch beyond the well-prepared food. After they cleaned up, they all adjourned to the family room where Ross had a nice fire going and the room was very comfortable. Ross was on the couch with his bride tucked under his arm.

Ross looked down at her and said, "Amy, I really do want to hear about your experience in Estherville."

Amy laughed and said, "It would be sad if it wasn't so funny. Aaron showed up and my impression was that he was trying to tell me that there was no place for me to go because his wife wouldn't let me in the house. He was so sure that I'd break down in tears that he was totally flabbergasted when I jumped for joy and told him good-bye. I congratulated him on his marriage and ran to the ticket agent to get my ticket back to Cheyenne. I couldn't help myself. It was like going from the gallows one second to ecstasy the next."

They all laughed at the visuals of poor Aaron being totally flummoxed.

Ross then said in a more serious tone.

"Papa, Mama, I know I mentioned this before, but I just want to see if I was right in my thinking. When I found out that Great Uncle Joe had left us both the ranch, I knew you both had a good reason. I'd like to know what it was, just to satisfy my curiosity."

Walter looked at Ross and said, "Ross, we always knew how mean Henry was to you when you were young. When we received notice of Uncle Joe's bequeath, we thought if he got a fresh start away from the farm, he'd change. We knew that Bessie wasn't happy with him, but we never understood why. We turned a blind eye to everything. I just never knew we could have raised someone who could be such a monster."

"Papa, it wasn't your fault at all. Some men are just bad. No one is to blame. I lived in the same house, had the same parents and no more or less guidance. I turned out okay."

His mother replied, "You turned out more than okay. We were so proud of you when you went to West Point and then when you graduated at the top of your class and were commissioned, we were even prouder. But do you know when we were the proudest? When you resigned that commission that you loved so much rather than do something you felt was wrong. Not many men had that kind of moral courage. No, you're much better than okay, Rossie."

Amy added as she turned to look at Ross, "I'll go even better, I think your son is miraculous."

Ross smiled back at his bride and then asked his parents, "I know you have some questions about our trip, so let's have them."

Emily asked, "Did you really shoot all those Indians?"

"The two that were going to kill Amy or the eight that were trying to kill us both?"

"You never did go into details. All we've gotten are snippets."

"My wife and I can correct that right now, isn't that right, Mrs. Braxton?" he asked as he looked down at Amy.

She smiled and said, "I thought you were talking about your mother."

He kissed her, then they began their joint narration of the long ride across the Great Plains.

Ross gave a more detailed account of their journey from southwest Dakota Territory to Cheyenne than he had before, and Amy assisted in the details from the start.

When the story finally ended, his father said, "The army lost one of their best, I think."

Amy replied, "But if they hadn't, I wouldn't be alive and have him for my husband. I'll take the trade."

His father then asked, "What are you going to do, Ross?"

"I think tomorrow or the next day, Henry will go over to the Mandrake's to collect his money. They'll say they gave the draft to me and he'll come here to claim it. I'm going to try to talk him into surrendering, but I doubt if he will. It may come down to one of us killing the other. I don't know how good he is with his pistol. I know I'm better than most, but it's always an iffy proposition. I'll have to play it by ear."

"You do what you need to do, Son. I know this is hard. He may be a monster, but he's still your brother."

"The sad thing is, Papa, that I don't think he'd have a second thought about killing me. As long as he could get away with it, he'd do it."

"You may be right."

―――

Six miles away, Henry was thinking about the cattle, too. He was on his horse and headed for the Rocking M to collect the money that would make him a free man.

―――

Ross asked them about the farm, and his father told him it was doing very well, and they had a good farm manager, which allowed them to make the trip. The dairy business was booming, and they had expanded their line of cheeses which were going to be sold as far away as San Francisco and New York.

―――

A few miles away, due south at the Rocking M, Henry Braxton had turned down the access road. He was almost giddy knowing that he was going to make it after all. He must have passed a half dozen wanted posters with his name on them, but no one noticed him. He trotted his horse right near the front steps and stepped down, not bothering to wait to be invited. He walked across the front porch and knocked.

Less than a minute later, it was answered by Mildred Mandrake, who swung the door wide and stood staring, shocked to see him there even though they were warned he might be coming around after the cattle sale.

"What do you want, Henry Braxton," she finally said with venom in her voice as loudly as possible without shouting.

On hearing his name, the children did as they'd been told, and hustled into a bedroom, closing and locking the door behind them.

"I've come to collect my money that you owe me. Where's your husband?"

"You stay right there. You smell so bad that I don't want you in my house."

"Well, too bad. Just for that, I'm coming in."

He pushed the door open and walked inside past a stunned Millie who was already covering her nose with her handkerchief.

"Mandrake! Where are you? I want my money!" he shouted as he strode across the parlor.

Arthur had heard the exchange between his wife and Henry and had started to rise as soon as it started, unhooking the hammer loop from his revolver as he stood. He normally didn't wear one, but after he sold the cattle, he was expecting this visit. He walked out into the main room and was assaulted by Henry's powerfully bad odor.

"What are you doing in my house? I specifically heard my wife tell you not to enter," he snapped.

"I just come for my money. Give it to me and I'll be out of here."

"I don't have your money. Your brother Ross showed up and showed me a certified copy of the deed showing that he was a half-owner of the ranch, and threatened to sue me, so I gave the voucher to him. He's at the Box B now."

Henry exclaimed, "*My brother? Ross is at the Box B?* That no good bastard! *Who does he think he is coming here and taking my money?* Well, you'll just have to give me that amount or I'll sue you, too."

"It doesn't work that way. You'll have to hash that out with your brother. He said if you had a problem, you could try to take it away from him. Personally, I can call one of my hands right now and have you thrown off my property. I'll notify the sheriff as well."

At the mention of the sheriff, Henry changed his tune.

"Alright. Alright. Don't get your dander up. I'll go get my money from my little brother. He'll be sorry he ever messed with me."

Henry turned and headed back out the door, leaving it open as he crossed onto the porch.

As soon as he was mounted and riding away, Millie said, "Open all the windows, Arthur. I don't care how cold it is. I thought I was going to pass out from the stench. I'll throw some more wood on the fire, too."

———

Henry was more than just angry, he was mind-crushing furious. He knew that Ross's name was on the deed, but Ross hadn't done a damned thing in the past eight years except be a cute little soldier-boy. He didn't know the army let such sissies be officers. *What was next? Were they gonna give women guns and let them go to war?* And now he had shown up and taken what was rightfully his. He reached the gate, unlatched it, and swung it wide, not bothering to close it. If the cattle got out, too bad.

Twenty minutes later, Henry looked down at the ranch, saw the smoke rising from both the fireplace chimney and the cooking stove pipe and knew that Ross was there. He set the horse to a trot and rode down the long rise toward the house, then slowed the horse to a walk to reduce the noise as he headed for the front of the house. He saw the two buggies out front with the gelding tied off behind one of them, and wondered who was visiting, but it didn't matter. He was in charge now.

He stepped down, flipped his reins over the hitching post, then pulled his Colt, cocked the hammer and stepped quietly onto the porch. He could hear laughter inside, and somehow that irritated him even more than he had been before, but he'd end that soon enough.

He reached the door, yanked it open, and quickly stepped inside, his pistol leveled.

He was momentarily stunned when he saw his parents sitting with his baby brother and that bizarre gray-haired woman as they all stared at him, but they were just as surprised as he was, and he quickly recovered.

"Well, well. What do we have here? A family reunion?" he asked with a sarcastic laugh.

He glared at his parents and then switched to Ross.

"Ross, you drop your guns, or I start shooting, starting with our dear mother. She always did favor you because you were more of a woman than she was."

Ross was stunned that Henry had shown up that early and was threatening to shoot his own mother. He had no choice, so he unbuckled his guns and let them drop to the floor, already trying to come up with some way to stop him.

"Now, kick them over here."

Ross kept his eyes on Henry as he kicked the guns six feet across the floor to his older brother. He had read his eyes and was sure that he'd shoot every one of them even if he got the money. Somehow, he had to take control of this situation.

"Well, you finally did something smart. Where's my money?" he demanded.

"What money?" Ross asked.

"My six thousand dollars from Mandrake! Don't go trying to fool me!" he shouted.

"I haven't gotten a dime from Mandrake. I went over there a week ago and showed him the deed, so I could get some information. I never asked for any money. I don't need it. He must have been saying that so he could get rid of you and get some of his hands together for protection."

"You're lyin'!" he snarled.

"You know better than that. I don't lie. Besides, I only came here to see how you were doing. As it turns out you've been downright evil, big brother. Beating your wife and finally killing her. The sheriff put out wanted posters on you and has notified other law enforcement agencies. Now, I would like nothing more than to give you your money and let you get out of here without hurting anyone. So, why don't you give up the gun, surrender to the authorities and go to trial. You'll get a fair trial, and there are no witnesses to the murder other than young children, and they make terrible witnesses. You might even get off. If you run, you'll be gunned down by someone for sure.

Be smart for once in your life, Henry. You've got no chance on the road."

Henry actually gave it some thought. He knew he'd be hunted, and he knew that sissy he may be, his brother never lied. That damned Mandrake had tricked him.

"Well, little brother, all pleasantries aside, I don't think I'll take your suggestion. I'm gonna head back to Mandrake's and he's gonna give me that money or I'll just plug his wife. He may even have to give me a lot more."

"You'll never make it, Henry. As soon as you get near to the house, they'll gun you down. That wanted poster is dead or alive."

It wasn't as far as Ross knew, but it could be.

Henry had to come up with a solution, then he looked at the faces looking up at him and smiled.

He shifted his pistol from Ross to their mother and said, "Now here's what's gonna happen, little Rossie. I'm gonna take our mother with me as a hostage. I'll have a gun pointed right at her head, and if I see one of your toes step outta this house, she dies. You got that, baby brother? And her dying will be on your head."

"I understand. No one will leave the house."

"You promise me, honest boy?"

"I promise you that no one will leave the house."

"Let's go, mama," Henry said as he twitched the pistol's barrel up and down.

"No. Take me," said Amy as she stood.

Henry turned to Amy, sneered and asked, "Who cares about someone like you?"

"I'm Ross's wife," she replied as she stared defiantly at him.

Henry smiled, and said, "Is that so, little brother? You finally grew a pair and found some stupid woman to take you? But I like the idea anyway. I figured he'd worry some about his old mama, but now, he'll worry a lot more about his precious new wife. Maybe she volunteered because she wants to get away from you, girlie boy, and sample a real man."

Ross knew that Amy was only thinking of his mother, and his plan for saving his mother would actually be easier with Amy because she knew first-hand what he could do.

He looked into those bright green, defiant eyes and said, "Don't worry, sweetheart. Stay sharp. Remember the first time we met, Sioux."

Henry didn't remember her name, because he didn't care, but said, "Now, isn't that sweet. Let's go, Sue. I'll be right behind you with this Colt."

Amy looked at Ross and nodded, letting him know that she got his message. Ross was going to go for a long shot with the Sharps and he'd be in the house, so Henry wouldn't see the gunsmoke. She'd be trusting her new husband with her life yet again and didn't doubt for a moment that she'd be returning to him soon. It was their wedding night, after all.

"Alright," she said, then turned her green eyes to her husband of just four hours and said, "I trust you, Ross."

Ross kept his eyes on her and smiled at her to let her know that she was safe.

Henry shoved the gun muzzle into Amy's spine, and backed out of the house. It wasn't too cold out there, about forty degrees, and the weather was very much on Amy's mind as she felt for the wind. One of their many conversations was about his long shots when she had first seen him, and he had explained about the effects of wind, temperature and altitude on the bullet's flight. She was pleased to note the absence of any appreciable wind.

Once outside, Henry turned her around to walk down the porch steps. She mounted Ross's gelding and Henry stepped to his horse, keeping his pistol on Amy, before they started walking the horses toward the south and the Rocking M.

"Swing wide," Henry ordered, "I want at least a hundred yards when we go past the house."

Amy angled the gelding to her right to add the distance, and also adding some concern because Henry seemed to think that Ross might shoot him from the house with a Winchester. She could only hope that once they were more than two hundred yards away, he'd stop looking behind him.

"What can we do, Ross?" said his father said as they all stood in the front room.

"I have to stay in the house, Papa. I promised I would."

"That promise doesn't matter. He has Amy and you have to do something."

"All promises matter, Papa, or none do, but I am definitely going to do something, and Amy already knows because I told her."

He wanted to give Henry enough of a lead that he would think he was safe.

His mother asked, "When did you tell her? I didn't hear you say anything?"

Ross looked at his mother and said, "Her name isn't Sue, Mama."

She didn't understand what he meant but didn't ask for clarification as it would soon be too late to do anything. Why Ross wasn't hurrying surprised her.

"So, what can we do?" his father asked.

"We wait for another thirty seconds."

"Then what?"

"Then, Papa, I fulfill my promise to Amy."

Neither parent had heard a promise in what he had said to his new bride but didn't say anything as there just wasn't time.

After another few seconds, Ross started walking to the kitchen as his parents followed.

Ross looked out the kitchen window from the back of the kitchen and could see Henry and Amy about two hundred yards out.

Ross yanked open the kitchen window, pulled the chair from next to the table and placed it a few feet behind the open window, then turned and opened the pantry. He pulled out the first Sharps and then his parents understood his plan, and his mother understood why he had called his wife Sue.

Ross slid a giant round into the breech and closed it, then cocked the hammer. He had already run the variables a half a dozen times in his head after he made his decision about what to do. They were at almost seven thousand feet, and the temperature was about forty degrees, with a light wind blowing from the west at about three mph. He set the ladder sight for six hundred and fifty yards. He knew they'd be further away, but those were the numbers he came up with.

Almost six hundred yards away now, Henry knew he was safe. He had checked his back twice but hadn't bothered after three hundred yards. Little brother kept his word as he knew he would and had remained in the house. Henry figured he might just take his woman with him. She was a real looker once you got past that hideous gray hair.

Using the windowsill as a support, Ross sighted his target and aimed slightly left of Henry's chest. He released the first trigger, held his breath, then slowly squeezed the second.

The Sharps' hammer dropped, the firing pin struck the cartridge, igniting the powder inside and the chemical reaction began. A small fraction of a second later, the large bullet spun down the long, rifled barrel ahead of the rapidly expanding cloud of hot gases and by the time the .45 caliber projectile left the muzzle it was traveling at almost fourteen hundred feet per second. The angle of the barrel was a little more than seven degrees, and the loud sonic wave followed the round. It would catch up to the slowing bullet just before it found its target. The cloud of gunpowder residue filled the kitchen as the loud boom of the gun echoed throughout the house.

The bullet raced toward its target, rising as it did. It climbed until it was nineteen feet above the ground, then began to lose speed and momentum as gravity tugged it back to earth, the drag slowed it down, and it began to drop. It was still traveling at over seven hundred feet per second as it descended toward Henry and was only eleven feet above the ground when it struck. Ross had aimed for the center of his brother's chest to give him some margin for error and he needed it, because he had slightly miscalculated the effect of the altitude and missed his aiming point by seven inches.

Instead of the center of his chest, it struck high. It hit Henry at seventh cervical vertebral body, just at the base of the neck. He suddenly felt the punch as the massive piece of lead transferred its kinetic energy to destructive force that destroyed the critical bone and the protection it afforded the spinal cord.

Henry didn't die immediately. He lost all control of his muscles as the large bullet ripped through his spinal cord and then out through the front of his neck. His heart and lungs stopped working and he toppled over. As he fell to the ground, still conscious and seeing the world slide past him, he heard the report of the big gun and knew. His sissy younger brother had kept his promise, shot him from inside the house and killed him anyway. He watched as the ground suddenly filled his vision and still felt the impact for a fraction of a second before he died, then twisted in a cloud of dust.

Amy heard the report at the same time that Henry fell from his saddle, knowing her trust in her husband had not been unwarranted. She watched Henry slam into the dirt, but didn't wait to see if he was dead or alive as she wheeled the horse back to the ranch house and set him to a gallop.

Ross had exited the house after he had seen Henry drop and knew he couldn't have survived both the shot and the fall, but he wasn't worried about his dead brother. Now he just wanted his wife back.

His father turned from the still-open window, then turned to his wife, put his arms around her and said, "It's all over, Emily. Henry is dead. Ross got him and Amy's coming back."

She rested her head on his chest and began to cry quietly. Not for her dead son, but for her live daughter-in-law who had offered herself in her place. They heard her horse come racing into the yard, and they both looked through the window.

Amy didn't wait for it to stop, as she leapt down and landed in her husband's arms.

She kissed him, then said, "I never had a doubt, Ross. I knew what you were going to do."

"I had to be really sure, Amy. I spent a little extra time having to be positive about my calculations, but it all doesn't matter now. You're back with me."

Ross took control of his horse and tied him at the back rail, then they stepped up onto the porch, walked into the kitchen and found his parents looking at them.

Emily walked up to Amy and hugged her tightly, saying, "Thank you, Amy. That was a brave thing you did."

Amy looked at her mother and replied, "Mama, I knew what Ross was going to do and trusted him. I wasn't afraid," she paused and looked at Ross, and added, "I'm never afraid when I'm with Ross."

Ross looked at his wife and said, "I'm going to go and put Henry on his horse, then I'll follow my parents back into town and see the sheriff to let him know what happened. Then I'll come home, okay?"

"Don't be too late, Ross. It is our wedding night," Amy reminded him.

"I haven't forgotten, sweetheart."

He turned to his father and said, "Papa, I'll need you and mama to stop by with me at the sheriff's office. They'll probably want statements."

"Okay, Son. Do you need help with Henry?"

"No, Papa. I'll handle it. I'll be back in twenty minutes"

He walked out of the kitchen, closed the door and stepped up on the gelding. Amy watched him from the kitchen window. It was still open, but she wanted to watch him as long as she could.

"How many other women have wedding days like this?" she thought.

When she thought a bit longer, she couldn't recall any that had hands-off, no-words-of-love courtships that involved fighting off Sioux warriors, either. She just hoped that their wedding night would be just as memorable as their wedding day, and knowing her husband, she didn't doubt it for a moment.

———

After reaching Henry's body, Ross saw that Henry's horse had stayed right where it had been when Henry had been hit. Ross thought it odd until he got close and saw that Henry's foot was still caught in the stirrup and had rolled, twisting the leather into a corkscrew. He was on the ground acting as an anchor to the horse.

He stepped down and looked at the odd positioning and had to get Henry's body onto the horse, but he didn't want to ruin the saddle, so he rolled Henry twice counterclockwise which allowed him to pull his foot from the stirrup.

Ross tied a trail rope to Henry's horse and hitched it to his gelding, then knelt down closer to Henry's body.

"Good God! Does he stink!" he exclaimed as his eyes watered.

Ross held his breath and hoisted him onto the horse, tossed him over the saddle and then tied him down.

"That's three disgusting smelling corpses I've had to deal with," he thought.

Henry may not have reached the level of bad odor exuded by the deserters, but he was getting close. He hoped his coat wasn't too foul.

He rode the seven hundred yards back to the ranch house and attached both horses to his rented buggy.

He returned to the house finding his parents already dressed for the cold.

"Okay, Papa you drive the first buggy and I'll follow you into Cheyenne in the second trailing the horses."

"Okay, Ross."

Ross then walked over to Amy, gave her a soft kiss and said, "Will you be all right, Amy?"

She nodded and replied, "I'll wear my pistol, but I don't think it'll be necessary. I'll be fine. Just come home to me as soon as you can, husband."

He smiled, touched her cheek with his fingertips, then pulled on his gloves and said, "I'll be right back."

He and his parents walked outside, boarded the buggies and set out for Cheyenne as Ross followed them with the two trailing horses. His father set a rapid pace, knowing that Ross had Amy waiting for him.

As they were driving, Emily turned to her husband and asked, "Could we have stopped this, Walter? Could we have done anything about this monster that we created?"

Walter answered without looking her way, saying, "No, Emily. It's like Ross said, some are just born bad. Let's just be grateful for the son we do have. Ross is happy with his wife and it's easy to understand why. Amy is a wonderful woman, and they are absolutely perfect for each other. All we can do is thank God that Henry didn't hurt anyone else. The children will be well-cared for and hopefully they will forget all this. We have a son and daughter-in-law to be proud of, and, unless I am sadly mistaken, we'll have a new grandchild within a year."

She smiled at him, hugged onto his arm tightly and said, "Thank you, Walter."

Ross had told them where to turn to get to the sheriff's office, so as soon as they reached the jail, they parked the buggies in front and stepped down. Ross held the door open for them as they filed inside.

"Hello, Ross. What can I do for you?" asked Deputy Brewster.

"I need to see the Sheriff again, John. You're welcome to sit in. These are my parents from Minnesota."

"Nice to meet you, folks. Come on back."

They walked back to Elias' office and Brewster did his perfunctory knock on the door jamb.

"Sheriff, Ross is here with his parents."

"Come on in, Ross," he said, and when Ross and his parents entered, he asked, "What can I do for you?"

"Elias, we're going to need a bigger room. I'll need at least four chairs. Five if you want John to take notes."

"That serious, huh?"

"Yup."

"Let's go across the hall. John, bring in an extra chair."

Deputy Brewster grabbed the chair from the sheriff's office, and they all entered a large interview room. Ross and his parents sat on one side and the two lawmen on the other.

"Okay, Ross, what do you have?"

"This afternoon, about two hours ago, Henry entered the ranch house with his gun drawn. He got the drop on me and threatened to shoot our mother. He demanded his money, but I told him I didn't have it and that Arthur Mandrake had never given it to me. He was going to take my mother hostage to the Mandrakes to get his money. My wife, Amy, volunteered to take her place."

"Hold on a second, Ross. Amy is your wife? Isn't that the married woman that you brought across the territories with you? The married woman you were all aflutter about and still sent her to her husband in Oregon three days ago?"

"The very same. Her old husband had annulled the marriage because he thought she was dead and then remarried. Had two kids, too. She got there, found out, and came back this morning. We got married a half hour later."

"Damn! Oh! Excuse my language, Mrs. Braxton."

"That's perfectly understandable, Sheriff," she said smiling.

"Anyway, he made me promise that we would stay in the house while he kept the gun on Amy. I promised, and he knows I never break promises. But Amy knew what I was going to do. She rode out with him across the fields toward the Mandrakes. She knew I was going to use the Sharps and began drifting slightly to the right to give me a little more flexibility. Then, I just opened a window and took him out with the Sharps."

"What was the distance, out of curiosity."

"Seven hundred yards."

"Seven hundred yards?"

"It's a good rifle, Elias."

"So, do you want to make a statement tonight, or tomorrow."

"Tomorrow will be better. We can stop by around nine o'clock or so, and then my parents can return to the ranch. My father and I are going to do some target shooting with the Sharps."

"I wouldn't mind that, myself, if you'll let me."

"After the statements, come along, but we have his body outside. We probably need to get it out of the street. Just a word of warning, though, it smells really bad."

"We've seen 'em before, Ross. John, do you want to take care of that? I'll see you folks here at nine."

He shook Ross and Walter's hands and tipped his hat to Emily.

They went outside, and it didn't take long for Deputy Brewster to realize that Ross hadn't exaggerated. John was untying the horse with Henry's body and said as he walked away with his nose crinkled, "Smelling bad doesn't do this justice, Ross."

"Sorry, John."

They were preparing to enter the buggies when Emily asked Ross, "Was it that bad, Ross?"

"When Amy and I ran into those two deserters in Dakota Territory, I had to bury them both and I thought they were the foulest-smelling men that walked the face of the earth until I got a whiff of Henry. I don't think he'd taken a bath in a month. I'm surprised you didn't notice in the house."

"I was too terrified."

"I understand, but I'm sure that Amy has the windows open and is burning some of the birch that was out back in the woodpile to help."

His parents boarded their buggy, and Ross climbed aboard his as they left the sheriff's office. Ross dropped his parents off at the hotel, attached the second buggy to the first, then drove them back to the livery where they had been rented, and mounted his gelding. He rode east so he could swing by the Mandrakes to let them know, and the sun was setting when he entered the access road.

He stepped down and wrapped his reins around the rail, then stepped up onto the porch, walked to the front door and gave it a hard couple of raps. The door stayed closed and he heard Mildred shout from inside, "Is that you, Braxton?"

He almost laughed, but shouted back "Mildred, I am a Braxton too, you know."

The door was yanked open and she said, "Come in. Come in, Ross. Henry stopped by earlier and we didn't know what happened."

She shouted, "Arthur, Ross is here!" as Ross entered, and then closed the door.

A few seconds later, Arthur walked out of his office and was obviously relieved that it was Ross who had returned and not Henry.

Before either could say anything, Ross asked, "Could I speak to Alice and David, please?"

Mildred said loudly, "Alice, David, your Uncle Ross would like to talk to you."

Ross heard a bedroom door open and then light footsteps before Alice and David popped into the room with smiles on their faces. He swore they looked like they'd gained weight already, but even if they hadn't, they looked so much better.

They walked up to Ross as he sat on his heels and said, "Alice, David, I just returned from talking to the sheriff. A little while ago, your papa showed up and threatened to shoot your grandmother who had come with your grandfather to see you both, but he took my new wife, Amy, the pretty lady I was with instead, and when they were riding away from the house to come here, I shot him. Your papa is dead for what he did to your mama, so you don't have to worry about him anymore."

Alice asked, "Then are we going to go home with you, Uncle Ross?"

"Do you want to come home with me, or would you rather stay here and grow up with Mildred?"

Alice turned and smiled at Mildred, who had her hand over her mouth as tears formed in her eyes, and said, "We really like you, Uncle Ross, but David and I want to stay here, if that's alright."

Ross glanced up at Mildred, smiled, then looked back at Alice and said, "I think that's a wonderful idea, Alice, and they will adopt you, so they will become your new papa and mama."

Alice and David both turned and trotted to Mildred who was happily crying as she dropped to her knees and hugged both children.

Ross stood and looked over at Arthur who was wiping tears from his eyes as he watched his wife, then looked over at Ross.

"I'll tell you the full story later, Arthur."

He nodded, then Mildred stood, turned to Ross and gave him a hug then kissed him on the cheek.

Then she stepped back, and asked, "Did I hear you correctly? You just got married?"

"This morning. She's waiting for me at the ranch house."

"Then what in God's name are you doing here?" she asked firmly, but still had a big smile on her face when she did.

"I was returning from Cheyenne, so I thought I'd swing by. Trust me, I'm not staying long."

"Before you go, Ross, here's the draft for the sale of the cattle," Arthur said as pulled the draft out of his pocket and handed it to him.

Ross thanked him then folded it and put it in his pocket.

"Aren't you even going to look at it?" Arthur asked.

"I trust you, Arthur. I don't need to."

"Maybe you should, Ross," Emily suggested.

Ross took it out and instead of the $5796 he expected he saw $8694.

"This is way too much, Arthur."

"No, Emily and I decided that if you were getting the money, you'd get the full price of the cattle. I made a few hundred off the sale, so don't feel bad."

"I appreciate it, Arthur."

They shook hands and Ross gave a wave to the happy new family, left the house, popped down the stairs, jumped onto the gelding and rode north across the pastures at a fast trot. He went through the still open gate, closed it behind him, then rode down to the house. Forty-five minutes later, he had unsaddled the gelding and trotted into the house.

He noticed that the windows were closed and wondered if Amy had opened them while he was gone.

After they entered the house and closed the door behind him, he was hanging his coat when he heard a rush of footsteps, turned, and was violently assaulted by Amy, who came charging out of the hallway and threw herself into him.

Ross caught her in his arms and wasn't sure if he kissed her first or she kissed him. It didn't matter, as they stayed locked together for as long as they could before they needed some oxygen.

When they finally separated and just smiled at each other, Ross said, "Well, I have to admit, that was one welcome welcoming, my beautiful bride."

"You deserve it, my incredible husband. I've been waiting here anxiously. We've waited so long. There were times out there in that tent that I wanted to slip out of my clothes and bedroll and slide in next to you."

He stepped back and noticed that she was wearing the dress she wore in Scotts Bluff.

"Can I tell you now that when you were in the hallway of that hotel in Scotts Bluff in that dress that you took my breath away? And then, when you wore those riding pants, I thought I'd died and gone to heaven. You were nothing short of spectacular, Amy, and it killed me not to tell you."

She smiled and said, "I thought you weren't interested. I was interested when I saw you taking your bath that day and wanted you to watch me taking mine."

"I know you watched, and I wish that I had. But, now, my love, I'm going to get to see what I missed."

Amy pulled herself against him and whispered in a sultry voice, "Take me into the bedroom and I'll do more than let you watch."

He kissed her and then took her hand and they walked slowly to the bedroom, and once inside Amy turned to close the door, then saw Ross's smile and said, "I guess there's no point in closing it, is there?"

"No, my love, we have the whole house to ourselves with no prying eyes to see us."

Amy was already excited just by her anticipation of what was going to happen, but even she couldn't have imagined what did. She had done her wifely duties with Aaron in the few months they were married before he left, but that was years ago and wasn't very inspiring, but Ross inspired her from that first kiss.

When he began to touch her softly, she began to let herself go and Ross talked to her and told her what he would do to make her feel his love and become aroused by his caresses, and then told her to tell him what she wanted, which surprised and pleased her.

When they first started, Amy just made short, quiet requests, but as her passion and pure lust began to explode inside her, she found that she could barely restrain herself as she almost ripped Ross's clothes from that masculine body she had seen stepping out of the river.

Then, as they finally stood naked in the bedroom, he stepped back holding her hands, admiring her, then said, "You are so perfect, Amy. And now, my wife, I will make you feel every bit of pleasure that you could imagine."

Amy closed her eyes and said, "Please."

Ross then scooped her up from the floor, as she held onto his neck with her eyes still closed and laid her gently on the bed.

Amy let him explore her body with his kisses and touches for almost two minutes as she let her hands wander over him, all with her eyes still closed to savor each gentle touch, each kiss.

Then, she suddenly opened her eyes, and pulled him close and kissed him passionately and Amy threw all inhibitions aside and their lovemaking escalated to a frenetic, and boisterous exhibition that only they could see and experience.

Ross wanted her so badly that he was in agony as he continued to kiss her and feel her perfection. Her gray hair flew about the bed as her bright green eyes flashed and danced.

Amy didn't care anymore, she wanted Ross and she wanted him now as she shouted and demanded that he take her, and Ross knew he couldn't resist her for another second.

The house echoed with shouts and cries of passion as they consummated their marriage with just as much excitement as they had begun their relationship, and probably even more.

———

Early in the morning, before the sun had risen, they awakened under the blankets and quilts wrapped together having spent most of the night either resting or not resting.

After a quick run to the privy, sans clothing even in the cold air, they returned to their cozy bed and resumed their tightly held positioning.

Ross brushed aside some of her gray hair, looked into her eyes and asked, "Amy, have I told you that I love you yet this hour?"

"Twice. But I'm not really keeping track," she replied as she snuggled in tighter.

"Amy, I forgot to mention that I picked up the payment for the cattle on the way back"

Amy had no idea of cattle markets, so she asked the perfectly innocent question, "And how much was that?"

"$8694."

Amy bolted upright. An event not without its advantages to Ross's eyes.

"How much?"

He repeated his answer, but before she slid back under the blankets, he slid his hands under her magnificent breasts and kissed each one to let her know that their wedding night wasn't ending with the sunrise.

After another passionate hour, they lay under the quilts, bathed in perspiration as Amy's head lay on his chest.

She sighed, then asked, "Are you going to keep interrupting me like this?"

"Show me your breasts again and I'll interrupt you every time."

She smiled then said, "I'll remember that," then asked, "What were we talking about?"

"The money from the cattle?"

"Oh, that's right. I seem to have forgotten for some reason. So, what are you going to do with all that money?"

"I have no idea. It's our money now, sweetheart. So's this ranch. I just don't know what we should do with it. I don't want it. Maybe we should just sell it after I get a job."

"Have you decided what you want to do?"

He slid his hand along her hip and said, "What I'd like to do and what I need to do are two different things, but I think I'll apply with the Union Pacific. It'll probably mean a move, though, probably to their headquarters in Omaha. It's a lot bigger than Cheyenne, and it's also closer to my parents' farm."

"Well, let's worry about that later and do what you want to do now."

"Again? You must think that I'm some sort of stallion."

She pulled the quilts back, then took his hand and placed it on her left breast before saying, "I thought you said that this would inspire you?"

It did, so his necessary trip to Cheyenne was delayed, at least for another hour or so.

When the sun had been up for an hour, Amy was making breakfast, Ross was dressed and walked up close behind Amy and kissed her on her neck.

"Amy, I'll be riding to Cheyenne to write my statement about Henry, then swing by the bank and deposit this little piece of paper, and after that, I'll be coming back with my parents and maybe the sheriff. He and my father want to try the Sharps. Did you want me to bring anything back when I return?"

She turned, look into his hazel green eyes and said, "Nothing that I can think of. I'm still trying to believe that I'm here with you and not in Oregon with Aaron. It was so scary, Ross, the thought of never seeing you again."

"I felt the same way. That's why I bought the necklace. For some inexplicable reason, I felt that if you had it, you'd come back to me. That's why I gave you so much money, too. I was hoping you'd buy a return ticket. You have no idea the lengths I was planning to come and steal you back."

She fingered the opal necklace and said, "I'll never take this off, you know."

He hugged her softly, but had to admit he was exhausted, but it was a very satisfying exhaustion.

She smiled and said, "You'd better have something to eat. We both burned off a lot of energy last night."

"And this morning, and will do so again tonight, I believe."

"Naturally. Now, eat."

They sat down and had their breakfast of bacon, eggs and coffee as Amy remembered that first time that she had bacon and eggs with Ross on their second day. She could never have imagined at the time that it would lead to this breakfast.

————

Ross left the ranch and arrived at the livery and rented the buggy again for his parents. He found them in the lobby and took his mother's arm outside to the buggy.

It was as cold as it normally was in early December in the high plains, but his parents grew up in Minnesota, so this wasn't bad at all to them.

They rode to the sheriff's office and wrote out their statements. He had expected that they might need Amy's as well, but the sheriff told him that it wasn't likely. The prosecutor had already declared it justifiable homicide, so there was no chance of charges being filed.

After leaving the sheriff's office, Ross stopped briefly at the bank and deposited the large draft from the cattle sale and then they headed back to the empty ranch with the sheriff trotting behind them bundled up on his horse.

They returned to the ranch just before noon, and everyone stayed around the big fire in the main room to enjoy the heat, and after they had warmed up, Amy served a hot meal which was deeply appreciated.

After lunch, cold or not, the men went outside to shoot the big gun. Ross brought both Sharps and set up targets at four hundred, five hundred, and seven hundred yards. That took a while just to get ready, but when it was done, they took turns using the same rifle so there was no advantage gained.

Walter hit the four hundred, but neither of the others. Elias hit the five hundred, but neither of the other two. Ross, of course, hit them all.

Finally, the cold drove them back inside, and after he had warmed up, the sheriff made his farewells and returned to Cheyenne.

After he was gone, Emily asked, "Well, Braxton boys, was freezing your back end off worth it to shoot that big gun?"

Walter replied, "It was. And as our generous son has given me one of them, you might as well get used to it happening when we get back to Minnesota."

"What are your travel plans, Papa?" Ross asked.

"We already have our tickets for tomorrow morning's train. The same one that Amy arrived on yesterday."

"After we see you off, I plan on stopping by the Union Pacific office and applying for a position as an engineer. Most likely, I'll be assigned to their Omaha headquarters, although it's possible I'll be assigned to the field. We'll see. If I am assigned to Omaha, then it'll be a fairly short train ride up to the farm, and we'd be able to visit more often."

"Rossie, that would be wonderful," said his mother

"What will you do with the ranch?" asked his father asked.

Ross turned to his new wife and asked, "Amy, what do you think? It's your ranch, too."

"Ross, whatever you decide is fine. I have no real attachment to the place," she answered.

"I think I'll go and talk to Arthur. If nothing else, I'll let him use the pastures and keep an eye on the ranch house."

"Ross, how do you carry one of those big guns on the train? Do you put it in the baggage car?"

"I've never had the problem before, but I don't know if I'd put it in the baggage car. Ideally, you'd get a case made for it and carry it with you, but I'll tell you what. I'll ship the Sharps, the Winchester and the Smith & Wesson to you rather than you having to take them with you. They'd be a bit heavy to take, anyway."

"That would be good."

"I'll include ammunition for all of them. I've been keeping an eye on those new Winchester '76 models that are showing up. They use a different cartridge but have more power. I suppose it doesn't matter if I'm living in a city like Omaha, but it sure looks nice."

Amy and Emily prepared a fancy dinner as Walter and Emily would be leaving in the morning. After dinner, Walter and Emily departed for their hotel, leaving the newlyweds to their privacy. They hadn't even turned onto the road to Cheyenne before Ross and Amy were taking advantage of that privacy.

————

Ross was up early and started the cookstove fire and then built up the one in the fireplace until it was blazing and filling the chilled room with heat. He returned to the bedroom, stopping for a short while to give Amy a morning kiss and cold hand on her warm body that brought a rapid and unwelcome response, but after his hand warmed up, the response was much better.

He started breakfast as Amy made the hazardous journey to the privy and back. She was freezing when she returned and wrapped her arms around Ross and got a little payback when she placed her freezing right hand on his nice warm neck.

They had breakfast, then prepared for the cold ride into Cheyenne, and Amy decided to add her cut up union suit to her day's wardrobe. Ross went outside and saddled their horses then brought them out front.

"Amy, I hate to do this to you. Are you sure you don't want to stay? I'm sure my parents would understand."

Amy stepped out onto the porch, her breath leaving clouds before her face.

"I'm not going to let your parents go without saying goodbye. It's just a little cold. You forget I grew up in Dakota Territory."

She boarded her horse and Ross climbed on the gelding. After the initial shock of hitting the cold saddles, things warmed up a bit from the heat of the horses, but it was still nasty cold. Ross guessed it was close to zero and there was that damned wind. It wasn't too bad, but it was coming straight out of the west into their faces. He would look over at Amy every minute or so to make sure she was all right, and just simply to look at Amy. She had her scarf over her lower half of her face, but she still looked cold. Ross had the horses going at a fast trot, but it would seem like a much longer ride to the hotel today.

They reached the hotel forty minutes later, stepped down outside, and Ross insisted that Amy go inside while he left the horses in the relative warmth of the livery. Amy gratefully accepted his offer and trotted inside while Ross dropped them off and quickly returned to the hotel lobby.

He was just beginning to feel like he was human again when his parents arrived from their room. They had eaten breakfast earlier, so they all settled into seats in the lobby to await their train. There was a schedule board posted in the hotel lobby showing the progress and estimated arrival times of the trains. As the trains made their stops, quick messages would be sent to stations down the line with any changes. The nine o'clock train was running on time and would arrive in Cheyenne in thirty minutes.

"Papa and Mama, I'm happy that you came. I know it was difficult, but I was glad to have you meet Amy and be here for our wedding."

His mother said, "Ross, that will be the most memorable day of our lives. I know it ended with a tragedy, but it was far outweighed by the joy we saw as you and Amy were reunited. I can't imagine what those days leading up to that moment were like for the two of you, but the end was worth all the angst, I'm sure."

"It was, Mama. I can't tell you what it was like reading that telegram from Amy saying she was returning as Amy Sorensen. Did I tell you that I gave the messenger a ten-dollar tip? I told him it was worth every penny."

His parents laughed and Amy asked, "Do you still have that telegram?"

"Of course, I do. Right now, it's in my money belt. Once we're settled, I'll keep it someplace more secure. I'm never losing it."

She smiled at him and took his hand.

A few minutes later, they heard the train whistle and had to start getting ready for the departure. Because of the cold, they, along with the other departing passengers, decided to make their farewells in the hotel lobby.

Ross shook his father's hand and received a massive bear hug. As his father was hugging Amy and receiving his goodbye kiss, Ross picked up his mother and kissed her gently on the cheek.

He returned her softly to the floor and said, "We'll be visiting soon, Mama."

She nodded and wiped a few tears from her eyes.

One last wave and his parents left the hotel lobby, then boarded the east-bound train for Omaha before they would have to head north to their equally cold home in Minnesota.

"Well, Ross, do we head back home now?" Amy asked.

"Let's stay for some coffee before we brave that weather and give the sun a chance to warm it up just a little bit."

She smiled and said, "You are a brilliant man, my husband," as she latched onto his arm.

Three hours later, they were sitting on their couch locked together as the fire popped and crackled before them.

"This is so peaceful, Ross. I'm waiting for some evil man to crash through the door with guns blazing. We need a few days of just being able to relax as husband and wife."

While still looking at the fire, Ross replied, "If we're spending time as husband and wife, I don't see much relaxing in that."

She smacked him in the back of the head as she laughed, then said, "You know what I mean."

He laughed and replied, "You left yourself wide open. I had to take advantage."

"Yes, I did. You seem to always take advantage of me when I give you the chance."

"And there are advantages to you when I take those advantages, ma'am," he replied with a smile but expecting another head smack.

Instead of a head smack, Amy pulled him closer and said softly, "Then take advantage of me often, sir."

They enjoyed the next three days taking advantage of each other often, and just enjoying quiet times as a new husband and wife.

There was still plenty of food and Amy showed her skills in cooking many things that Ross had never had before.

On the fourth day, the weather finally warmed to a balmy thirty degrees. They shared breakfast, which included flapjacks in addition to their normal bacon and eggs.

"Amy, I'm going to go into Cheyenne to apply for that job today. I'm also bringing in the guns to ship to my father. Did you want to stay or come along? It'll be boring."

"I'll stay. I want to bake something different."

"That's fine. I'll be back a little after noon."

He gave her a goodbye kiss. Well, it was a newlywed goodbye kiss, so it lasted a bit longer.

He took one of the Sharps, a box of ammunition, the second Winchester and the outlaw Smith & Wesson along with four boxes of ammunition. It was a heavy load.

He saddled the gelding and put the pack saddle on the pinto. He put all the ammunition and the pistol and belt into a pannier and hooked it on, then slid the Sharps and Winchester on the other side and strapped them down.

Then he set off to Cheyenne. His first stop was to S. Bon Boots, Shoes, Leather and Findings on 16th Street. He went in and explained what he wanted to a very interested clerk, who called over a leather smith who listened to Ross. The craftsman was familiar with the Sharps and after talking to Ross for almost ten minutes got the design drawn on a sheet of paper. Both men were excited with the final plan, and the he said he'd have it done in three days. His next stop was the shipping firm where he dropped off the weapons and ammunition and gave them his father's address in Minnesota. They assured him that they would pack the weapons carefully, so they couldn't move, then he paid for the shipment and got his receipt.

His last stop was the Union Pacific office, and after talking to the receptionist, he was sent to the director of the

Cheyenne headquarters and was welcomed into his private office.

After they took their seats, he asked, "Mr. Braxton, you have an engineering degree from the Military Academy?"

"Yes, sir. Class of '71."

"How were your grades?"

"I finished first in my class."

The man's eyebrows rose as he asked, "Could I ask why you left the army? Usually those who do that well stay until they are generals."

"I loved being in the army. I just decided that I wouldn't take part in raids to attack defenseless Sioux villages, so I resigned my commission."

"Are you friendly with the Sioux?"

"Hardly. I can speak Sioux, but I never had the slightest qualms of killing their warriors. It was my job. But I drew the line at killing women and children. If you and the Union Pacific have a problem with my viewpoint, I'll just leave you now and seek a position elsewhere."

Ross started to rise, and the director said, "No, no, Mr. Braxton! Have a seat, please. I have no such issues. In fact, I applaud you for having the moral courage to do so. Too many of our officers may have similar misgivings but opt to risk their souls rather than their careers."

Ross sat back down.

"Mr. Braxton, I will be honest with you. When I heard that you were a West Point trained engineer, I was ready to offer you a position on the spot. The company is always looking for qualified engineers and is in constant competition with the seemingly never-ending spate of new railroads entering the business daily. Too many of our competitors use self-taught engineers with the expected results. The Union Pacific won't do that. We expect our bridges to stay up and our tunnels to remain open.

"It is difficult to find men of your background and I just needed to be sure you hadn't done something that would cause us problems in dealing with the army in the future. Your explanation dispenses with any such concerns. Now, insofar as your position is concerned. We would initially assign you to our main office in Omaha. Usually junior engineers are then sent to different locations where we are expanding our lines. However, given your background, I will recommend that you be assigned to the Omaha offices. They may not do so, but that will be their decision. I just wanted you to know they could send you elsewhere. They could also send you out on temporary assignments to troubleshoot problems at various sites."

"That could prove interesting."

"If you like excitement, it could be. Your starting salary will be eight thousand dollars per annum. Does all this sound acceptable?"

"Quite."

"Wonderful. I'll have my secretary make up the necessary paperwork. It should take him about a half hour. By the way, are you married, Mr. Braxton?"

"Yes, about a week ago."

"Well, congratulations. Just to let you know that you will be issued a pass that will allow you and your wife to travel on our lines at no cost. We also have agreements with most other major lines to honor each other's employee passes."

"That's a good benefit."

"There are others as well. Mr. Smithers, my secretary will give you all the details. I've set your starting date as the first Monday in February. Is that acceptable?"

"Perfect. It'll give me time to settle my affairs here."

They shook hands and Ross stepped to the outer office and filled out some paperwork. He also gave Ross his railroad pass and a second for Amy.

By the first Monday in February, he and Amy would have plenty of time to take care of all of their issues here in Cheyenne.

He rode east to stop by and see the Mandrakes and the children, arrived less than an hour later and stepped up to the door and knocked.

The door opened, and a small blonde head appeared.

"Hello, Alice," he said as he smiled at the little happy face.

She grinned back at him and turned her head and shouted, "It's Uncle Ross, Mama!"

Ross noticed the 'mama'.

Mildred appeared and opened the door wider.

"Come in, Ross," she said warmly.

Ross stepped inside the cozy house and watched as Alice happily skipped across the floor and turned into what he assumed was her bedroom as Millie closed the door.

"Ross! How are you?" Arthur said loudly as he walked across the main room with David perched on his shoulders. It was a close fit and David's head must have been three inches from the ceiling, but he didn't seem the least bit concerned.

"Fine, Arthur. The children seemed to have adapted well."

Arthur lowered David to the floor and said, "Go play with Alice for a while, David. I need to talk to your Uncle Ross."

"Okay, Papa," David shot off to his sister's room.

Ross smiled at the sight and asked, "What can I do for you, Arthur?"

"Come on and sit down if you don't mind."

He sat and wondered what they had in mind. It sounded serious.

"Ross, we talked to the judge yesterday and asked about adopting Alice and David. He said as there were living close relatives, he would need to have you talk to him. We are apprehensive about the grandparents as well. We don't know if they would interfere."

"I've already mentioned it to my parents and they fully supported my decision to let you adopt. Bessie's parents both died while I was in West Point which was probably one of the reasons that she married Henry, so I'd be more than happy to do whatever you need to let you adopt them. Whenever you'd like, we can go to the courthouse and we can do all the legal paperwork."

Mildred smiled and said, "Thank you, Ross. You don't know what this means to me."

Ross returned her smile and replied, 'Oh, I think I do, Mildred. So, when do you want to meet with the judge?"

Arthur answered, "The day after tomorrow at ten o'clock. Is that okay?"

"Absolutely. I'll bring Amy along, but I stopped by to ask you another question, though."

"Go ahead."

"I just left the Union Pacific office in Cheyenne. I was offered an engineering position with the railroad in Omaha and I'll start in February. Now, I have no use for the ranch whatsoever, so I was wondering if you just wanted to use the pastures for grazing and keep up the house until I decide what to do with it."

Arthur scratched his head and said, "Now, that's a funny thing, Ross. I was going to ask you what your plans are for the place. I was wondering what Henry would do with it once all the cattle were gone, and I'd really like to buy it. I'm running short on grazing land already and keep having to increase my purchase of hay. I can make you a good offer, plus the house would be ideal when either Alice or David needed a place of their own."

"You are thinking ahead."

"Now, the ranch is four sections, or twenty-five hundred acres. Good grazing land is running four dollars an acre, plus the house, that comes to just under eleven thousand dollars. I can give you a draft and we can go to the land office and do the changeover after we meet the judge. You and Amy stay there until you are ready to go to Omaha and it's a great deal for everyone."

"Arthur, that's way too much money."

"No, it's a fair price. You could sell that ranch in two hours to half a dozen ranchers. You walk into the Cattleman's Club and tell them you're selling, and you'd have it gone quickly."

"Well, let's make it an even ten thousand dollars then. Just to keep it easy to remember."

"I can live with that, Ross," he smiled as they shook hands on the deal.

"Would you like some coffee, Ross?" asked Mildred.

"Normally, I'd accept, but my bride is waiting for me, and I don't want her to think that I'd run off with some floozy."

They laughed and waved him on his way.

He left the house, stepped up on the gelding and rode across the fields, reaching his now temporary home with loads of news for Amy.

But first, he had to put the gelding and pack horse in the barn and brush them down. After he took care of all the necessary jobs to keep the horses healthy, he trotted to the house and stepped quickly to the kitchen door.

When he opened the door, he was met with a delicious aroma. Whatever Amy had baked had filled the entire house.

She heard him enter and bounced into the kitchen, having almost finished *Nicholas Nickleby.*

Ross heard her coming and had just finished hanging his jacket when he was bowled over again as Amy smashed him against the empty wall. Trapped, Ross had no other options than to go on offense himself. Discussions could wait.

An hour later, they were warm and in their now accustomed positions as they finally were able to talk.

"So, what kept you, my husband?" she asked quietly as her head rested on his shoulder with her gray hair spread everywhere.

"Only momentous things could keep me from having my way with you, my perfect wife."

"And what were those?"

"The mundane was shipping the guns to my father. Then I went to the Union Pacific offices. It seems there is great competition out there for engineers, and they offered me a position in Omaha starting on the first Monday in February."

She turned her face toward him and exclaimed, "Ross, that's wonderful!"

"The salary is eight thousand dollars per year."

"Why so much?"

"Because there are a lot of railroads and other construction and manufacturing concerns out there looking for qualified engineers. There's a shortage of really good ones. A lot of companies are making do with self-trained engineers, but that doesn't work for big projects, though."

"That is big news."

"That's not all, Amy. I stopped by and talked to Arthur and Mildred, so I'll need to go to Cheyenne and talk to the judge about their adoption of Alice and David. Did you know that the two children on their own decided to start calling them mama and papa? You should see how happy they are, too. That'll be at ten o'clock, the day after tomorrow. Then, I asked if they would like to use the ranch as grazing land until we decided what to do with it and Arthur told me that he really had planned on buying it from Henry for a while. So, after the meeting with the judge, we are going to the land office and transfer it to Arthur and Mildred. He offered me the market price, but I couldn't do that. So, I gave him a discount."

"That's fine, Ross. We really don't need the money."

"I know. That's why he's only paying ten thousand dollars for the ranch."

Again, Amy sat up and looked at him while Ross just stayed laying down and looked, but decided to give her a break this time.

"Ten thousand dollars? And that's after the discount? I didn't know they cost so much."

"Neither did I. I know my parents' farm in Minnesota is worth a lot more than that, but I figured with homesteading and everything, it wouldn't be worth that much, but Arthur knows such things, and he said if I wanted to, I could have gotten more from any other rancher."

Amy finally plopped back down, and Ross watched that, too, but he still pulled the blankets and quilt over her to keep her warm.

"Ross, we'll have almost twenty thousand dollars in the bank. That's a lot of money."

"I know. But we'll have to buy a house in Omaha, and my love, you get to go crazy furnishing it."

371

C.J. PETIT

That brought a twinkle to her green eyes, and she said, "I can manage."

"Now, that's the last of my news. No more talking."

She didn't answer...verbally.

———

The following day was spent in normal day-to-day things. Amy showed Ross her baking creation. It was what she called a strudel cake and had apples inside with a brown sugar cinnamon crust. Ross ate two large pieces for breakfast and told her she'd have to work it off him later, so she offered him a third slice.

Ross brought some more wood in and told Amy they'd have to have more delivered to get them through till February.

After an eventful night in which Ross worked off the cake and then some, they finally were able to get some sleep.

———

The next morning was surprisingly warm, already above freezing when they got out of bed.

Ross' breakfast consisted of one more slice of her cake and a cup of coffee. Amy had to admit, she was fond of the cake as well, but didn't want to eat too much. She had seen many of the wives in town who obviously enjoyed their own cakes a bit too much and vowed she would never gain weight. She wanted Ross to want her as much ten years from now as he did last night, and every night they'd been together after she stopped being the Witch.

They rode their horses out of the ranch at eight-thirty, arriving at the courthouse an hour later then waited in the courthouse lobby and watched as Arthur and Mildred walked through the doors holding the hands of their two skipping children. Amy watched them and hoped she could enjoy her children as much and, like Ross, could see the improvement.

They all walked down the hallway to the judge's chambers, the judge's clerk showed them in, and introductions were made.

"Mr. Braxton, as the children's closest relative, are you willing to forgo your rights to the children and allow their adoption to proceed?" asked Judge Porter.

"I am, Your Honor."

"I am personally acquainted with the petitioners and know them to be of high moral standards."

"As am I, Your Honor. When I first met my niece and nephew a short time ago, they were malnourished, dirty and had little clothing. You can see them now. I fully trust Mr. and Mrs. Mandrake to bring them up as model citizens. I have already discussed this decision with my parents and they wholeheartedly supported it."

"That was going to be my next question. With no other objections, I so authorize the adoption of the two minor children, Alice and David Braxton to Arthur and Mildred Mandrake."

He shook Arthur's and Ross's hand and smiled at a weeping Mildred who was hugging the children.

Ross turned to Amy, and said quietly, "Every so often, some good comes out of something bad."

They all left the judge's chambers, then made a quick stop at the land office and transferred title of the Box B to the Mandrakes. Arthur gave the draft to Ross and then they all went to a restaurant for lunch.

After lunch, which was paid for by Arthur at his insistence because of the discount on the ranch, the Mandrakes drove the carriage home, leaving Ross and Amy in Cheyenne to take care of their other tasks.

They went to the bank first, where Ross had them add Amy to the account. When she signed her new name for the first time, it gave her goosebumps, and Ross made sure she had several bank drafts. Then, he deposited the big draft and withdrew four hundred dollars, and gave half to Amy, who protested about the amount, but knew she had no chance of winning the argument. But she knew she had some shopping to do, so she acquiesced and slipped the bills into her pocket and wondered if she would ever wear clothes with pockets after they moved to Omaha.

When they were leaving the bank, Ross stopped and turned to her.

"Well, good wife, what do we do for the rest of the afternoon? Perhaps some shopping is in order."

"That sounds perfect. I know where I'd like to go, but I don't think you want to be there."

"Probably. Well, I'll tell you what. I'll meet you here in two hours. Is that long enough?"

"I think so," she replied, then gave him a quick kiss and a quicker wave before scurrying away.

Ross watched her walk away, then turned and headed to Harrington's Clothing, and once inside, walked straight to the women's section and told a clerk what he wanted. After he described Amy's size, the clerk showed him to the selection of women's coats and found one that he liked with a fur lining and fur trim. It was a dark green velvet, which was important. Once he selected the coat, he walked to where he remembered Amy admiring the emerald green silk dress the day that he had bought her the kid gloves before she left him for Oregon. They had one in her size, so he asked if both could be boxed and placed in a bag that disguised the source as they were Christmas presents for his wife. The young clerk smiled at him and said, "She is a very lucky lady."

Ross replied, "Not nearly as lucky as I am."

He followed her to the counter to pay the bill, and only paid forty-six dollars for them both. He'd have to remember how much silk dresses cost for future reference.

In a total juxtaposition, Amy had gone to Bergersen's Guns & Firearms. She walked in, smelled the familiar odor of gun cleaning solvents, then headed for the counter.

"May I help you, ma'am?" asked the gunsmith.

"I'd like to buy a new Winchester Model 1876 for my husband for Christmas, and I'll need four boxes of the cartridges. He mentioned that they were different than the '73 model he has now."

"A wise choice, ma'am," he said as he pulled out a new Winchester and began stroking it like it was his lady love.

"This weapon may look similar to the '73, but it has more power, and some say increased accuracy, but I'm not going to sell it on that basis. It has a ladder sight and I think a smoother action and only uses high-carbon steel in the receiver. It's a fine weapon. It comes with the cleaning kit, of course. This model has the twenty-six-inch barrel and fires the .45-75 cartridge. Now this particular rifle is very special. As you appear to wish it for your husband who obviously understands his weapons, I'm offering it to you. It's what they call *one of a thousand*. When rifles are produced at the factory, they have a range of acceptable variances, but every once in a while, one comes out that is perfect. This is one of them. Each part of the rifle is stamped with the rifle's serial number to distinguish it from the other production rifles. Naturally, it's quite a bit more expensive than the other Winchesters at seventy-five dollars, but to me, it's worth every penny."

"Could I have it inscribed?"

"Most certainly. In fact, it's included as part of the price as it's a very special rifle."

"It sounds ideal. Now, the only question will be how to get it to the ranch without him knowing."

"If I may suggest a possible solution. We could deliver it in a large disguised package on Christmas Eve. We would just leave it on the porch."

"Perfect. It's the Box B on the northeast road."

He took down the information, including the inscription.

Amy was excited with her purchase. She couldn't believe her good fortune in being able to buy such a unique gift for Ross. She paid for the rifle and ammunition, feeling the pleasure of finally being able to give something to Ross that he would appreciate, other than the gift she had given him on their wedding night, but that had been a mutual exchange anyway.

Ross's selections were far less destructive, as he picked up his order and was pleased that it was in a plain cloth bag. There was no indication of its origin anywhere.

He left the store, returned to the restaurant, and had barely touched boot to ground when he saw Amy walking toward him and felt a rush of warmth and a smile grow from the inside out. He didn't know if he'd ever get over the sight but hoped that he never did.

"So, my wife, did you find what you wanted?" he asked when she was close.

"Yes, but I didn't pick it up, yet."

"Did you find what you were looking for?" she asked.

"Yes, I think so."

"What is it?"

"Amy, I decline to answer that question. It's for your own good."

Amy had her suspicions that Ross had been doing exactly what she had been doing as Christmas was only days away.

But before they left, Ross told her that they needed to buy some gifts for the children, so they stopped at the leather shop and bought a child's saddle. Then they stopped at a mercantile and Amy picked out a little girl's brush and mirror set, some children's books, some ribbons for Alice's hair, and some paper and colored pencils for drawing.

———

The next few days after they had done their shopping were interesting. Amy knew he had bought two unmarked boxes but couldn't find them anywhere. Not that she looked intentionally. It was that as she went about her daily routine of dusting or arranging things, she'd casually glance around, or look under beds. She was caught once by Ross, who, although appreciative of the view, asked her what she was doing looking under a bed.

"Checking for dust bunnies," she replied as she stood.

"Oh. I thought you might be searching for hidden Christmas gifts."

"Did you buy me something? Really?" she asked, as if she didn't know.

"Could be. I can't recall."

And so, it went. Amy never found them because Ross had them hanging from the rafters in the barn's loft. He'd retrieve the bag on Christmas Eve.

He had found a perfect tree in a pine stand in the corner of the property, and two days before Christmas, he went out with his saw, cut it down, took it to the barn and built a simple cross stand. After it had been put in place, they added some decorations, but not much. Just enough to acknowledge that it wasn't just another tree.

The snow started that night. It wasn't a howling blizzard, but it was a good, deep snow, so they stayed indoors and enjoyed their fireplace and just being able to be with each other. Ross had arranged for a large load of firewood, so they didn't have to conserve wood, which meant they had a large, crackling fire warming up the room while Ross sat on the couch and Amy was lying with her knees bent and her head on his lap.

"Ross, can I tell you something that I've kept bottled up for a while? It's been nagging at me and I thought you should know."

"You can tell me anything, Amy."

She sighed and said quietly, "On our first day in Cheyenne, when we were in this house. You were talking to Henry and I was talking to Bessie. Bessie told me what had happened, but then she asked me how we had met. I told her about how you had fought off the Sioux. Then she looked at me and said, 'So, you're in love with him, too'. I told her I couldn't be because I was married, but then she said that she was married too, but she wasn't afraid to admit that she still loved you.

"She said she always had but that because she wanted you so badly, she reduced your relationship to something very superficial. It was only after you had gone that she realized that she really did love you. She said she only married Henry because she thought he might be like you. I thought you'd want to know."

Ross blew out his breath and said, "I know. She told me when I gave her the hug. It's been gnawing on me, too, but only because I feel like I got her into this. If she had picked a different boyfriend, maybe she'd still be alive and happy."

"Ross, you know you can't play the what-if game. It'll drive you crazy. She couldn't have picked another boyfriend for the same reason that I couldn't go back to Aaron. We both were in love with you. So, just put it behind you and spend the rest of your life loving me as I will be loving you."

He leaned over, kissed his wife and said, "You're a very special lady, Amy."

———

Christmas Eve arrived, and the weather was spectacular. There was no wind, the temperatures were in the mid-twenties, and the snow made it seem like Christmas. Amy asked Ross if he could clear off the front porch, which he did, before going out to the barn and returning with his big bag.

He stomped the snow off his boots and entered the house, catching Amy's eye as he closed the door.

"You hid it in the barn?" Amy asked with wide eyes.

"I figured you'd scour the house looking, so I'll leave them under the tree as long as you promise not to open them."

"If you'll give me the same promise about yours."

"I didn't see anything strange around the house, or the barn, for that matter."

"It's not here yet."

"Wise woman," he replied.

He slid the two cold boxes from the bag and slipped them under the tree.

Two hours later there was a thump on the front porch and Amy knew her gift for Ross had arrived. She waited a few minutes and then went outside to check, while Ross remained on the couch, suspecting that his gift must have just been dropped unceremoniously on the porch.

Amy was impressed with the mysterious packaging. The gunsmith must have used a second box to make it seem larger and then wrapped them both together, so it looked wider and less like the Winchester it was. It was a bit awkward when she picked it up, but she was able to get it under the tree without mishap.

Then she returned to the couch, slid against Ross who put his arm around her.

"Well, that's impressive, Amy. I thought you were ready to fall over there for a second. If you weren't so determined to do it by yourself, I would have helped."

"I wouldn't have let you carry it, anyway."

————

They slept in a bit on Christmas morning, and sun was already up when they had breakfast. They pretended that neither was the least bit curious about what lay under the tree.

As they sat, sipping their coffee, Ross finally said nonchalantly, "I suppose we could go and open our presents. Unless you had something else to do."

Finally, Amy swatted him and said, "Oh, stop it! Let's go!", then they trotted into the main room, stopped before the tree and sat down on the floor.

"Who goes first?" asked Amy.

"Well, you have two boxes, so you open one first."

"Okay."

Amy slid open the top box containing the silk dress, then opened the box and slowly pulled the shimmering green dress from its box.

"Oh, Ross. This is exquisite. It's so beautiful. Every time I went into that store, I'd take time to walk over and see this dress. It's absolutely perfect. Thank you, my perfect husband."

She leaned over and kissed him.

"Your turn," she said as she smiled anxiously, waiting for his reaction.

Ross literally had no idea what it was. He opened the wrapping paper and was momentarily confused by the empty brown box used to expand the shape, then he saw the Winchester logo and his face lit up.

He reverently opened the box and slid the rifle from its container, marveled at the silver inlay and the solid construction and immediately noticed the subtle differences between the '73 and '76 models.

When he noticed the inscription: *Ross Braxton 1 of 1000,* he was astounded. Amy had bought him one of the rare *one of a thousand* Winchesters.

He spent a few seconds acting just like the gunsmith, and Amy watched with an appreciative smile as Ross ran his fingers across the smooth metal and polished wood.

"Amy, this is extraordinary. I never would have bought this for myself. I can't wait to fire it and see how it shoots, but not today. Thank you, my love. I couldn't have asked for a better gift."

"I suppose I'll open my last one now," Amy said as she reached for her second gift and slid it onto her lap.

She opened the second box and was greeted with fur. She pulled the coat from the box and stood up, slid her arms through the sleeves and wrapped it around her.

"Ross, it's so elegant and warm. Can I go and try on my dress and then put on the coat? I want to see how they are together."

"I can't wait to see how you look either, Amy," he replied.

She scurried into their room, but didn't close the door, so Ross sat back and watched the only thing that could keep him from examining his new Winchester.

Amy stepped out a few minutes later and looked ready to attend an opera or a fine gala.

"What do you think?" she asked, as if she didn't know by the expression on his face.

"I was already impressed watching you get undressed, but I have to admit, you look stunning in your new dress and coat."

She walked over and hugged him. He kissed her and then began seeing how she felt under silk, so it didn't take long for them to share another Christmas gift.

———

An hour later, they dressed in warmer clothing and packed up Alice's gifts in the same bag that Ross had used for her gifts. He took the child's saddle and went out to the barn, brushed down the pinto and saddled him with the child's saddle.

Then he saddled his gelding and Amy's horse, led them back to the house, and after loading Alice's bag of gifts, they mounted and cut across the pastures to the Rocking M trailing the pinto. The gate was left open now as it was all Rocking M property. When they arrived at the front of the ranch house, they stepped down and Ross tied the pinto by itself off to the side of the hitchrail while Amy picked up Alice's gifts before they climbed the porch stairs and knocked on the door.

Arthur opened the door, wished them a merry Christmas and had them enter. Because they had hitched the pinto at the far end of the hitchrail, it wasn't visible by anyone standing inside the house.

The Mandrakes had their own, bigger tree, and Ross and Amy could see the pile of toys and clothes nearby as they took off their coats and scarves and hung them near the door.

The children had been out in the kitchen with Mildred as she baked Christmas cookies, but soon came streaming into the room and hugged Amy and Ross. Mildred trailed with a warm smile on her lips.

"Alice, we brought you some gifts for Christmas," said Amy.

She gave the bag to Alice who grinned at first and then turned to Ross.

"But what about David? Can I share my gifts with him?"

"No, Alice those are all yours. Where is that young cowboy?" he asked, looking over the top of David's head.

"Here I am, Uncle Ross."

Ross picked him up, then asked, "David, what does every cowboy need?"

"Cows?"

Everyone laughed, even Alice.

"Yes, that's true. Without cows, there would be no cowboys. So, if you already have cows, what does the cowboy need to round them up?"

"A horse?"

"Yup. A horse. So, David, are you a cowboy?"

"Not yet. I haven't got a horse."

"Are you sure?"

"Yes."

"I think you're wrong, cowboy. I think Santa Claus brought you one last night when he went past the house. At least it looks like a little boy's horse and saddle in front of the house. Did you want to look?"

David's eyes grew wide as he exclaimed, "Yes, please!"

Everyone followed as Ross carried David to the front door, swung it open and once they stepped out just a foot, David saw the pinto staring at him.

"I have a horse!" he yelled.

Then he turned in Ross' arms and yelled to everyone in the room.

"I have a horse! I have a horse!"

"It's getting cold in here, David. So, I'll close the door for a while."

"Okay. But I have a horse!"

Ross put him down and he was bouncing all over the room reminding everyone that he had a horse.

When he finally calmed down to come over and thank his uncle, Ross crouched down and said to him.

"Now, David. That's not just an ordinary horse, you know."

"It isn't?"

"No, he's just the opposite. Why just a few months ago, he belonged to a fierce Sioux warrior. He was chasing after your Aunt Amy with a tomahawk in his hand and was going to hit her over the head with it, but I shot him off the horse and the other Indians ran away. I let your Aunt Amy ride him for a while, but then we found the tall horse she rides now, and she didn't need him anymore. And you know what?"

387

David shook his head.

"That horse followed us hundreds of miles without a rope just to come here so he could be your horse. I'm sure your papa will show you how to ride him, too."

David turned to Arthur and said, "Wow! Really? Papa when can you show me how to ride him?"

"When there isn't so much snow."

"Okay."

David sprinted off to tell Alice about his horse.

Mildred asked, "Out of curiosity, was that story true?"

Amy answered, "Every word. The warrior was less than twenty feet from me when Ross's shot hit him. I was scared to death. Then after we released the pinto two days later, he just followed us. We only put a rope on him after Scotts Bluff because we put a pack saddle on him and needed to make sure he wouldn't wander off."

"Now, there's a story that will make every boy in his school jealous."

They shared a nice Christmas dinner with all the trappings. The hands had all been gifted earlier with nice bonuses and had gone to Cheyenne to celebrate.

When it began to darken, Amy and Ross said their goodbyes and returned to the ranch house.

Later, when Ross and Amy were wrapped together in bed, Ross said to her, "You know, Amy. I did modify my true belief about why the horse followed us when I told David."

"Of course, you did. The horse wouldn't know about David."

"But I do know why that horse followed us."

"You do?"

Ross slid his hand down her back and across her rounded form.

"If I had this behind sitting on my back, I'd follow it anywhere."

Amy laughed for a little while but decided to show Ross that the horse had a good reason to follow.

———

The only thing that happened over the next few days was that Ross went into Cheyenne and picked up his custom piece of leatherwork from the shop. It was perfect, and it was elegant, too. It cost twenty-four dollars, and the shop owner said he had never seen the like.

When he brought the piece home, he showed it to Amy.

"It looks like a gun case, but I'm not sure," she said as she looked at it.

"You are correct. That is exactly what it is, but it's really more of a 'guns' case. Watch."

He opened the case. Then he walked into the kitchen and pulled out the Sharps and his new Winchester, which he still hadn't fired. He also picked up box of ammunition for each, returned to the main room and sat down next to the new case.

"The man who made this is a true craftsman. I told him I wanted to be able to carry my Sharps and my Winchester together. He asked if I wanted to add some ammunition as well, and I did. So, watch this."

Ross opened a leather door at the back of one side of the case. He slid the Sharps in barrel first. It fit snugly against a built-up leather pad in the center. Then, he closed the door. He turned it around and opened another door on the opposite end and slid the Winchester in until it rested against the other side of the pad.

"He built it so that the barrel length was relatively unimportant, as long as it wasn't over thirty-six inches. Now the ammunition cache was very clever. He had all this room on the top between the handles. The rifles were underneath, so they'd provide the ballast. The ammunition is stored in these two pouches on the top. You simply pull this one strap for the big rounds or the Winchester's rounds. Of course, the new gun has bigger cartridges than the old one, but that's not an issue."

Ross leaned back smiling.

"Won't that be a bit heavy?" she asked.

"Not bad. About thirty pounds or so."

"You're going to take that on the train?"

"Of course, I'm not going to trust my guns to the baggage car. Besides, one is very special gift from a very special lady."

Amy just looked at Ross and smiled.

CHAPTER 9

The remainder of January was uneventful and cold. A big blizzard hit the area on the twelfth of the month, locking Amy and Ross in the house for a week, but they found ways to pass the time.

On the morning of the twentieth, the weather warmed to above freezing and people began to dig out as best they could. The warming stayed with them for another five days, which turned the roads into a quagmire of thick mud, and when the cold weather returned, people were grateful as the mud was hardened enough to make transportation possible.

Finally, it was time for Ross and Amy to depart for their new home in Omaha. They left their first home at six-thirty and rode across to the Mandrakes.

They said their goodbyes to Mildred and the children and left their horses at the hitching rail having no more need of them. Arthur drove his carriage with Amy and Ross in front with him and all their baggage in back. They arrived at the station and let the porter take all their bags except for Amy's toiletry bag and Ross's gun case.

Ross shook Arthur's hand and Amy kissed him on the cheek. It was time for Ross and Amy to get on with their new life.

They sat together on the couch in the hotel lobby as they waited for the eastbound train.

"Isn't this all amazing, Amy? Three and a half months ago, I didn't even know you, and I had no idea what I would do with my life. I was wandering. And then I saw an old squaw being run down by four Sioux warriors and everything in my life changed. All because of you, Amy."

"You did so much more for me, Ross. Even after you saved my life, I knew I had to go to Oregon and a life I didn't want. I had lived six weeks of adventure with the most incredible man I had ever met, and I was doomed to a boring life with a dull man. But fate intervened. and I returned to Cheyenne with an opal necklace and a happiness that I could never have hoped for. And that, my dear husband, is because of you."

Public decorum be damned. Ross leaned over and kissed his wife with as much passion as he had kissed her when she had gotten off the same train they would soon be riding to Omaha and their new life.

They heard the whistle and the passengers began moving to the cold platform. They had first-class tickets by showing their Union Pacific passes and boarded the first train car, Amy with her small toiletry bag and Ross with his long gun case.

They sat in comfortable seats and Ross leaned his gun case against the side. They had bought new books for the eighteen-hour trip, and there were only eight other passengers in the first-class coach, so it should be a peaceful journey, which contrasted greatly with the one they had taken to get to

Cheyenne. The train began moving and they settled in for the ride to Omaha and the start of their long future together.

The entered Nebraska a short time later and turned eastward from their previous southeastern heading. The landscape was unexciting, so Amy and Ross began reading, as the other passengers either read or slept.

Ninety minutes later, the train began to shake, despite being nowhere near a stop. There was high-pitched squealing as the drive wheels began to buck the forward motion of the train and rotate backward as the engineer tried to bring the train to a stop without the benefit of the brakeman's work.

"Ross, what's happening?" Amy asked anxiously.

"Nothing good. It could be a bridge out or something, but I don't think so."

He pulled out his left-hand Colt and handed it to her.

"This shoots the same as your Smith & Wesson. It has five shots loaded," he said.

Amy didn't say anything, but simply nodded and took the pistol.

He reached over to his case and opened the Winchester door, slid the new rifle out, then flipped the ammunition case open and grabbed ten more cartridges which he slid into his jacket.

"I'm going up front. Stay seated and hide the pistol under your purse."

Amy nodded again and watched him leave.

Ross took off at a lope and reached the front door, opened the door and stepped outside. It was cold, but not too bad. The train was still slowing as he stepped across to the coal car and climbed the ladder to the top. He looked in front of the train and saw that a large boulder had been rolled across the track. That meant it was a robbery, so he scanned the area looking for trouble but couldn't see anyone which meant the robbers must already be on board. They wouldn't have paid for first class passage, but they might come in and try to rob the wealthy passengers when they finished trying to open the train's safe.

He climbed back down and re-entered the car, closed the door behind him and turned to the passengers.

He said loudly, "There's a large boulder that has been rolled onto the track. I believe that there will be a robbery attempt shortly. Do any of you have guns with you?"

No one did, which surprised him.

"Alright, I'm going out the back way. I think the robbers must be on board in the regular passenger cars. They'll have their horses in the stock car. When I leave, you should all move to the back of the car. My wife is armed and can handle anyone that comes through the door."

The other passengers all stared at the young, gray-haired woman wondering if she was carrying a derringer and what good would it do.

After his announcement, he trotted the length of the now-stopped car and opened the back door. He halted and tried to see inside the first standard passenger car and spotted a man standing in the aisle with a pistol raised. Ross slowed down and stepped across to the second passenger car. He cocked the Winchester and then went to the door.

He yanked it open and pointed the Winchester at the man.

"Drop it now, or you'll die in three seconds. One, two…"

The man dropped his gun, which was immediately picked up by a passenger, who said, "He said he was gonna shoot us if we did anything."

"You, ex-gunman. Sit your ass down in that empty seat. Now."

The man complied. Ross turned to the man who had picked up the gun.

"Aim it at his head. If he so much as looks funny, kill him."

Ross started to go past and then stopped next to the outlaw and said, "Oh, to hell with it," and cold-cocked him with his new Winchester's barrel.

"Now, make sure he doesn't do anything."

Ross trotted back to the second car. Again, he saw a man holding a pistol at the passengers. He stepped onto the new car and yanked open the door, then pointed his Winchester at the man and said loudly, "Same thing mister. You have till the count of three to drop that pistol or you'll lose your head. One, two..."

This man must have thought he was smarter or faster, but he was proven wrong when he quickly turned to face what he thought might be a pistol but saw a big Winchester pointed right at him, but it was too late to change his mind, because as soon as he began his turn, Ross fired. At that range, it was messy. Luckily, no passengers were behind him as the bullet passed right through him and out the back window. Ross didn't take time to wait. He levered another round into the chamber and the expelled brass flew away as he trotted back to the next car, leaping over the dead would-be robber.

Next was the baggage car. There was an express car behind that. He guessed it was the target, but he also knew that they had heard his Winchester, so he lost his surprise advantage. His edge now was that he knew they would have to get to the stock car to retrieve their horses, unless someone else waited with their horses near the big boulder blocking their path.

He had to gamble, so he jumped down and chose the left side for no particular reason.

Ross crouched as he ran looking for movement under the cars but didn't see anyone moving. The only sound was the venting of the steam engine far behind him, but as he passed the express car, he heard voices.

"Open that damned safe. We ain't gonna waste a lot of time."

Could it be that they didn't hear his shot?

He started moving again and passed the express car and ran around the outside, circled around behind the caboose and then looked down the other side of the train. He could see the express car, and the door was open.

Now it was decision time. He figured they had to come out of the express car with their money. If he tried to make a move now, he'd endanger the expressman and not know how many were in there, so he decided to wait.

What he hadn't seen was another member of the gang leave the treed area near the boulder and sprint to the first-class car. He swung onto the car and opened the door with his gun drawn, and he quickly pointed it at the passengers.

"Everybody stay where you are! While my friends are taking care of the safe back in the express car, I figure you high-fallutin' folks don't need all of your money or jewelry. So, it's time to pay up," he said loudly as he scanned the passengers and counted three women and six men.

"Alright mister," he growled, pointing his gun at one of the smaller men, "get up here and open your wallet."

The man stood and walked slowly forward.

Amy had the gun in her right hand, and just needed to cock the hammer as quietly as possible. She began pulling it back, then she coughed, and pulled the hammer back at the same time.

The robber looked quickly at her as she coughed, but then looked back. Amy watched the man and waited for the right moment, just as Ross waited for his near the caboose.

Her moment came first.

He had collected the first man's money, and now he brandished the pistol and focused on a second man in the back of the car.

Amy drew the pistol slowly upward and then quickly raised it to eye level and pulled the trigger. The .44 caliber round traveled four feet hitting the robber on the side of his chest almost instantly, the bullet ripped through his right lung, then passed through his left before exiting his body and lodging in the wood of the car's front wall. The robber's pistol clattered to the floor as he slowly turned and saw the gray-haired woman standing there with her green eyes and her smoking Colt. He fell to his knees, still staring at Amy before falling onto his face.

Amy sat back and put the smoking revolver on the seat next to her, her heart was still racing, and she let others go and pick up the man's pistol as she waited for Ross to return.

Ross heard the shot and knew someone had just been shot in one of the passenger cars. Even though he knew the possibility that it was Amy was remote, he still felt panic rising, and almost jumped the gun. He took one step forward, then caught himself, just as the two robbers in the express car reacted to the pistol shot, mistakenly believing that a member of their gang had shot a passenger.

So, the boss of the operation, Jeff Plunkett, told his comrade to go and check to see what happened. The second man hopped down from the car and began trotting toward the passenger cars. Ross couldn't chance it. If it meant that the expressman might die, it would be too bad. It was his job. The passengers paid for a safe trip.

He brought his Winchester to bear and squeezed the trigger. The more powerful round found its mark and spun the trotting gunman until he faced Ross for a second, shocked at what had just happened to him. Ross quickly fired a second, unnecessary round just to be sure, putting the round in the center of his chest. The outlaw's expression never changed as he fell face forward into the hard, rocky surface near the rails, his head bouncing off a wooden crosstie before coming to rest.

Ross levered in a new round and waited.

Plunkett heard the two rifle shots and knew he was in trouble. All he had was the expressman, and he made a lousy hostage. Nobody cared about employees, but it was all he had.

Ross sprinted back around the caboose and trotted to the back side of the express car, then dropped to the ground and waited. Someone would have to get out of that car sooner or later.

Plunkett grabbed the expressman and told him to go outside and stand still. He did as he was told and hopped down then remained where he landed. The expressman didn't see the shooter but saw the dead outlaw on the ground with two bullet wounds in his back, so he knew there was a lawman nearby. He thought about running, but then realized if he took one step, he'd be shot, so he stayed where he was hoping the lawman would take care of the last bad man.

Plunkett waited until there had been no shots fired at the expressman. He thought they came from the back end of the train but wasn't sure.

He walked to the doorway and scanned outside, but couldn't see anyone straight on, so he took off his hat and quickly stuck his head out looking backward finding no one there. He waited ten seconds and repeated it looking forward this time, but there was no one there either, other than the expressman.

"Start walking slowly forward," he commanded as he hopped down from the express car, still scanning behind him and then quickly returning to the front.

Ross didn't hesitate and was sure that the man in back had to be the robber. He aimed as high as he could at the man's leg and squeezed the trigger. The Winchester spat out its .45 caliber round and hit his right leg just at the knee. It passed through the right leg and took off his left kneecap.

Plunkett screamed and hit the ground hard as he grabbed at his legs, letting his cocked revolver hit the dirt. It went off, sending a large cloud of debris into the air as the .44 caliber bullet punched a crater into the earth.

The expressman turned and looked for the shooter, but there wasn't anyone in sight.

Finally, Ross trotted around behind the caboose, levering in a new round into place as he rounded the red car and shouted, "There is one unconscious robber in the first standard passenger car, a dead one in the second. Take this guy's gun and let him bleed to death for all I care. I have to go and find out what that shot was in the passenger cars."

The expressman reached over picked up the pistol and looked down at the screaming robber then kicked him once in the chest before returning to his express car.

Ross passed the dead gunman and stepped up to the last passenger car and went inside.

"Is everyone all right? Where did the gunshot come from?"

Three of the passengers pointed toward the front.

Ross sprinted that way and exited that car and quickly entered the second. He asked the same question and got the same response.

He entered the first-class car and saw everyone huddled around Amy's seat. *Not Amy!*

"Amy! *Are you all right?*" he shouted as he raced down the aisle.

Then he saw that gray head rise and turn to him wearing a smile, and he slowed down, bent at the waist and finally exhaled loudly.

The other first-class passengers separated and allowed Ross to reach his wife, then he saw the dead outlaw a few feet away, knowing that Amy must have shot him.

He reached his wife, put down his Winchester, wrapped her in his arms and kissed her.

Then he let her go a bit and asked, "Did you do that?"

"I had to, Ross. He was waving that pistol around and threatening everyone."

"You did a great job, Amy. I'm proud of you for protecting everyone."

"What happened out there?"

"I've got one incapacitated in the second passenger car, one dead in the third, another dead outside and a fourth severely wounded as he was robbing the express car."

She handed him back his Colt, which he replaced in his holster and automatically flipped the trigger loop over the top.

He turned to the passengers and said, "We need to clean up this mess and see if we can't get the train going to Omaha. Is anyone here a doctor? I have a severely wounded man a few cars down."

"I'm a dentist," said the first man that the robber had called forward.

"Good. Come with me."

He led him outside and down to the express car, but there was no need for a doctor or a dentist. He had bled to death.

"Never mind with this one. We'll deal with him in a while. Let's go check on the one that I conked over the head."

They entered the middle passenger car finding the bandit still unconscious. Ross checked him over for other weapons and found a small pistol in his jacket and a knife. He removed both, then pulled the man's belt and wrapped it around his wrists.

"That will hold him when he wakes up. Who is familiar with firearms?"

"I was in the army," replied a passenger two rows back.

"Good. Here's his other gun. When he comes to, question him about the others. Tell him he's the only survivor. He'll talk."

"Will do, captain."

Ross smiled, and said, "I never made captain," then tapped the man on the shoulder.

Then he got out of the car and walked out front to talk to the engineer and fireman, wondering what happened to the conductor in the caboose. The conductor, he would learn later, had simply hunkered down in his rolling bunk with the brakeman and waited for the shooting to stop.

He hopped on board the engine and said, "Gentlemen, the planned robbery attempt has failed, and four of the five men are dead. One is in custody. What's the plan for getting the train to Omaha?"

"We can't, sir. We'll have to back it up to our last stop until they get a crew out there to move that boulder. I don't know how they got it there."

He pointed to the right and said, "See that hill, I'll bet it was up there and they just got it going. The tough part would be getting it stopped as it rolled down the hill. I don't know how they managed it, unless they dragged some logs or something and laid them on the other side of the track. Anyway, we'll get that out of the way in about thirty minutes. I may need you to provide some power, though."

"Mister, if you can get that rock out of here so we can still make schedule, I'll give you all the power you need."

"I'll count on it."

Ross hopped down and went over to the boulder. It was a good six feet high and probably weighed forty or fifty tons, but it was reasonably round. It wasn't dead center on the tracks, either, so he'd try to get it moved to the right, where there was a slope.

First, he jogged around to see if there were any of the outlaws' horses around, and it didn't take long to find them. There were five good looking mounts tied to some trees to the right. He left the horses but took the five ropes.

He tossed the ropes near the base of the boulder, then walked back to the middle passenger car.

"I need some ranch hands. As many as I can get."

There were three volunteers in the first car and five in the second. They walked back to the stock car and found another eight ropes and in the baggage car, a spool of rope, giving Ross some hope that his engineering skills might be able to get the boulder free.

First, he told the cow hands what he needed. They all understood and followed him out to the front of the locomotive and began roping the boulder. The first and biggest loop was dead center. As each one was looped moving upward, Ross had them tie off the rope at the right side where he wanted the rock to go.

Then when all eight ropes were in place, he took two more ropes and ran them perpendicularly to the eight loops the cowboys had made, and that was tied down. It was critical that the loops stayed in place. Then he had them wind the eight ropes into a thick cable. At the end of the cable he had them create what appeared to be an oversized hangman's noose by looping it over, creating a hook, then winding the rope from the reel around it to keep the noose in place. There were two hundred feet on the spool to start, and Ross guessed he had one hundred and sixty feet left. He'd only get one shot at this.

They ran the eight-rope cable to a cottonwood just off the track, the noose barely clearing the base of the tree, then took the spool and ran it to the still huffing engine, and ran it through the cow catcher, back through the noose, back through the cowcatcher and through the noose again. There were four thicknesses of rope when they were done, and he wished they had more. The trick would be to exert the pressure smoothly.

He hopped aboard the engine and said to the engineer, "Alright, we're ready to go. I need you to back up slowly. We can't snap those ropes."

The train engineer could see what he was doing, understood what Ross needed and said, "Here goes."

The engineer increased his steam pressure and pulled back the throttle slowly. Ross almost held his breath as the train began backing slowly. Ross was concerned that the ropes weren't taut enough and listened for the sound of popping ropes. The cowboys had all moved far out of the way in case it snapped and whipped all over the place but watched their creation as it stretched.

The ropes tightened and creaked loudly as the train moved back a few more feet. Ross watched the boulder closely as the ropes tightened even more around its girth.

His eyes were squinting waiting for something to happen, and finally, it did when the boulder moved. Not much at first, but as the train moved back it suddenly popped free of the tracks and thundered down the small embankment that had been created when the track had first been laid. As it rolled the ropes came loose and shot around the cottonwood like a whip. The engineer had been waiting for it and slammed the throttle home.

"Whooeee!" he yelled, "That was fun."

Ross replied, "Maybe for you. Give me ten minutes to clean up the mess and we'll be out of here. We'll need to spend a few more minutes at our next stop and notify the law."

The cowboys were all cheering as Ross headed back that way.

"Guys, I appreciate the help. Now, if anyone wants that rope, you're welcome to it. If not, I will personally give you enough to replace them. Can some of you move those five horses that the outlaws were planning on using to escape and get them in the stock car? I'll go start moving bodies."

They all waved and headed over to the horses.

Ross headed back to the first passenger car, and as he entered, said, "We need to move this body out of the car, then we'll be rolling shortly. The boulder is off the tracks."

Two men stepped forward and slid the body out the back of the car. The blood the railroad could take care of later. With the help of the other passengers, the other three bodies were all moved to the stock car and placed under a tarp. The wounded man was secured with some pigging strings that the cowboys had with them. He had said he was with the Plunkett gang. That was all, but that was enough.

They got some hot water from the engine and quickly washed down the blood from the two cars and they finally got under way forty minutes after the robbery had started. All things considered; the engineer couldn't be happier.

No one had even paid attention to the freezing temperature.

Ross finally made his way back to Amy and collapsed next to her.

She looked over at her husband and said, "You continue to amaze me, Ross."

He smiled at her and replied, "Not as much as you astonish me, Amy."

They stopped the train at Sidney, and the bodies and the lone survivor were removed from the train, and as he had expected, he and Amy had to stay in Sidney and fill out their statements as to what happened while the train left for Omaha. The engineer blasting the whistle several times as he departed.

The sheriff was a likeable man and had them both sit while he and his deputy listened while Ross and Amy told him what had happened. He was totally silent as they provided a very detailed account, and was impressed with their accuracy and demeanor, especially when Amy mentioned that she had coughed to disguise her cocking the hammer of the Colt. When they had finally finished, the sheriff sat back.

"Do you both understand how incredible this story is? We've had law enforcement agencies in three states looking for the Plunkett gang. In less than five minutes an engineer and his wife take them all out of action. Not only that, you had the train moving forty minutes after it had been stopped. Go ahead and write your statements, and we'll get you set up in the hotel. In the morning, we can have you review everything and see if it's correct. You don't have to worry about any prosecution. We are extremely grateful for what you did."

Amy was carrying her small bag of personal items and Ross was lugging his heavy gun case as they walked to the hotel and stopped in the restaurant to eat. They had lunch and then walked up to their room and fell asleep with the sun shining outside, but after a three-hour nap, they awakened and felt better.

"Ross, are we ever going to get past this kind of thing?" a fully-clothed Amy asked as she laid beside her husband.

"Amy, once we get to Omaha, we are done with Indians and bad men. We are going to go to the theatre, dances and other social events. You and I will have our children and not have to shoot anyone ever again."

"Didn't we have this conversation twice before?"

"But I don't think I mentioned children before. Did I?"

———

The next morning, they reviewed the accuracy of the documents, signed them and headed for the train station.

They got on the train at 11:45, and their train arrived in Omaha fourteen hours later without another gunshot having been fired. But the trip had taken its toll and they were exhausted when they arrived.

They put most of their items in storage and found a nice hotel, and Amy was first into the bath and stayed there longer than usual. Ross didn't begrudge her the extra time.

The next morning, they went to the hotel restaurant, where they expected a nice quiet breakfast, which they had, but when they exited the restaurant, they were greeted by the president of the Union Pacific and his entourage.

He introduced himself and told Ross how proud he was that Ross had decided to join the company. What he had done had saved the company thousands of dollars and he had shown his engineering expertise with the removal of the giant boulder. Ross introduced Amy and the president told her that he had heard of her actions in the attempted robbery and was glad she was on their side. All the toadies laughed as required.

After a few more minutes of backslapping, he ended the interview with the standard, "if there's anything I can do for you…' line.

They all piled out the door and Ross turned to Amy and said, "Well, I guess we're in Omaha."

Amy stayed at the hotel while Ross went to the Union Pacific headquarters where he was welcomed and shown around. He mentioned that he had to find a home, and they directed him to their personnel offices, where he had to sign some forms to be added as an employee and then one of the clerks showed him a listing of departing or retiring employees who had homes for sale, which they usually did as a service to incoming hires.

He took the list and returned to Amy at the hotel, who was looking forward to picking out their new home. Her first real home and she would be sharing it with Ross.

The following day, which was brisk, even by Omaha in January standards, they began looking at houses. The first two lacked some of Amy's desires, but the third home was perfect. It was quite expensive, at thirty-six-hundred-dollars, but it had everything that Amy could have hoped for. It had two full bathrooms, a huge kitchen and six bedrooms, and all of the rooms were large. The house came mostly furnished, so all they would have to buy were accessories and some kitchenware and dinnerware as well, but Amy was in love and Ross could not deny her anything. The house had a ten-acre lot and a carriage house with a carriage already present. They would need to buy four horses; one matched pair for the carriage and another two for riding, but they could be easily found. They had transferred all their funds from their Cheyenne account to a new one in Omaha's First National Bank and moved in four days later and had totally settled in by the 15th of January.

———

Ross started his job on February 3rd and fit in quickly. Everything was going better than planned.

A week after he began work, he and Amy were lying in their customary late-night positions on their new four-poster bed under new, heavy quilts and blankets.

"Ross, this is all real, isn't it?" she asked softly, her head laying on his chest.

"Yes, my love, this is all real. It's a dream come true, but it's real," he replied just as quietly.

Amy sighed and said, "I don't want to ruin our dream, Ross, but I do think our lives will change now, but not because of angry Sioux warriors, pistol-carrying outlaws or crazy men. It will change for the best of reasons, my beloved husband. You're about to become a beloved father."

Ross didn't leap up in surprise. He just laid there with a big smile as he stroked his wife's gray hair.

"I'm happier than you could imagine, sweetheart. I'm also so very content with our lives now and after you have our first child, we'll get busy on the second."

Then he simply leaned down and kissed Amy softly. Amy sighed and snuggled in closer, feeling the same contentment and happiness that Ross experienced.

———

They were visited by Ross' parents twice in the next six months. They had plenty of room in the house and they stayed for a week each time. They were excited by the prospect of a new grandchild.

Amy made friends of the wives of other company engineers and executives. They were mesmerized by her gray hair and the stories she told of how she had met her husband. None of the other wives could come close to anything nearly as exotic or as romantic.

Ross did well in the company and was soon designing buildings as well as bridges. He was already the head of a division when Amy went into labor. She was a strong woman and had a relatively easy delivery, if there is such a thing. She gave birth to their daughter on September 11th at St. Joseph's hospital. They named her Bessie.

Ross sat on Amy's bed as she held their new daughter close to her. Both her parents were amazed of the miracle of their little baby girl, as most new parents are.

"She's got blonde hair, Ross," Amy said with a smile.

"I know, sweetheart, but I was kind of hoping she'd take after her beautiful mother."

Amy laughed and said, "Now, why would you wish that on her?"

"Because, my love, I couldn't imagine anyone being as pretty with boring colored hair."

Bessie's grandparents arrived a week later and were ecstatic with the baby girl, as were her parents.

When Amy returned from St. Joseph's hospital with their new daughter, she walked up to their new nursery, laid her precious bundle in the crib and covered her with a blanket as Ross stood next to her.

"Have your dreams all come true now, Amy?" he asked quietly as he put his arm around her waist.

She turned to her husband with almost a beatific smile on her face.

"Oh, yes, Ross, every dream I have ever had his complete now. I have a wonderful home, a perfect baby girl, and a husband who loves me. No woman could ever dream for more."

He took her hands in his and asked, "Amy, you know how you're always wondering what we'll do with all these bedrooms?"

"Yes, but if it's okay with you, I'd really prefer not to fill them all with children."

"No, but while you were in the hospital, I did have one room modified."

He kept hold of her hand and led her down the hallway to the next bedroom, or what used to be a bedroom.

He opened the door and she looked inside.

There was a desk and a file cabinet, bookshelves with all sorts of reference books, and sitting next to the desk on its own table was a machine.

"Ross, what is all this?"

"This, my wonderful wife, is the path to your other dream. The one that you confessed to me while we made our fateful journey across the plains."

Amy felt a cascade of warmth flood over her. *He had remembered!*

"What is the machine?"

"That, my love, is a Remington typewriter. You can type your novel rather than handwrite it. You can do either, of course, but I hear that the editors in New York love these contraptions. You hit a key and it prints the letter on the paper."

"Really? You put all of this together for me to write? Do you really do think I can do it?"

"I always believed in you, Amy. Now, I'm going to get a nurse for Bessie, a cook for us and a maid so you don't have to clean."

"Ross, I don't mind."

"I know you don't, sweetheart. But writers write, and you need time to dream, to organize and to write. You'll still be Bessie's mother and my wife. But you are yourself, too. You still have a dream, Amy, and this room can help you reach that dream."

Amy started to cry. She didn't know if it was because she just had a baby, or she had the most wonderful husband in the world, but she didn't care as she hugged her husband and laid her gray head against his chest, listening to the heart that belonged to her.

She now could begin to work on the only dream that she still hadn't fulfilled.

———

Their life settled into a serene routine. Ross would ride to his office in the morning, while Amy would care for little Bessie, but devote her spare time to writing, having more spare time due to Ross's thoughtful hiring of domestic help. Amy finally decided on a subject, but it was not about Boudica or an English knight.

As she wrote, she would sometimes take the opal in her hand and let it change hues in the light. She would look deep inside as she turned it in the light and could see her own face as she left Cheyenne, despondent and lonely. And then, if she turned it another way, she could see her face again, rapturous and radiant as she was returning. Not to the place, but to the man.

EPILOGUE

Seven years later, Ross was the vice president in charge of engineering. His gray-haired, and still beautiful young wife was a staple at social events. Their three daughters were all that any parent could hope for. None had gray hair, but each one had Amy's bright green eyes. After Bessie, came Sarah and then Grace in successive years.

Ross was bringing one of his new young engineers and his wife and daughter to dinner. He had just been hired and Ross was impressed with the young man.

The young family arrived and were shown into the parlor and Ross was surprised and pleased to discover that they had bought a house just six doors down that had been owned by a retiring vice president.

They spent some time in the parlor where Ross introduced them to Amy and his three daughters.

"Amy, this is Carl Ritter, our newest and brightest engineer, his wife Barbara and their daughter Beth."

He turned to Beth Ritter and said, "Beth, these are our daughters, Bessie, Sarah, and Grace. Bessie is almost exactly your age, Sarah is six and Grace is five."

Beth smiled at the three Braxton girls and waved hello. They waved back, then Bessie led all the girls up to her bedroom, so they could let the adults talk about all that boring grownup stuff.

"Carl, I hear you met Barbara in Wyoming?" asked Amy.

"I did. Ross was telling me that you two met on the trail in the Dakota Territory."

"We did. How much did he tell you about our journey?"

"Quite a bit."

Before, during and after dinner they exchanged stories of their adventures in the Wyoming and Dakota Territories. As it turned out, both couples have had their share of entanglements with bad men.

The girls listened to them talk and decided that grownup talk wasn't so boring after all.

The two couples became good friends and saw each other often in the company of another Union Pacific executive and his wife, Tom and Emily Wilson. The Wilsons had also shared in the Ritters' adventures in Wyoming.

———

It was a beautiful spring day in Omaha. The postman had stopped by and dropped off a thick stack of letters, which wasn't unusual, as they were a sought-after couple in the Omaha social sphere. Ross picked them up and started to quickly scan the senders.

He stopped at one, raised his eyebrows, set the other mail down on a table, and called, "Amy, can you come down here for a minute, please?"

Amy stepped down the staircase as Ross looked up at his still perfect wife, and felt that familiar warm rush down his neck, and the desire to smile from the inside out, answering a question he had asked himself years before. Just the sight of his wife still gave him a thrill.

"What do you need, Ross?"

"The mail just came in and you have a letter."

"I hope it's not another invitation. I'd like a few nights at home with my husband."

"No, I don't believe it is, my stunningly beautiful wife," he replied as he handed her the envelope.

She flashed him a brilliant smile, but when she glanced at the return address, the smile disappeared, her lips tightened, and her brows furrowed.

Her hands were shaking as the opened the letter from New York, quickly read the first few sentences and let out a shriek as her face exploded into rapturous joy.

She held the letter out to Ross, letting another piece of paper drift to the floor. Ross read the same opening lines and grinned widely as he scooped his wife into his arms.

The girls all came running and saw their parents hugging and kissing, so they turned away and returned to their rooms. It wasn't anything special.

It may not have been special to the children, but it was to her parents. It was from the publisher in New York who had reviewed Amy's final manuscript and were very pleased to offer her a contract for publication. A draft was enclosed, but it had floated to the floor. It didn't matter.

As her heart and soul soared in the arms of her loving husband, Amy had reached that ultimate goal, because fulfilling her dream was all that mattered…her first dream and now the last to be satisfied.

———

Six months later, Amy's first novel was a bestseller.

The title, *Captured By The Sioux*, was a romantic adventure novel in which the heroine is captured by hostile Sioux and escapes, only to be rescued at the last second by her hero, who then leads her on a long journey narrowly escaping death at the hands of Sioux warriors, outlaws, and despicable wrong-doers.

The hero bravely escorts her to safety while they both fall deeply in love as they travel through hostile lands, but because she is betrothed to another, neither can express that love, and he loses her to an unloving man. They are heartbroken to separate, but must travel different paths, until she finds that her betrothed had wed another, and she is suddenly free to joyfully return to her true love. They marry and still must face added dangers before they finally find contentment and a love that never diminishes.

It was listed as fiction, but to many in Cheyenne who knew better, the story was very true.

And if there was ever a question, in a large house in Omaha, Nebraska, there was a bag in the attic with eight Sioux knives and eight Sioux war tomahawks.

BOOK LIST

1	Rock Creek	12/26/2016
2	North of Denton	01/02/2017
3	Fort Selden	01/07/2017
4	Scotts Bluff	01/14/2017
5	South of Denver	01/22/2017
6	Miles City	01/28/2017
7	Hopewell	02/04/2017
8	Nueva Luz	02/12/2017
9	The Witch of Dakota	02/19/2017
10	Baker City	03/13/2017
11	The Gun Smith	03/21/2017
12	Gus	03/24/2017
13	Wilmore	04/06/2017
14	Mister Thor	04/20/2017
15	Nora	04/26/2017
16	Max	05/09/2017
17	Hunting Pearl	05/14/2017
18	Bessie	05/25/2017
19	The Last Four	05/29/2017
20	Zack	06/12/2017
21	Finding Bucky	06/21/2017
22	The Debt	06/30/2017
23	The Scalawags	07/11/2017
24	The Stampede	08/23/2019
25	The Wake of the Bertrand	07/31/2017
26	Cole	08/09/2017
27	Luke	09/05/2017
28	The Eclipse	09/21/2017
29	A.J. Smith	10/03/2017
30	Slow John	11/05/2017
31	The Second Star	11/15/2017
32	Tate	12/03/2017
33	Virgil's Herd	12/14/2017
34	Marsh's Valley	01/01/2018
35	Alex Paine	01/18/2018
36	Ben Gray	02/05/2018
37	War Adams	03/05/2018

Made in the USA
Middletown, DE
04 August 2021